T0156551

THE
DISTANT VOICES

THE VOICES SAGA

VOLUME 1

WILLIAM L STOLLEY

iUNIVERSE, INC.
NEW YORK   BLOOMINGTON

The Distant Voices
The Voices Saga

Copyright © 2009 William L Stolley

iUniverse books may be ordered through booksellers or by contacting:

iUniverse
1663 Liberty Drive
Bloomington, IN 47403
www.iuniverse.com
1-800-Authors (1-800-288-4677)

ISBN: 978-1-4401-3182-0 (pbk)
ISBN: 978-1-4401-3183-7 (ebk)

Printed in the United States of America

iUniverse rev. date: 3/31/2009

I would like to dedicate this novel to my son, W. Michael Stolley, whose inspiration guided my hand to start writing. He had constant faith in my ability and offered emotional support. I also dedicate this book to my mother, Annamary Kelly-Stolley, who insisted I should be a writer from an early age. I would like to mention two important people. The first is the esteemed Dr. Milton Gipstein, a good friend who encouraged me to stop writing a travelogue and tell the story. The second is my lifetime friend Elaine McKeough. She advised me that any sentence which began 'there was' lacked imagination. Both individuals – successful and brilliant in their career fields – took the time to offer me unbridled advice. Finally, I wish to acknowledge the continual support of my wife, Lori A. Stolley. Thanks to her long hours of hard work, this first novel is possible.

"Space is the greatest desert – a vast hostile wasteland filled with boiling gases and frigid silent realms. Amidst this barren void float tiny oases, seemingly unconnected across the great distances of time." WLS

Contents

CHAPTER 1

BREAKING THROUGH

"MAY I HAVE THIS DANCE?" he politely asked as he bowed. He then stumbled toward a bush.

Stuporous, he imagined that in this pitch-black place with only the light of the stars overhead, the round bush before him resembled the plump social instructor he once knew years ago from his private school – her arms outstretched as she beckoned the young man to waltz.

He tossed the empty wine bottle in his hand backward. It flew over his head and crashed on the white rocks alongside the tracks. The bush did not reply to his request. When he reached for a branch that he mistook for an arm, leaves brushed into his face, which startled the young drunk. He jerked his head back and frowned.

"Hey! It's my birthday," he declared as he backed up. "How dare you refuse me? Granted," he thought as he recalled his tortured past, "it's a whole lot better than the one I had ten years ago," he half-smiled and then unsteadily turned away. He almost fell down. "Some partner," he mumbled while he rubbed his nose. The sorrowful young man made his way in the dark along the railroad tracks whose steel path led him away from Hattiesburg. "Perhaps I'll find more agreeable company this way…"

Tall, pale, thin, this young man – this poor wretch, this unfortunate ghost of a once promising self – reached the end of his rope, his road a dead end, his current life the sad final chapter, the hopes of his father dying with each weakening step.

If only he had listened. If only he heeded the words that drove him to

1

madness. Where was the voice that stole his youth and took the joy from his heart? He ran out of medication days ago. He feared that at any moment, the voice would return to plague his troubled mind. The same voice he feared would drive him back to a pleasant room, with pleasant staff, in a peaceful setting, where doctors would write on his progress daily while he slowly went insane. He clung to his ragged freedom like a piece of flotsam that drifted through an ocean of indifference while waves of apathy swept over him and threatened to drag him under.

"Please, someone help me…"

At approximately 8:45 AM, much earlier that bright Wednesday morning on the first day of July, an overly confident balding effete man strode into the Simsbury, Connecticut branch of the Santa Fe Bank. Wearing a half-priced, tan sport-coat with dark brown trousers and a yellow tie, Burt Loomis smelled of too much inexpensive cologne as he strutted toward his private office. He never glanced at any one else. He only had one purpose in mind when he arrived at work, a task he treasured each day.

"Mr. Loomis, sorry to bother you…" his secretary spoke up.

He stopped in mid-stride just outside his office door.

"What is it, Ms. Simmons?" he caustically addressed his secretary.

A tall kindly white-haired woman with a regal bearing stood up. She towered over Loomis. With only two years left before her retirement, he had trouble letting her go, lest she file an age discrimination lawsuit against him. The last thing he wanted was an investigation at the bank.

"I was wondering if you thought about Michael…" she started.

"Tyler?" Loomis interrupted. He nervously glanced around and showed his hand. He leaned close to her and lowered his voice. "Why? What have you heard?" he asked. His eyes peered over his bifocal glasses.

"N-nothing, sir," she stammered. His close face made her feel uncomfortable. She resumed her seat. "It's just that no one has heard from him in quite a while…"

"What is your point, Ms. Simmons?" he said as he straightened. He stared down his narrow nose at her.

"He seems to have disappeared," she continued. "I've tried to locate him, but my inquiry letters to shelters keep coming back unanswered. I've scoured the entire area. Don't you wonder what happened to him?"

"No, nor should you," Loomis answered as he brushed aside her comments. "He refused free treatment at the adult center after his release. He went out on his own instead. You saw him in here, on drugs and alcohol, begging for money. When he feels desperate, he'll show up to ask for more. Meanwhile, we have a bank to run. Don't we, Ms. Simmons?"

"Yes sir," she replied and casted her eyes down. She returned to her computer screen.

Burt Loomis slipped into his office and breathed a sigh of relief. He knew he would have to fire Ms. Simmons one day to prevent her snooping. He would wait until he found a better replacement. She knew too many important people from nearby Farmington Downs. He dismissed her concerns as petty. Excited about his latest dividend, he rubbed his hands together and headed for his computer to play further with the Tyler fortune – siphoning off the bottom.

Ms. Simmons glanced over at the portrait on the wall of Anthony Tyler, grandson of the bank's founder and father to Michael. She remembered the little brown haired boy with those piercing blue-gray eyes as he ran through the lobby ahead of his father. Mr. Anthony Tyler had command of the bank in those days, an institution originally founded by his grandfather, Pierce. Ms. Simmons often wondered how the bright and curious little Michael Tyler would turn out. She recalled the disappointment she felt when his parents placed him in the juvenile center for violent emotionally disturbed children.

She gazed at Loomis office door. She felt a tinge of guilt, as she knew that Burt Loomis mismanaged one of the largest private trusts in Connecticut while the actual owner wandered some city street as a homeless man.

"Wherever you are Michael, I hope someone is watching over you…"

A tall slender young man with shaggy brown hair and piercing blue-gray eyes stumbled down a railway track. He had no destination. The hot humid July night pressed in on him like a vise. He desperately needed a drink. He ran out of wine and money hours ago. He over-indulged when celebrating his twentieth birthday. He blew his last buck on booze and drank it all before noon. He cradled an empty bottle in his arms for the last six hours like some misbegotten child, until he finally chucked it onto the train track when he considered dancing with a bush. On this warm night, he would soon pay for his lack of foresight. He began to shake and shiver, a certain sign of his withdrawal from alcohol. He felt as if ants crawled over his skin. His body craved the drug that he could no longer supply.

"I can beat this," he mumbled.

His lower lip trembled as drool hung from his unshaven chin. He clenched his fists as his gut sent him on a roller coaster ride. He leaned to one side and heaved what little stomach contents remained onto the ground. Weak and unable to stand, he laid down on the ground while he stared up at the heavens. He could only hear his labored breathe and the occasional mosquito buzz in his ear. He rubbed his sore tired eyes. More pain shot through his gut.

"Please, someone help me," he muttered with his arms wrapped around his middle.

"I can help, if you will let me," a voice responded.

"Oh no, not now, please go away! You've done enough to me!" he barked at the stars.

The stars said nothing in return. They twinkled back at him – distant orbs of light that shimmered in the night sky. No person stood nearby. No spirit spoke from the heavens. The young man who lay upon the empty train tracks was quite alone.

He grabbed his gut, ready for another round of agony. Right before his pain reached its crescendo, it stopped.

"What the…" he thought.

He sat up and looked around as if he sensed another presence. The cold steel rails ran off silently to the horizon. The trees nearby made no sound. The city of Hattiesburg lay miles behind him.

"I told you I can help," the voice spoke, "if you will allow me to help."

The annoying resonating metallic tone of the voice was once a constant nuisance to Michael. Every time he heard the voice, he erupted with violent behavior until he started regular doses of medication at the tender age of ten. They told the angry youth that his medicine would chase the ghosts away. Only now, he was out of medication. The ghost had returned.

"You? Help me? They told me you're just a delusion," he said back to the voice that only he heard. He spit out his words with anger. "I mean, how could you possibly…"

He paused to consider the coincidence of that offer with what just happened.

"Yes, but you never… well, if you can help me now, why didn't you help at the home or when my parents died?" he wondered.

"I cannot remove that pain – a terrible loss for you," the voice spoke.

"What would you know?" he told it. "You're just a figment of my imagination."

Michael Tyler stood up. For a reason he could not explain, he felt better. Then his stomach growled. It reminded him he had not eaten in a long time. He reached into his pockets and found no help there – no loose change, not a penny.

What did he expect to find? Homeless, alcoholic, friendless, unshaven, unkempt, stubborn, unwilling to listen or follow advice, this tall frail young man was but a thin shadow of his late successful father, Anthony Tyler.

"Voice… nameless voice… good for nothing voice… you drove me to distraction… you made trouble for me… if you can cure the sick, then why can't you grant me wishes!" Michael exclaimed as he swayed. "I wish you had that power," he mumbled and swatted away a buzzing pest. "I'd wish for some cash right about now."

"For what purpose," the voice quickly replied, "to purchase more wine? I have tried to tell you, Michael, you are damaging a vital asset to your future…"

"Future? What future?" Michael yelled at the night air. He gestured back toward the light on the horizon. "I have no future. In that direction is the town of Hattiesburg, Mississippi," he indicated to his right. He turned left, "in this direction is peace and quiet. True, I could have a hot meal and a warm bed if I go into town. Of course, they'll lock me up again… crazy Michael, nutty Michael, fruitcake Michael, vagrant, delusional, he hears voices in his head…" his words slurred, "…and they don't go away! They stick around just to pester me!"

He sat down on the ground feeling forgotten and lost – a broken man. He sobbed into his hands.

"You must control your emotions," the voice said.

"Like you? You heartless bastard!" Michael blurted as he raised his face. "It's because of you," he said while he pounded his fists against his head, "that I'm in this shape."

"Michael, that is not true," the voice retorted. "I am not responsible for what happened at your tenth birthday party or the reaction of your parents. Nor am I to blame for Dr. Hami's treatment. I have been trying to communicate with you for over nine of your years. You have refused to listen. Tonight, you have finally run out of medication to block me. Would you please take a few minutes to listen to my words and accept my counsel? What have you to lose?"

Michael lay back and wiped away his tears. On such a clear July night in the darkness of the countryside, he could see practically every star. Their bright twinkling light seemed to reach out and invite him. Then he recalled his psychiatric treatment for the voice and his momentary feeling of solitude fled.

"You've spouted that drivel into my head long enough. I'm so sick and tired of it. Do me a favor – just go away," he uttered. He rolled onto his side. "I'll be better off," he mumbled. He gazed up the endless steel rail next to his head. "Leave me to my end out here under the stars." He turned onto his back and took in the tiny points of light overhead. "It's been a long time since I saw such a clear night," he thought.

"I have a suggestion," the metallic-sounding voice spoke.

"Would you stop bothering me!" he yelled.

"I would like you to look at the stars. That is all I ask. Would you do that?" the voice prompted.

"Will you promise to go away?" Michael requested.

"Please Michael," the flat mechanical and unfeeling voice begged.

"If you insist," Michael sighed, "then go away."

The young man stared up into the black inky sky.

"Ok, I'm looking… now what?" he said with a half-smile.

Off to his right, one star suddenly shined brighter and flared with a brilliant bright bluish-white light for a second. Michael frowned. He shook his head and closed his eyes.

"I must be sicker than I thought," he mumbled.

He opened his eyes and stared skeptically at the same region of sky.

"I thought so," he confidently nodded as he saw no change in the stars.

Then the same star in the same region of sky twinkled brightly again. It clearly stood out from the rest of the celestial firmament.

"Was that real?" he wondered. He sat up and rubbed his eyes.

"Now will you believe me?" the voice spoke inside his head.

"How did you do that?" he asked. He tipped his head back and stared upward.

"Through the portal in your mind," it told him. "You have a very unique attribute Michael. You can perform many actions by using your mind, if you will allow me to make an alteration," it requested.

According to his original medical file, ten-year-old Michael Tyler reported to the psychiatrist that he heard an annoying metallic-sounding voice inside his head that no one else heard – an abrasive voice similar to squeaky car brakes in tone. When it spoke, he reacted violently to the voice out of frustration. It drove him to fits of anger. He swung his fists at his invisible foe. Hence, the reason he unintentionally struck a young girl at his tenth birthday party. Yet, during eight years of institutionalization for psychosis and adolescent delusional schizophrenia, he never witnessed a manifestation like the one he just observed. Emancipated by the state at the age of eighteen and free for the last two years, he kept the voice at bay by using the free samples of medication he carried in his pockets – medication he finally ran out of three days ago.

"Do that again," he requested. He frowned at the night sky.

The star unmistakably flashed and shone brilliantly. Its light and location were in the exact place as the other times. He knew this was not some defect in his eyes from rubbing them. The affect appeared in the distance with the same intensity similar to fireworks seen from afar.

"Who are you?" he began to wonder.

"May I explain?" the voice asked. "Will you listen?"

"I suppose I don't have any choice," Michael stated and sat very still.

"Where to begin," the voice started. "I am not simply a voice in your head Michael," it tried to explain. "I am an alien being communicating with a human being from Earth via a new and very special conduit that recently formed in your species. I can enhance this connection by entering your mind and manipulating an energy influx that will alter neuronal and blood vessel pathways. This will form a new area inside your brain surrounding this portal. Then you can manipulate this form of energy too," the voice explained.

"Whoa, whoa, whoa!" the smelly young man replied. He dismissively waved his arms. "What are you saying? I wanted some money, not surgery," he stated. "You see, I always pictured my fantasy voice as a benevolent fairy robot that could grant wishes. I don't want some alien poking around my head altering pathways." He paused, still defiant. "You did say alien, didn't you?" he questioned. "Until now, you've only been an annoying voice. They told me you're a delusion... con... convinced me," he stammered. "Are you trying to tell me you're... real?"

"Michael, I am as real as you, only I am located on a planet that is very far away – hundreds of millions of light years as measured by your science," the voice told him.

"Ha!" Michael exclaimed. "Now I know you're a delusion," he nodded and grinned with self-satisfaction. "That's impossible. You wouldn't be able to speak to me if that were true. Your voice takes time to travel..."

"On the contrary," the voice cut him off, "the tiny portal – actually a conduit located inside your brain – has made this form of communication possible. Your species has developed a new trait which has emerged in a small number of humans," the voice explained. "This trait is also prominent on other worlds. I have one too. We are exchanging thoughts via this portal."

"A small number on this planet..." Michael conjectured. "You mean that other people like me hear a voice in their head and it's just some alien trying to communicate?" Michael asked.

"We are wasting valuable time," the voice said. "You must decide if I am to perform this action."

As the voice spoke, Michael's hunger, his delirium tremens and his continued despondency over the death of his parents apparently vanished.

"What can it hurt?" he declared as he shrugged his shoulders. "I'll probably be dead before morning anyway. Go ahead, do your worst," he beckoned. "Oh, this is so stupid! Why am I listening to my own delusion?" he wondered as he started to rise.

"Why must you persist in this self destructive attitude?" the voice responded. "I am offering you a chance to be your world's first ambassador to the galactic collective and you refuse based on some antiquated notion? I implore you," the mechanical voice stated.

Still weak, he swayed back and forth. He decided it was safer to remain on the ground. He stared up at the stars again. They did nothing – no twinkling, no shining and no brilliance. They all appeared the same – eternal and fixed. He took in a deep breath and sighed.

"Fine then!" he declared as he closed his eyes. "Fiddle with my mind if you must or what's left of it."

"You will not regret this, I promise you," the voice said.

"… and I promise you, that if I am not somehow different when I wake up, we will end this once and for all," Michael threatened.

"Michael, do you intend to take your own life?" the voice asked. "You must not do this."

"If it means ridding my mind of your chattel…" he stopped before he completed the thought. "I…I grow tired of this. Do what you must or leave me alone!"

Michael Tyler lay back on the ground with his eyes closed. The warm humid night no longer pressed in on him. Across the vast reaches of space, special energy flowed through an extremely tiny portal inside his head. A great and wondrous change took place within his brain, which made him most unique.

CHAPTER 2

CONFRONTATION

ELEVEN MONTHS PASSED SINCE THAT fateful night between Michael and his voice.

On a quiet and lazy Thursday morning in early June, no one bothered to look toward the bank's front door when it opened. A well-groomed, tall and distinguished young man entered – dressed in a dark gray hand-tailored suit, he wore a deep maroon silk tie that stood out over a hand-made, Italian-linen, white shirt. He quietly walked into the Simsbury Branch of the Santa Fe Bank. The perfectly coiffed young man – with his neat brown hair and piercing blue-gray eyes – boldly strode up to the remaining misfortunate teller still waiting to take her coffee break.

"I would like to see the bank's manager, Mr. Burt Loomis. Is he in?" the young man asked. His voice sounded firm yet polite.

"Do you have an appointment?" she responded while she counted receipts. She did not bother to look up.

"I believe he'll wish to see me," the confident young man answered. He reached into his jacket.

"May I ask your name, please?" the teller requested while she counted.

"My name is Michael Anthony Tyler," he replied.

Completely frozen, the woman stopped counting money and stamping receipts. She stared down at the counter afraid to look up. Her jaw dropped open as if she wanted to say something, but the words caught in her throat. She knew, as did everyone at the bank, the Tyler fortune created the original

Santa Fe Bank of Connecticut. The Tyler Trust was its largest account – its assets, investments, and holdings were worth billions.

Yet, no one in the bank had heard from crazy Michael Tyler for over a year. A social worker in Mississippi simply informed them that she spotted the young man wandering near the town of Hattiesburg. This report arrived after the bank's manager reluctantly posted a reward for his whereabouts at the insistence of Ms. Simmons. To the secretary's relief, she discovered the homeless young man was still alive. Since that time, he slipped into obscurity.

The teller remained motionless, as if she was frozen to the spot and too stunned to move. Her eyes slowly traveled up to the tall young man's handsome face. She very clumsily tried to regain her composure. She cleared her throat about to ask for his identification.

"May I see some…"

Sensing her request, the suave young man held open an official U.S. Passport for her inspection. Not bothering to give her eye contact, Michael turned his head while he swept the room with his senses.

"It can't be him," he heard her thoughts as she stared at his face. "Sure looks like him though."

Her eyes flickered down upon a dark leather-bound, checkbook-sized document unfolded in his hands. She saw his color picture and signature. The document was stamped and verified "The United States of America, State Department," with its golden-inlaid seal and hologram embossed on the opposite page, including his digitized thumbprint with a recent date, May 12, 2016. They issued the passport only a few weeks ago.

"You were right," he thought, "this is more impressive than a driver's license."

"Everything about you is impressive today Michael," his voice spoke to his mind.

The teller glanced over his shoulder at the portrait of his father in the corner, moved away from Burt Loomis' office a few months ago. The tall young man had nearly the same identical face. Her eyes bounced back to that commanding face.

"Is Mr. Loomis here or not? I have a busy schedule today, if you please," Michael insisted.

"Yes sir, right away… uh, Mr. Tyler sir," the young woman stuttered. She started to move in one direction, changed her mind, and then moved another way, before going back in the first direction.

Michael tired not to smile. For months, he worked with his alien voice preparing for this moment. In a series of complex communications, the alien took Michael on a figurative journey inside his mind, expanding his general knowledge on a variety of subjects. Working together, they transformed the haggard young man both physically and mentally into the confident, assured, and handsome male Adonis standing before the teller. He felt older and wiser than his current age of twenty years.

In another month, he would be twenty-one years old, owner of the largest private trust on the eastern seaboard, and personally worth over a billion dollars. Michael knew a bit about what to expect long before he walked into the bank, thanks to his good friend on another world, and its ability to tap easily into our electrical-based computerized systems.

For months, Michael toyed with the idea of seeking out the other psychics scattered about the globe. He and his voice began to devise a plan. For the first part of this plan, he needed to reclaim his trust as a legitimate source of funds he could use later. With the help of his alien friend, Michael obtained practically anything he wanted via the Internet, including access to the world banking system.

He thoroughly examined every detail of the Tyler Trust. He learned everything he could about the bank his family founded, its employees, and Burt Loomis' encrypted pages that showed every single embezzled penny. He came to confront the manager. By default, Loomis took over as the trust's administrator when the court ruled Michael mentally incompetent after his father's death.

Michael's eyes followed the unsettled bank teller as she hurriedly scooted out from behind the counter. The young woman's high heels scraped the tile floor as she wiggled in her tight dress to a short hallway off to the side.

"I'm expanding my sensory area," he thought to his voice. "Are you catching this?"

"I sense what you sense," the voice answered.

With their current connection, the voice could now hear and see everything that Michael did, including the thoughts of others.

"Michael, I sense excited activity to your left," the voice indicated.

A tall slim white-haired woman wearing a two-piece pale yellow suit walked toward him, taking big strides.

"I'm trying to act nonchalant," he thought back to his alien friend.

"Michael?" the woman kindly spoke as she approached. "Michael Tyler? Is it really you?"

Michael turned to face a smartly dressed tall woman nearly able to look him in the eye. She had a pleasant affect and welcoming smile. He sensed her genuine affection, as she knew his father quite well and remembered the boy before his committal.

"Ms. Simmons," he nodded, "you remember me?"

"How could I ever forget you?" she answered. Her eyes bordered on tears.

"We thought you were… I mean… let me rephrase that…," she said and smiled. "I'm glad to see you've recovered. You look great!" she beamed.

"Thank you," he curtly replied. He had not expected this kind reception.

"Oh, yes," she quickly caught on while she glanced back over her right shoulder. "I suppose you wish to see Burt… uh, Mr. Loomis, right away, don't you?"

She had a half-expectant expression as if she waited for the other shoe to drop.

"Yes, I would appreciate it," he said and used a business tone.

"This way," she offered while she thought, "I can't wait to see this!"

She did not know that Michael could hear her thoughts. He suppressed any expression and fell in behind her.

"Please wait here," she said as she indicated a chair. She then entered Loomis' office.

Behind the door, pandemonium broke out when Ms. Simmons dropped the news in Loomis' lap that Michael Tyler waited outside his office to see him.

As if expecting an attack, an older fat man wearing a cheap suit with a polyester tie and balding hairline timidly popped his head out the door. He smiled a big phony smile. He stared intently at Michael's face while trying to be certain of his identity before proceeding.

"Mr. Tyler?" the man asked with a squeaky voice.

The slightly effeminate tone made Michael cringe. Inside Loomis' mind, Michael sensed the man's fear that his worst nightmare just came true.

"Yes?" Michael replied as he stood.

Loomis' eyes squinted as he peered over the top of his reading glasses. The bank manager carefully crept around the door and stared up at the tall young man. He wondered how this new version could be the same man that once appeared unshaven – the bum who reeked of urine and body odor two years earlier that fumbled into his bank and begged for money after his release.

Michael's facial features did not lie. Loomis only had to glance across the lobby at the portrait of his father, Anthony Tyler, to see the resemblance.

Michael obtained skin rejuvenation knowledge from his alien friend that completely erased the signs of his alcoholism and lack of hygiene. After eleven months of treatment, his skin glowed with youthful luster.

"I hardly recognized you Michael," Loomis began. His eyes searched the young man's face. "Would you mind coming back into my office?" he asked. He stood still a second. "Are you really…" he swallowed, "Michael Tyler?"

"Yes, I am!" Michael snapped. He quickly produced his passport once more, "How many times must I say it!"

Burt Loomis glanced down briefly for confirmation and then back up at Michael. He made a toothy grin while he gestured at the same time toward the inside of his office. The man reminded Michael of a vampire baring his fangs.

Ms. Simmons sat down at her desk and thought, "Good luck, Michael," as he passed.

Michael immediately noticed the "Tyler Trust Financial Report" that sat on Loomis' desk. The rotund manager quickly slid the report into a drawer.

"Did you see that?" his voice injected. "Those are the latest figures about your trust from this morning!"

"Mm," Michael silently concurred, "the same figures we examined yesterday right after the market closed."

Once the two men sat, an awkward silence followed as neither man spoke. Loomis smiled broadly at Michael, but Michael did not smile back. Loomis leaned forward.

"So, how are you, Mr. Tyler? What brings you to…?"

"Mr. Loomis, let's get down to business, shall we?" Michael stated.

He reached inside his upper suit pocket. For a second, Loomis wondered if he might be producing a gun and flinched. Instead, Michael pulled out an electronic device. A small screen sprang to life showing charts and figures.

"I'm curious as to how my fund – the Tyler Trust – has performed lately," Michael asked, trying to sound as innocent as possible.

"Oh, you want to know about your father's funds?" Loomis said. He made every attempt to sound in charge but stumbled – a trifle off mark.

"No Mr. Loomis," Michael replied while he continued his no-nonsense tone. "I'm talking about the trust fund my father set up in my name, the Michael Anthony Tyler Trust Fund, which will revert to my control on my twenty-first birthday in about a month from now."

Michael never took his eyes off Loomis' face.

Loomis smiled again, "Oh yes, quite right…that fund! You are correct. My mistake. You know, I've been meaning to contact you about…"

"My lawyer and I spoke on Tuesday with your investment broker," Michael said as he glanced down at the electronic pad.

"You spoke?" Loomis gulped.

Michael continued and did not skip a beat.

"He informed us that over the past eight months, you invested millions of dollars in highly speculative ventures to maximize your return. He said you made a "killing," – his choice of words, not mine. Is that correct?" Michael asked. His eyes focused on Loomis' face.

He then noticed skepticism in Loomis' expression.

"Technically Michael, I don't need your authority to make those investments," Loomis declared. "Your father put me in charge of the trust, since the court passed judgment against you..."

"That decision is reversed," Michael said. He produced a folded piece of paper – an official court document, which he showed Loomis. The fat man nodded after he looked it over briefly. "I am not here to address your improper purchase of investments that might jeopardize the fund," Michael put to him. "I am here to discuss your other involvements in the trust," he continued, "such as the numerous withdrawals for personal expenditures that exceed the parameters of the trust's provisions entitled to you. I acquired the services of an estate attorney in New Haven – a Mr. Arnold Wilson. He would like to meet with the bank's officers and go over the fund's history. You do have legal representation, don't you Mr. Loomis?"

"History of the fund?" Loomis asked. He swallowed hard as his mouth became dry with fear setting in.

"Yes, we managed to obtain a complete read out of all your transactions over the past two years. I believe we discovered some discrepancies. Mr. Wilson is eager to discuss the matter with you," Michael delivered cheerfully. "Imagine," he said, "Mr. Wilson actually wanted to call the SEC and the state's Attorney General's office. I said I would discuss the matter with you first. Would you like to explain your actions to me, or shall I call my lawyer?" Michael asked. "This is a cell phone."

Michael pulled up the number of his lawyer and then placed the device face up on Loomis' desk with his finger poised over the send button.

For a moment, Loomis stared straight ahead. The impact of what he heard from this brash young man had not yet fully sunk in. He dropped the artificial smile. His eyes fell to the device on his desk.

"How could he know about my activity unless he had me investigated?" Loomis thought.

Michael clearly heard those thoughts. He decided to end this cat and mouse game with Loomis.

"What is it you want?" Loomis muttered.

Michael took out a card from his other inside pocket. He pushed the card across the desk until it stopped in front of Loomis.

"This is Mr. Wilson's phone number. He wants you to call him at the end of this meeting. I believe you will find him a fair-minded person. We are looking for justice, Mr. Loomis, not prosecution," Michael stated.

Loomis gazed off into space. His head swam with visions of headlines, a jury trial and possible incarceration.

"Do you understand me, Mr. Loomis?" Michael said while he requested an answer.

Sweat beaded up on Loomis' forehead. His stomach did flip-flops. He could only nod in reply.

"The Tyler Trust will be closely monitored from now on," Michael said as he pressed him. "Your days of pilfering my fund are over."

Burt Loomis wanted to speak. Instead, his mind raced with images of police hauling him out of the bank in handcuffs. He nodded up and down so rapidly that the sweat gathering on his forehead spattered the desk in front of him.

Michael did not wish to gloat or send this pathetic man to prison where he belonged. He righted the wrong instead and put the man back in his subservient place. He took in a deep breath. However, he did it so quietly that Loomis did not detect it. Michael wanted the meeting to end. He could barely stand to be near this man.

"Do you have any questions before I leave?" Michael asked.

"Questions?" Loomis spoke absently.

He finally glanced down at the business card. He saw the attorney's name and phone number. He realized in that moment Michael Tyler turned out to be more like his father than he thought he would be.

"No questions? Good!" Michael said as he stood up. "I must leave. I have other appointments."

Michael started to move toward the door and then turned back.

"Oh yes, I almost forgot," he added, "I told Mr. Wilson you would call him by eleven. If you do not, I instructed him to take immediate punitive action today," Michael stated.

He glanced up at the office clock and gestured.

"Better start moving, Loomis. It's almost eleven o'clock," Michael pointed.

Burt Loomis jumped up from his chair as if someone gave him a cattle prod.

Michael opened the door, speaking over his shoulder as he walked out.

"Good-bye, Mr. Loomis," he said, the anxious smiling-eyes of Ms. Simmons followed him. He casually strolled out of the office with the same confident smooth stride that brought him inside the bank.

Burt Loomis remained standing at his desk, stupefied. He glanced down and realized Michael left his cellular device on his desk.

"Oh, my! Mr. Tyler!" he shouted as he tore from his office. "Mr. Tyler! You left your organizer!" he cried. He ran out his office door and waved it in his hand.

Michael stopped and turned slightly.

"Keep it. Consider it a gift," Michael told him. He then glanced over Loomis shoulder at Ms. Simmons watching the two men. "One more thing," he stopped to add, "I'd like Ms. Simmons to receive a raise – make that a large raise in her salary and retirement benefit. I would say the bank owes her that after being saddled to you all these years. In fact, donate the entire amount that you generously siphoned from my trust to her. Do we understand each other?"

Behind Loomis back, Michael saw the white-haired woman make a silent "Yes!" gesture as she pumped her fist and mouthed the word. This time he managed a half-smile.

"Oh, yes, Mr. Tyler," Loomis swooned, "whatever you say, Mr. Tyler."

Suddenly aware he appeared conciliatory Burt Loomis nervously glanced about him. The bank's employees resumed what they were doing. They pretended not to notice the nervous sweat that poured off his balding head. He then looked up in time to see the bank's clock about to strike eleven. He scurried back inside his office to call New Haven. He hoped that Mr. Wilson would go easier on him than Michael Tyler had. Mr. Burt Loomis would have a very unpleasant day, especially after Arnold Wilson read him the new tighter rules regarding activity on the Tyler Trust.

As Michael turned to leave, he could hear the sound of Ms. Simmons laughing.

Outside the bank, the picture perfect sky seemed to reflect the young man's mood. Michael touched his thumb to a soft flat pad on a keychain inside his left pants pocket, deactivating the security device. A light chime sounded, the front lights flashed, and the car door automatically opened for him. He sat in the driver's seat sideways. The seat turned and then Michael swung his legs in. The seat slid forward into position as the steering wheel dropped to his pre-set level.

Silent yet very swiftly, he pulled the sleek imported electrically powered luxury sports car into traffic and quickly sped from the bank.

"Whew! I'm glad that's over," Michael linked as he loosened his tie. "I think we actually pulled it off too, thanks in no small part to you my distant friend."

"That's why I'm here Michael," the voice droned. "Phase one of your plan is complete. You have your trust back. The significance of the trust will come into play much later when the future aspects of your plan come to fruition. Now you can begin phase two, all roads lead to China," the voice spoke to his mind.

"Rome," Michael corrected. "The phrase is, 'all roads lead to Rome,'" he reminded his voice.

"I understand it is an ancient expression meaning that no matter what path a person takes, their course is set," the voice quoted. "Would that be considered predestination?"

"I wouldn't know," Michael retorted. "When you gave me lessons in philosophy, you grouped them together with religion," he said as he shook his head. "I am thoroughly confused about the validity of both. At any rate, I wish our destination was Rome instead of China," Michael linked. "I could openly drive my car and eat the best Italian food on the planet. Speaking of paths, my journey to China will not be that easy. According to your sources, you've managed to pinpoint only two areas of the world with potential psychics… one in Canada and the rest is a group in China. Crossing over into Canada is one thing. However, going to China and smuggling out a dozen or more people is going to take more than just secrecy and money," he mused.

"Money you have," the voice replied. "I recognize that the secrecy aspect will be difficult. That is ahead of us. Tonight, my Earth-bound friend, you will relax and celebrate your triumphant victory. I want you to be happy."

"Hearing your rough metallic voice and knowing I am not insane makes me happy," Michael shot back.

"Seriously Michael, I am only trying to…"

"Help," Michael finished. "The voices created such an elaborate protocol, satisfying my physical and emotional needs, even providing luxury apartments and imported sports cars, how convenient. Every human should have one."

"I adjusted my protocol for your particular needs," the voice explained. "We operate with optimal communication efficiency. By the way, I chose a very expensive penthouse suite for the celebration. I paid for it out of our dummy corporate account before I closed it. The cost will not be connected to the trust."

"You really want this celebration to happen tonight?" Michael thought uneasily. "Aren't we behaving just a bit premature? This is only the beginning. I won't feel secure until the entire plan is finished and we have all of them together in one place."

He readjusted his grip on the steering wheel.

"I've been thinking about our plans," Michael continued. "I'm still having doubts. You know my abilities. I'm not certain I have what it takes to pull this off. I'm very worried about the outcome and…"

"I am here to help," the voice interjected.

"Yes… yes you are," Michael replied as he tried to regain his confidence.

He considered the history of this voice. He began to think over all that happened in the past eleven months or for that matter the previous ten years. He took in a deep breath.

"I'm lucky to be alive," he uttered. He felt both cursed and blessed by his hidden voice.

CHAPTER 3

SOMETHING LOST, SOMETHING GAINED

THE CONNECTICUT COUNTRYSIDE QUIETLY SLIPPED past as Michael made his way from the bank. He spoke to the car: "Michael Tyler, voice activation, entertainment system," he requested.

"Entertainment system on," a feminine-sounding voice responded.

"Classical music, Rachmaninoff Symphony No. 2, Eugene Ormandy and the Philadelphia Philharmonic version, volume level four," he ordered, "start."

With New York City at least an hour away, he reflected over the past ten months since his miraculous transformation while the soothing mood music played in the background.

His mind drifted back to the night of July 1, 2015, nearly a year ago. He replayed that fateful evening when the alien only he knew as his voice melded with him and converted his mind. Upon waking, Michael discovered many new things during those first moments. Initially, he realized he had been lying unconscious on a train track.

"Not the best place to rest," he thought as he rose.

Although he wanted to stand, he found he had no strength. Weak and unsteady, he finally stood up. He could not walk. Instead, he stumbled around; his head throbbed with a severe headache. As he swayed back and forth, different voices – human voices that spoke other languages – began to flood his mind.

"What happened to me?" he wondered as a cacophony of sound bombarded his brain.

At that precise moment, Michael finally acknowledged that the mechanical voice in his head was not a delusion. The new voices he heard sounded very different from his old nemesis. They spoke coherent thoughts in sentences while expressing their feelings at the same time.

"I did change," he thought as he straightened. "You are real…" he added. He referred to his special metallic voice.

These new voices continued to bombard his mind. He tried to adjust his senses after receiving the alteration to his brain made possible by his alien voice. However, he could not focus. The voices, while different, distracted his conscious mind – as if he stood amidst a crowd of people shouting their thoughts and ideas at him. He could not turn them off like some spigot.

"What am I hearing?" he shouted.

"You are hearing the thoughts of other psychics located around your planet," the mechanical voice instructed. Michael heard its distinct unfeeling voice clearly above the rest.

He felt a chilling energy surge through him, like a cold wind descending from the north, giving him goose flesh. He tried to shake it off as the voices continued their onslaught.

"I feel as if I know them. Who are they?" he asked. He sought his voice's advice.

"They are people like you, not as potent or powerful," his voice informed him. "Consider their minds pre-psychic, the same state as your mind was an hour ago."

"Psychic?" Michael questioned.

"That is as close a definition to your condition as English words permit. These other humans have the same potential as you did. You hear them because they are not aware of broadcasting such thoughts, nor do they understand any thoughts they hear. They must make the same conversion you made if you wish to link with them."

"Link with them?" he asked. "You mean others on Earth can become psychic like me if they go through this conversion? We'll be able to share our thoughts?" he asked via his now stronger link with his voice.

"That is correct Michael," the voice reassured him. "Together as a group, you can link your minds and do even more than that."

"More?" he inquired.

"Yes, Michael," the voice linked. "Your mind has significantly more capability than you currently comprehend."

Michael closed his eyes. With increasing effort, he could reach out and hear the internal dialogue of several strong minds around the planet, especially the internal monologue of one Chinese man. Gradually his thoughts and the other voices faded into the background until they vanished.

"Hey! What happened to them?" Michael asked.

"They are far away, relative to your current position. Their signals are weak compared to your current strength. Initially, you heard them as the Earth's first psychic being. However, your mind naturally filtered these other voices out," his alien voice informed him. "When you walk into a crowded room, you do not listen to every conversation. The same is true with your psychic mind. You would go mad if you tried to listen to all the psychics at the same time."

"I'll try to avoid that," Michael stated. "If I can't hear them because of energy and distance, how can I hear you so clearly?"

"You do not 'bend space' when you link with your fellow species," his voice informed him. "Addressing us opens the portal in your mind. Psychic energy between our two species flows through this conduit."

"What is psychic energy?" Michael questioned.

"Psychic energy is a low level form of energy created by certain circumstances or creatures such as humans beings. It is very miniscule and difficult to measure. Most humans discard it. The energy continuously dissipates from the body. The new area inside you mind gives you the ability to concentrate and apply this energy for many purposes," the voice explained.

"Our species is very similar to yours," it told Michael. "Many hundred-thousand of your years ago, we developed the same portal in our minds. We learned to harness this energy by helping to convert each other. For centuries we thought we existed alone on our planet, until, quite by accident, one of our fellow creatures developed a listening device that amplified our ability to sense psychic energy on other planets. We reasoned that if we mentally contacted another species, we might exchange thoughts rather than trying to travel via a space ship. The concept seemed wise at the time. However, that first contact proved disastrous. We did not properly prepare our first encounter with this species. We discovered that the intergalactic conversion process is difficult for species to make without our assistance. When we converted the first few contacts, they used their power for personal gain. Rivalries erupted. Soon, conflict followed. We watched helplessly as they destroyed their planet, unable to stop it."

The voice paused as if reflecting on the severity of that memory. The silence that followed left Michael feeling quite alone for a few seconds. In the past, the voice's irritating quality drove the young man to commit violence. Strangely, its metallic tones now seemed a comfort to him. The voice returned and continued its brief historical perspective.

"After that first encounter, we cautiously studied species before making contact. We made a new goal, to reach out across the universe and find those with a similar trait. Then we would help them gradually develop their psychic ability by listening to our counsel. We built a great structure on our planet to help us achieve this goal. This structure gives us the ability to reach far beyond our galaxy. Many worlds belong to our collective. They speak to each other through us. With the new area inside your brain, you may now utilize psychic energy. Eventually, you will expand your abilities and interact with other species when you wish," his voice concluded.

"If you say so," Michael responded. The amount of information overwhelmed him.

Despite his dismissive skepticism, a surge of good will passed through him. He leapt into the air and swung his fist. He felt like shouting, but did not wish to attract attention, in case someone might be near.

"I only know that I feel different," he said as he gazed down the railroad tracks, as if he had a destination in mind. "For the first time in my life, I feel... confident."

From that moment on, Michael referred to the alien he heard in his mind and the others of its kind as the 'voices.' While he walked south along train tracks, the two engaged in conversation. His voice continued to inform him about how their organization worked to benefit others. Michael learned the voices often take years, even decades to study a planet's cultures before contact. They learn to translate languages and use the unique idioms that exist between species to address each side's cultural uniqueness. The voices then act as liaisons as well as facilitators in bridging worlds together.

Michael and his voice spent the next few hours adjusting to the new relationship, the first between a human from Earth and a being located many millions of light years from our galaxy. Now that Michael listened to his voice, the two began a dialogue that dispelled the youth's fears and anxieties. Michael opened his mind and expressed his thoughts freely.

"Do you make contact this way with other worlds?" Michael asked.

"Not every world welcomes our intrusions," the voice explained. "New subjects often react with the same revulsion you had as a boy of ten."

"On this planet, children do not hear voices," Michael responded, "it's a sign of insanity."

"Not just your planet, Michael," his voice said. "We cannot force beings to link with us," it stated. "Once we make contact, we try to minimize our impact and work to facilitate communication."

"Do you always succeed?" Michael wondered.

"Mostly we succeed, but not always. Each planet's species is unique. As you know, our first contact ended in disastrous results. After that blunder, we changed our protocols," it explained. "Our approach varies from species to species."

After walking up the tracks for a few miles while conversing with his voice, Michael emerged into the northern edge of another town. He tried to avoid any entanglements with the police as he made his way along the tracks. However, the bright flashing lights of one large establishment intrigued him. Drawing nearer, he discovered a gambling casino open twenty-four hours, not far from the local train station.

"Convenient," he thought. His lips were dried and cracked. "Perhaps I could slip in and find a drinking fountain."

He left the tracks and boldly headed over to the huge place with its front exterior covered by bright designs and colorful neon lights. He only wanted a drink of water. He cautiously strolled into the front lobby, though several security cameras automatically swung in his direction. A metallic glint caught his eye. As a harbinger to his recent change of fortune, he glanced down and saw a coin lying on the carpet.

"I shouldn't be here," he thought as he regarded his dilapidated appearance.

He picked up the shiny dollar coin. Rather than pocketing the valuable object, he reached over and put the coin into a large fancy slot machine resting just inside the front lobby. He pulled down the over-sized manual lever meant mostly for show than practicality. The machine accepted the coin. It began to whirl and make noise. He did not wish to attract attention. Michael turned to leave when the slot machine flashed bright lights and loud sounds declaring that he won.

"How is that possible?" he thought while he stared at the machine that tallied up a total figure which seemed absurd to him. He glanced down and noticed that he had been touching the side of the massive electronic device the entire time.

"You said you wanted cash," his voice thought to him. "I tried to help."

"You did that?" Michael asked with fear rising in his voice as he backed away. He reverted to his thoughts. "They might have me arrested for tampering with the slot machine," he reasoned. He turned to run out the front door, when a security man approached him.

"Wait!" the large uniformed man shouted across the lobby.

Michael froze, afraid the officer might shoot him. He wondered what would happen next.

"Sir don't leave," the big man said, walking up to him.

For a second, the officer took in Michael's homeless appearance and wrinkled his nose at his smell as he realized the lowly character of the man standing before him. However, he also knew that security cameras located all around them recorded everything they did or said.

"You cannot leave sir," the officer said to Michael.

The pale young man faced the officer. "Why not?" he wondered still frightened.

"Your winnings," the security officer stated. "Legally, they are yours. I saw you put the coin into the machine. If you'll wait just a moment…" he began. The security officer turned to look at the machine's readout.

The display stated twenty-five thousand dollars!

The man's jaw dropped. He pushed a button on his radio and spoke into his collar. In seconds, security officers and casino personnel flooded into the lobby. A man dressed in a dark business suit, presumably the night manager, approached while rubbing sleep from his eyes as if he had been napping in his office.

"What's going on?" he demanded.

The lobby officer regarded Michael a second before he spoke and then turned to the manager.

"This man just won the jackpot, sir," the officer stated. "We're reviewing the security logs now."

A few tense moments followed where Michael – wearing his smelly dirty clothes – stood amidst a crowd of big burly security men and a doubtful scowling night manager. The officer's radio squawked. He spoke into a special microphone on his collar. He nodded a few times listening to a voice speak through his earpiece. He then turned to the night manager.

"It's true sir," the man said. "Security confirmed it. They reviewed the images from ten different angles and ran remote tests on the machine. He won the money. Legally, it's his."

The manager eyed Michael and closed his eyes. He shook his head.

"I cannot take his picture and put it up in the lobby," he muttered, "they'll have my job! Cut him a check and send him on his way," the man said. He started to turn away when he gazed at Michael with something akin to pity, taking in his obvious poor condition. He then spoke in a low voice to the officer. "Better yet, give him the cash and tell him never to set foot inside this casino again. Is that clear?"

The officer nodded. He led Michael through several security doors and down a few corridors until they made their way to an office, where another man asked for Michael's signature. When Michael could not offer up any identification, they accepted his word that his name was Adam Smith and his promise to pay the taxes he owed. The officer stuffed the young man's pockets with several bundles of hundred dollar bills – two hundred and fifty of them to be exact. The officer then escorted Michael to the exit, and told him never to return to the casino. He practically pushed the young man out the front door.

Michael walked out of the casino onto the street wearing a broad grin across his face. He fondled the cash in his pockets – the most he ever possessed in his life. He glanced up the street and saw the small neon sign to a corner neighborhood bar.

"You promised to stop drinking," the voice reminded him.

He considered the voice's advice for a moment and then nodded, "I did make that promise," he linked back. He fought for a sense of pride. "I believe its time I changed my clothes," he thought, taking in his appearance, "and had a shower." He straightened his filthy clothes and made his way up the sidewalk with his head held high.

Michael did not walk far before he spied a patrol car slowly making its way up the street. He nervously glanced about him. The casino owned a reputable hotel next door. Michael decided that since he had the cash, he would stay there for a while – at least, until he figured out his new ability. He entered and paid for a large suite two weeks in advance, stating he had to rush from one of his 'numerous' construction sites.

"These are my work clothes," he told the skeptical night clerk.

After she accepted his excuse and his cash, Michael crossed the lobby to a small clothing store just opening for the day. He purchased several outfits, including socks and new shoes. Once he made his way to his room, he discarded his old clothes and took a very long hot shower.

The soothing warm water seemed to wash not simply the dirty away, but his previous emotional states of mind. Depression, fear, and anxiety flowed out from his body, relaxing the tortured man's soul. For the time being at least, he did not crave the drink that once drowned his sorrowful thoughts. Instead, a new goal preoccupied his mind, one that would grow into an obsession by a year's end.

Stepping from the shower, the tall pale young man stood before a full-length mirror naked. After he shook his long shaggy brown mane, he noticed sores and red areas on his skin. His ribs stuck out, and he had dark circles under his blood-shot eyes, gross stubble covered his face. In short, he was a physical wreck.

"What can I do to change that?" he linked to his voice while indicating his image in the mirror.

"I have consulted another psychic studying your species," it linked to his mind. "She recommends skin treatments…"

"Wait a minute," he interrupted. "Did you say another species? Am I to understand that other species have been studying us?" he questioned his voice.

"We are wise but we do not know everything!" his voice quickly linked back. "We must consult experts, too. Our specialty is language. Other psychics in our collective specialize in areas that emphasize their strengths. I have spoken to psychics that specialize in healing. They are always interested in new species. I am here to act as your guide and assistant, if you will allow me. Together, we shall embark on a journey to heal your mind and your body, Michael Tyler."

"I look forward to that relationship," Michael said as he turned from the mirror, "but first I must do something I've needed to do since my conversion…"

"What is that?" the voice wondered.

"Sleep," he said. He tumbled over onto the bed and instantly closed his eyes.

The following day, Michael deposited the remainder of his cash into a bank account, obtaining a temporary debit card. He followed the advice of his voice by calling a toll free number and ordering a fully loaded laptop computer. His voice informed Michael that in addition to manipulating the slot machine, it had the ability to enter the realm of electronic cyberspace.

"Is that why you insisted I buy a computer?" Michael asked after he placed the order.

"Computers operate by using pulses of low voltage energy. I can enter the circuits of anything electronic and manipulate the flow of that energy as long as you are near the source, just as I manipulated the slot machines," it told him.

"What about security?" Michael asked it.

"The energy stream is continuous on your planet," it stated. "Wherever energy flows, I can go, whether by airwaves or by current. Your world's feeble attempts at security are a façade to us."

The computer arrived via express delivery the following day. Michael's voice then entered the world's Internet system. It deciphered and manipulated data systems to their purpose. It created a new identity for the twenty-year-old, giving Michael a personal history he never lived. It then generated a new social security number and a new driver's license and sent them via express delivery service to the hotel. After Michael received a special 'download' about driving in his sleep that evening, he then purchased a new domestic car the following day – everything arranged by his voice on the Internet. The dealership delivered the vehicle to the hotel after Michael paid for all the charges in advance: taxes, license, handling, everything.

Michael recalled that his life changed dramatically during that first week with the voice as his guide. One evening, when Michael flipped through Internet sites, the voice started scanning investment pages for information.

"This Wall Street is important for generating capital," the voice stated to him.

"If by capital you are referring to investments that generate money, currency, cash, and the like," Michael responded, "then I would say yes, Wall Street is very important. I thought you researched American culture. New York is the world's financial hub. Every market from around the world connects there," he responded.

"Then you must go to this financial center Michael," it advised. "You must go to New York City."

"You want me to go to New York?" he asked incredulously. He could not believe that the voice would make such a request. He had never been in large city the size of New York. Michael felt apprehensive and fearful about going there.

"I can better manipulate your funds if I am in closer proximity," the voice told him. It sensed his rising anxiety. "Having large amounts of money is an important aspect of life on your planet. You could achieve your goals with greater efficiency should you become wealthy."

"I can see how you would come to that understanding," Michael responded. "Many humans regard wealth as a sign of intelligence. Nothing could be further from the truth." His father often reminded him that money corrupted the weak-willed individual. "Actually, I am already a wealthy man," Michael laughed while he tried to hide his pain. "It's funny. When I checked my father's bank, I discovered he left me the bulk of his fortune in a trust… for all the good it has done."

Michael stood up and paced. "I've come to believe that the guardian placed in charge of my trust has turned out to be its embezzler!" He shook his head and stared at the bank's website on the screen. "I also believe the temptation of free access to my father's money has filled Burt Loomis' obsessed mind with avarice. That is why he hated to relinquish or share any part of that money with a mentally defective person. It's so clear to me now. That is how greed can cloud judgment."

"You should go to Connecticut and reclaim your trust," the voice stated.

"Like this?" Michael said glancing over at the mirror on the wall. "I look a wreck. Loomis would simply enforce the decree that kept me from my inheritance. They'd lock me up for my own benefit. No, you were right to suggest I need to restore my health first before I attempt anything else. New York might be just the place with the resources I need." He went back to the computer and sat. He then pulled up a New York real estate site.

"You've turned out to be a valuable resource my friend," he said absently while working out an idea in his head. "New York is sounding better all the time. With my new identity and a padded bank account, perhaps I can straighten out the mess in my head before I confront Loomis. Then, who knows? I should investigate the source of these other voices…"

"What will you do if you find them?" the voice put to him.

"Create a community," Michael thought, "a shared community… away from humanity."

"You could use your trust money to support this community," his voice suggested. "However for now, we will keep you anonymous until you fully recover."

"Good idea," Michael sighed, astounded with his voice's perception of him, "Why didn't you help me this way years ago?"

"Remember the listening problem?" the voice reminded. "Consider this the beginning of your new life, Michael Tyler," the voice indicated.

Michael took an extensive download that employed several models of economics while emphasizing how to set up and run a business the size of a corporation. He and the voice spent the next few days creating a dummy company by using investment capital they obtained from disreputable banking sources. They privately raided disguised accounts created for illegal gun merchants in Singapore, and drug dealers in Bolivia. They invented a new corporation and opened a line of credit with a large east coast bank. By the end of the first week, the voice made Michael a wealthy man, on paper at least.

Michael and the voice then decided it was time he moved to New York City. He could now afford to take a fashionable apartment in lower Manhattan, as close as Michael could bring the voice to Wall Street. On the way to New York, his voice created a series of text messages to arrange a meeting on the phone with a Manhattan real estate agent. With four hours of drive time remaining until he reached the city, the real estate agent finally contacted him.

"Did you say the selling price was thirteen-point-eight million?" he asked into the cell phone as he drove.

"The location you requested is very exclusive, Mr. Sawyer," the woman told him. "I have several names on a list for this prime…"

"I'll take it," Michael interrupted.

"Beg your pardon?" the woman replied.

"I said I will buy the condominium," he told her.

"You haven't seen the property…" she began to protest.

"I can bring you a cashier's check for the full amount by this afternoon. Will that be satisfactory?" he asked her.

A long pause followed.

"Hello?" Michael asked.

The woman practically spit her response into the mouthpiece as if she had choked on the idea of him handing her a check for the full amount.

"You'll need to fill out the paperwork first," she spoke hesitantly. "Is it possible to meet you at the building, say around three? I'll tell the attendant to reserve a space in the basement lot," she informed him. "I've sent the location to your phone."

"I'm forwarding all the necessary information via text to your office. See you at three," Michael added. He touched a button on the steering wheel, shutting off the embedded phone. "They've improved these since I last saw one," he thought. "You'll arrange for that transfer of personal information for the agent?"

"Of course Michael," the voice responded.

Hoping to make New York in time, he pushed his foot down on the accelerator. His electrically powered vehicle rapidly changing lanes as he easily avoided the other cars on the freeway. When he came within range of state police "road scanners," the voice sensed its presence and jammed the patrol car's radar systems. The voice did the same with the road sensors, too. He arrived at the Manhattan apartment building just before three in the afternoon. He then began to frantically search for a parking spot when he remembered she reserved a space in the basement lot and pulled in.

He had so focused on his rapid driving that when he left the car and headed for the building's elevator, the city's dense population suddenly affected his new brain center. Hundreds of thousands of thoughts pressed on his mind. Dizzy with the bombardment flooding into his head, his eyes could not focus on the floor controls when the elevator door opened.

"I need to stop this," he practically pleaded as his vision blurred.

"I sense your dilemma," the voice broke in. "Rein in your field of perception," it cautioned, "shut your psychic senses down Michael – pull your awareness back!"

Fighting his way forward, Michael managed to press the right floor number and the doors closed. He took in a few deep breaths, closed his eyes, and concentrated. He managed to withdraw his undisciplined range to within a few meters. By the time he stepped from the elevator, he began to regain a sense of normalcy, and his vision cleared. A woman stood in the hall, waiting for him.

"Punctual," she thought after she glanced down at her jewel-encrusted watch.

Despite hearing her loud thoughts, he pressed forward. She extended her hand but did not smile. He shook it. He then reached inside his jacket and pulled out the bank draft.

"What is this?" she asked. She realized that the paper was not a cashier's check.

"It's a bank draft. I own the corporation," he told her. "Phone it in," he suggested. "The bank's number is on the front. I can assure you that the check is genuine. Don't lose it," he added. "I made it out as cash."

All at once Michael heard, "What a hunk!" leap into his mind when the woman took out her cell phone. She held out the paper to call the number and glanced over at Michael. "A little rugged perhaps," her thoughts continued, "but I like that in a man."

Her strong emotional attraction nearly knocked him over. Michael decided to put some distance between them. He walked through the large empty rooms as she called to verify the check. Within a few minutes, she closed the phone, satisfied with what she heard. Michael felt her staring at his back for a second. She punctuated the moment with a single, "Huh!" He turned around to face her.

"Is there anything else?" he asked as he glanced around the large space.

"No Mr. Sawyer," she told him while she walked up to him. She placed the keys into his hands. "Your application is more than qualified. The apartment is yours. I'll notify the building's owner of the sale. The orientation guide is on the kitchen counter," she added and then paused. "I understand you are single," she put to him, "If you'd like a personal guide to the…"

"I can manage," he said and cut her off.

"Welcome to New York," she smiled briefly. She cocked her hip and looked the young man up and down. When Michael did not respond to her flirtation, she headed for the door.

He walked to the window hearing the door close behind him. He had a nice view of the surrounding street from the twenty-seventh floor. He found out later that every person in the building was at least a millionaire.

"I hope you know what you're doing," he said to his voice.

"Central park is just a few blocks from here," the voice told him. "You can use that area for outdoor exercise. Access to medical treatment, ingredients to create a new skin treatment formula and most shopping is within walking distance," the voice added. "You will recover with greater efficiency in this location."

"Thanks for the vote of confidence," Michael said. He stared out at the skyline while he searched his feelings. He wondered if he shared the same optimism the emotionless voice seemed to express. He had his work cut out for him.

During those first few weeks after he arrived in New York, the voice helped Michael adjust his mind to living within the city. He learned to cope with his alcoholism and rejuvenate his sagging spirit. Every morning the voice woke him. He ran a few miles in Central Park. When he returned to his apartment, Michael and the voice worked on building up his investments. The voice revealed a skin treatment formula based on research performed by other species offering to help. Michael took his voice's advice and followed every recommendation. He completely cured the sores on his skin and rejuvenated his youthful appearance. Soon, he regained the commanding stature and appearance of his father.

By year's end, Michael lived an extremely comfortable life. He knew his opulent lifestyle was only temporary. The only reason he needed the money was to carry out his mission. Therefore, he did not "decorate" his apartment per se. He had a few sticks of very expensive furniture, a bed, sofa, chairs and table. Yet he had no curtains, pictures on the wall, plants, rugs, bookshelves or any other domestic accoutrements that make a place home for most people. The plain white walls nearly resembled his old juvenile asylum minus the calming pictures. He remained isolated in his apartment and never left except when he ran through the park or shopped for life's necessities.

As Michael sat alone in his austere apartment late one February evening, he studied the details of a world map on a holiday present he purchased in late December – a new laptop computer with a satellite link that allowed him Internet access anywhere in the world. He sat propped up in his bed with a half dozen pillows piled up behind him as he balanced his computer on his lap. He nursed a cup of hot sweetened tea while he contemplated his journey.

He knew his ultimate destination would be China. He had yet to determine how he would travel or if he should seek help from a closer psychic before he went to Asia. However, he did not initially hear any psychic voices that spoke English which concerned him.

"Do you know the precise location of these pre-psychics?" he asked his voice that evening.

"We assign each person a voice – as you call us – the moment we detect his or her presence. Many of us fill this structure where I operate," it told him. "Finding those individual voices will take time. However, I will make an attempt to locate them."

"Meanwhile, I suppose I must be patient," Michael responded. "If you could, find the psychic nearest to my location," he requested. "Perhaps together we can link and figure out a course of action. Meeting them will be the first leg in my journey once I start out from New York."

"Have you given the trust more thought?" the voice put to him.

"I doubt you've studied the intricacies of jurisprudence. I'll need help with that," he thought back. "I'm going to enlist the services of an estate lawyer. They must be licensed in Connecticut."

"I can search databases," his voice suggested.

With the Santa Fe Bank located in Connecticut, Michael's trust required a lawyer with local credentials. He and his voice searched the state's files for attorneys until they found a reputable one with many years of estate practice. When Michael called to make an appointment for a consultation, the lawyer stated that he knew Michael's father. That is when Michael realized he would need to resume his actual identity. He had to be Michael Tyler once more.

"I'll need identification with my real name this time," he requested of his voice after speaking to the attorney. "When you generate a Connecticut driver's license," Michael suggested, "use my father's old address."

"I believe something more sophisticated is in order Michael," the voice told him. "You should carry a form of identification that can be used anywhere, in any country," it proposed. "In addition to the driver's license, I will generate an American passport. Creating one will take some manipulation," it told him. "I will send for the license first. Use the computer's camera to take your picture."

The voice first arranged for Michael to receive a Connecticut driver's license. After arranging the license, it then generated an official U.S. passport. During the weeks that followed, Michael and the voice took the opportunity to investigate the trust further. They uncovered the extent of Burt Loomis' illegal discrepancies that Michael suspected had existed. During his first meeting with the lawyer, Michael laid out the facts before the Connecticut attorney, Mr. Arnold Wilson of New Haven. Seeing the evidence, the lawyer agreed to take Michael's case. He helped the young man regain control of his trust.

When the time approached for Michael to confront Loomis, his sense of urgency to locate and meet the other psychics grew into an obsession.

One afternoon in mid-May, a week before his confrontation in Simsbury, the world's first psychic was feeling isolated, desperate and hopelessly alone despite having an intelligent voice as his guide.

"This is no longer an option," Michael called on his voice. He anxiously paced in front of his large living room window. The view and clear blue sky over the city did nothing to cheer his mood today. "I need to contact these other psychics or I feel I'll go mad," he informed his voice. He stopped long enough to look around the room at the material items he accumulated. "None of this matters any longer. Only *they* mean anything to me," he gestured out the window. "I will leave New York and set out to find them – the sooner the better. Whether I return someday is a matter of conjecture. Of course, I'll leave my possessions… the car, the electronic gadgets, furniture – everything we've purchased."

"What will you do with these things?" his voice asked.

"I don't care what you do with them," Michael tossed back. "Donate them to charity, give them away – they no longer matter," Michael directed to his voice. "Material possessions are transitory. Shut down the corporation. Put the condominium on the market. Disburse the capital. Give some of the proceeds to charitable organizations and send the rest to the various levels of government since we haven't paid any taxes."

"That's a sizable sum of money…" the voice began when Michael jumped in.

"Don't you understand what I am feeling?" he practically yelled.

"I sense confusion, an increase in anxiety, and anger," the voice stated. "Have I offended you?"

"No…" Michael answered.

"Do you feel…" the voice tried to guess.

I don't know what I'm feeling!" the young man declared. He threw his hands into the air. "I only know I must seek out and find these other… voices… human voices," he relayed. "Perhaps if we could form a group, then I can begin to understand why we are here."

"I will help you in any way I can," the voice added.

"You've helped me already," Michael replied after he calmed down. "I realize that I should listen to your advice. However, if I am the beginning of a new phenomenon on this planet, then I must be the one that seeks these others out," he reasoned. "I must be the catalyst for the rest. Please… find him, find this other psychic voice so that he and I can… link."

The following day, when Michael stepped out to buy some last minute groceries for the few remaining meals at his current address, his voice suddenly opened a contact. As he waited for the elevator in the lobby of his building, the alien – eager to help Earth's first contact – rushed to impart its new information into Michael's mind.

"I've located a potential human subject to the north," the voice blurted.

"Whoa!" Michael linked back. He nearly dropped the bags in his arms. "Warn me first before you do that!"

"Beg your pardon?" a man said coming off the elevator.

"Nothing," Michael mumbled. He pushed his button and made a hasty retreat to his apartment.

"Are you settled?" the voice asked a few minutes later.

Once Michael stepped inside, he kicked the front door closed with his foot.

"Tell me more about this contact," Michael requested while heading for the kitchen.

"I do not have an exact location. You must find and convince the person to convert, Michael, if you want their assistance in your journey," the voice declared.

"Find? Are you telling me I have to wander the countryside until I feel their presence?" he reflected as he put away his groceries.

"I only know the general direction of the subject from your current location based on psychic energy levels. I have not located the subject's specific voice. Once you move further toward the north, I can obtain more information," the voice indicated.

"North… you mean this person could be a block north of here?" he asked.

"No, this distance is further," it stated. "The energy source is difficult to pinpoint. While the surface of your planet is not very large, its reading is relatively weak. I am acting through your conduit. Have you ever heard of the technique called triangulation?" the voice asked.

"I have," Michael replied. He folded the reusable grocery bag. "Take two readings and measure the distance between them. Use the angles formed when you connect them to a third point and you can determine the third point's distance from the other two."

"Correct," the voice confirmed. "When you meet with the Connecticut lawyer next, I will attempt another scan. With two directional readings, I can place the location of your subject to within a few kilometers," the voice stated. "Armed with that information, I can scan the collective to find the corresponding voice," it told him.

Michael stared at the wall in his kitchen. For a moment, he thought about what it would be like to have another true psychic in his presence.

"Meeting another psychic…" Michael's thoughts rambled.

"Excuse me?" the voice replied. After interacting with Michael for months, it knew the correct "polite" responses to use.

"Just some pre-meeting anxiety," Michael relayed. "I can tell this is going to take a bit of finesse on my part," he thought to it. "After all, I've never met another psychic person. What if they visualize my approach and send images into my brain of tigers ripping me to ribbons? On the other hand, we might just hit it off and become great friends. Who knows?" he said, before he realized how unprepared he felt. "This whole idea of just running off around the world and confronting strangers is starting to make me feel nervous."

"Perhaps you should perform some strenuous exercise to release the tension. A run through the park for example," the voice suggested.

Michael followed its advice and ran five miles around Central Park. The workout did help him sleep better that evening.

When Michael met with Mr. Wilson for the second time two days later, his voice gained enough direction to pinpoint an urban area where this psychic might live. As he drove back to New York after the meeting, the voice informed Michael it narrowed the search to a city.

"I can give you a specific location for the nearest pre-psychic," it told him. "That person lives in Battleford, Canada."

"Are you certain?" Michael asked.

"Yes Michael," his voice told him. "Although I have not located this person's voice, my scans of the collective should produce results within a week by your time standards," it stated. "Is the province known as Saskatchewan currently a long way off from your present location in New York city?" it asked. "You are bipedal creatures."

"Yes we are bipedal," Michael responded and smiled. "However, Canada is a long way for my species to walk," he told it. "I wish I could fly there," he said while trying to picture his mode of travel. "It would certainly be faster."

"As in an aircraft," the voice observed.

"Yes," Michael replied. "Unfortunately I have no choice. I'll have to drive. I can't risk taking any other form of transportation and move about inconspicuously."

"Can you do that alone?" the voice asked him.

"I'm running out of options," Michael observed. "If I take public modes of transportation – by bus, train, or commercial flight – anyone could trace my movements. I must begin to use stealth in everything I do. The cash and other items I've been able to accumulate can buy our passage to China. I should have enough valuables to barter for two passports once the smugglers bring this other psychic and me into Russia."

"If the person in Canada agrees to conversion and travels with you," the voice added.

"I only hope I've made the right kind of contingency plans if they don't," Michael thought.

In a carrying case, Michael collected a small treasure in the form of large denominations taken from a variety of commonly used currencies along with four sheets of bearer bonds, a small case filled with twenty perfect five-carat diamonds, ten twenty-four carat gold bars, ten bars of platinum, and the advanced laptop computer with satellite connective capability. Michael always kept this briefcase near him. He and the voice used the dummy corporation to purchase the items, hoping their lucrative value would help Michael negotiate his way around the world.

"Before I set out for Canada, I'll need a few things," he requested.

"Please give me your list," the voice indicated. "Then turn on your computer and connect me to your system. I will have your items express delivered."

"First, I'll need identification to cross the border," he thought to his voice, "a Canadian driver's license, a Canadian plate for the car and two blank Canadian passports for possible use later," Michael indicated as he opened his case and started his computer.

"Ordering," the voice replied.

"Also, I'll need an older, less-conspicuous domestic model car other than this Italian sports car," he asked, "one without tracer chips in it – perhaps an older model that uses liquid fuel," he suggested.

"Searching…" the voice stated.

"Of all my possessions, I'll miss you most," he stroked the contoured leather seat.

"I have begun to generate everything you have requested," the voice indicated. "You have three days before the meeting with Loomis. That should be enough time."

An ambulance – lights flashing, sirens screaming – flew past his car going in the opposite direction and startled him.

Michael's mind returned to the present. From that last moment when he recalled driving home in his sports car a few days ago to the current time, Michael's rumination over these last eleven months passed quickly. His Manhattan apartment was only minutes away. He had remembered the night he acquired his new psychic ability, the day he moved to New York and began to manipulate the markets. He recalled when he learned new subjects, recuperated from alcoholism, acquired the estate attorney and regained control over his trust.

With his mind now focused on the present, his firm grasp on the wheel relaxed as he made his way into lower Manhattan just as the orchestral music reached its symphonic climax. Michael leaned back into his soft faux-leather seat while the sleek and stylish car made its way home. He left his thoughts about the trust, Loomis and Connecticut behind him and began to dwell instead on the difficult tasks that lay ahead with his morning departure for Canada.

"Time is precious," his voice reminded. "I booked the hotel room for one night."

"I hope I am doing the right thing," Michael linked.

"Have faith in your own ability Michael," the voice encouraged.

"Faith," Michael deadpanned. "A being on another world that has no idea how religious values shape human morality is telling me to acquire something it can't sense."

"I tried to use human expressions to help bolster your…" the voice attempted to explain.

"Yeah yeah, it's part of your protocol. I understand," Michael replied as he neared his high-rise. "I'll switch this car with the clunker I parked in the apartment's garage yesterday. Well, aren't you going to wish me luck?"

"Michael…" the voice began.

"I know," the young man sighed, "it's just an Earth expression. Sometimes we humans need reassurance."

"Only sometimes Michael?" the voice asked him.

"I'll concede," Michael chuckled. "We need it most of the time."

"Earth language… do you realize with all of your quirky familiarities, how difficult the English language is to translate? I suppose Chinese is next on the menu."

Michael shuddered at the thought of learning yet another language.

"Don't remind me. I can hardly wait to fill my mind with a hundred thousand different characters!" he flipped out his remark.

"Seriously?" the voice asked. It then realized that Michael slipped into using sarcasm. "In other words, you dread the prospect. I am catching on."

"Do you mean to tell me that my voice finally understands how to banter?" Michael laughed aloud for the first time in days.

He smiled as he pondered his current state. His life was not that bad he considered. He had an incredibly powerful alien as an ally. He changed into the world's first truly psychic human. For the moment, he drove a posh expensive European sports car. As a bonus, he finally had the trust back! Why should he not smile? He positively grinned from ear to ear, letting out a great belly laugh as the orchestra thundered its last refrain, 'Rach-ma-ni-noff!'

He switched cars in the garage and reluctantly parted company with his handmade Italian sports car. He could not drive it to Canada without being too conspicuous. Its distinctive sleek styling stood out. Besides, he already donated the car to charity. He figuratively kissed the car good-bye.

"It was fun to pretend I was rich and famous if only for awhile," he thought. Then he manually erased the auto's memory chips and wiped down the car for any prints he left.

Chapter 4

A test of character

Michael drove his older model car to the five-star hotel to spend one night in a penthouse suite that his voice reserved. He surprised the valet when this perfectly coiffed, expertly dressed young man stepped from such a pitiful beast and tipped him two one-hundred dollar bills to watch over his heap.

"At least I'm properly dressed for this superb ambience," he thought. He glanced up at the grand, refurbished and historic New York hotel. He took in a deep breath. "Relax," he thought.

Riding the elevator up to the luxurious accommodations, he began to look forward to spending the night. He would have extended his stay if time permitted. However, any delay in the start of his journey might increase the chance that something terrible would happen to the extremely rare humans he would soon pursue.

After the usual escort to the highly touted room by a uniformed bellhop, Michael flopped on the large bed feeling like a pampered kid again. Symbolically, he held his breath all day, wondering how the encounter at the bank would end. Full of fresh confidence, he stretched out his arms and let the air out of his lungs like a balloon shooting around the room.

"Ahhh!" he sighed.

"Feel better?" the voice broke in.

"Oh yes," he lied.

As he lay on the bed and stared up at the ceiling, his anxieties began to plague his mind. The overwhelming details of his fragile plan, the stress of the day and the idea of having to share his uniqueness with others along with its uncertainty, preyed on his nerves. Old memories and feelings surfaced… his parent's tragic death… his brutal treatment by the psychiatrist, Dr. Hami… and his two years of alcoholism returned to haunt the young man on what should have been a joyous evening. His stomach lurched. An old familiar pain shot through his middle.

"Oh god!" he winced. "Why do I suddenly feel like I'm back on those tracks in Mississippi?"

Michael felt tremendous pressure during the last month with no one to share his feelings except a shapeless cold alien voice. He wrung his hands together as he bit his lower lip.

"This is too much," he gritted his teeth. "I don't know if I can handle this."

Rather than call on his voice for help, he jumped up and moved over to the locked liquor refrigerator. Its chilly insides held beer, little bottles of liquor and bottles of dessert wine inside. He stared at the cold wine bottles inside and licked his lips – relief lay just inches away. He took the red plastic lock in one hand and gave it a firm grasp. He closed his eyes and swallowed hard.

"If you take a drink, you will dull your senses Michael, not enhance them," his voice sprang into his thoughts.

"You still here?" Michael linked. Moisture gathered on his upper lip. His mouth felt dry. His breathing quickened. The programmed signs returned in an instant. "I need a drink," he confessed. "I only want a little one."

Michael stared at the wine bottle. He recalled the welcome numbing sensation of being drunk. More than anything in the world – at that instant – he wanted to open the bottle and take a long welcome chug of cool wine to fill his belly. Then he could be stuporous and forget about the voice or any of his troubles…

"That's the old Michael speaking," he thought. "But I only want a little drink. A little drink won't hurt me… will it?"

"Are you certain?" the voice broke in.

"You don't know how much this means to me!" Michael declared. "I might be psychic but I'm human, too!" he declared.

His hand trembled as sweat broke out on his face. It would only take a quick snap of his wrist and he could return to the days when a drink calmed his nerves. As an alcoholic, he knew he could drink his way out of a crisis. The pull of alcohol felt very strong.

"Remember the plan," the voice broke in.

"Damn the plan!" he grunted through clenched teeth.

He forced his eyes closed and concentrated on control even as pain swelled in his stomach. Sweat broke out on his upper lip. His hand started to shake.

"After all the treatments, the clinic visits, working your mind and body into shape… you want to throw all of that away for a drink?" the voice asked him.

"You don't know the strength of this feeling!" he said. He wiped across his mouth with his free hand.

"Yes I do know your feelings Michael," his voice quickly responded. "I know exactly how you feel more than anyone you have ever known. I know every nuance of your feelings," the voice linked. "That is also how another psychic will interact with you. They will know exactly how you feel about everything. That is why you wish take this journey. Remember?"

"Sorry," he dipped his head. With his free hand, he tried to rub away the pain in his stomach.

"Please let me help you Michael," the voice offered.

Michael resisted the voice's intervention. He wanted to beat this on his own. However, his hand holding the red plastic lock shook so violently, he could not stop it. He had to put his other hand around his wrist to keep it still. Yet for some reason he could not let the plastic lock go.

"Anything!" he shouted aloud. "Help me! Please!"

"Breathe deep Michael," the voice began.

For once, the screeching metallic tones of his alien's voice sounded almost soothing. He felt energy flow through the conduit within his mind. In seconds, his pain, along with his craving subsided.

"Thanks," he said. He nearly collapsed on top of the bar's refrigerator.

With considerable effort, he regained his control and let go of the little plastic red lock. His shaking hand pushed back the matted hair off his moist forehead.

"I don't want to be weak… I want to be strong," he said, moving away.

"Your healing process will take time. Try to relax. Take in the comforts of the suite," the voice offered. "You've spent the last eleven months preparing for your confrontation with Loomis. You played your hand well. You had your judgment reversed and you have regained control of your trust. This is a moment of celebration Michael. Let your mind be free of stress this night."

Rather than link, Michael nodded his head in agreement. He went around the large room and turned off the lights. He drew back the curtains and stepped out onto the terrace. A refreshing wind blew across his sweaty face. He slowly removed his pricey handmade clothes – the last remnants of wealth. He let each piece of expensive clothing fly away in the breeze.

"May you find some homeless person," he called out. He tossed each item over the side of the balcony – including his fourteen-hundred dollar handcrafted shoes! They floated off in the breeze.

"That's done," he said as he brushed his hands together. He wore only his birthday suit.

Naked, he strolled back inside the suite and stood before a full-length mirror. He noticed that most of his healed sores had vanished. Instead of a bum, he saw a six-foot six-inch tall young man staring back at him – trim, slightly muscular, handsome with neat brown hair and bluish-gray eyes. He nodded and smiled to reassure the figure in the mirror. This gesture did not erase the doubt in his mind. He slumped into a large chair and gazed out upon the twinkling skyline of New York City.

"I wish my mother and father were still alive. I miss them," he thought.

His eyes swelled with emotion recalling their images.

"I must have come into this world for some purpose," he reasoned. "It was not just to grab all the riches or be the most powerful person on the planet either."

Michael took in a deep breath. His insolent side – the part of him from that upper class home in Connecticut – wanted to be cuddled, spoiled and pampered. He traveled a rough unforgiving road to manhood. Only now could he begin to feel good about his new emerging self. The very thing he once cursed – a voice inside his head – became his consolation and salvation. Yet, when he considered his current position, the psychic energy he possessed surged through his body. It filled him with not just confidence but a feeling of power.

"Do you realize that with my advantage," he considered and sat up, "I could be the wealthiest man in the world and perhaps the most powerful?" he thought. This statement contradicted the one he just made. "After all, who would stop me? I could be the master of Wall Street or President of the United States. I'd read their minds and use that to my advantage. Why don't I?" he cried out as he stood up. "I will rule the world!" he declared. He spun his naked body around with his eyes closed and his arms stretched out.

He stopped, lowered his arms and stared at the nighttime New York skyline.

"You people are so vulnerable," he whispered.

He remembered his father, a man who worked hard his entire life to maintain the family firm, Tyler Engineering. With no successor, Tyler Engineering failed and broke up. Only the trust remained. Recalling his father's greatness, Michael's head dropped in disgrace when he saw the image of his father's face before him. His father had been a man who took great pride in his family's heritage, despite his one shame – a mad violent son. After all he had been through, all his parents put him through, Michael still sought his father's approval.

"No, I won't rule over you," he spoke aloud while he watched the flow of traffic on the street below, "because… well, because I know that it is wrong, that's why. I am my father's son. I won't make you ashamed of me father! You taught me better than that."

The strong temptation to use his power for domination washed over him and then retreated, like the tide from the shore. Michael took in a deep breath and turned away without regret.

"If that was a test," he pondered as he started to shiver from the breeze, "then I think I just passed."

He felt a surge of good will and confidence pour into his mind. He walked back to the phone inside and called down to the front desk. He remembered passing a Brookman's men clothiers in the lobby. They connected him to the store. Within minutes, he ordered several sets of casual clothes for his journey.

As he sat naked in the dark, a being on a world many millions of light years away contemplated Michael's most recent actions. His voice quietly observed human morality as it rested at its workstation on another planet.

"In their thirst for power and greed, many psychic beings wasted their opportunity and destroyed their worlds. You have risen above that temptation. We admire you human for your tenacity and moral courage!" its thoughts echoed through the collective.

Michael never heard any of these comments. He sat quietly gazing at the nighttime bustling city for several minutes in silence.

"Snap out of it Michael!" he finally spoke aloud. "Tonight is supposed to be one of celebration. I have my trust back! Phase one of the plan is complete! Right?"

At that moment, he heard a knock at the door. Michael ran into the bedroom for a robe. He then let in a waiter who pushed a large cart. The voice ordered several items off the menu electronically when it placed the room reservation: smoked salmon, asparagus with hollandaise, specialty cheeses, pastry, fresh fruit, chocolates, plus a variety of hors d'oeuvres.

The waiter spread the scrumptious treats out on the bar. Michael then watched the waiter place two chilled bottles of sparkling white grape juice into a large bucket of shaved ice.

"Your clothes will be up in few minutes," the man informed him.

Michael generously tipped the delivery person and then turned to the bucket.

"This is the only drink I need," he said. He pulled one of the bottles from the pile of crushed ice.

Twisting off the top reminded him of the cheap wine bottles that once held sway over his life. Michael poured out a glass of the bubbly liquid and took a long cool drink.

"This actually tastes good," he stated. He knew he could never drink real wine again. He walked out onto the terrace. "I swear that I will never regret giving up alcohol or feel the temptation to drink!" he yelled and he did not care if anyone heard him. "I promise that those urges will never control me again," he added.

Silence. No voice. He walked back inside and contemplated the bar of treats. He attacked the spread of hors d'oeuvres by taking a bite out of this and that. He wanted to taste everything. He suddenly felt the urge to be carefree. The idea of a diet did not concern him. He tore into the feast as one who was famished.

"I believe you will carry out that promise," the voice encouraged a minute later. "You seem to demonstrate all that is good in human beings."

"I wondered what happened to you," Michael linked as he chewed. "Things grew a little too quiet in there for a moment," he thought to his voice. "You're missing the celebration."

"That's the spirit!" his voice linked. Its comment made Michael smile.

"By the way, nice pitch for an alien," he linked back. "You sound more like a football coach. Your language skills are improving."

"To be honest, I did recall the expression from your television watching experiences," the voice confessed. "However, I have been looking forward to this evening Michael," the voice said.

"So have I my alien friend. So have I," Michael affectionately replied.

He munched on the gourmet delicacies until he had his fill. Stretching his mouth wide with an enormous yawn, he made his way to the spacious bedroom. Exhausted, he paused before the bathroom mirror before hitting the bed.

"I'm not certain what you'll find in Canada," he addressed the man in the vanity mirror. "I only know that if you find a nut case or raving lunatic, we'll have that much in common."

The following morning, Michael dressed in the semi-casual clothes brought up from the hotel's lobby shop. He then set out on the first leg of his quest. After a day and a half of long hours behind the wheel with very little rest along America's westbound interstate highways, he finally arrived in the dead of night at Whitetail, Montana.

A few miles before the border crossing, he pulled the car off the road and changed his license plates. He only brought his clothes and personal items along with the briefcase, which he concealed inside the front seat of the car – hidden from the border's x-ray machine by the clunker's old metallic framed seats. He pulled up to the border crossing at one o'clock in the morning. His voice indicated that according to statistical averages, Michael could enter

Canada at this location with relatively little interference from the border officers.

At 1:22 a.m., local time, Michael crossed into Saskatchewan, Canada, without arousing anything but a friendly greeting from the officers on duty. He flashed his Canadian driver's license to the U. S. Border agent. They might have searched his car thoroughly had his destination been America. After just a few minutes of simple questions and a quick look around his car with a flashlight, the agent waved Michael on. He drove through the night. Despite his low level of energy, his anxiety regarding this new psychic man kept Michael awake. By noon he pulled into downtown Battleford, and found a room to rent, paying with cash, as he had when crossing America.

Once inside his room, he collapsed onto his bed after using up the last of his energy reserves. He slept continually for the next 18 hours.

Meanwhile, his alien friend tried to locate this particular person's corresponding voice on its own world, a task made easier with Michael being in close proximity to its energy pattern. When Michael awoke, he tried to make contact with his voice. Instead, he opened a link to a different alien voice – the first time it ever happened to him. This new voice volunteered to act as facilitator between Michael and another destination, if he wanted. He declined the offer.

Michael thanked the voice and disconnected his link. He decided on patience and waiting as his best course of action. He took a walk and stopped by a diner to eat before he returned to his room. Lying down, Michael just closed his eyes for sleep, when he sensed his conduit open.

"Michael, I found the contact's voice," his own voice boomed into his brain.

Michael jumped up off the bed and practically flew across the room.

"You're back!" he exclaimed. "Thank goodness," he said as he breathed hard for a few seconds after being startled. "I was beginning to think I dreamed the whole thing up and that I was destined to be trapped in Battleford for the rest of my life while waiting for a delusion to respond!" he chuckled.

"Sorry Michael, the search took longer than I expected," the flat voice informed him. "I realize my absence caused you some anxiety. This facility contains large numbers of voices linking many psychic minds scattered around the universe. They relieved me of duty during my search. I finally located the voice responsible for the Canadian contact. We exchanged information. You may find this news comforting," the voice said. It imparted a slightly excited tone.

As much as Michael adjusted his style when speaking with his alien voice, the voice gradually discovered the kind of human emphasis on expressions that put Michael at ease or fulfilled his need to encounter suspense.

"What?" Michael finally blurted.

"The contact is a young female named Cecilia Beaton," the voice explained. "She is seventeen-years-old having graduated from high school last week. She lives near the intersection of Twenty-sixth Street West, and Second Avenue. The address is two-six-three-four Twenty-sixth Street West."

"A young woman, huh," Michael answered, "Not what I expected. I supposed I'd better rush over to see what she looks like," Michael answered while gathering up a jacket.

"We should be cautious Michael," the voice suggested. "I recommend surveillance first – to observe the young woman for any anomalies."

"Anomalies?" Michael shot back.

"Find out as much as you can about her before you attempt contact," the voice went on. "Her voice tried an interaction about six years ago with terrible consequences. She left school, upset and crying. She told her mother she heard strange voices in her head. Fortunately, her parents did nothing – except offer her support. The voice then withdrew but kept her under observation."

While Michael tried to figure out what to do next, the voice added another caveat.

"We have one thing in our favor," it stated, "she feels free to broadcast her inner feelings. Her voice compiled many details, which it shared with me. For one, she yearns for adventure. She loves to read romantic fiction. Her fantasies include a handsome young man rescuing her from a dull life in Battleford. You seem to fit the bill."

As Michael pondered those facts, he considered an experiment. He was not certain if he could link directly to her mind. However, if the young woman's voice opened a contact to her, perhaps he could link directly to her mind via his own voice. They never tried this type of link. It seemed his only course of action to impress her.

For the first time in the history of the planet, two people would openly share their thoughts. Michael considered that the risks involved with such an interaction were formidable. Yet, he had to convince her in a way that would inspire belief.

"No superficial barriers separating a man's thoughts with those of a woman. The very thought frightens me!" Michael shuddered.

He wondered how much honesty their open minds could endure.

CHAPTER 5

THE FIRST MIND LINK

MICHAEL WATCHED CECILIA BEATON'S MOVEMENTS and mannerisms from a safe distance for two days without garnering unnecessary attention.

"What's taking so long?" the voice finally asked Michael on the second day.

"I see you've begun to comprehend our time scheme," Michael shot back.

"I thought you wanted to be at the rendezvous point by now," the voice replied.

"This young woman is very intelligent," he tried to explain. "I may need her help. I can't go charging in and demand she turn into a psychic being, then drag her clear across Canada hoping she'll be receptive! This will take time. I must use finesse. I need to have the right approach."

"You are running out of time, Michael. You must confront her and stop making excuses," it practically demanded.

"That's easy for you to say," Michael responded. "Do you recall mating?"

"Vaguely," it stated. "We don't mate as often as human beings."

"This is similar in that I lack experience," Michael pointed out. "Interacting with the female of my species isn't like dealing with Burt Loomis. Remember, I've never dated, or even kissed a woman," he confessed. "I cannot take a download in developing personal skills overnight the same way I learned a subject. Being on an all male ward and then homeless after that kept me separated from females most of my adult life."

"I wondered why you never acted on the sexual impulses that I sensed while you lived in New York," the voice asked him.

Michael hesitated to answer. He had profound difficulty expressing desire after his isolating experience in the juvenile facility. The medicine he took suppressed every sexual thought or desire he had. While living in New York, Michael only expressed his desires during dreams. He may as well have been a eunuch. He had never lost his virginity. Even now, the idea of sex embarrassed him.

"I wasn't ready," Michael shot back. "I doubt I'll ever be. I have trouble expressing… affection. Enough about me," he said, dismissing his feelings. "I must consider whether this young woman is a proper candidate for conversion at this time. For some reason, I always pictured someone like me – that is, a young man to pitch in and help when I needed it. I never thought about my choice being a… young woman," he said, staring down at his feet. "I only hope she can offer us some assistance."

He saw the complexities, far clearer than his voice, especially about leaving one's home, a painful memory for him when forced into seclusion at the age of ten. Perhaps Cecilia Beaton had loving parents, close friends, familiar surroundings, fondness for her home and school.

To remove her from this environment, take her by force to some other location, and expect her to cooperate, might be asking too much of anyone, let alone a new high school graduate with very little experience. Michael knew he had to find a way to speak to her. However, his time to plan for ideas and solutions ran out.

Desperation sometimes calls for drastic measures.

"Michael, a thunderstorm is forecast for tomorrow evening," the voice said after having scanned the local broadcast channels on his computer. "That might give you enough cover in case you must kidnap the girl and make an emergency getaway," the voice suggested.

"Kidnap?" Michael linked back.

"I was trying to make suggestions," the voice stated. "Did I use the wrong term?"

"I'm afraid this is one aspect of humanity you've interpreted incorrectly, my alien friend," Michael replied. "I'll either convince her to join me or move on without her. Either way, I'm not using force. Each person must decide to choose the kind of life I've chosen. If I cannot set up a psychic community of willing participants, then I will continue alone. Let me approach her tomorrow morning," he suggested. "I'll wait outside the house. When she comes out, I'll speak to her via a mind link, but I'll do it my way."

The following day started out hot, humid and sunny. Michael arrived shortly after dawn and parked the car on the street a few houses away. He slumped down in the front seat while sipping hot sweetened tea from a foam cup.

The cute and shapely young blonde teenager left her house early that morning. She planned a busy schedule. First, she intended to visit her friend and share her new collection of songs from their favorite groups. She walked alone with no distractions. The street seemed deserted, an excellent opportunity for Michael to act.

"Make the connection," he requested of his voice.

Cecilia's voice tapped into her thoughts. Michael felt the connection open. All at once he heard her stream of thoughts. He hoped she would hear his.

"Cecilia…" he thought.

He spoke to his voice with his mind. His voice relayed those thoughts to the other voice inside the collective connected to the girl's mind. That voice then relayed Michael's thoughts back to Earth inside her mind. The two young people – about thirty meters apart – had an intergalactic link that extended over hundreds of millions of light years. The girl stopped dead in her tracks when she clearly heard her name pop into her head. She whirled around.

"I'm not behind you," Michael linked. "I'm speaking to you inside your head, Cecilia. Don't be alarmed. I've been waiting to speak with you. Nod your head if you can hear me."

Wondering what she would do next, Michael closely monitored her reaction. As he spoke, she put her hands up to her ears to block any sound. When that did not work, she slapped the side of her head, and then stopped because it hurt.

"Please, don't hurt yourself," he tried to sound at ease. "You aren't crazy. You have a special talent that few people possess. Please stop and listen to my voice for just a minute."

Michael tried to focus in on her thoughts.

Her mind blank, the teenager stood very still.

"You can communicate with me if you try. Focus your thoughts and try to think something back to me," Michael informed her.

"Can you hear me?" she shyly asked.

"Yes I can," he answered slowly.

"Then shut up and leave me alone!" she yelled aloud and started to walk away.

"I can't, wait, please! Cecilia, you are someone special and unique. Please stop and listen to me," he begged.

Her hands on her hips, Cecilia stopped once more with a defiant expression.

"With your special abilities, you can be a great assistance to me. You will help me, won't you Cecilia?" Michael asked. He wondered what her next reaction would be.

"I… I don't know," she said while she softened her assertive stance. "What kind of help?" she asked as she looked all around.

Michael put his hand down on the handle of the car door.

"A man is going to walk up to you. Listen to him for a minute. Don't be frightened. He won't hurt you. He just wants to talk," Michael told her.

"How are you doing this? Who are you?" she demanded. Her head spun around as she tried to find the voice's origin. "Is this some kind of practical joke or something?" she asked half-smiling.

"Just a few minutes ago, after you downloaded your favorite music into your player, you danced around in your pale yellow underwear trimmed with snowflake lace. You sent your friend a text message. This happened in the privacy of your room less than five minutes ago," Michael linked as he watched her carefully. "No one watched you. You closed your curtains as well as your door. Am I right?"

Cecilia froze. His words spoke the truth. Everything happened exactly as he described it. Perhaps he had some hidden camera in her house.

"Let me explain," he continued. "I do not have a camera in your house," surprising her as he said it. "I can see into your mind Cecilia. I know your thoughts. I also know you are scared and suspicious. Talk to this young man. He will be walking up to you in five seconds."

"What?" she questioned. She spun around and searched the immediate area with her eyes.

Michael opened his door and stepped out of his car.

"Four," he counted, as he crossed the street.

"Wait! Stop!" she shouted.

"Three," he continued toward her.

He stepped up on the sidewalk. Still moving toward her, his advancing form finally caught her eye.

"Two," he linked as he moved in closer.

Without opening his mouth, he spoke directly into her mind. Cecilia started to back up.

"One," he finished. "It's me, Cecilia. I am the one talking to you." he spoke to her mentally. He stood before her with his tall imposing frame.

"I don't believe you," she bravely declared, although inside he detected her fear.

"Believe me," he answered aloud, "you are an extremely rare individual," he added via the link.

"But how are you…" she began. She stared up at Michael's face.

"I'm using a mind link with you," he answered via his interstellar connection. "Please don't be upset, Cecilia. You'll begin to understand once I explain everything," he added, smiling. "The explanation is very simple, if you'll listen."

Defiant yet confused, she bravely faced him while her emotions hovered between fear and anger.

"I'm sorry," he softened. "I'm being rude. I didn't introduce myself. My name is Michael Tyler. I drove across America to find you. I am here because you – that is – we have a gift, you and I, a gift that other people don't have. We can send our thoughts great distances, but we can also learn to receive thoughts from those around us."

He carefully watched her reaction to this news. Questions and fear filled her mind. She started to speak, but Michael held up his hand.

"It's ok," he told her. "I hear your thoughts and your feelings. I understand that what I am telling you is a lot to take on faith. I had trouble understanding it too at first." He glanced around them and paid particular attention to the neighbor's open windows. Their position on the street seemed vulnerable to him and far too exposed. "I'd like to speak with you for a few minutes – but privately," he conveyed over the link. "Would you mind coming with me – either in my car or to a public place – if you like?" he asked while gesturing toward his parked car. "Personally, I'd prefer some privacy where we can discuss this. I promise you that talk is all I have in mind. I need your full attention," he gazed hopefully at her youthful face.

"Slow down!" she said as she backed up. "This is just a bit too much for me. Can you just give me a moment here?" she asked and turned her head.

"This is crazy," she thought. "What is going to happen to me if I go with this guy? I don't even know him! I swear, if he tries anything, I'll scream and kick him!" she thought.

"I appreciate the fact you'd consider speaking to me," he interrupted her thoughts, "but please don't kick me. I promise that I will be a perfect gentleman," he linked.

"Oh, my gosh! You can read my thoughts!" she exclaimed, startled.

"Cecilia," he said, glancing about nervously. "I don't mean to rush your decision, but we must leave here before we attract too much attention."

She hesitated for another second. She considered her judgment of another person's character sound. She saw Michael as a clean, tidy, fastidious young man who spoke sincerely to her. She did not detect a hint of deception on his part.

"Ok," she spoke softer. She caught on to his hint. "I'm too well known around here," she said, beginning to agree with this stranger. "I know a place nearby. Let's go in your car," she said. In her mind she added, "Oh, God, please let this be on the level. Don't let this guy be some molesting jerk!"

"I can assure you," Michael replied in his link, "I am neither a molester nor a jerk."

He raised his eyebrows and betrayed that he heard her accusation.

She meekly smiled back, "Guess I'd better be careful what I think!"

"If it will make you feel any better," he reached into his pocket. "Here are the keys to my car. I can't drive without them. We'll just sit in the car and talk. Does that make you feel more secure?"

Cecilia took the keys and nodded.

The two crossed the street and entered Michael's old car. Sitting in the passenger seat, she turned to him.

"You'll have to excuse my... hesitation," she thought to him. "This is the first time I have ever placed this much trust in a stranger. I'm more than just nervous. Ok? This better not be a put on. Is it?"

Without moving his lips, he thought directly back into her mind.

"Believe me, Cecilia, this is very real," he linked to her.

She sensed that the expression on his face seemed as sincere as her father's was when he lectured her. She did not need any more convincing than that. She nodded, and faced forward. She closed her mouth, took in a deep breath, and thought back to Michael.

"The park is usually deserted this time of day. Drive to this corner, and turn left," she linked as she gave him directions.

"I'll need my keys for that," he requested.

Cecilia handed Michael back his keys with a sheepish expression.

"Sorry," she thought.

He started the car.

"This way?" he pointed while pulling the car away from the curb.

Cecilia nodded once more. Whether she was too afraid to think or not, he could no longer be certain. The alien voices remained silent.

Michael drove to the edge of a small park, not far from the residential area. The park had a small grassy field with swings and a practice field bordered by woods. The spot was abandoned at this time of day. He shut off the engine and turned his head toward Cecilia.

"I am linked to your mind through what I've come to call 'my voice,'" he explained. "Only we can hear them. These voices are not human, but you can ask me more questions about them later."

The frowning teenager stared at him with skepticism.

"This is so weird," she said. "I mean you aren't moving your lips or anything, yet I can hear you so clearly!" she thought back. "Are you able to read minds or something cool like that?" she asked.

Michael shook his head and held up his hand – a gesture that made Cecilia pause. He took a serious tone.

"Cecilia, I really do need your help," he thought to her. "A task needs to be done. It is one that involves the future of humanity – believe it or not."

"Right now, I'd believe anything," she linked back.

"Good, because some of what I'm about to say will seem fantastic at first," he began to explain. "In order to accomplish this task, I'll need help from someone with my ability."

"You mean… me?" she gulped.

"Listen to me carefully," he turned his whole body in the seat to face her. "It was your power that drew me here. If you wish to use this ability, these voices only ask one thing in return…" Michael paused as he searched for the right words.

"What is it?" she blankly asked. She feared the answer.

"You must freely open your mind to them. Only then will they convert your brain. After that, you will be… changed," he tried to explain.

"Convert… changed… in what way?" she frowned.

"You already possess a unique feature, which they enhance by altering certain pathways. When they finish, you will be psychic," he told her.

"Will I remember my past?" she asked.

The thought of altering her mind concerned Cecilia, as she feared some sort of attack. Michael sensed it at once.

"Please don't worry about your brain. Nothing bad will happen to you," he said, yet he started to perspire and wiped his forehead. Convincing Cecilia to convert stressed Michael more than he thought it would. "I'm not very good at explaining this, am I?" he addressed his voice.

"You are doing fine, Michael," his mechanical-sounding voice interjected.

"What the hell was that?" Cecilia asked. The sound startled her. She looked around as if the voice originated in the car.

"That was an alien voice," he replied. "They are benign beings from a distant galaxy. They hear our thoughts and sense our emotions. They know everything about us. They directed me here. During this conversion process, they will enter your mind and change its structure."

Skeptically shaking her head, Cecilia frowned.

"Thank you, but I'm not having anyone mess with my mind. I like the one I have," she stated and turned to confront him. "What if they screw up and turn me a drooling idiot? No thanks," she said as she threw up her hands and dismissed Michael. She reached for the door handle.

"Wait! Cecilia, it's not like that, I promise," Michael pleaded to her mind.

He wanted to reach out and touch her hand, but he hesitated. "I went through the same process. Do I look goofy to you?" he asked her.

"Well…" she hesitated as she glanced back over her left shoulder at him.

"I might be clumsy – especially trying to explain this – but I'm definitely not crazy," he said with conviction. "Let me explain some of the benefits. Then let us know what you think."

"Us?" she asked and turned back.

"The voices and I work together," he told her. "Oh, and not to pressure you or anything, but we need your answer now. If you say no, I must leave here at once, and we will probably never see each other again."

Cecilia sat there and gazed at Michael's face for a moment, when a strange sensation came over her. His clear blue-gray eyes seemed to glow as she stared into them. His creamy complexion, strong chin, and small straight nose took on a soft appearance. Her eyes traveled down his tall and trim muscular physique. All at once, everything about Michael seemed so inviting, so handsome. The air around him grew foggy. Her imagination kicked in. She suddenly envisioned Michael riding up on a horse...

"May I take you from this place?" he said to her using a throaty masculine voice. He wore a white shirt that hung open revealing his rippled hairless tanned chest. His long brown hair fluttered in the breeze as he stretched his muscular arm down from the horse to lift her up.

"Such a handsome face," she thought, "just as I thought you would be…"

"Pardon me?" he interrupted her thoughts.

She shook her head. "Whoa! Get a grip, girl."

"What was that?" Michael perked up.

"Nothing," she quickly shot back as she changed her thoughts. "I need to be certain before I decide."

"Give your mind whatever reassurance you need," Michael thought to her, "only I don't have any time left. What is your decision? Tell me now," he requested. "Will you open your mind or do I take you home?" he asked, putting his hand on the keys.

She cocked her head and wondered if her next step would be her last.

CHAPTER 6

THE TIMID SECOND

"CECILIA? MAY I COME IN?" the muffled voice requested.

Mrs. Beaton knocked softly on her daughter's bedroom door.

Cecilia glanced over at the door. Her mother's sudden appearance at her door caught her by surprise.

"Just a second, Mother," she called out.

She quickly pushed her suitcase under her bed.

"Ok, come in," she said in as sweet a voice as she could muster. "What is it?" she asked as her mother entered.

"Oh, nothing," her mother said. "I just wanted to talk with you for a minute..." she said, her voice trailing to silence.

Cecilia watched her mother staring at the posters and cutouts of teen idols from her favorite magazines. She plastered one wall with pictures of young men.

"Why do these men always wear earrings and tattoos?" her mother thought.

Cecilia started to reply '...because it's sexy, mother!' and then realized that for the first time in her life, she clearly heard her mother's thoughts. The effect caught her off guard. She started to protest but stopped and changed her expression as her mother turned to face her. She tried to appear calm on the outside – as if she did not hear them.

"How are you feeling?" her mother asked. She was puzzled by her daughter's change of behavior. "You didn't eat dinner. Usually, you're famished after you work out with Shanna. This afternoon, you seem so… preoccupied. Any thoughts you want to share?" she asked as she moved closer.

Cecilia could feel her sincere intentions. Inside, however, she also heard her mother's contrary thinking.

"I wonder what she's up to. She's being so secretive," she thought though smiling.

She felt her mother's genuine concern for her. She would miss her mother more than anything or anyone in the world.

"This is so weird," Cecilia thought as she smiled back.

For the past year, Cecilia carefully considered what she would do after she graduated from high school. She sent out applications for college, yet did not focus on one in particular. She had no goals and no specific plans. Although several responded, she hesitated to commit.

In less than a month, she would turn eighteen.

"Too bad I'll miss your surprise party next month, mother," she thought. She read her mother's intention secretly to invite all of her friends.

Her encounter with Michael Tyler today changed everything about her future. She discovered, for the first time in her life, new feelings, desires, and a new sense of direction. Once Michael explained his plan, she also realized that she had a special purpose for her life – a secret mission that required her involvement to fulfill. She knew that the journey to China would be dangerous and perhaps even life threatening. Yet, Michael easily convinced her that their combined efforts might change the world's destiny. This was a chance for greatness – one better than any college course offered.

"Besides," he commented at the time, "this could be your dream adventure."

"Get real," she told him flatly.

She patiently listened to her voice explain the extent of their contact, after which she consented to the conversion. Several minutes passed, the voice sent the initial "download" – a unit packet of physiological changes and knowledge that expanded her consciousness regarding her immediate environment.

When she awoke, she initially heard the same fading voices Michael first heard. After several uncomfortable, nearly catastrophic moments between them, he eventually drove the recovered Cecilia back to within a block of her home. She walked the remaining distance and reflected over everything that had happened and wondered what was to come.

Despite taking an extra-strength pain-reliever that she found in her mother's bathroom, her head still pounded from the experience. She reached out with her thoughts and tested the link with Michael. He sensed her inquiry immediately.

"Cecilia?" he linked.

"Sorry," her tone sounded slightly bashful, "just checking if this works."

"I hear you," he linked to her. "The connection is very clear. Everything ok? Do you need me?"

"No, I don't need you. Everything is still on for tonight. See you then. How should we end this… contact?" she asked him.

"Try concentrating on something else," he suggested.

When she thought about packing, her link to him seemed to fade. She then realized that the psychic link established earlier connected them directly, without the assistance of the voices.

"Does that mean our minds will be open and linked forever?" she wondered.

When she first walked inside her house, Cecilia seemed distracted as she was thinking about Michael and their improbable future together. However, with her mother standing this close in her bedroom, she could only hear her mother's thoughts, as if the woman shouted them at her.

"I wish I could tell you how much I changed today," Cecilia reasoned as she watched her mother. "Perhaps you'll understand what I'm about to do… one day."

Cecilia went to her mother and hugged her hard while whispering in her ear.

"Oh, mother, I love you, so very much," she spoke softly.

Her mother stood still for a moment, perplexed, almost shocked at her daughter's sudden burst of feeling. After all, she did not show much affection lately. All that seemed in the past to the new Cecilia. More than ever, she felt less like a teen and more like a young woman leaving home with the hope of accomplishing many great things.

She melted when her mother warmly returned the embrace.

"I love you, too, dear," her mother responded.

Something on the dresser caught Cecilia's eye. Slowly she reached behind her mother, and slid the envelope further under her jewelry box. The note inside explained that she intended on traveling to America and find a job. She told her mother not to worry. She promised to send her new address. She wrote this note to divert the authorities for she knew her mother would call the police. Her mother pulled back.

"Are you sure you're all right?" she asked.

"Yes mother, I'm fine really," Cecilia said, avoiding eye contact. "I never realized how much I loved you until I graduated. I suppose I appreciate you more than ever."

Her mother regarded her daughter for a moment skeptically. Then she gave her a warm smile.

"I guess you're more grown up than I thought," she said as she brushed her daughter's long blonde hair from her face.

The two women laughed and embraced again.

"Hungry?" her mother asked.

"Not really," Cecilia lied. "I'll eat later," she told her.

"Sure?" her mother questioned.

Cecilia nodded and tried to keep from crying.

"Ok. I'm going over to Millicent Brown's to play cards. I'll be home around 10:30. If you feel hungry, I put the leftovers in the fridge," she told her daughter.

"Thanks, mom," Cecilia said, still fighting back her tears.

Her mother turned and left the room.

"Good bye, mother," she quietly said after the door closed. A tear ran down her cheek. She could not fight her emotions any longer.

CHAPTER 7

UNFORTUNATELY LINKED

NO ONE IN THE WORLD realized that just a few hours before Cecilia's touching departure, the most momentous occurrence in the history of humanity took place – the first moment in which a man and a woman truly understood one another.

Cecilia, having just finished her conversion process, leaned back in the front seat of Michael's car with her eyes closed. The unassuming Michael sat in the seat next to her and stared off at the trees with his mind blank and open as the conversion took place. The attractive pert young blonde-haired woman in her summer shorts and cut-off blouse relaxed in the front seat. She was unaware of the world around her. A new area of her brain had recently formed.

At that precise moment, a series of bizarre events took place that neither Michael nor Cecilia expected. Within such close proximity, their minds began to merge thoughts, which flowed freely between the two naïve and relatively innocent young psychics.

"I don't want to!" a child's voice blurted, startling her.

"What did you say?" Cecilia heard, as Michael's mental energy unwittingly poured into her mind. The sound of this new voice frightened her.

She figuratively opened her eyes and took in her surroundings. She discovered that she sat in the corner of a large room decorated for a child. The room had colorful figures painted on the walls and a myriad of toys and electronic devices scattered on the floor. The room had enough toys to make any youngster overjoyed with the prospect.

However, her point of view appeared distorted, as if she were lying down on the floor. Her head tilted back. A tall woman stood over her.

"Michael, you must listen to me…" the tall stately woman began, leaning down toward her face.

"But mother!" the words involuntarily erupted from her mouth.

"Please listen to your governess from now on," the beautiful woman with auburn hair and hazel eyes said. "She's in the kitchen… she came to me, crying."

"I'm playing!" the boy protested. "I don't want to take a shower. She can't make me!"

"That's enough!" the woman said, standing up. "I know a little boy who will sleep in one of the guest bedrooms tonight if he doesn't listen to his governess. I'll pick the scariest one… you know the one…"

Cecilia's head bobbed up and down.

"Now, take those clothes off and go into your shower, young man!" the tall beautiful woman insisted.

"Wait!" Cecilia pleaded inside her mind. "I'm not who you think I am…" she protested.

She tried to sit up but the images kept pouring into her mind, as if she stood in the middle of a swift flowing stream. She fought a current impossible to stop.

The room faded away. She stood with a row of other boys in the courtyard outside what appeared to be a castle with tall pillars framing the entry. Gray columns rose to meet an antique patined copper roof. The place resembled something out of movie about wealthy ivy-covered prep schools.

"Good morning gentlemen," a well-groomed middle-aged man stated as he walked along the line of boys in uniform, as if inspecting the troops.

The man had a golden insignia over his left navy-blue jacket pocket – a coat of arms, she suspected. Cecilia glanced down. She had the same insignia on her jacket.

"His private school," she thought, "day one."

A man in a limousine parked across the courtyard waved from an open window. Unable to alter the memory, her hand rose to wave goodbye until she felt the un-approving stare coming from the school's headmaster. She could feel Michael's angst as he watched his father's limousine pull away. That memory faded.

She next ran through a beautiful garden emerging onto a large wide patio made from enormous pieces of polished granite attached to the back of a great sprawling manor house. She could tell that a professional decorated the space for a child's party.

"Happy Birthday!" a chorus of people cried.

Heading toward the center table with a beautiful sculpted cake and a stack of fancy presents nearby, a strange sensation of dread arose within her.

"I have a terrible feeling that this was not a happy birthday for Michael," she thought, as she watched the young man relive the anger and pain of that horrible day – the same day his voice first spoke to him. Right in the middle of blowing out the candles, the voice spoke for the second time that day.

Swinging at the air in anger and lashing out at the voice, Michael struck a little girl in the face. Cecilia watched in horror as the little girl reeled backward with blood spurting from her nose a second after Michael swung his fist at the invisible menace. It was an accident.

"I didn't mean to do it," the boy's anxious voice cried, "it was the voice… it spoke to me… it made me do it…" he pleaded.

No one believed the little boy's story. They stared at him with contempt on their judgmental faces.

She next sat in a plain room with two-way mirrors on the wall. A man with a receding hairline and thick lips entered holding a yellow pad in his right hand. She immediately sensed him as being detestable in every possible way. His slick demeanor and wiles did not deceive her or the young man, whose point of view she shared.

"Dr. Hami, the psychiatrist," she realized as the history of Michael's life played out in nonstop realistic images, "the man who took advantage of the Tyler fortune by imposing his diagnosis of "childhood schizophrenia and delusional paranoia with violent mood swings" on Michael. He imprisoned Michael in his adolescent clinic for eight years!" she thought.

Scene after scene continued to unfold with Cecilia trapped inside a young man gradually aging and entering puberty. She experienced his adolescent fantasies, along with every emotional traumatic pain-filled moment within the asylum – from the padded rooms, to the time when an uncaring Dr. Hami coldly informed Michael of his parent's death by a drunk driver.

Finally, she went through his bout with alcoholism after the state declared him emancipated. Every traumatic memory rushed unobstructed into her open mind. She experienced every time that Michael raised his fist to empty a bottle of wine into his gut.

Meanwhile, Michael sat in the driver's seat, staring out the window. He did not pay attention to Cecilia but instead, waited for her to finish the conversion. He thought her initial download kept going, as she seemed to writhe on the seat next to him. The moment he closed his eyes, Cecilia's memories transported him to a different place and time.

"I said stand up straight, young lady!" a woman's voice shouted at the frightened young girl.

Michael glanced around. He no longer sat in the car but stood in a large room with a wide wooden floor and tall open windows along one wall. Off to his right, a row of young girls wearing pink tutus and stern faces glared at him. The large woman who spoke marched over and stopped right in front of him. She held a determined and unkind expression on her face.

"Face the mirror as the other girls do!" she ordered.

He turned around to see the reflection of a little girl. Her blonde hair was in pigtails and she wore a leotard and pink tutu with ballet slippers on. Her bottom lip quivered with fear and frustration. The little girl put out her hand and placed it on the bar that ran in front of the mirror. The other girls turned and placed their hands on the bar too.

"Wait a minute!" he tried to protest to no avail.

"Up, down, up, down!" the woman shouted while banging a stick against the rail in tempo with the music playing.

As he watched in the mirror, he noticed tears welling up in the young girl's eyes as she continuously bent her knees and rose repeatedly. She did not like this dancing. Once she donned the outfit, she thought it would be so easy to transform into a ballerina. She only stayed in the class to please her mother.

The room darkened around Michael. Someone pulled off a blindfold. He stood in front of a kitchen table. Family and friends crowded in around the kitchen table.

"Surprise!" people shouted.

He noticed several familiar children seated around the table. The young girls talked to each other and ignored Michael as if he were not there.

"Happy Birthday, Cecilia!" an older man exclaimed.

"Her father," Michael guessed.

At first, he could not sense why this birthday should be so traumatic for the young girl. The man stepped up with a camera in his hands. Michael could feel the revulsion inside the young woman's mind.

"Smile!" he ordered unkindly.

She smiled with her lips, but she would not reveal her teeth, being ashamed of her shiny metal braces.

"How embarrassing," Michael thought.

"Smile!" the young girls shouted and teased her. "Smile, Cecilia!"

He shut his eyes, but when he opened them, he found his arm reaching into a locker for a book. When he closed the door, a smelly boy with a greasy pimply face and bad breath stood uncomfortably close.

"Wanna go to a movie Friday?" he asked with a cracking voice.

Michael felt the conflict in her mind as she weighed in on how to react to his request. She did not wish to be rude, yet she loathed this stalking pest. As she stood before this bothersome teen, she felt a trickle of liquid down her left thigh. A severe cramp rushed through her abdomen… her first menses! When Cecilia's female hormones rushed through her body, throwing her thoughts and chemistry into turmoil, Michael felt them… the anger, the frustration, the surges, the changes in attitude and her wild fantasies… as a man, he struggled to endure every feminine-filled moment of her changing life as he rushed through her timeline.

"Stop!" Michael cried, as cramps took hold of him for the fortieth time. He took in a deep breath. He opened his eyes, scrambled to find the handle, and shoved the door open. He jumped out of the car. "I cannot be a woman! This is impossible!"

"I can't take it either!" Cecilia echoed, leaving the car on her side. She was also out of breath.

She swayed for a second before taking two steps and nearly tumbled over. Michael fell back against the car until he saw how badly the experience shook Cecilia. She was pale and gasping for air. He realized that she must have been living his life. He walked up behind her shaking shoulders and wished that he could reach out and comfort her. He sympathized when he discovered that she just relived his alcoholic past. Yet, he hesitated to touch her. He was unwilling to risk offending a young woman he really did not know.

In the past few minutes, both Cecilia and Michael knew more about each other's true feelings regarding their life than anyone else in the world did.

"What is happening to us?" he cried out, hoping his voice would answer.

She spun around and put her hands out, strongly clasping his arms in a way that startled him.

"Memories, Michael," she blurted with a mixed expression, "mostly traumatic ones! Our minds are open to one another. Every thought in our heads is flowing between them. I am becoming you and you are becoming me. I can't take any more of this. I'm sorry to say this, but being you is making me sick. Right now, we are only exploring the strongest memories. Soon we'll start seeing each other's fears. We all have nightmares, dark images, monsters buried in our heads. I don't want to go there, Michael. I'm afraid. We must stop this flow of information between us or we'll go mad!"

Michael backed up as he pulled away from her. This was not how he pictured their first meeting. He did not expect this kind of reaction. He always contemplated how great their union would be. He thought he would feel jubilance and rejoice when their minds first merged. He forgot about the other side of humanity, the ugly side of the human brain that made possible cruelty, torture, rape, and murder everyday events in the world.

He shook his head but the images from Cecilia's mind continued to flow. He fell back into the memory of a recent heavy menstrual period. Cecilia started to experience Michael's withdrawal from alcoholism, including the dry heaves from intense nausea. She bent over with nausea. He grabbed his abdomen as intense pain shot through it.

"Help!" they cried out simultaneously. "Help us!"

Across the universe, their powerful cries shook the entire psychic collective. No being in its eight-hundred-thousand-year history ever reverberated with such intensity as did these desperate psychics from the planet Earth. The humans from Earth brought not only new psychic voices; they also radiated incredible raw uncontrolled power. Their initial level of strength was unique in their organization. Using the open mental conduits, the voices somehow shut off the flow of energy between the two.

The images that flowed back and forth between Michael and Cecilia fell silent, as if an invisible curtain of steel dropped down to cut them off from each other's thoughts. Both psychics experienced temporary relief when the images and accompanying emotions suddenly halted. Cecilia quizzically tilted her head as she stared at Michael. He shook his head.

"It wasn't me," he said aloud, unable to link to her. "The voices must have…"

"Control," their voices advised simultaneously into both minds. "You must learn control. Ease out your awareness. When in the presence of another psychic, guard your thoughts, unless you wish to unify your minds."

The two young psychics stared at each other, wondering what to do next.

"Be prepared to act when we stop our interference," the voices spoke again. "Adjust your energy level in the presence of the other without intruding. Experiment until you find a range of comfort."

The moment he sensed his control return, Michael pulled his awareness back just as he learned to do in New York. Having done so, he barely felt Cecilia's power next to him.

"No," she said at first, backing away.

Then she began to nod her head as her voice communicated something private that Michael could not hear.

"Better," she finally said, "yes, much better. Thank you."

She slowly and timidly moved closer to Michael.

"Michael I'm sorry," she told him. "I assumed this is what happened to you after your first…"

"I had no other psychic person around," he countered. "I should apologize. I lost focus during your conversion."

Cecilia seemed at ease. She discovered that as he linked thoughts to her, she also understood his feelings along with his thoughts. She sensed soothing and calm feelings – very different from the mechanical and uninvolved voices.

"These thoughts coming from you… they are not like speaking. I understand everything your thoughts say to me so clearly," she linked, "they are beyond words."

Her eyes sparkled as she gazed into his eyes.

"Uncanny," she sighed, losing focus on his kind face.

"I wondered what this experience would be like," he began. "Very different than I imagined. Standing in that pink tutu…" he started to explain.

Cecilia laughed and then suddenly stopped. She remembered Michael's disastrous birthday party that led to his confinement for eight years.

"Oh Michael, your birthday party – Dr. Hami's cruelty – and then your parent's death," she linked to him, the smile falling from her face. "Those images must have haunted you for years. I feel so bad about what you went through…"

"Let's not revive traumatic memories unless you wish to discuss your first menstrual period at school," he countered.

"You went through that?" she shuddered at the thought.

"Uh huh," he said, curling his lip with disgust.

"Some of our personal experiences are better left unspoken until we are ready to share them openly," she concurred. "Shall we move on, then?"

"Agreed," he said extending his hand.

Cecilia accepted it. The two of them shook hands and spontaneously laughed. Michael quickly broke off the handshake as he sensed a different flow of energy when they touched. It made him feel uncomfortable.

"By the way," he asked as he wiped the sweat from his forehead, "who was that creep standing at your locker?"

Cecilia stopped laughing when he brought that up.

"Ernie? You were me cornered by Ernie in the hall at school when I started to…" she began to ask.

Michael nodded, then shook his head and shivered as if shaking off a chill.

Cecilia recalled the very unpleasant experience.

"He used to chase me around school. I never did go out with him," she said.

"I hoped you had better taste in men," he wondered.

She gave Michael an almost uncomfortable look of sincerity.

"I'm so glad you arrived when you did," she thought. "Thank you for rescuing me Michael Tyler."

She moved closer to kiss him on the cheek. However, Michael quickly took a step back away from her. She sensed at once his struggle with showing or receiving affection and understood the reason behind it.

"Then you'll help me?" he queried, anxious about her reply.

For a second, he could not judge her emotions. Whether conscious or not, she did something that stopped him,. She had a far away expression, as if she considered every aspect of her decision and weighed it very carefully.

"Of course, it won't be easy leaving my home, my family, and my friends," she muttered under her breath, as she walked back to the car.

She turned back to him before opening the door. In spite of his apparent strength, he seemed a bit helpless underneath. She gave him just the hint of a smile.

"Yes, I will help you, Michael Tyler," she said to him, "and go with you."

"Thanks, Cecilia," he sighed gratefully. He knew better than to follow his next impulse which was to hug her. "Not a wise move," he thought – unaware he had also transmitted those feelings to Cecilia.

She noticed his feelings at once. Instead of being offended, she understood his willingness to keep his distance and not to allow any emotional involvement to interfere with their relationship – for the time being at least.

She also admired the moral stand he took in New York, having seen that memory as well. Then, she wondered how much Michael actually picked up from her mind, such as the fact that she secretly adored his kind handsome face.

Michael knew all of her thoughts – every single one – including her fears, which he would not openly acknowledge. Nevertheless, he decided to avoid any personal feelings for the sake of their mission. Meanwhile, he had a great deal to accomplish before nightfall. She in return, understood.

"I'll take you home," he told her as he drove off.

CHAPTER 8

A FRESH START

THE PREDICTED SUMMER STORM ARRIVED on cue late in the evening. Michael stood in the pouring rain with his recently purchased rifle. During one loud clap of thunder, he aimed for and shot out a crucial component at a power station – a component the voice indicated would have a cascade effect. A shower of sparks rained down on the ground as he ran from the site to avoid electrocution. Automatic breakers tripped. The lights in the town went out.

He quickly drove to the next location where he destroyed a crucial communication junction. He then shot the power line to a necessary microwave relay tower. The voice then shut down the town's satellite link. It also took out the 'Compu-link' system at the main police station effectively cutting Battleford off from the rest of the world.

He ditched the weighted-rifle into a pond, and drove as fast as he could to the street corner a block from Cecilia's house. In the darkness and dripping wet, the shadowy figure of a seventeen-year-old young woman waited in the pouring rain for Michael. All of her life's possessions were in two small suitcases by her side.

Michael hopped from the car, took her two suitcases, and threw them into the trunk as Cecilia slipped into the front seat of the car. He then drove up the street in the direction she indicated and headed out of town as fast as he could. He finally turned the car lights back on once he took the car onto the westbound highway.

Inside the relative quiet of the car, an awkward silence separated the short distance between the Earth's only truly psychic persons. The demure yet coquettish Cecilia glanced sideways at the handsome twenty-year-old man, his head cramped into the top of the car's interior. She decided to break the ice.

"I thought you did a nice job, destroying the town," Cecilia linked, trying to inject some humor.

Michael nearly ran off the road when her thoughts suddenly leapt into his mind. He was not used to her different presence in his thoughts. He did not reply. He remained focused on driving.

"I saw the sparks up on the hill," she continued. "That was you, wasn't it?"

"My voice recommended…" he started.

"…to cut the power and phone lines…" she completed his thought.

"Yes," he nodded.

"What is next?" she linked. "Is my life going to be an open book when you're around?" she asked, her questioning eyes examining his face.

Michael stared ahead into the darkness saying nothing. He was unwilling to respond – afraid he might convey too much emotion to her. He found it very difficult to express his feelings after hiding them for so many years. He could only imagine what she must be reading from his mind. He tried not to peer into her mind out of courtesy. However, as each mile passed, he sensed increasing unease in Cecilia. He tried to offer some reassurance.

"This is only the beginning of our journey," he linked in a polite way. "Things may seem difficult at first. Our voices will help us along the way. You'll see."

Cecilia noted Michael's platitudes and patronizing tone. She realized that he lacked interpersonal tact because he had only interacted with his voice and not another psychic human. His words, while well intentioned, only served to confuse Cecilia. She stared out the side window at the pouring rain. She could feel the presence of her mother and family slipping away in the darkness. They were replaced solely by Michael's powerful intruding thoughts. Despite his promise of protection, she knew her survival depended on her mastering this new ability.

"Are you feeling alright?" Michael asked, concerned, as he glanced her way, sensing her anxiety.

"I'm ok," she turned back with a quick dismissive grin. "I miss my mother already. She means so much to me. Eventually, I must write to let her know how I am."

Michael started to think a note of caution back to her, but she stopped him.

"I know, I know," her thought interrupted his, "You were going to say it's too dangerous, that she'll have the police investigate, and you'd be correct thinking that way," Cecilia told him, "but, Michael, she is my mother. I can't just leave Canada and never speak to her again. It would hurt her. We must find a way so that I can reassure her."

"Ok," he thought back. "When we complete this mission, we'll find a way."

"Thanks," she started to reach for his hand, stopped, and returned to staring out the window.

Cecilia gave up on conversation for the moment and decided to take a rest in case he wanted to share driving.

With his journey delayed by a day, Michael felt determined to make up for lost time. He pressed on through the night. Not sensing any radar traps, he pushed the car to its limit as they raced west across the Canadian plains on Canada Sixteen, the Yellowhead Highway. If the authorities decided to place a roadblock in their path, it would effectively cut off the only direct road to the west coast.

Michael hoped that the further they ventured from Battleford, the better their odds to escape without confronting authority. After driving most of the night, he pulled into a cheap roadside motel just west of Edmonton.

"What's going on?" Cecilia asked, waking.

"I need some rest," Michael told her as he stopped in front of the motel's office.

Before she could respond with an offer to drive, Michael stepped out of the car and disappeared inside the front office for a few minutes before returning.

"I sensed they had a night clerk on duty. He accepted cash," Michael stated, "and he didn't ask questions. We have a room with two full-sized beds."

"I'm hungry," Cecilia yawned, stretching. "Any chance we could find some food?"

"Why did I think you would be hungry?" he replied, tossing her a plastic-wrapped package.

"What's this?" she asked, feeling a large lump in her hand.

"The clerk had some turkey sandwiches. I bought two cans of soda. Isn't that brand your usual choice?" he asked, handing her one.

"It'll do," she said, peering at the container in the dark.

Inside the cheap aging motel room, Michael pulled down the yellowing blinds. The two nibbled their food in silence. More tired than hungry, Michael fell on the bed, turning away from Cecilia's side of the room. He closed his eyes. He had too many important things on his mind.

CHAPTER 9

TOO LITTLE PRIVACY

TO BE AWARE OF EVERY thought coming from the person sitting next to you – including his or her deepest desires or darkest fears – would unsettle anyone. Yet despite their youth and inexperience, Michael and Cecilia handled the new intrusive ambience surprisingly well.

Still they struggled with the idea of knowing each other's intimate thoughts – whether they wanted the other person to know them or not. For the very first time in the human race, no filters existed between the thoughts of a man and the thoughts of a woman. This fact alone spelled trouble.

Although the voices advanced their understanding of Earth's languages, they still did not fully comprehend the complexities of human mores, ethics, social customs, and cultural practices that separate civil men and women from behaving with primitive responses. One good rush of mutual emotion and the fragile wall of civility between most young men and women easily crumbles into undeniable attraction.

Without thinking how it would affect Michael, Cecilia decided to take a shower before she laid down – her usual habit.

"I want to clean up," she casually threw out after she sniffed her armpit in a rather unladylike fashion. "I won't be a minute."

Her simple words caught Michael off guard. He did not intend to use his imagination to picture the young woman without clothes – as any normal healthy young man might.

Instead, he clamped his eyes tight and tried to keep out bad thoughts concerning Cecilia –thoughts that she might accidentally grasp. That futile act did not stop his imagination from suddenly conjuring up an image. He could not deny Cecilia's physical beauty. In addition to her lovely facial features, her trim and curvaceous teenage body made her a very attractive young woman.

Michael briefly opened his eyes and saw in the television glass the reflection of a slender and very sexy young woman emerge from the bathroom after her shower. She toweled off her dripping head and dressed only in her underwear. Not wanting to embarrass Cecilia with an obvious stare, he closed his eyes.

He tried to suppress his feelings by thinking about anything other than her. He tried to picture other people he knew at the homeless shelter – ugly, homely, ordinary people. However, each time he pictured them, he saw them standing around in their underwear. He took his pillow and pulled it over his head as he groaned.

Cecilia caught Michael's unintentional broadcast and saw a flash of his imagined thoughts. At first, she giggled at the silly image. She did not realize that someone as handsome or sophisticated as Michael would find her attractive.

She stopped at the full-length mirror. "Not bad, Cecilia," she said turning.

Michael represented a male ideal to her – a heroic figure from fiction. For Cecilia, Michael was the lord of the estate – a kindly baron astride his noble steed and searching for his country bride. He was the exact opposite of the awkward, pimple-faced, high-school country lads.

"Oh, no," he groaned once more from under the pillow.

Michael tried to ignore the innocent yet naïve visual he caught from her mind, as he struggled to suppress his own private feelings.

Neither directly linked to the other. Still, their thoughts jumped around the room like echoes impossible to ignore. While Cecilia thought the idea initially cute, she could not stop the flow of information that made her feel increasingly uncomfortable. As the discomfort grew, Michael's tension boiled over.

"I can't take this!" he said. He sat up and faced the door.

"I can't either," she said as she sat on her bed and faced away from Michael.

The two psychics temporarily repressed their feelings. The result left the room with an odd silence that fell between them with a resounding thud. For the moment, both felt grateful for the brief privacy that followed. Michael clumsily tried to change the subject.

"It would be best if we traveled by night," he thought to her with his back turned. "Would you mind?" he asked.

She understood the reasoning behind why he said it at once. She flung her towel across the room and pulled the rest of her clothes on.

"Night travel would lessen the chances of running into the authorities," he added to explain.

"I understand. Good idea, Michael," she stated when she finally dressed.

"Then we should try to sleep now and rise later this evening," he said and turned to her, "You tired?"

"I could still grab some more sleep," she factually stated.

"Ok. Let's try to sleep least six additional hours or so before we hit the road," he suggested.

Cecilia lay down on her bed and stared at the ceiling. She wanted to say something considerate to Michael. Perhaps she should apologize for the way that she appeared in her underwear. She felt her private thoughts too exposed, as if Michael knew what she personally thought about him most of the time. She remained silent and reached over to pull the bed cover over her.

"Night," she said quietly.

Michael stood up and turned out the lights. He stopped in the darkness to gaze down at her shadowy form across the room. He wanted to express his regret for the way he thought when he saw her undressed. Then he realized – just as she did – that thinking about her for any length of time opened his mind to her.

He returned to the bed and rolled on his side away from her in order to leave his mind blank. He hoped that this would be enough. Within minutes, Michael and Cecilia, mentally and physically exhausted, fell into deep sleep.

At first, Michael slipped into heavy slumber that held no dreams. He remained undisturbed in deep sleep for hours. Later, when he entered the dream phase of his sleep cycle everything changed.

He woke up on the ground and noticed Cecilia nearby.

"Where are we?" he asked her, but she did not answer.

Michael rose to his feet. He stood on the shore of a great blue ocean with strange plants and rock formations behind him that stretched out beyond the beach. The hot light of a nearby star beat down on the white sand as ocean waves crashed upon the shore lifting a moist cool salty breeze into the heated dry air.

A darkly tanned Cecilia lay on a large white cloth. A round colorful beach umbrella partially protected her with shade from the intense sunlight. Michael wore a white open vest and baggy pants, as if he were in some Arabian tale of the desert. His hairless bare abdomen and muscular chest exposed.

Cecilia wore a thin veneer of white cloth over white skimpy undergarments, similar to those she currently wore. A large white hat cast a shadow over her face. Her dark-tanned body stood out in contrast to her bright surroundings. She playfully smiled when she glanced up at Michael and gazed at him through dark sunglasses. She held out her hand. He reached down and grasped it. The moment they made contact, the two quivered at the touch. Sensations rippled through their bodies, as if an electrical current passed from one to the other.

Michael joined her by lying down on the blanket. His body pressed against hers. Neither spoke a word. They embraced and began to kiss softly and slowly at first until they kissed passionately.

All at once, they both woke up.

Cecilia and Michael sat up in their separate motel beds, and stared across the space between them. The each breathed heavily as if they'd just run a race. Michael still lingered inside Cecilia's thoughts. Sweat trickled down his face. He could feel her pounding heart beat and her warm panting breath.

Ashamed, Michael pulled back from her mind. Cecilia reciprocated. They gratefully stared down at the space between the beds as if it was the Grand Canyon keeping them safely apart.

"Were we just lying next to each other on a beach?" Cecilia blurted.

"Cecilia," Michael started to apologize, "I didn't mean to intrude…"

"Did we almost… I mean, in that dream, did we?" Cecilia spoke, half-breathless, and sweating.

Michael nodded his head up and down.

"Everything seemed so real," she said slowly, "as if I was really there. It was more real than any dream I've ever had."

Michael could only nod his agreement – unable or unwilling to speak.

"We need to guard our thoughts," she said once she had calmed down. "Otherwise, things could become… complicated."

Michael did not say a word. He simply nodded again. The two young psychics sat there in their motel room, not speaking, afraid to link.

Michael swung his legs over the side of the bed to face away from Cecilia. He quietly began to link with her.

"In all the months I spent with my voice, I never felt any emotion with a psychic contact. We had a perfectly platonic relationship. My initial co-dependent role gradually grew into that of an independent person," he thought to her.

"When I contemplated meeting other psychics, I knew things would change. The interaction would be…" Michael twisted his head and stared into Cecilia's eyes, "…different. Only I didn't suspect how personally different until now."

Cecilia understood him completely.

"Before we met, I was afraid of you," Michael confessed. "I imagined some pretty gruesome characters. Then I figured you'd be man. I never pictured a teenage girl. When the voices said you just graduated from high school, I thought that I could deal with that. I presumed that I would act as an older brother and serve as a guide into the new psychic world. Now, I see I was wrong in making that assumption. I did not foresee how we would interact if our minds dwelled on things like… sex. It never occurred to me I would have that kind of interaction, because… well, I simply never thought of it. I made a mistake. To be honest, I'm more afraid than ever that involvement between us could destroy my goals."

He turned all the way around and faced her.

"I like you Cecilia. I really do," he addressed her. "However, I have to be a respectable person. That is, I must behave responsibly. I don't know if I can control my private thoughts or desires. I judged the situation incorrectly. Perhaps I should take you home."

"First of all," she spoke up, "you are not taking advantage of me – so don't start feeling guilt – at least, not yet. Nothing happened and nothing will happen. We're just friends. We should keep it that way," she stated. "Still, I've changed Michael. I can't go back home – not now, not after this," she pointed to her head. "You and I will just have to make a truce. I believe we can do that, don't you?"

The two young psychics regarded each other for a second.

"Ok," Michael spoke, "so we make a truce. We still have the problem of keeping some of our thoughts private at times. Any suggestions on how we do that?"

Both realized the problem went deeper than a simple solution could solve. Michael sat back on the side of the bed. He watched Cecilia rise and begin to pace on the other side of the room.

"We need to find a way to keep our thoughts private," she pondered, "a way to experience our own thoughts without having to share them."

"Perhaps we can erect some sort of mental barrier?" Michael suggested.

"That's it, Michael!" Cecilia acknowledged. "I think you just hit on something. If we create a strong mental image – something very solid – perhaps that will give us the privacy we need. We can at least try. Can't we?"

"What do you suggest?" he asked.

"Create a mental construct around the psychic area of the brain. It can be anything solid enough to cut off the flow of energy," she thought to him.

"Let's try it," Michael agreed.

The two concentrated for a few minutes. Michael thought of a thick solid wall. He created a brick house and went inside. Cecilia simplified matters by walking into a bank vault and pulling the door shut tight. Their conscious effort stopped the flow of psychic energy. It remained unclear whether the mental image only guided them to this action.

"Can you read my mind now?" Cecilia asked aloud.

"No," Michael said trying to probe her mind. "I sense nothing."

"Good," Cecilia replied. "I'm not sensing anything from you either. At least we can use this technique to keep our thoughts private from time to time."

Michael stood up and walked over to the window to pull back the shade.

"That was too close," he thought. He was glad she could not overhear his thoughts. "I must be more careful."

The sun had set behind the tall western slopes of the Rocky Mountain range. Michael glanced over at the clock radio. To his surprise, several hours passed as they slept. He hoped that next time it would be without incident. He would be grateful for that. He walked over and gathered up their belongings.

"Ready to press on, or would you like to go back?" he asked her.

"Commitment isn't anything a woman takes lightly. Let's keep going," she replied, heading for the door. "You'll find that out as you know me better."

"Believe me Cecilia," Michael replied, "I know it now."

As the hours dragged on, Michael and Cecilia eventually crossed the remainder of the continent. They were on track toward the west coast of Canada. Michael decided to drive straight through without stopping. Cecilia helped for a stretch and thus allowed Michael to take a needed rest, albeit in the cramped backseat. After a day of driving, the young couple finally arrived in little Prince Rupert, a jewel on the bay.

Chapter 10

A promise of cot and breakfast

Prince Rupert, British Columbia, rests on a sparkling bay just off the Chatham Sound, part of a picturesque setting that encompasses this entire area. Called the fjords of the northwest, forest-covered mountains thrust their steep green roots into the bottoms of deep blue inlet waters.

Just outside the western edge of town, a small bed and breakfast lays tucked away in the back of a family-run inn with a few advertised cramped rooms for rent according to the hand-made sign in front. As soon as the owner handed over the key, Cecilia skipped off to inspect their lodgings while Michael paid for the room.

"Do you have any cots?" Michael asked.

"I thought you two was married?" the owner asked.

Michael dropped his left hand to his side.

"We are," Michael told him, "Only my wife and I sleep in different beds at home," he added recovering.

As she enthusiastically bound around the old wood-frame structure, the view behind the tavern made Cecilia pause. A steep forest-covered mountain plunged straight down into the dark blue water of an expansive bay. Billowy cumulous clouds stood out against a light blue sky. This place was very different from her home on the flat plains of Saskatchewan.

"I've fantasized about a place like this," she sighed.

Then she recalled their experience in the motel.

"I'd better take that thought from my head. I don't want to share another dream fantasy with Michael. Our mission is too important to jeopardize," she gulped.

"I can help with that," Cecilia's alien voice interrupted. "A mental discipline known as seeded thinking," it explained. "It might help you keep certain issues private."

"I'll be grateful for anything," she told it.

After signing for the room, Michael drove around to the room, and parked the car on the side. He then took the bags out of the trunk and spotted Cecilia almost at once. An old wooden veranda dotted with unfinished rocking chairs surrounded the back end of the building. She stood at the opposite end outside the open door to their room. As Michael walked along, each board creaked under his weight.

"How quaint," he mused before entering.

The small cramped room held one full-sized bed and a dresser, with a shared bathroom down the hall. Michael turned his tired eyes away from the inviting large multicolored down comforter on the bed. The owner, having emerged from a backdoor, wheeled a cot up to the room door, grunted something unintelligible, and left.

Michael set up the cot. Cecilia took a shower down the hall. Taking advantage of her absence, he used his laptop to make a satellite link. He sent his contact a brief coded message with the help of his voice to confirm their arrival and his intention to meet tomorrow night at the pre-arranged rendezvous position. They returned a single letter acknowledging receipt of his message before cutting off their end. His voice warned to keep these communications brief.

Michael sensed Cecilia coming up the hall. He closed the laptop and put it in his briefcase. The moment she entered the room, she knew he had something to hide.

"What were you doing just before I walked in?" she asked toweling her hair.

"Checking the weather…" he threw back.

"Michael, you cannot lie to me," she said, turning to face him.

"I was confirming the coordinates with the smugglers for tomorrow night," he relented.

"A submarine?" she questioned, seeing it in his mind.

"I couldn't spend two weeks at sea on a freighter," he commented.

"Two days on a sub will definitely be better," Cecilia said as she stowed her shower gear. "But why not fly a plane? It would be faster."

"Planes, even private ones, can be traced. For our purposes, we need to travel incognito," he told her.

"The Russians have private submarines for hire?" she wondered.

"No," he explained, "about two decades ago, when the old Soviet Union broke up and a wild surge of capitalism took place, a cartel sprung up…"

"The Russian mafia," she guessed, having read about it once.

"That was one cartel," he clarified. "Another group, one financed by those in the government, took its place," he told her. "This cartel has influential connections, from some of the highest levels of government. They are very secretive. They include members of the old Russian KGB and even some retired members of the American CIA. The two organizations needed a way to continue certain aspects of their organizations while keeping their operations clandestine."

"You mean that when they elected…" she started.

"Let's say that they had help in high places from both sides of the Pacific," Michael said as he cut her off. "One of the things they established was a way to smuggle items and people in and out of Russia, as well as other places. They try to avoid contact with the United States Navy. Of course, it's not an easy thing to do."

"I would think it was impossible!" Cecilia broke in.

"One would think," Michael said. "My voice and I discovered secret files. Let's say that this organization has ways to level the playing field. The result is mutual benefit. The CIA is aware of everything inside the Kremlin, and the Russians, well, they do not lack for knowing anything about us."

None of this surprised Cecilia, as she knew Michael spent nearly a year alone with his voice in New York and that they performed extensive and virtually untraceable searches via the Internet.

Michael went on to explain how he arranged for their transportation via submarine to the Kamchatka Peninsula. From there, he planned to travel around the Sea of Okhotsk to the Russian city of Yakutsk. He would then meet a man named Kazif, a member of the smuggling cartel. Kazif could provide official documents to enter China via Mongolia. He and Cecilia would pose as university archeologists.

"…so your briefcase contains the computer to arrange this?" she asked.

"Uh huh," he nodded. "I had to alter the original plan when you agreed to join me."

"Haven't you noticed," she stated wisely beyond her years, "the plans of men usually change when a woman is involved?"

CHAPTER 11

AN INCREDIBLE DISCOVERY

AWAY FROM PRYING EYES, MICHAEL and Cecilia munched on lunchtime sandwiches in one of the tavern's dark corners. They kept their conversation to a minimum. Afterward, they retired to the back porch outside their room where they rocked away the afternoon on the creaking veranda like some old lazy married couple. They drank iced tea out of a tall plastic cup while enjoying the serene setting and gazed out at the blue ocean water with Digby Island sitting off in the distance.

Cecilia stared down at the drink in her cup.

"Did you ever drink iced tea before now?" she linked to Michael.

"No, did you?" he linked back.

"I just wondered why we should be drinking tea instead of soda. Maybe it's a psychic thing," she wondered.

"I thought of tea when I ordered the drinks. Funny," he glanced at his cup, "I don't recall ever liking tea before my conversion," he shrugged his shoulders. "I seem to like it now."

A middle-aged married couple, staying two doors down, sat at the other end of the veranda. They discussed travel at this time of year and complained about the poor condition of the room, the bad food, and so on.

Michael and Cecilia, on the other hand, engaged in a different sort of conversation. They linked freely and allowed a private mental communication to flow between them as they rocked. Cecilia expressed her feelings over their plan to go to China.

"I suppose you obtained maps, memorized routes, know exchange rates, local customs, things like that," she enquired.

"Of course, I did," he began.

"Transparent as water," she sipped her tea.

"Well… I researched…" he started.

"Of course, you did," she echoed his earlier sentiment.

"Look, I'm familiar with everything you've mentioned. It's just that…" he began to defend his planning.

"You aren't as concerned with the details as I am," she finished.

"I suppose…" Michael hesitated.

"I reviewed some research provided by the voices on China," Cecilia put in. "Most rural Chinese family households have very strong support systems. Two or three generations might live in the same house for many years. It may be more difficult to separate people raised in such a system," she suggested.

Her statement triggered some rather painful and sensitive memories of Dr. Hami tearing Michael away from his parents. He threw up a block to keep those feelings private.

"I'm sorry," Cecilia immediately sensed his discomfort. "Did I say something…?"

"No, Cecilia," Michael shot back as he brushed aside her sympathy. "It's just that, for me, the separation from my parents occurred under different circumstances…"

"I understand," she grew quiet.

He was about to change the subject when his voice broke into their link.

"What action will you take if you are not successful in China, that is, if you fail to convince any others?" it questioned.

"I can't accept that as an alternative," Michael immediately replied. "I will try to make the most convincing case I can that we must join together for our mutual success," he said while trying to sound confident for Cecilia. "I hope that by the time we arrive in China, our mission will be clearer."

"By the way, how will I understand anyone speaking Russian or Chinese?" Cecilia asked.

"The voices have studied Earth's cultures for many years," Michael replied.

"Michael," Cecilia broke in. "I've never spoken any language except English and a smattering of French. How will I learn to speak Russian?"

"When I first arrived in New York, my voice explained that with my corporate account, I could have anything I wanted. I told it I wanted an expensive sports car, one made in Italy. Before we went to the dealership, I thought it would be convenient to speak Italian. My voice arranged for me to have a language lesson while I slept. When I woke the next morning, I spoke and understood Italian. I asked it how it accomplished this. It said it placed the data in my memory. That's when I started referring to those educational sessions as downloads."

Cecilia stopped abruptly and turned in her chair. She looked over Michael's shoulder at the other couple on the porch. They had a peculiar expression on their faces as they stared back at them. Cecilia frowned and gave Michael a nudge.

"What's wrong? Why are they staring at us?" she thought.

Michael glanced over at them for a moment and then turned back.

"Well, we've been sitting here a long time, nodding and exchanging glances, yet saying nothing. We aren't signing as if we were deaf. Don't you think that appears rather strange?" he pointed out.

An idea suddenly occurred to Cecilia that made her sit up.

"You say the voices can remotely manipulate memory. Can we do that?" she put to him.

Almost afraid to link, Michael stared back at Cecilia.

"What are you saying?" he asked her.

"Have you ever tried to manipulate people's thoughts?" she wondered.

Michael did not speak. Cecilia understood his reluctance.

"You felt it an intrusion? Why, Michael?" she asked.

"I was alone in New York, trying to recover from being sick. I did not want to take advantage of anyone, as others did to me," he confessed.

"Michael," Cecilia leaned back, "While I admire your moral convictions, I would remind you that we are now a team stuck in the middle of nowhere. We should use this new ability to the best of our advantage or at least try? Please?"

"Do you mean trying to influence someone's behavior with our minds to make them do something they wouldn't ordinarily do?" he offered as explanation.

"That is only an aspect of what I meant," she slowly replied. "Doesn't entering someone's mind elicit other possibilities in that brilliant mind of yours?"

Michael hesitated as he mulled over her implied meanings.

"We must probe deep," he thought, "centering on the part of their motor functions as well as their conscious thought to make the choices. That's a very complex link with a non-psychic brain…"

"Where do we start?" she asked.

"I'm not really certain," he began.

Michael closed his eyes and created a mental picture he could share with Cecilia. Over the past ten months, he and the voice explored many subjects such as history, art, mathematics, chemistry, biology, and human anatomy. After reviewing the extensive data he had accumulated on the brain and its functions, he then suggested certain anatomical pathways, memory centers, and motor functions. She followed his path through the brain's physiology.

"Yes…" she replied as she watched, "I see."

She paused trying to focus her own thoughts without any distractions.

"Let's perform a simple test, something infallible," he offered. "We'll implant the suggestion to this other couple to stand up, bow, shake hands, and then skip back into their room. We would know right away if our intrusion worked. Are you ready?"

"I think so," she thought back.

"You take her. I'll manipulate him," he said.

"Got it," she answered.

They turned toward the couple, and stretched out their senses until they entered the mind of the man and woman. After only a few seconds, the couple stood, bowed, shook hands, and skipped all the way back to their room.

Michael and Cecilia burst out laughing.

"I didn't think I could do it!" the two thought simultaneously.

They laughed harder. What they accomplished stunned them. Then, the ramifications struck home, and the potential for what they could do, changed their mood to a sober one. Their faces fell as they realized that someone with their ability could order people to do things against their will – bad things as well as good things.

"Do you realize that with this power we could…" she began

"Yes," Michael linked back quietly. "We can manipulate anyone to do anything we want, or see anything we want. We cannot only alter memory," he pointed out, "we can even change the way people feel about other people." He took in a deep breath. "We possess tremendous power over the rest of humanity."

"Michael, you were right. Perhaps we shouldn't meddle…" Cecilia began.

He held up his hand, closing his eyes, while suggesting Cecilia do the same. They sat in silence, privately sharing their concerns and feelings regarding this new ability.

As if he had opened a door to a new realm of possibilities, Michael suddenly understood the importance in finding others of their kind. Alone he would never have performed such a feat. With Cecilia nearby, they sharpened, honed, and increased the scope of their abilities. Then he wondered what else they would discover?

Into this quiet contemplation, Michael's voice returned.

"Do you finally see the significance of forming a group, Michael?" his voice asked.

"Now I do," Michael hesitated. "I thought you were wired for non-interference."

"True," his voice replied. "We also realize your species is quite unique. We would welcome a community of psychic humans. Our galactic organization is both large and diverse. Just as a satellite communications network orbiting in the space above your planet connects your civilizations around your globe, we connect many species on over a hundred different worlds and translate their languages. I have never considered a label for our organization, as the translation to English did not correspond to one particular idiom. However, you can now refer to us as "Galactic Central," Michael."

"Galactic Central," Michael considered. "You've seldom mentioned any specific details of your home world. Why now?"

"The beings that comprise Galactic Central would like to explain our existence in a way that will convince more than one psychic, so that you may share this experience with others of your kind," Michael's voice explained to both psychics. "We are the hub at the center of a great hive of colonies that are scattered across distant galaxies. Your Milky Way, as you call it, lies on the fringe of the zone we can affect. Of all the worlds in your galaxy, only yours emits psychic energy. Our species act as both facilitators and interpreters. We freely allow the psychics on these worlds to communicate with one another to share thoughts and ideas while upholding a universal code of ethics. We work for our mutual advancement of knowledge and understanding."

Suddenly the wooden deck and chairs disappeared around Michael and Cecilia. As if someone shut off the sun, the world turned dark. Michael could only see Cecilia and she could only see him. Everything else around them appeared black.

"What's happening, Michael?" Cecilia asked, frightened.

"I don't know!" he replied with alarm. "This has never happened to me."

"Michael, I can see you," she linked, "at least, I can see an image of you." She saw Michael, yet she could see through him, too, as if he were a ghostly form.

"I can see an image of you, too," he replied as he stared with disbelief at her semi-transparent body.

"Look Michael, behind us!" she stated. She reached out and rotated his floating form.

Michael turned his head in time to see their spirit bodies zooming away from planet Earth to some other cold dark region in outer space – a region surrounded by a great field of distant stars and galaxies.

Michael maneuvered next to Cecilia so that the two floated side by side. The light of one star seemed to sparkle more brightly to Michael.

"Did you see that?" he linked to Cecilia. It reminded him of what his voice had done that first night on the rail tracks.

"Michael," she linked back, "I feel it pulling me." He sensed her fear.

"Me, too," he thought to her.

Their bodies lurched forward at a dizzying rate.

"I feel as if I'm falling," she thought.

While the rest of the universe turned into a blur, stars shot off at all kinds of angles. One tiny shimmering light gradually grew larger until a galaxy of stars filled their vision. One particular star near its mid-section sparkled. Again, Michael and Cecilia felt pulled in that direction as they streaked down toward a star-filled section whose lights grew further apart until only one enormous ball of fire burned before them. Despite the intensity of the light, their 'eyes' naturally tolerated its brightness.

"We're in some kind of planetary system. Look over there!" Michael pointed as their bodies flew past the star.

They moved toward a large greenish-colored planet with three moons circling nearby. At this range, they noticed a surface similar to Earth's. It was covered with huge expanses of green continents and large wide "rivers." They saw only a few major bodies of water around the equator. In contrast to Earth's oceans, land dominated this much larger planet.

Zooming down through an atmosphere of high wispy clouds, they plunged toward the night-side surface. Michael and Cecilia saw groups of lights and other signs of civilization below them. Racing around the planet, dawn rose over the terminus between night and day.

Cecilia held her collective breath as their ghostly bodies plummeted down toward the surface at break neck speed – like some wild carnival ride out of control. Their flight leveled off just under a cover of clouds. A vast forest of gigantic trees spread out beneath them. Onward, they streaked toward the sunrise.

She gasped at the sight. "Did you ever see anything so beautiful?"

A rich golden light pierced the clouds all around them. It sent down shafts of illumination that could not penetrate beyond the top of the forest canopy.

"I've never seen trees this large. This stand covers thousands of miles," he whispered as the horizon rushed toward them.

The massive trees stretched upward from the forest floor over a thousand feet in height Michael estimated. Yet the foliage did not resemble anything he ever saw on Earth.

"The circumference around the base must be hundreds of feet," he reasoned as he glanced down at them while rapidly passing by.

"What's that?" Cecilia noted, pointing toward a distant object poking up through the canopy, its top disappearing up into even higher strata of clouds.

Michael stared into the rising sun. "I can't tell yet."

The atmosphere cleared as they made their way toward the sunrise. They saw what appeared to be a single spire of metal sticking up through the trees until its top reached high into the atmosphere. It stood alone, like some tall thin sliver of shining silver metal with no equal anywhere on the planet. The base disappeared beneath a covering of white mist that hung over the forest canopy.

Far away, the scale seemed small to them. However, as they grew closer, the tower began to reveal its true size. They realized this metal spire was not narrow but actually quite large.

A small door opened in the side of the tall metallic spike. Their course changed as they headed directly toward the portal. The spike began to take on larger proportions as they grew nearer.

Soon, the tower filled the entire sky in front of them and demonstrated its true size and proportion. It was the largest structure Michael had ever seen – with nothing to compare on Earth. The shiny metallic edifice measured thousands of kilometers in height and at least a hundred or more kilometers wide, he estimated. No civilization on Earth could ever build such a gigantic thing.

Michael realized at once its true nature.

"This is Galactic Central," he gazed at it with awe. "They said they've been around for hundreds of thousands of our years, yet this tower appears new. How had it stood for so many millennia without any sign of corrosion?"

"What's that on the outside?" Cecilia pointed to something moving.

Michael noticed tiny shapes scrambling around the surface of the tower. As the two visionaries flew nearer, these specks grew into intricate robotic creatures that worked all over the surface – polishing, cleaning, and fixing as they hurriedly moved about from place to place.

"No wonder the tower is immaculate," she thought to Michael.

"They're worker robots," he realized. "They probably spend their entire existence on the outside in order to keep the tower in perfect condition."

What first appeared to be a small door in the distance, turned out to be an enormously huge opening in the side of the great spire. As their rate of approach began to slow down, they entered the gargantuan structure through the large opening in its side. By this time, the width filled their entire peripheral vision.

"I can't see the bottom," Cecilia pointed downward.

"Nor the top!" Michael pointed up.

As they flew inside, a large floating craft flew out in the opposite direction. The sheer size of the vehicle dwarfed them into tiny specks. Michael and Cecilia speculated that this great floating vessel somehow took its passengers away on some sort of break or vacation.

"Are the passengers inside the voices taking leave?" she wondered.

Michael shrugged. Before either could pursue that line of thought, a force whisked their spirit bodies inside.

They found the complex interior behaving as one giant living machine with millions of moving parts. Some pieces flew about in different directions. At first, everything appeared chaotic. Some of the flying objects just barely missed others, as collisions in the air seemed imminent. Yet, no contact ever took place, as if they timed the path of each piece to the millisecond.

The couple sped toward the center hub of activity. Thousands of columns ran parallel to the sides with groups of work stations bundled around each column at various intervals. Neither Michael nor Cecilia could see a top or bottom to the place as it stretched out of sight in either direction. It was dizzying to witness.

They moved closer to one workstation. Each possessed several large curved rectangular-shaped screens displaying different worlds. At the bottom of each screen, a crawl of different symbols of varying types ran past. The screens encircled a large dark rectangular tank.

"Is that language?" Michael wondered.

Cecilia nodded, "It must be."

The same force acting on them now moved them around until they came to a workstation where the screen had English words scrolling by.

"Is that language?" the words moved across the bottom and were followed by, "It must be."

Michael and Cecilia just exchanged those thoughts. On the large screen above the scroll, they noticed a detailed three-dimensional view from the back of the bed and breakfast in Canada. Michael realized their physical bodies still sat in the rocking chairs.

A large tank the size of a semi-truck's trailer rested on the platform and was filled with some sort of brackish liquid. Something definitely moved around inside the tank's dark fluid. Many cables and wires connected to each tank. Some of them pumped fluids in and out. Devices similar to cameras were positioned around the tank and pointed toward the screens, as if something inside could see them.

"The screens replicate visual acuity," Michael thought.

"How do you know that?" Cecilia questioned.

"I don't know how I know," Michael replied, "I just do."

As Cecilia peered down into the murky soup, a small robot popped up from inside the liquid and startled her. Just as they witnessed robots working on the outside of the great spire they realize that several robotic machines tended the tanks in order to clean and adjust them. Although they could not see it clearly, the travelers noted that a singular massive organic object occupied the inside of the tank.

Occasionally, a colorful flying machine would attach to a place above the station and glow brightly. Then after just a second, the object would fly off and replaced by one of a different color. The screens at other workstations showed continuous images of strange and wonderful worlds.

"I still think it's strange that they have all of these screens," Cecilia stated.

"Do you feel it?" Michael linked to Cecilia as his thoughts scrolling across the screen.

"Feel what?" she responded.

"Time is slower inside the spire," he observed.

"What makes you say that?" Cecilia replied.

"I don't know how I know these things," he said while staring around him. "I just feel the truth of it. This place operates outside the normal realm of physics. They've created some kind of spatial dampening field that slows down the rate of time here. See those objects, coming and going?" he pointed, "They represent translated thoughts that are performed elsewhere. Each being must specialize in some aspect of language or cultural idiom. This structure houses countless voices – hundreds of millions, perhaps billions of these creatures."

"You may be right," she replied, as one of the colorful objects passed right through the couple's shadowy forms.

Some powerful force drew them upward like an express elevator to the very top of the spire. Approaching the top, the couple noted bright shafts of strikingly colorful light shoot like arrows around the narrowing space.

"What amazingly intense colors," Cecilia thought.

"Yes," Michael muttered, also impressed.

Pulses of white light struck large suspended clear crystals of enormous dimension. The light split into thousands of colored shafts – each one entered specific colored stations. Millions of the flying objects, like those they had seen below, waited in tight color-coded formation flowing in with dull color. As they left those workstations, the objects' colors were bright and vibrant, as if invigorated.

"Why would they need colors?" Cecilia questioned.

"It isn't the color. It's the wavelength," Michael guessed. "Just as with the screens, they perceive bands of energy – only our eyes perceive color."

"How do you know these things?" Cecilia wondered.

"You keep asking me, but I'm not certain about anything, Cecilia. I feel I just know these answers," Michael replied. "Besides, they must possess visual acuity. Why else would they have display screens?"

Near the very top of the enclosure, a clear shell covered a complicated and intricately timed machine moving so fast that its moving components visually blurred. Their spirit bodies moved through the shell's exterior into the center of the machine.

A tank, similar in construction, yet larger and more complex than the others, hovered in the center with thousands of mechanical tentacles sticking out in all directions. These appendages touched this and adjusted that at extreme rates of speed. They only saw this device move as a blur from the outside. Michael sensed a very powerful level of psychic energy. He realized that time flowed slowest in this space, and that great intelligence emanated from within the central tank and guided these choices.

"This is the heart of Galactic Central," he felt.

One tentacle paused before a screen, whose strange pattern only the creature could decipher.

"It knows we're here," Cecilia thought to Michael. He sensed it too.

For a brief moment, the two young people felt the being's awareness of them. The tentacle touched something and severed the link with Earth. The moment the connection broke, Michael and Cecilia had the sensation of falling. Dizzy, they struggled to open their eyes and sputtered to breathe while fighting back nausea.

Michael briefly glanced down at his watch. The second hand did not move. Then it changed, ticking away the seconds. Michael realized that no time had passed during their long arduous journey through space. They still sat in their rocking chairs on the back porch of the family-owned inn. Their eyes met.

"Did we just see the home world of the voices?" he thought to her.

"I think so," she answered as she took in a deep breath and became reoriented. "Let me see if I understand this correctly," she stated. "We are psychically linked with living organic beings with large minds suspended in some sort of sterile organic soup that connects them to massive computers. That living machine at the top of the spire routs the thoughts of the Galactic Collective down to the individual voices. The whole tower acts as some sort of giant antennae that processes the thoughts of psychics from worlds all over the universe." She smiled and folded her arms. "That's about it in a nutshell, don't you think?"

Michael stared skyward for a few seconds without speaking. He knew that he and Cecilia could not have made that journey on their own. The voices somehow made it possible. He could not determine why they did that. He tried to absorb everything they saw and make sense of it. He finally turned to Cecilia.

"I'm tired," he yawned. "I believe I've experienced enough for one day."

"Feel like turning in?" she asked.

He nodded. The two exhausted psychics headed inside their bungalow.

On a world many hundreds of millions of light years away, two beings acknowledged their part in the beginning of Earth's first psychic colony.

"Do you think the humans understood?" one linked.

"Let us not underestimate their capacity for understanding," the other voice replied.

Chapter 12

A rough crossing

The next morning, Michael and Cecilia ate an early breakfast, and prepared to take the ferry over to Graham Island. The experience from yesterday infused the two youths with increasing confidence. They no longer feared most figures of authority. They could mold any mind how they saw fit, since they discovered this new talent of psychic manipulation.

"I'm still uneasy about doing this," Michael commented, as they headed back into the tavern after packing the car.

"Would you rather people remembered us or traced our movements? You are the one that emphasized stealth," Cecilia pointed out.

"I did. Very well, I will agree to this… psychic manipulation," he relented, "but only if it will make it easier for us to achieve our goal and we limit its use."

"Sounds reasonable to me," Cecilia sighed.

To try out their new powers in earnest this time, they focused on the owners of the Prince Rupert Inn. They erased all trace of the two from the owner's minds and anyone else in the tavern who saw them. Outside, Cecilia checked with Michael.

"Still feel we did something bad or that it's a waste of time? They have no memory of us. No one inside does!" she stressed as they moved into the car.

"Ok… I concede," Michael replied as he threw up his hands in resignation. "This technique does have certain strategic advantages."

The young couple headed to the docks, and proceeded to take a free ferryboat ride to Graham Island. The operators would not remember them either driving on or leaving the ferry. On the island, Michael drove the final leg of the Yellowhead Highway north to the end. A small community of local anglers lived there. He found an isolated place to park along the north shore and chose to remain with the car until nightfall.

Later after dark, he and Cecilia removed everything from the car. They wiped down the entire inside of the car – hoping to remove every trace of them. Michael then fixed the steering wheel and placed a rock on the accelerator. He slammed the gear into drive and jumped free as the car drove off an old pier into the ocean. It sank out of sight.

"It served its purpose," Michael said as they walked to the local boat docks.

After inspecting the boats and examining the minds of their owners, they found a boat with sophisticated onboard navigation and communication equipment to meet their needs.

Without any moon, and only the faint light of stars glistening on the black inky water, Michael powered the boat slowly out of the harbor into the strait. Having never piloted a boat, he did everything as his voice suggested. Navigation during the day is one thing; in the middle of a moonless night on the surface of water that constantly bobs up and down, it is something else entirely.

After a while, Michael steered the craft to the final coordinates. He shut off the engine and turned on the radio, setting it to the agreed frequency. He picked up the microphone and tapped the front in the 'on' position using the agreed code. He did this several times before he set the mic back down and shut the device off. They waited in silence, with only the sound of the water, lapping against the side of the boat.

"You used Morse Code?" Cecilia asked about the tapping.

Michael nodded, "Very similar, but tougher, with a progressive changing code. I learned to translate it into English and then answer back into Russian."

"We're here? This is the location?" she questioned.

"Yes," he said, glancing around. "The cartel recommended the code as the simplest and safest means of communicating. They timed the rendezvous to avoid any regular shore patrols. Now we wait. Hopefully they'll locate us with their sonar."

"Do they smuggle many people?" Cecilia asked, sitting on a deck chair.

"On this trip, I believe we are their only passengers," he stated. "Although it would be highly unlikely, the Russian cartel required a hefty down payment for this favor in case the sub is discovered."

"How big is hefty?" she wondered.

"I had to cover the cost of their cargo, fuel… I believe I wired about twenty million to their Swiss account," he casually stated.

"Twenty million… dollars?" Cecilia questioned, "Michael, where did you…"

"Wait! Stretch out your senses," he said and held a finger to his lips.

They heard the sound of water splashing, followed by a metallic crunching sound, and then men speaking in hoarse whispers. Out of the darkness, a powered raft rapidly approached the port side of their boat with two men aboard. Michael and Cecilia waited with luggage in hand, having already wiped the boat clean of their prints. Michael quietly greeted the advancing men. He spoke fluent Russian.

"The night is cold," he called out in Russian.

"The sea is colder," a man from the raft answered, also in Russian.

"More code?" Cecilia linked. Michael barely nodded back to her.

The craft pulled alongside. The men urged Michael and Cecilia to jump.

"Come! No time to waste!" a Russian voice hoarsely whispered.

The raft sped back into the darkness. Within moments of pulling up to the long black metallic vessel, Michael and Cecilia scrambled down the narrow hatch. They stood in the control room onboard an older model Russian submarine built in the mid-to-late twentieth century. The crew passed along their luggage and prepared the aging vessel to dive.

"How did the cartel manage to purchase a nuclear submarine?" Cecilia linked to Michael as they waited for the captain.

"You can buy anything if you have enough cash. Isn't that so?" he linked as they stood side by side.

The smell hit Cecilia first. She nearly fainted.

"We should introduce them to deodorant and air fresheners," she linked.

Michael did not reply this time. He concentrated on trying to read the mind of the man wearing the specialized cap.

"Hatch is secured," one crewmember yelled as he slid down the ladder behind them.

Cecilia's eyes darted toward Michael.

"I understand everything they're saying," she linked.

"Your Russian download from last night is working," he linked back.

She suppressed the urge to smile.

The sub's captain shouted to his helmsman.

"Dive! Quick man, before the Americans know we're trespassing and blow us out of the water!" he snapped.

The Russian submarine slipped quietly back into the deep, dark, cold waters of the strait, and made for the open sea of the northern Pacific Ocean. Michael grabbed a railing nearby as the bow of the sub dropped to a steep angle before leveling off somewhat. Cecilia simply grabbed his arm for support.

"We probably tripped every buoy alarm in the fleet just now. Stay alert," the captain ordered, as he glanced from station to station. "Let's get the hell out of here!" he barked to his second in command. "Flank speed!"

The crew sprang into action. They were used to avoiding coastal patrols.

The old tub wheezed and hissed, as the weight of the ocean pressed down on the aging walls of the Russian submarine sinking further into the cold water attempting to gain speed as it dove to avoid detection.

"Surface vessel on scope, captain!" one seaman spoke excitedly.

A few seconds of nervous silence followed. No one in the command center moved.

"A fishing vessel," the man calmly indicated.

"Take us down to 800 meters and maintain course! Hug the bottom, Yuri," the captain instructed his helmsman.

Once a proud officer of the Russian Navy, the white-haired retired seaman sat in his chair and contemplated his risks. His pittance government retirement pay did not support his family. The smuggling cartel offered shares in the profits. The captain sent his shares home to his wife and children in Minsk. Heavily creased skin and sunken eyes displayed the face of a man that led a very hard life.

"Vlad!" the captain growled to one of his men. "Show our guests their spacious quarters," he sneered, turning back to his maps.

"His name is Chulya Vertov, a once proud submarine captain in the old Soviet Navy," Michael informed Cecilia. "He supports sixteen family members back home, which includes his in-laws. Judging from his medical history, he doesn't have long to live," Michael added. "He plans to keep on working until his death for his wife and children – so sad."

A tall broad-shouldered man maneuvered up behind Michael and Cecilia in the cramped quarters of the control room. Grease stains blackened his big hands. He wore a tank top and the coarse black hair on his chest and arms stood out. He stooped as he navigated the narrow causeway. Michael quit linking to Cecilia when he felt the seaman's presence behind him.

"This way," Vlad grumbled, gesturing, he herded them toward their room.

He soon opened the door to a cramped room with two small bunk beds that seemed more appropriate for children than for adults.

"The Captain confined you to quarters until he gives you leave," the seaman barked in Russian. "Do you understand?"

"We understand," Cecilia answered aloud, astounded at the words coming out of her mouth.

"Tell the captain the room is entirely unsuitable," Michael injected as he stooped low to enter.

"Two officers gave up this room for you," the seaman shot back.

"If this is the best you have, it will do," Cecilia added, catching on.

Michael turned away not wanting the sailor to see him smile.

"You must eat alone," the seaman continued, "captain's orders."

The seaman then slammed the door shut. Moments later, Vlad stood before his captain with his report on their comments.

"Spoiled brats," the Captain mumbled while rubbing his scraggily white beard. "Do they think they hitched a ride on a cruise ship?"

"Captain, how do you suppose these wealthy Russians came to be in Canada? Spies?" Vlad asked him.

Captain Vertov shrugged his shoulders, examining an underwater geography map.

"I never ask questions about cargo, Vlad. Curiosity killed the crewman," he stared up at the man, and then glanced down at his table. "Make ready for the open sea!" he barked.

Alone in the room, Michael scanned for listening devices and did not sense any. Cecilia learned as she watched Michael use his scanning abilities.

"We can speak freely unless you wish to link," he told her.

"I have a few questions," she said as she turned to him.

"Shoot," he responded as he sat.

"First, where did you obtain twenty million dollars?" she asked directly.

"Money has never been a problem since the voice and I started," Michael relayed to her. "The voices can manipulate electrical impulses, alter signals, and even change permanent memory circuits. They are very useful when it comes to anything electronic."

Michael then explained in detail the story regarding the night of his conversion. He told Cecilia about his luck in the casino. He then described how he arrived in New York as the head of a dummy corporation – a wealthy man.

"The voices certainly have a way with computers," he fondly recalled.

"You didn't need the trust. You could have been wealthy and stayed in New York. What changed your mind?" she asked.

He wanted to be intimate with his feelings, since he knew Cecilia so well, better than he knew any person in his life. Yet he remained distant – fearing personal involvement.

"Cecilia," he tried to explain, "the voices informed me that possibly a hundred or more psychics live in various stages of readiness around the planet.

The Chinese are apparently the most ready for conversion. Yet, these same extremely rare people may also be in danger if they should use their untrained ability in the wrong way that attracts attention. Their circumstances may become worse than mine were. I could not leave them to flounder as others did to me. Besides, I need someone human I can relate to…"

He turned from her but tried not to display too much emotion.

"You didn't have to make this journey," Cecilia went on. "When you obtained your trust, you still could have lived a privileged life in New York. Why didn't you?"

"Life means more than money or possessions to me," he linked to her, his back still turned. "Besides, my trust has other purposes in the future," he told her. "I hope that one day we – that is our community – can…" he stopped and yawned, stretching his muscles. He had not slept well in days.

She wanted to reach out to him in order to offer him some comfort.

"We'd better grab some sleep," he cut off her protective impulse.

He pulled up a chair to the end of the bottom bed and tossed a blanket on the seat before jumping into the bunk. His legs stretched clear off the bottom with his feet resting on the chair.

"Good night," he mumbled as he rolled over away from her.

Cecilia turned the lights out and climbed up to the upper berth.

"Night," she whispered.

The lumpy mattress pushed into her back like a sack of potatoes.

"Ugh, this is terrible," she said, struggling for a comfortable position.

Michael did not wish to share his experience of sleeping on the ground for nearly two years.

"You have no idea what bad is," he privately thought, "until you wake up and find bugs crawling in your underwear!"

A day at sea came and went. The second day offered no change in their venue. Michael and Cecilia spent little time outside their cramped room except to eat. If Cecilia thought their living quarters were terrible, she found the food was even worse. The cook offered them a concoction of boiled beets, onions, cabbage, carrots, and tough grizzled brown meat cooked into some kind of thin soup.

"What is this stuff?" she asked regarding their second meal of the same dish.

Michael, who once ate anything he could dig out of a garbage can, hoped he had not overburdened the ingénue.

"It's called borscht," he informed her, "although I ate a more enjoyable version in New York. It tastes better with fresh ingredients and sour cream."

She took a spoonful to her mouth but could no longer eat the stuff.

"Don't they ever change the cooking pot?" her lip curled up in disgust. "This tastes the same as yesterday's soup, only stronger."

"I believe I'll start the submarine diet," Michael linked as he pushed his bowl away. "I think I'm still digesting yesterday's meal," he burped while staring at a stale cup of black coffee.

Adding to their misery, the crew smoked the strongest cigarettes. The odor infiltrated every living space on the ship. Cecilia yearned for a breath of fresh air. After two days at sea, both started to turn green. To pass the time, the couple spent hours playing chess or cards – games that they found in one of the drawers. During this time, they hardly linked. Neither wished to delve too deeply into the thoughts of the other.

On the end of the second day, Captain Vertov called Michael and Cecilia to his sparse quarters. Cecilia thought she would pass out from the body odor when they walked through the bridge. The smell even affected the seasoned Michael.

"How did you happen to be in Canada?" the captain asked Michael.

"It is not your business to know," Michael said pointedly. "Contact the cartel, if you want answers to questions."

"I do not take orders from a child," the captain's eyes narrowed.

"This child is paying for your trip. I suggest you treat us like guests, or things may not go so well for you in Moscow, captain," Michael quickly threw back.

The captain hesitated, chewing those words.

Cecilia watched this exchange with curiosity. Clearly, Michael spoke with authority and all the arrogance of a person from the upper class.

"An act?" she wondered. If it was, he pulled it off well.

However, the voice briefed Michael on what to say and how to address the captain.

"Very well," the captain replied. He waved his hand and quickly dismissed them. "Return to your room. Pack your things. Be ready to leave."

Within the hour, the submarine began the cautious run of Russia sensor buoys. The cartel paid a high price for their exact locations. As the sub approached the coastline, the captain took a chance surfacing but checked first by using both his radar and periscope. The overcast night appeared perfect for smuggling. A mist in the air obscured visibility. The sea remained calm.

The submarine approached until the captain ordered "all stop" to avoid grounding on the bottom.

The crew, already assembled on deck, sprang into action. The captain ordered the signalman to risk a short burst of light. Immediately, a light flashed back from the shore.

"Send the signal," the captain spoke in a low voice.

The signalman and shore exchanged several timed bursts.

"That's it," Captain Vertov hoarsely whispered. "Start the crew unloading!"

A series of motorized rafts began to arrive from the group on the shore. The crew unloaded the cargo into the rafts. Soon a chain of the boats hustled back and forth from the shore to side of the submarine and back again. Knowing a patrol boat might come upon them at any moment, the crew worked feverishly.

"Vlad, bring our guests up on deck," the captain ordered.

Moments later, Michael and Cecilia crossed the short gangplank dropped on their behalf to a waiting raft. The captain, far too busy, did not bother to look in their direction, as their small vessel broke away. Michael sat on the raft's stern and stared back at the captain. He used extra care to wipe the captain's memory clean. Cecilia's mind swept over the crew, altering their recollection of seeing two young people onboard.

"The captain has no memory of going to Canada," Michael thought to her. "He'll destroy his personal records when he goes below."

The two jumped from the raft onto the beach and moved along the shoreline away from the smugglers loading trucks. They headed in the direction of some lights – a small town probably a mile or more away.

"At last," Michael thought to Cecilia as the two walked up the beach, "back on dry land. No more oceans to cross."

"…and no more horrible food!" she added with a smile. "I can't wait to shower!"

The legend that psychics foresee is pure myth.

Chapter 13

Paths diverge

When Michael first planned to cross the Pacific, he never considered having a young woman along as a partner. He always figured the psychic in Canada would be a man. He did not know why he thought that way. Perhaps some men presume that only another man would be helpful in a crisis.

Yet as he walked along the beach, feeling Cecilia's presence beside him, Michael kept his personal thoughts blocked when he realized he did not make special hygienic provisions that any teenage woman might require. Only one of many aspects of his plan he neglected when he agreed to take Cecilia.

"Will she be helpful or a hindrance?" he wondered, his mind flooded with doubt that first evening about whether to bring her along.

"Where to?" she intrusively asked through her thoughts. She was eager to start.

"In that direction naturally," he pointed toward the lights.

Cecilia immediately sensed uncertainty in his mind link.

"You don't know where we are going, do you, Michael?" she asked as they neared the village.

He chose not to answer. Cecilia sensed his block going up. Instead of confrontation, she stayed with him – stride for stride – until Michael stopped in front of a small ocean-facing house. He noticed an older model Russian car parked in the driveway.

"I say we borrowed this car," he gestured, hoping to divert her attention away from his lack of preparation. "The tank is filled with fuel. That should take us a good distance from here."

"Planning on asking permission first?" she quipped.

He tapped his skull and smirked as he headed for the front door.

"What are you going to do?" she wondered.

"Keep it quiet by not disturbing anyone," he whispered.

Michael walked into the owner's house, silenced the dog with his mind, found the car keys, and implanted in the sleeping man's mind that he had never owned the automobile.

Michael explained to Cecilia that when confronted by his wife the following day, the Russian man would repeatedly deny owning a car even if his wife could produce pictures of him with it.

"Clever," Cecilia said as they moved into the front seats, "putting the dog asleep and convincing the man he never had a car," she linked with a touch of sarcasm. "Why didn't you convince him that he wasn't married? Then he could go out on the town tomorrow night!"

"Stop," he said while trying to keep from laughing.

Michael noticed the car had three pedals. He knew the right one was for acceleration.

"The middle one must be the brake and the left one… the clutch!" he thought, "…a manual transmission… now, let's see," he said as he started the car and ground the car's shifter into first gear.

The car lurched forward out of the driveway into the street and stopped. He started it back up and it lurched forward, stopping again.

"What's wrong?" Cecilia asked.

"I've never driven a manual car," he said.

"What do you mean?" she asked him. "Do you mean you never used a clutch? I thought you drove a sports car?"

"This is the twenty-first century. I drove a variable automatic," he said pushing the shifter into a different position and again ground the clutch.

"Is that your idea of keeping it quiet?" Cecilia linked. "You're going to wake the whole neighborhood! You really don't you know how to use a manual transmission?" she demanded, out of frustration.

"Sure," he shot back, "just not one with a clutch." He struggled with the stick shift. "I can't put the car into gear."

"Push your left foot in," she pointed.

"Like this?" he responded.

"Yes," she told him, "now, move this lever up here. That's it. Now, ease out the left pedal as you press down on the right," she patiently instructed.

The car jumped forward, but did not stall this time. The car then jerked several times, but Michael kept going. He was determined to leave the village. Cecilia copied Michael's technique. She reached out with her senses and put several waking people back to sleep. Michael started to smile at his new accomplishment, driving a stick shift, until he saw the concerned on Cecilia's face.

"Do you want to drive?" he asked her

"I don't know how to drive a clutch, either," she told him.

"I thought you knew!"

"I saw it once on TV."

The Russian car crept up the street in first gear slightly faster than someone taking a brisk walk would. After several agonizing minutes, he managed to put some distance between them and the small seaside village. He finally pulled the car off the main road into a small side road surrounded by woods.

Out of desperation, Michael called on his alien counterpart for help.

"What is it, Michael?" it asked.

"I must drive an automobile that has a manual transmission," he requested.

"You cannot master this device without calling on us?" it replied.

"It's a mechanical component of a car and rather complicated. I can't use it without special instructions. Can you help?" he requested.

"One moment, Michael," his voice replied. Its energy signature faded and then quickly returned. "We examined your analytical and conforming abilities finding components missing from your conversions. We will correct that anomaly."

The couple exchanged glances as they overheard the exchange.

"Missing?" Michael questioned, confused with the voice's statement.

"What did it mean by anomaly?" Cecilia wondered.

Before they knew what hit them – a powerful energy download poured into both minds, knocking both psychics senseless. For several minutes, the youths sat unconscious in the front seat of the Russian car while the voices from Galactic Central fine-tuned the area around their portals making additional alterations in each brain.

When Michael awoke several minutes later, he immediately noticed the dramatic change.

"What happened? What did you do to us?" he questioned.

Banging in his ears, his words sounded like thunder. He not only experienced an increase in the sensitivity of his hearing but he also noticed that his senses of touch, sight, and smell had enhanced. The surrounding forest filled his nostrils with a myriad of odors that drifted through the open window. The pleasant smell of flowers in bloom mixed with pungent odor of rotting plant material. His hearing not only detected a slight wind but he could also even determine the wind's direction. His eyesight zoomed out the front window until he focused in on an ant crawling up the bark of a tree some twenty yards away.

Cecilia noticed similar affectations when she awoke. She stretched her senses out far beyond her body. First, she encompassed the entire surrounding environment, and then she sent her senses even further into the countryside.

Both Michael and Cecilia experienced the eyesight of an eagle, the hearing of a bat, and the smell of a bloodhound, all of their senses amplified.

Cecilia turned to Michael. He had his eyes closed and covered his ears with his hands. She placed her hands on his arms and gently lowered his hands.

"This new level requires greater control," she whispered into his mind. "Pull your senses back."

For once, Cecilia gave out the most sound and rational advice. Michael opened his eyes and gazed into Cecilia's. He instantly understood what to do. Slowly, their new sensory ability returned to normal levels.

"We must learn to extend these new powers only when we need them," she spoke wisely beyond her years.

He nodded in agreement – not wanting to either speak or move for fear he might create a sound like a blasting foghorn.

"I have a confession to make. Want to know something?" he linked while sitting back in his seat.

"What?" she questioned, unable to read him.

"I had my doubts that you were the right person to help me. After tonight… well, I'm very glad you came along," he said as he put aside the concerns.

"Why, thank you, Michael… I think," she straightened. "Are you able to drive a manual transmission?"

Michael took hold of the steering wheel. His new power rippled through the automobile. He could sense every detail of the car, right down to the smallest part. He did not have to learn to drive a clutch. He knew every aspect of what a clutch is and does. He realized at once how to work it properly.

He started the car using his mind. He pushed the clutch in with his left foot, put the car in gear, and gradually eased out on the clutch pedal as he pushed down on the gas pedal. The car smoothly moved back to the road as he continued through the remaining gears. He glanced over at Cecilia with a confident air.

"That's a start," she said relieved.

"It's exhilarating," he confessed.

He loosened his tense grasp and relaxed as his confidence increased.

"I feel as if I know every part on this car. If I concentrate, I can see inside the pistons to watch how the water pump works and see the crankshaft turn inside the engine block," he linked to her, his tone an excited one. "At the same time, I can peer inside the chest of a bird on that tree. I feel its fluttering heart beat."

Cecilia nodded agreement. She had the same sensations and picked up sights and sounds everywhere.

"What's happening to us Michael?" she wondered. "What are we becoming?"

"I wish I knew," he mumbled.

His awareness sharpened on his ability to drive. He could sense the oncoming pavement. The sensation felt empowering, uplifting, and exhilarating. He pulled his mind back when he noticed Cecilia stifle a yawn.

"I feel as if I'm running out of energy," she confessed. "Do you mind if I try to rest?"

He could sense her energy level weaken and drop off.

"Sure, rest," he told her. "I'll drive until I need relief. You can drive a clutch now, can't you?"

"If I must…" she linked as her thoughts faded.

In the next moment, her head slumped over, and she fell asleep.

"Using these abilities drains our energy," he thought. "I wonder how we are supposed to replenish it – sleep, I suppose."

Michael fought the urge to sleep. Determined, he continued inland away from the coast, driving the unfamiliar bumpy stretch of road in the dark, and trying to dodge potholes. He never saw another car.

After what seemed like an hour passed, he slammed on the brakes, shoving both feet to the floor. The car skidded to a halt. Cecilia's seatbelt grabbed her before she slid off the front seat. The engine died.

"What's wrong?" she woke from her nap, startled. "Are we out of fuel?"

The neglected rural road, which Michael drove to cross the southern tip of Kamchatka, arrived at a T-junction. One fork of the road went due north, the other path turned due west. This was not a matter of which road to take. This decision would affect the rest of the journey.

Michael reached in front of her and pulled out a map he sensed from the glove compartment. He stared at the map trying to reason which route would be best. Whether from fatigue or frustration, his mind went completely blank. He could not determine which way to go. His Galactic Central voice did not respond when he tried to raise it. Sweat broke out on his forehead. He crumpled the map in his hands and buried his head in the wrinkled map.

"What's wrong?" she asked.

She had never seen Michael this shaken. His hands trembled uncontrollably as he licked his lips. He tried to block her out.

"It's all wrong," he blurted. "Why did I drag you into this mess? I didn't plan properly. I'm sorry, Cecilia. I don't know which way to go," he said as his head lowered. "Let's face it. I'm too weak to be an effective leader."

She could feel the fatigue and level of frustration pressing on his mind. She also knew that old ghosts from his past haunted him during times of increased stress.

"What are you saying, Michael?" she sat up and remained calm.

"Look at this!" he said, waving the map. "The Kamchatka Peninsula is larger than I first envisioned," he began. "My plan to drive around to Yakutsk seems ridiculous!"

"What's wrong with driving around the peninsula?" she asked.

"The city of Magadan alone is over fourteen hundred miles away," he said, slapping the map. "Yakutsk is miles beyond that. If the roads are anything like this one, we could be driving for weeks. Suppose that the weather worsens, or that the car breaks down in this mountainous terrain. We might be stuck in a wilderness location," he gestured at the crumpled paper. "I can't risk taking you into the unknown like this. We should just find a way home. I've failed in my mission."

"I would hardly call you a failure – although everything you've mentioned makes perfect sense to me," she calmly linked.

"Cecilia, I don't know where this road leads," he gestured. "It isn't on the map. It might as well be a dead end."

Cecilia closed her eyes. Michael sensed her power growing.

"What are you doing?" he asked while staring at her perplexingly.

"Remember why you sought me out? I'm helping," she responded.

She extended her new senses, stretched out her mind, and took on a new perspective of their surroundings. Rising high above the ground, she saw the countryside for hundreds of miles.

"We cannot go to the north," her link sounded distant. "Most of the roads over the mountain range will be impassable until the beginning of July unless we want to abandon the car and cross using a tractor."

She turned her sensory field toward the west.

"At the end of this road, I see a small fishing village nestled around a calm bay with two diesel trawlers still in port. One would be perfect for crossing the sea," she relayed her vision to him. "The boats are slow but reliable. We must start out soon or else…"

She collapsed into the seat having run out of energy. She slumped down with her head hanging toward her chest. All at once, Michael could not detect her presence. Alarmed, he reached for her fearing that the new ability harmed her.

"Cecilia? Cecilia!" he gently shook her. She did not move. He thought about life saving measures when he sensed her breathing and heartbeat as normal. "Weak… you're weak," he realized. "You drained all of your energy, that's all," he thought, taking in a deep sigh of relief. "You brave beautiful girl… thank you," he whispered. "How did you do that?" he wondered as he marveled at her new ability.

Michael walked around the car, gently gathered her into his arms, and then laid her down on the back seat. He glanced over and noticed his briefcase, with his satellite computer inside. It rested on the floor in the back. He had been so tired that he had completely forgotten about it.

"I could have used the computer. My voice would have suggested it…" he thought.

For a second, he wondered how much influence his voice had on his life. Then his stomach growled. He could not recall their last meal.

"See you in the morning," he said to her as he carefully closed the door. "Sweet dreams."

He took the road she suggested and drove the rest of the night while pushing his body past sleep and fatigue. He finally arrived on the western side of the Kamchatka Peninsula just before dawn.

CHAPTER 14

SEA OF OKHOTSK

MICHAEL NOTICED THE SKY BEGINNING to lighten overhead. Just as he rounded a long curve in the road, he came face to face with a vast sparkling blue body of water that seemed to stretch to infinity. The first reddish rays of dawn struck the tops of clouds hovering above the western horizon. The road then took a downward turn toward the sea. Michael opened a connection to Galactic Central. His voice responded as Michael stretched out his senses to include his voice in his vision of the coastline.

"Can you identify that body of water?" he asked his voice.

"You are gazing upon the Sea of Okhotsk, an inlet sea some seven-hundred miles wide," it described in terms Michael understood. "Only through the giant sieve-like opening along the eight hundred mile long chain of the Kuril Islands to the east can boat traffic gain access into or out of the sea," it droned.

"Thanks for the information," Michael muttered before cutting the connection as he fought to stay awake. "Right now, I need a strong hot cup of tea," he thought while scanning the fishing village ahead.

He drove toward a little shantytown that consisted of old weathered buildings crowded around an inlet bay. A hundred or more white seagulls hovered over the shore like a great living cloud, shifting with the morning breeze. Michael noticed that local anglers moored a couple of large white fishing vessels just off shore, exactly as Cecilia described in her vision.

"Probably left for repairs," Michael reasoned. "I only hope they're in working condition."

He pulled up next to the village tavern by the water's edge. The owner tied up a couple of goats to the corner of an aged, gray, wooden chicken coop sitting next to the crumbling old structure of the tavern with filthy panes. Michael doubted that the owner had ever cleaned them. Judging from the goat's heavy bellies, the animals most likely provided fresh milk. The moment he stepped from the car, he smelled the inviting odor of freshly baked bread mixed with some other cooking concoction.

"Here's an answer to a prayer," he said as he pushed open the tavern door.

He took in a deep breath. The aroma filled his nostrils with a dizzying perfume. An old woman tended a stove and moved gingerly about with her routine.

"Let me see…" he thought while taking in a deep breath and concentrating on what should be his first priority.

He first entered the elderly woman's mind and changed it so that she did not see him. Now invisible to her, he next turned to the boiling pot of water on the stove. He threw a tea bag into a cup of hot water and added what he thought was cream into his cup. He swallowed a large gulp only to discover the tea had an unusual pungent flavor.

"What is that?" he wondered as he picked up the cream and smelled it. "Goat's milk," he realized though too late. He downed what he could tolerate of the remaining tea before he turned to the soup – hoping to satisfy his hunger.

"I'll need some provisions," he thought. "Let's start with that fabulous breakfast waiting for me."

Michael easily convinced the old woman to give him a few loaves of fresh bread, and to pour out some of the soup simmering on the stove. He grabbed a wooden spoon and quickly scooped down the steaming bowl and stuffed his mouth with freshly baked bread while the old woman filled up an empty crate with the standard provisions for a fishing trip at sea – an idea that he suggested to her mind.

The hot soup – full of sausages, various pieces of fish, crumbs of goat cheese, potatoes, carrots, cabbage, and leeks in a hearty stock – warmed and invigorated his chilled bones.

"This is definitely better than borscht!" he chuckled while sopping up the remainder of the broth with a piece of steaming warm bread.

Satiated, he returned to the car and roused Cecilia. He opened the car door and had her sit up. He held out a steaming bowl of soup.

"I take it you drove to the fishing village," she said while blinking away the bright sunlight. She held out her hands to obtain her bearings. "What is this?"

"Soup… it's quite good," he told her, holding out a spoonful.

She took the spoon into her mouth and relaxed in the seat.

"I can manage," she said as she took the bowl, a hunk of fresh bread, and the spoon from him.

Michael watched with delight as she eagerly dug into the food. She was as famished as he had been. He returned a few minutes later with two steaming mugs of tea.

"Here, this will help," he offered.

"Now what?" she asked, taking one.

"Hot tea with sugar," he indicated.

For a second, she tipped her head, as if contemplating some point. She set the mug down and returned to slurping up the hot hearty soup. She broke off pieces of fresh bread and dipped them in the broth exactly as Michael did.

"This is delicious!" she exclaimed via a link. "The old woman inside knows her stuff."

He turned back toward shore and gazed out over the expansive water. He wondered about crossing the sea and all the problems associated with operating a boat. The strong tea gave him enough stimuli to keep going. He sipped his hot tea while he waited for Cecilia to finish.

The humble meal revived her.

"Much better!" she yawned. She then stretched her cramped muscles.

The sun crept over the eastern hills behind them and filled their world with its golden glow. The sky cleared overhead.

"A good day to start a sea voyage," Cecilia stated, trying to stand. "Oh, I feel weak," she groaned and sat back down. "You'll have to give me a few minutes."

"Stay put. Try to regain your strength. Finish your tea," he suggested. "I'll check out these boats."

Leaving behind the women, children and the elderly, most of the men from the village were away with the rest of the village's fleet, fishing in the northern part of the sea. Michael chose to inspect the larger of the two vessels that the fishermen had left behind. He took a skiff out to the boats anchored in the harbor.

Bow to stern, the larger boat showed obvious wear and tear from having been in service for many years. However, some recent fresh paint and renovations here and there, demonstrated to Michael that the owners tried to keep the sea-going vessel in decent running condition. The front of the boat had a wide wooden deck and a deck plate covering a vacant place in the bow for a crane. Another covered opening led to a cooler below. The wheelhouse sat up higher from the deck near the center of the boat and had a wide window in front.

At the stern, he noticed another deck plate secured with heavy bolts. Michael assumed correctly that the space represented the area for the machine that hauled in the net. Their absence lightened the boat, and therefore it would probably use less fuel.

The moment he put his hands on the pilot wheel, his mind spread throughout the vessel and into the engines. He knew every aspect stem to stern. He started the engines. They purred like a tiger.

"Recently overhauled," he noted. "That's a relief," he thought and shut them down.

At the back of the wheelhouse, a worn wooden staircase led down to the crew bunks and a primitive galley, a stove with four burners, a fixed table, and benches. Further inspecting the living quarters, Michael noticed six crew beds had fresh linen. Perhaps they intended to make this vessel seaworthy soon.

Michael returned to the galley and opened the box that he brought aboard the ship. He privately thanked the old woman for arranging the provisions neatly inside – jugs of fresh water, salt, sugar, tea, flour, two dozen fresh eggs, smoked meats, a slab of bacon, a bag of carrots, a bag of potatoes, shortening, baking powder, matches, canned goods, and two boxes of chocolate biscuits.

Returning to the pilothouse, he checked the fuel tanks and oil levels. While going over the controls, he happened to glance out the window. A group of villagers gathered on shore and expressed alarm about the strangers. All at once, the group dispersed. Michael saw Cecilia's arm wave out the car window.

"That's my helper," he mused.

On his next trip out, he brought their luggage and extra fuel to the boat. He worked for nearly an hour in order to make the boat seaworthy. He then finally headed back for Cecilia. In her present weak condition, she could not stand. Michael carried her to the skiff.

"I'm so embarrassed," she whined, when he picked her up.

She wrapped her arms tight around him and leaned her head on his shoulder. He said nothing and did not link. Onboard the trawler, she sat on a wooden chair in the wheelhouse.

"Ready?" he asked.

"Not really, but if this is our only choice," she quietly linked to him.

"You were right. We will save time this way," he said.

"Then we'd better start before someone official joins that crowd," she pointed back to a fresh assembly of people onshore.

Again, the crowd moved off – thanks to Michael this time. He then cast off the mooring line, raised the anchor, and started the engines. He gradually eased the vessel out of the harbor into the open water of the sea. Michael set the ship's compass on a course due west. He opened up the boat's diesel engines to about one third of its top speed to conserve fuel. He hoped that they would be across the sea in a matter of hours.

At first, the vessel chugged merrily through the waves. The couple seemed hopeful about their decision to use to the ship as a shortcut. Cecilia rose and moved about. She became acquainted with the ship's areas and gradually gained strength. About an hour after leaving the port, the day rapidly deteriorated. A strong wind, along with dark threatening clouds, moved in creating large waves. A constant flow of ever increasingly large swells tossed the moderately sized fishing boat. The trawler rose up and down each wave like a piece of bobbing cork.

Shortly after the wild ride began, Cecilia ran to the railing and hung her head over the starboard side. She retched her guts out amidst the waves that sprayed an occasional salty mist across the deck.

"Oh," she groaned. "I think I just lost the soup."

"You'll adjust to motion after awhile," he suggested.

He initially found her predicament amusing, but not for long. Within minutes, he too felt his gut stricken and ran out to join Cecilia along the rail.

"Not much fun, is it?" she glanced over at him.

"No…" he muttered before relieving his insides again.

With the boat's engines pushing against both the wind and waves, Michael struggled to keep the fishing trawler on course. Despite his nausea, he returned to the wheel and carefully watched the fluctuating compass. The storm appeared to rage on without end. Frustrated with fighting the surf, he brought out his laptop and tapped into a satellite to monitor their location and check the weather.

Clang! He heard a loud distracting sound come up from the galley.

Michael tried to stay focused on tracking their exact location. He made changes to navigation maps he found on the boat and marked their current location. The boat rode up another large swell.

Bang! Clang! This time several objects broke loose below. They made loud noises as they rolled around the galley's floor.

"Will you be alright if I go below?" he asked Cecilia, "…seems I must batten down the hatches," he linked as he recalled the nautical terms.

"Go ahead, I'm keeping the railing attached to the side of the ship," she droned back. Her knuckles were practically white from her firm grasp.

With the ship violently rocking up and down, he carefully maneuvered down the slippery wooden steps. Cups, forks, spoons, knives, and several pans had spilled out of open cupboards and drawers and slid around the floor. Michael slipped and fell on the moist floor as he chased after them.

Busy catching the loose items, he neglected to tie off the helm wheel. This caused the ship's rudder to drift, turning the bow gradually south. As the ship bounced through the waves, Michael's laptop computer inched its way toward the edge of the table. After a few minutes, he eventually picked up and secured the last of the loose items.

"I wondered why these cabinets and drawers have latches," he noted as he secured them closed.

Suddenly, a large wave pushed the boat up. Instead of the bow cutting into the wave, the boat turned sideways to the wave and listed over to one side. Michael was tossed on his ear.

"Hey!" Cecilia cried out, holding onto the rail to keep from falling.

Crash! Michael heard the sound of breaking glass above. The boat flipped back as he ran back up to the wheelhouse.

"Where's my…"

The window next to the table had a small shattered hole in it. He caught site of his laptop precariously balanced on the edge of the deck as it teetered toward the water.

"No!" he cried as he rushed out the door.

Another wave pushed the boat into the air. He dove for the computer just as it flipped up and then fell overboard. He yanked off his shirt and started to dive into the water after it, when a hand reached out and grabbed the back of his pants.

"The computer we can replace," Cecilia spoke wisely from behind him. "The captain is indispensable."

"You don't understand," he whirled about. "That's my navigation system!"

"You'll just have to do it the old fashioned way, I guess," she shrugged.

Exasperated, he stomped back into the wheelhouse and searched the drawers for something its crew used for navigation, as the owners had stripped every electronic device from the control room – probably for use in another boat. He found additional maps and a large exquisitely crafted black wooden box. Inside the rectangular box, he pulled out a delicate polished brass instrument, shaped like a triangle with mirrors and lenses.

"What's this?" he thought as he held it up in front of his face.

"A sextant," he heard a feminine voice in his mind. He glanced out the front window. Cecilia leaned against the rail and watched him.

"Do you know how to use one?" he asked.

"Nope!" she quickly replied.

"Don't tell me that you saw it on TV," he suggested.

"No, but I saw a picture of one in a book once. Mariners used them for navigation. I don't know how they work. You're the navigator," she linked to him. "You'll figure it out. It's why the crew elected you, captain!" she quipped.

"What does that make you?" he frowned at her.

"I'm your first mate!" she smiled.

"Ha!" he threw back. "If you're first mate, then hoist the sails or swab the decks!"

"Trust me – I'm doing plenty of swabbing down here," she earnestly answered, turning back to the rail.

She gracefully curtsied as he spun the wheel back. He turned the bow directly into the wind and the next wave. This sent the front of the boat back up into the air. The vessel crested the wave and slid down the other side. Fighting the elements and her motion sickness, Cecilia turned back to the railing as she fought to keep her nausea under control.

Keeping the swaying boat on a westward course, Michael maintained constant watch on the wheel and compass. Eventually the continual rocking took its toll on him too. He grew tired of fighting his nausea. Before he linked with Cecilia, she reached out to him.

"Michael, I can't take this anymore," she pleaded. "I could use some help."

"Me too," he confessed as he swallowed hard. "Let's help each other adjust," he suggested.

Michael diverted his attention from the boat to form a healing link with Cecilia. The two psychics worked on the balance part of each other's brain and helped one another to conquer their motion sickness.

"Better," she replied while trying to stand on the swaying boat.

"Hang on, Cecilia. We'll help each other through this," he reassured her.

She attempted a weak smile in reply to his patronizing tone. Soaked to the bone, she finally went below and found some dry clothes. She changed, toweling off first. She tried to rest on one of the bunks. However, the water banging against the side of ship bothered her. She did not wish to go down with the boat in heavy seas. She lay awake and stared at the wooden structure over her head, until she finally stood up and returned to the wheelhouse. Standing next to Michael, the pair leaned left and right as the vessel swayed with each wave.

"I remember the putrid air in that confined space, but I believe that after a few hours of this, I'd rather tackle the sea inside a submarine," she confessed to Michael. "This surface travel is too rough for me."

"Have you forgotten how bad the crew smelled?" Michael retorted.

"I could never forget that. However, after today, I won't be requesting a cruise anytime soon," she told him.

"I hear the food on a cruise ship is very good," he commented.

"Please don't mention food right now," she said as she leaned against the wall.

Cecilia glanced over at Michael. He swayed on his feet as he gallantly fought to keep his eyes open.

"When was the last time you slept?" she asked him.

He shrugged his shoulders.

"I'll stay here and keep us on a steady course. You go below and try to rest for awhile," she practically ordered.

For once Michael did not argue. Fatigue finally caught up with him. He had no energy left. He went to the crew's quarters for some needed rest. For the remainder of the day, Cecilia monitored the course of the fishing boat as it chugged along – inching its way westward across the Sea of Okhotsk.

As evening approached, Michael came up and took over. Tying off the wheel, he managed a few additional hours sleep during the night by lying on a blanket in the wheelhouse while Cecilia slept in the crew's quarters.

The following day the sky cleared and the trawler continued on its slow crossing with only mild waves gently rocking the boat. They saw nothing around them but the wide-open sea. The sunlight took some of the chill off the air.

Encouraged by this change of events, Michael and Cecilia decided to eat something. After a rather light meal of sandwiches, Michael stepped out on the deck with his rather complex instrument in his hands.

"Is it working?" she asked.

"I received the download on how to use a sextant last night. I can obtain a rough estimate of our position, as long as I have the sun and stars to help pinpoint our location," he explained.

He checked the scope and realized that at their current pace, it would take them longer to cross the sea than he thought.

"I believe we have the slow boat to China," he joked.

"Slow and steady wins the race," she pointed out – using another cliché.

"I'm afraid the person who came with up that slogan didn't die of boredom on a fishing boat," he shot back. He tied the wheel off. "I'm lying out on the deck. Join me?"

"Sure!" she hopped up.

Michael peeled off his shirt and Cecilia discarded as much as she could. Both psychics tried to avoid staring at the other. They decided instead to give their psychic minds a rest, and enjoyed lying in the sun. They talked aloud about life in general – their likes and dislikes. They played a few hands of cards that they found in the crew's quarters.

After the noontime meal, they returned to the deck. Michael would hop up now and then to verify their westward course. The two psychics spread out a blanket and lay side-by-side on the front deck until the sky turned to inky black. They enjoyed the clear celestial view and catching a glimpse of an occasional passing meteorite.

"Have you ever seen so many stars?" Cecilia noted.

"Certainly is dark without a city nearby," Michael commented. "Right over there," he pointed toward a constellation, "is the location of Galactic Central."

"How do you…" she started to ask.

Michael shared with her the moment in Mississippi when his voice indicated its location to him. Whether he admitted it or not, over the course of the past week he and Cecilia had become very close – not just as the world's first two psychic human beings but also as a man and a woman.

"I've decided I don't want to be a princess," Cecilia broke the temporary silence.

"Is this some high school fantasy?" Michael wondered with a half-smile.

"No, I want to be queen of the world, instead," she flatly stated.

"What made you say that?" he asked.

"I mean, if we really wanted to Michael – think about it," she pointed out. "We could rule the world. You would be King Michael, and I, Queen Cecilia. Everyone would bow to our wisdom."

"You aren't serious," he leaned on one elbow to face her.

She propped on her elbow opposite him.

"Who could stop us?" she asked with all sincerity.

"That's a terrifying thought, Cecilia. Don't you think so?" he said, laying flat again. "I mean, imposing our will on others and forcing other people to obey us, instead of using their own free will? I can't say I would enjoy living in that world."

"We could create a great world with our power," she insisted.

"Scientists, futurists, politicians, capitalists, they all want to make the world a better place," he thought to her. "The world is fine as it is – at least most parts of it. True, we could establish more equity and justice. However, if you start imposing your way people will never learn from their mistakes. We base progress on failure, not success. Striving toward perfection takes us forward. Complacency would destroy us."

"None of what you are saying makes sense to me," she countered. "I say we make them all see the light."

"Who would willingly help you?" he asked.

"We'd put it in their minds," she answered.

"Remove choice. Impose a solution. Don't you see the fallacy in the logic, Cecilia?" Michael stated. "Mankind has to stumble and fall, if it is to learn."

"Yes, but they don't learn," she continued. "That's the problem Michael! Their hatred drives them to kill and torment each other. Would you sit by and do nothing if someone declared war on America?"

"Well, no…" he hesitated.

"What about Moscow or Beijing?" she pointed out. "People are people. If a foreign country attacked those nations, would you intervene? Remember, all of humanity needs our help."

"Help is one thing. Taking away freedom is messing with the natural order of history," he told her.

"We're part of that nature too," Cecilia said. "We weren't created in some laboratory on Mars."

"No, but we're the product of alien intervention and not a natural process," Michael said as he returned to his elbow and faced her. His face was quite close to hers now. "I've given this many hours of thought, Cecilia. I believe that we should remain secretively separate from humanity. Should we use our power for good? Yes, I'd like that very much. Should we interfere with human history by steering governments toward one particular philosophy or changing the course of elections? Never. If we do, I feel we'll be inviting disaster."

Cecilia stared at Michael for a moment.

"You know what I like about you?" she whispered.

"I can't imagine," he said – uncomfortable with her stare and close proximity.

"You are truly selfless," she told him. Their lips hovered inches away. "Any other man would take what he felt was his due. But not you. Well, you did amass a bit of money and possessions for a short time in New York. Yet your only purpose in doing so was to make this mission possible. Why didn't you stay in New York? You could have been the only psychic in the world – unchallenged."

"That is not my style," he mused.

"Yes, but you never explained this on the submarine. Why did you go through the trouble of taking back your trust? You could have created another," she wondered.

"I recall an old saying, and I paraphrase; 'steal my money and you have nothing, steal my name and you have everything.' Despite my parent's lack of faith in their son, I still love them," he explained. "I wanted my father's name to live on with honor."

"What will you do with the trust?" she asked him.

"This is difficult for me to explain, even through a link," he said with hesitation. "I want the psychics to form a community. I want it to be a very special place – open and sharing. Once we create this haven, I feel we can achieve our fullest potential as both humans and psychics," he told her. "Oh, I agree with you. We should help the world. We might even relieve poverty and misery where we can without attracting too much attention. The trust can help with that after we organize. First, we must achieve something special on our own. We could make the world's first true utopia, a place that is special for us and those other humans like us. From this base, we could launch missions to troubled spots all over the world. But taking over the world is for egomaniacs and not for understanding sympathetic psychics, Cecilia. Our contributions to the world must be subtle ones."

For a moment, Cecilia realized she could inch forward and kiss his lips if she wanted. Michael chose that moment to back away. He sensed her feelings. Cecilia shrugged it off.

"You're right about everything, of course," she said while lying down and staring back up at the night sky. "I suppose that in this idealistic haven you propose, I could settle on a new career. With Galactic Central's help, I could be anything, or anyone, but I definitely do not want to be a princess," she smiled, and then thought seriously. "Who knows, maybe I could become a doctor? What do you think?"

"As long as you are part of that community, Cecilia," Michael said softly as he lay down next to her, "you'll always be a princess to me."

Cecilia stared at the stars, and deeply sighed, "Aye, aye, captain."

CHAPTER 15

A WALL OF WHITE

MICHAEL STAYED UP LATE THAT evening. He remained in the wheelhouse and watched the compass while Cecilia rested below. He maintained the chugging vessel on a westerly heading. For several hours, he looked over maps, and took advantage of the clear night to check their position using the sextant. He pointed it at the stars to locate their latitude and longitude as best as he could calculate and marked their progress on the map. He finally rigged the wheel and managed some rest by lying on a mattress that he dragged up the stairs.

By early light, the sea calmed down considerably, nearly flat. Michael jumped up and realized that he had slept longer than he had wanted. He listened for a sound, but heard nothing – only the distant chugging that became part of the background. He could not hear the wind – not even a breeze. Everything seemed a little too quiet.

When he stuck his head out the doorway, he noticed a light blue sky devoid of everything, horizon to horizon, not a cloud, a bird, or even a buzzing insect, nothing. Only the sound of the fishing boat penetrated the morning air, as the motor churned up water, pushing the boat west.

Cecilia stood at the bottom of the stairs and spied the mattress on the floor.

"Did you...?" she started to link.

"Uh huh," he finished the thought as he bent down to grab a corner.

He did not catch the twinkle in her eye or perceive her thought on his gallantry.

"Mind if I make a pot tea?" she linked.

"By all means, go ahead," he linked back.

He dragged the mattress back down the wooden steps, and threw it on the bunk. He next plopped down on a bench in the galley.

"What's wrong?" Cecilia sensed trouble in his mind.

"I don't know," he said. His fingers nervously tapped the table. "I can't place it. I just feel it – like a pebble in my shoe."

She stopped and extended her mind.

"I don't sense any danger around us," she linked to him.

"Probably nothing," he said as he tossed it off. He swung his legs around the bench to face her. "I'm glad you made the tea. I could use a fresh cup," he said as he rubbed his scalp. "What about breakfast?"

"Ok," she capitulated, "I don't mind cooking unless you wish to cook."

"I'm afraid I wouldn't be good at anything this morning," he told her. "I can't seem to focus. Maybe I slept wrong," he said as he ran his hand around his neck.

"Next time sleep on the bunk. I can help with relief," she offered.

"I'm not used to asking for help," Michael replied as he glanced up. "Thanks for offering though," he told her.

As much as he anticipated Cecilia's culinary artistry, Michael could not sit still. He stood up from the bench and bounded back up the steps to the wheelhouse. He wanted to check the ship's location. He stepped out on the deck with the sextant and made another reading. He noted their location on the chart. From these readings, he supposed they were still on a westerly course – albeit their progress was slow. They had only crossed a quarter of the total distance – a fact that disappointed Michael.

He heard Cecilia making noise in the galley. A short time later, he smelled the tea brewing, the toast browning, and then heard bacon sizzling – its welcoming smell followed. Despite those homey smells and sounds instilling a feeling of familiarity, Michael could not shake the brooding sensation of impending doom.

He tried to think about what they would do when they reached the opposite shore. He leaned his chair back and tried to relax, yet something irritatingly nagged at his brain. His head kept bobbing up to check the view out the wheelhouse window. He stared out at the flat sea as if it would whisper some new secret. All at once, he felt Cecilia's presence behind him.

"Here," she handed him a hot cup of tea. She put a hand on his shoulder. "You ok?"

He nodded his reply and sipped the welcome brew.

"Ah, real cream!" he thought, knowing the old woman packed a can of cow's milk.

Cecilia's hand lingered on his shoulder. Her reassuring touch felt right for some reason, as if she instilled confidence in him.

"Stop worrying," he thought as he took another sip.

On the map table behind him, Cecilia laid out a feast. Michael turned to a plate filled with freshly cooked bacon, sunny-side eggs, and fried potatoes, even toast spread with melting goat cheese. If the way to a man is through his stomach, she convinced him with this meal.

"Cecilia, this looks great," he told her, enthusiastic at the prospect of eating.

Without thinking, he instinctively put his arm around her waist and gave her a quick hug. As he moved past her, he missed the startled yet pleased expression on her face.

"If that's all it takes," she privately thought, "I'll make breakfast every day."

Michael did not hear her comment. Instead, he focused on the plate and dug into the fresh hot food. He savored every mouthful of the flavorful meal like a gourmand.

"Thanks Cecilia," he linked to her. He stuffed his hungry mouth deciding not to hesitate. "Where's yours?" he asked, taking another mouthful.

She did not answer. Michael cleared his mouth with a swig of tea.

"Cecilia?" he asked, expecting a reply.

He turned around. Cecilia was gone. He stood up and went to the window. He noticed her standing in the bow. She stared straight ahead and shielded her eyes from the sun with her right hand. He reached back to take another quick bite of food before stepping outside. He tried to link but she blocked him.

"What is it?" he asked aloud, calling down to her.

"I don't know," she shrugged. "Probably nothing," she turned around with a fake smile. "I've decided to tan."

He briefly watched as she pulled off her sweater leaving only a 'sports' bra to cover her ample bosom. She then proceeded to spread out a blanket and lay down. She pulled out a pair of sunglasses and put them on as she lay on her back. The image seemed too familiar. It reminded Michael of the dream they shared back in Edmonton. He swallowed hard and tried to suppress any tinge of arousal he might be feeling.

Michael avoided his wandering thoughts and returned to the interior of the wheelhouse to finish his tea and breakfast. Just as he started to take his empty plate below, the strange feeling returned. It gnawed at his rising sense of anxiety. He put down the plate and moved back to the window. The crisp horizon line disappeared and was replaced with a fuzzy one. He could not explain what he saw, yet he noticed it moving toward them, very fast.

All at once, the temperature dropped. Michael could see his breath.

"What the devil?" he thought. His eyes squinted as he peered through the front window. The bright sunlight reflected off whatever approached the boat. "What is that?"

Even with his new keen vision, Michael could not comprehend the phenomenon developing before him. Before he could react, a giant wall of white thickly dense air rose up from the sea. Like an enormous ghost, it swooped down and quickly swallowed the moving ship.

"Fog!" he uttered. The frightening word caught in his throat.

Alarm bells went off in his brain. He wondered if he could navigate this old tub in such heavy fog. He could no longer see the bow. It disappeared!

Moments before, as the fog approached, Cecilia sensed an inordinate concern rising in Michael's emotional state. She had sensed his fear. She sat up and turned around in time to see his puzzlement turn to dread.

"Michael?" she inquired.

He stood at the window with a frozen contorted expression on his face – the skin on his forehead stuck in a great wrinkled frown as he gazed out to sea.

Then the cold enveloped her. She could see her breath. Pulling her sweater back on, she jerked her head around in time to watch an impenetrable fog rapidly engulf the boat. She stood up and moved to the bow. She tried to stretch out her senses. Nothing, she sensed nothing, as if she met with a solid formidable and impenetrable wall. She turned around. She could barely make out Michael's worried face through the dim yellow light in the wheelhouse.

"What are we going to do?" she asked him.

He shook his head. He did not have a clue, but he did not want to worry her.

"Give me a minute," he linked back as he tried to reason through the problems of navigation.

He thought about collisions at sea with a vessel. Thus far, they had managed to miss any large container ships or oil tankers that moved about in their regular lanes. Most of them came to or from the eastern Russian port city of Magadan, the principle destination for most the traffic in this part of the sea.

Without radar or sonar, they operated blindly to most dangers in this wide inlet sea. In a heavy fog, however, they could run smack dab into a rock formation, or even a big container ship. They would never see it coming until it sliced right through their boat. The Russians built their fishing boat for short runs and certainly not for crossing the sea as a passenger ship.

Michael cut back on the engine's throttle to twenty-five percent in order to slow their forward progress.

"What should I do?" he stressed, figuratively wringing his hands. He tried to block Cecilia out of his mind. "Think, Michael. Think!"

Piercing his troubled mind, he heard the sweet soft voice of Cecilia.

"Michael," she called to him. "Be of one mind. Join with me," she beckoned. "I will cut through this fog."

He opened his mind and lent Cecilia his psychic energy.

"Allow me," she linked.

Like a dolphin skimming the waves, he felt her thoughts reach out and touch the water. The surface acted as a conduit for her energy as it flowed out across the sea until she finally encountered the main shipping lane, dead ahead.

In those well-churned waters, both psychics saw large tanker and cargo ships going back and forth like planes taking off and landing at a busy airport.

"Michael, do you see them?" she asked.

"I see them!" he noted after having tapped into the image.

He scrambled to grab a pencil and mark their locations on a map. For Cecilia not only transmitted their heading, speed, size, and type of each vessel, but she also provided such details as the names of the ships, their cargoes, and destinations.

Michael furiously scribbled the information on his map. He noted the positions of those vessels relative to their own position on the chart as well. Cecilia's vision also indicated their current rate of speed and distance from shore. If they maintained their present rate, he could track all the ships including their own with just a few calculations and a watch. He reached out and checked the throttle controls and the engines rpm's.

"I've got it!" he chimed back to her.

Previously when Cecilia had applied that technique, it practically drained her psychic energy level to zero. This time she carefully tapped only a fraction of her energy level. Relieved yet slightly weary, she leaned against the mast at the bow for support.

Meanwhile, the thick white fog grew worse around the pair as it descended like an opaque avalanche of white to envelope the fishing trawler completely. The light faded around them – plunging the boat into near darkness in the middle of the day. Hoping to avoid collisions, Michael switched on their running lights, when he felt Cecilia touch his mind.

"Don't," she quietly mentioned. "I want to stay in the dark for a little while, if you don't mind."

"Not at all," he linked back.

Michael turned the outside running lights off. He kept the light on inside the wheelhouse to read the maps. The moment Cecilia pulled back from her vision, Michael feverishly worked over the charts and made numerous notations. After a few minutes, he stared down at a problem area – shoals.

He tried to determine how close they could take the boat to the opposite shore. However, the map indicated treacherous shoals marked in yellow along the western shoreline. If the fog persisted, or lasted for days, he might scuttle the craft if he attempted blind navigation through those dangerous waters. Going further north took them closer to the rendezvous but farther from China. His eyes traveled down to the bottom of the chart. The Sea of Okhotsk presented an opportunity he never considered – a direct route.

"What if we entered China by a different route?" he offered to Cecilia.

"Which way?" she asked.

"We could go up the Amur River and cross over to China where the river turns into border with Russia? What do you think?" he offered.

"Go up the river in this boat?" she responded.

"Not necessarily," he countered. "We'll ditch the boat along the southern shore of Okhotsk and find a car in one of the nearby cities. I figure we can probably drive all the way to Beijing. Cecilia?"

"Yes, ok, go ahead," she faintly linked her reply. She was apparently distracted.

"I'm changing our course to a new heading, southwest," he linked back.

Michael decided to head for the shoreline north of Nikolayevsk-na-Amure, which lay at the mouth of the great Amur River delta. He noted that only this particular area contained any stretches of sandy beach without an underwater barrier. They could approach land without fear of scuttling the ship on some reef formation.

He pulled out more maps and was grateful to the boat owners for having them. He pondered over a map of eastern Russia.

"This northern shore of the Khabarovsk, the "Horse's Head" Peninsula, has some wide sandy beaches. I'll have to swing wide to avoid the shipping lanes and Sakhalin Island. But if I make the correct maneuver here," he pointed to a spot on the map with his compass.

He measured the turn and made an arc drawing a line down the map.

"I'll come out here," he indicated with the point of the compass.

The direct line on the map showed their new destination.

"We can take the boat close to shore and either wade or swim the rest of the way. Hopefully we can avoid any patrol boats," he muttered, "if we have enough fuel."

An hour passed by as the boat chugged through the murky water surrounded by the endless fog bank. Cecilia sensed Michael putting up a block. She turned, cupped her hands, and yelled to him.

"We're about to enter the shipping lanes!" she shouted.

"Why are you yelling?" he shouted back as he stuck his head out.

"You were blocking," she replied and lowered her voice. "Besides, I'm trying to sound like a shipmate!" she started to smile, when something caught her attention.

She sensed danger ahead. Michael did, too. He peered out the front glass in the wheelhouse. He switched off the cabin light to see better into the pea soup.

"This is hopeless," he thought.

He could only estimate their visibility in feet.

"Michael! Look!" she cried out as she pointed just off the right side of the bow.

Through the dimness, both Michael and Cecilia could make out a huge black shape, like a giant flotilla with thousands of running lights heading north and fading away off the starboard side. Their little fishing boat, tiny in comparison, barely missed a very large container ship, more than a hundred times their size. Had their timing been off by a minute, the giant ship would have smashed the smaller craft into pieces.

"Cecilia!" Michael called out to her. "Come away from bow! The wake!"

She turned her head and keenly gazed into the darkness. Her eyes filled with fear as she backed away from the bow. She sped inside the wheelhouse for safety. Michael turned on the searchlight and aimed the light forward. Out of the fog, they could just make out the growing shadow of a large wave heading directly for the ship. It started to break right in front of them. The foam from the top of the wave crashed down on the bow. It splashed all over the front of the boat and even submerged the bow under the wave momentarily. Michael closed the doors to the wheelhouse and the pair remained dry as the wave washed down the length of the boat.

Cecilia turned to Michael and whispered, "Thanks."

"You're welcome," he answered as he turned to face her.

For the first time since their sea journey began, the two youngsters paused. They stared deeply into one another's thoughts and saw affection there. They lingered for only a second or two before turning away. No telling where it might have led if they held contact a moment longer.

"Too close," she mumbled, moving back to the bow.

"Are you referring to the wave?" Michael asked as he flicked the light back on.

"What else?" she linked back to him.

She found the box she'd been sitting on, righted it, and resumed her place in the bow. She glanced back over her shoulder at Michael in wheelhouse. For a moment, she thought about the repercussions if they became romantically involved.

"You need to stop thinking that way," she privately thought. "Funny thing, after my conversion, I've begun to think less like a teenager and more like a woman. Yet, here I am, still inside the body of a teenager and not ready for the world."

She worried that her inexperience might jeopardize the mission. Her intuitive insight, however, proved its value to Michael more than once. Still, she thought the voices' view of humanity rather naïve since she was convinced they chose her to be his traveling mate.

"We are hardly naïve," her voice intruded having detected her opinions. "We have studied human culture for many years. You manage to behave unexpectedly at times.

"Oh, I think that when we're up and running with Galactic Central," Cecilia said with confidence, "you're going to find out we humans are full of surprises."

"Of that we have no doubt," her voice replied.

CHAPTER 16

CRISIS AT SEA

THE COMMERCIAL SHIPPING LANES RECEDED behind them as the fishing trawler pressed on. Cecilia stuck it out as guide and stayed in the bow.

"I detect no obstructions along your new course, Michael," she informed him. Her mind pierced the condensed atmospheric phenomenon.

"You're English is too good," he countered with a smile.

"I have my voice to thank for that," she replied.

She smiled inwardly. The conversion process not only cured her use of local slang, it also instilled in her mind a new level of worldly knowledge that no university class could instruct. She did not believe that Intelligence Quotient tests applied to her level of thinking any longer.

"We're way past those," she privately considered as she bristled against the cold.

When the fog pressed in on them, it not only darkened their world, but brought a rapid change in temperature as well. Cecilia began to shiver as the temperature dropped. However burdened, she remained stoic in her position.

Michael made his turning maneuver and carefully watched the ship's compass as he steered the boat in the new southwestern direction. Monotony set in. With little else to do, he spent his time bent over the table. He stared at the charts and maps. He discerned ocean depths and compared treacherous coastlines with other information.

He reached out to check on Cecilia's condition and realized she hovered on the verge of collapse from extreme fatigue. He stood up and saw her leaning against the pole at the bow. She was nearly unconscious. He sprang to her side.

"Time to come inside," he requested as he ran to put his arms around her. Her skin felt cool to the touch.

"I'm not moving from this spot," she insisted as she shook her head awake. She gazed into those bluish-gray eyes of his. She straightened and shrugged off his arm. "I'm doing my part, which you know I can do better than you," she insisted.

He did not wish to argue. Yet, the level of discomfort she tolerated, and which he detected, troubled him. He rushed below and then returned with a thick crew blanket. He found an old cushioned wooden chair with arms to replace her box.

"Thanks," she linked. She sat down and wrapped up in the blanket. She then propped her feet up on the wooden crate.

He next brought her a fresh cup of hot sweetened tea. He made it strong as she suggested. For a while, at least, the blanket and tea kept her warm and alert.

Regardless of summer's seasonal approach, the air took on a fearsome chill inside the heavy fog bank. Finally, after another hour went by, she started to fall from the chair.

"No more objections. You're coming inside," he demanded as he left the wheelhouse and headed for the bow.

"Do you want us to crash?" she asked as she gazed up at him.

"No," he answered, "but if you stay out here any longer, Cecilia, you'll develop pneumonia. Even with our stores of knowledge, we don't have the medical supplies to treat the symptoms of a major illness," he explained.

She realized he linked the truth to her and that she reached her limit of tolerance.

"I thought the hot tea, blanket, and chair would be enough," she said, stirring, "I think you are correct, Michael. I will take a nap."

To Michael's relief, she retired to the sleeping quarters. He then checked their fuel supply. He feared they might run short.

"The gauges are on the slim side," he observed. "This course change lengthens our route."

He went below and emptied the last of the extra fuel canisters into the main tanks. Calculating the remaining fuel against the number of miles to go, he discovered his estimates might be dangerously close.

"If we run out of fuel, we'll have to swim," he thought looking around for a life jacket. Not finding one, Michael realized that he neglected to put them onboard. "What else will swim up and bite you on the butt?" he wondered, admonishing his own poor planning.

The ocean is a large place. It is sometimes filled with unsuspecting predators. Unknown to either Michael or Cecilia, a fearsome monster prowled this treacherous sea. A great black behemoth silently lurked in the cold depths far below their small vessel. It reached out with its own sensors and spotted the small craft inching its way toward the southern coastline.

The Russian Navy monitored the sea with alert buoys and radar. They also patrolled the Russian coastline with a number of vessels. When Michael changed their heading southwest, he took them right into the path of a Russian nuclear submarine on routine patrol. Though still miles away, their intersecting paths triggered alarms aboard the sub.

"Captain!" the Russian sonar man yelled out, "Unknown surface contact, bearing 117, no signal beacon. It appears to be a fishing boat, sir, moving very slowly. It's outside the usual areas for a boat that size," the seaman stated.

Captain Shimanovsk commanded this submarine for many years. His trimmed white beard not only reflected his age but also his experience. The crew trusted him. Some of the men served with him for over twenty years.

The captain considered this new sonar information for a moment. Russian anglers did not fish in these waters. Experience told him the surface ship could be either pirates or smugglers.

"Notify the regular Coastal Patrol ships," the captain droned softly, "Let them handle the brigands," he ordered.

"Captain," sonar answered, "satellite images show thick fog topside. Our patrols would have difficulty finding them even if we gave them their current position. Some of the surface boats don't have good radar systems, sir."

"Don't tell the Americans that," he joked with his men. "We'll have the CIA in fishing boats all over the Sea of Okhotsk."

Several of the officers on the bridge chuckled.

"Belay that radio order, seaman," the captain remarked. He turned to one of his commanding officers.

"Maybe they're lost?" his friend suggested.

Captain Shimanovsk turned back to the sonar control officer.

"Monitor the position of the boat. If they head to shore, then radio its position to the patrol boats," the captain ordered.

"Who would be in a little boat alone at sea?" a bridge officer mumbled under his breath.

"Maybe that's the Chinese invasion, sir," another officer responded quietly.

The other bridge officers chuckled and the captain joined them, smiling.

While keeping the country safe from invasion, this particular Russian submarine also engaged in shadowing another submarine, one from the United States. The US sub's course skirted the territorial limits to spy on

Russian, Korean, Japanese, and Chinese electronic transmissions. Not far away, the sonar man of the American submarine alerted his captain to the same contact.

"It might be a Russian spy trawler, sir. It doesn't fit the pattern of the other fishing boats, though," the young man related. "It's alone, not part of a group."

Captain Robert Conrad, Jr. came from a family with a long naval submarine history. His grandfather commanded a submarine during World War II. His father commanded a submarine during the height of the Cold War period during the mid-to-late Twentieth Century. Captain Conrad attended Annapolis and received his own command after being in the Navy for twenty years.

"What makes you think it's not just a fishing boat, sailor?" the captain spoke up.

"Captain, this boat is alone. Its course is south and away from the usual fishing grounds. The rest of the fishing fleet is to the north. It doesn't make sense sir," the young man informed him.

Captain Conrad turned to his Lieutenant Commander and friend.

"What do you think, Brad? Fishing boat or spy?" he asked him.

Bradley Jason Andrews had known Bob Conrad for years. In addition to trusting his judgment, loyalty, and advice, they started as friends at the Naval Academy long before Captain Conrad arrived at his current position.

Whenever a question arose that begged debate, Captain Conrad could turn to his friend for his keen insights. Lt. Commander Bradley Andrews helped Captain Conrad on numerous occasions.

Brad Andrews adjusted a special light. His eyes ran over the map laid out before them. He pondered the position of the boat for a moment.

Then he called out to communications, "What are the Russians doing?"

Communications answered, "They're maintaining radio silence."

Sonar spoke up, "they haven't changed course either, sir. They're still shadowing us off our port side."

"If we surface, we'll be in violation of territorial agreement, but not treaty. We're still outside the hundred-mile limit," he advised. "Sonar!" he added, "What's the weather topside?"

"They're socked in. Heavy dense fog sir – a solid white out," he spoke back, "I can give you a satellite visual from space, sir, if you want it?"

"Never mind," the captain responded. "Sounds like a spy ship able to navigate through a fog bank so easily," Captain Conrad stated as he sat back in his chair, "or else…"

"Or else what?" Brad spoke up.

"Well, either somebody's either real smart or very lost," Captain Conrad commented.

All at once an alarm at the sonar station sounded. Everyone's head on the bridge turned in that direction. The seaman reached up and shut the alarm off. He checked the screen in front of him.

"Sir! New contact," he called out to Captain Conrad, "bearing 2-4-0 at 20 miles and coming in fast, sir, at flank speed. She's a big fish, too... not Russian... running diagnostics now, sir," the sonar man stated as he stared at his screen.

"Come about, helmsman, to a new bearing of... 288, hard to starboard," the captain barked as he came up out of his chair. "Move us away from this Russian coastline."

Captain Conrad knew he needed lots of room to maneuver a boat that size. Having the Russians so close would limit his options. In addition, he wanted to lessen his radar signature to any approaching vessel.

"Aye, sir," the helmsman replied, "Coming about to 288 – hard to starboard, sir."

Everything in the big boat listed to the right as it sharply turned under the sea.

On this day of behemoths, the sea contained still another predator unknown to both the Russians and the Americans – one that felt equal to their opponent's vessels. It was a brand new Chinese nuclear submarine. Although the Chinese sub casually lumbered along more than 20 miles away, both the Russian's and the Americans' radar alerted them to its presence.

While China had few large vessels in their Navy, this new nuclear submarine spoke of nationalistic pride in the Chinese fleet. Neither the Russians nor the American intelligence knew the top-secret maiden voyage trial run started last night.

Chinese Captain Zhinlin Gu'an commanded one other submarine for less than a year with a crew as equally inexperienced as he was, when he received his transfer orders to run test trials of China's top secret vessel. He and his crew worked on simulators for weeks before testing the new submarine.

With the surprise launch less than twenty-four hours ago, the Chinese captain had orders to perform fake attack maneuvers against the Russian coastline in order to test the defensive system and avoid any other subs that might be in the area. If they encountered any Russian or American submarines, they were to avoid contact and quickly move away.

Even with the most sophisticated electronic gear they had available, their sensors did not detect the presence of competitive submarines when they entered the Sea of Okhotsk. They were not aware that the Russians and

Americans possessed advanced stealth-cloaking abilities or that they were hiding their wake signatures from Chinese naval radar for many years.

The Chinese sub approached the coastline at top speed not realizing the two submarines lay directly in its path.

Back on the Russian sub…

"Captain?" the Russian sonar man called out to Captain Shimanosk. "The Chinese submarine is on a direct collision course with the Americans sir!" asking for orders as the Chinese sub bore down on their position.

Captain Shimanosk paused to formulate a strategic plan. He glanced over at a map of the underwater shoals in that area.

"Change course, Helm. Come to a new heading of 255," Captain Shimanovsk barked to the helmsman.

"Coming about, sir, to 255," he answered.

"Captain," the sonar man called out to his commanding officer, "That will put us in very close proximity to the Americans," his officer at sonar responded.

"They'll have very little room to maneuver sir," his helmsman pointed out.

"I'm counting on it," he commented back. "Do it!" he barked at the helmsman.

"Yes sir," the seaman replied as he started his turn.

Onboard the American submarine…

"They're doing what?" Captain Conrad asked.

"They're turning, sir, and coming in very close to our port side. Very close," the sonar seaman stated.

"How close?" the captain asked as he stood up and moved closer.

"To within a thousand yards!" the sonar man stated back, his rising anxiety noticeable in his tone.

"That's insane! Is he crazy? What does he think he's doing?" the captain complained.

"He's forcing us to surface," his friend advised. "Go ahead. If you angle your ascent, we can skirt the territorial limit."

"Fine!" the captain said as he resigned to his forced move. "Helm, come to 145 starboard – up 15 degrees on the bow plane," Captain Conrad began.

At that moment, the American sonar seaman started shouting from his station.

Onboard the Chinese submarine…

"Fire dummy warhead," the Chinese Captain Gu'an ordered to his weapons officer. His vocal tone sounded bored and indifferent. He had run this same drill seven times today in different locations.

"Dummy torpedo fired, sir," the man informed him.

Captain Gu'an, confident with his drill practice so far, did not understand his actions might have precipitated World War III.

"Bring us about helm," the captain casually ordered as he sipped his tea. "Time the torpedo to impact and let me know if any of those Russian buoys start sending out signals."

"Yes captain," his sonar answered.

All hell broke loose aboard the American submarine…

"Torpedo in the water, sir! Torpedo in the water! It's the Chinese, sir!" the panicked sonar seaman yelled. "They've just fired on us!"

"Yes, sir," another seaman stated, "weapons confirms sonar's findings. A torpedo-type weapon bearing down on our position, sir, and closing fast!"

"What?" the captain shouted as he glanced over at his friend. Then he quickly addressed his steersman, "Belay that turn order, helm!"

Unfortunately, his countermand arrived too late. The submarine had already changed course. The ship's bow headed straight for the torpedo.

Onboard the Russian submarine…

The Russian experienced crew scrambled automatically into combat mode the moment they detected the torpedo. The Russian captain ordered his vessel to change course and head for the coastline, away from the American sub. He decided to put as much distance as possible between them and the Americans. An underwater explosion could damage his vessel, too.

"Besides," he thought, "I want no part of an international incident. Russia will stay out of any force expressed between China and America."

The sub turned at a steep angle to the port side and headed back into the heart of the Sea of Okhotsk and the protective coastline of mother Russia.

The Americans, having detected the torpedo the moment it fired, wanted to turn and miss the torpedo with countermeasures. However, modern torpedoes do not miss. They are sophisticated missiles that zero in on their target. Unfortunately, for the American Captain, he gave his order to come about too late. His huge sub lumbered directly into the path of the oncoming torpedo. The torpedo would strike the hull in a minute, not enough time to reposition.

"Sir the torpedo is head straight for our position," the sonar officer yelled out, "time to impact approximately one minute!"

Captain Conrad took only a second to realize his submarine was doomed. Yet, he would not go down without a fight. With little time to discuss why the other submarine fired, he had to respond, and act quickly.

"Plot a solution and return fire!" he quickly ordered – an order that no man on the bridge wanted to hear.

The crew stopped what they were doing and stared back at the captain. They stood frozen because they knew the implications of such an order.

"Did you hear me?" Captain Conrad yelled, "I said return fire! That's a direct order!"

Brad Andrews grabbed his arm, "You need an order from the President!" he reminded him. "That's not just a fishing boat out there. That's a Chinese nuclear submarine, Bob!"

"There isn't time," Conrad mumbled, resigned to their fate. "We were at war the minute the Chinese fired on us, Brad. If we don't fire back, they could use that platform to fire on Washington."

Captain Conrad struck an emotional chord in all the men with that statement. His men scrambled. A few seconds later, they returned fire. The weapons console called out the time.

"Torpedo fired, sir, 30 seconds to target. Our torpedo will strike five seconds after their torpedo strikes us, sir," the man's trembling voice added.

The men on the bridge stood by in silence as each man came to the realization that within seconds, they would be no more, and the sub would implode around them. Some men began to pray while others just closed their eyes for the inevitable.

The captain turned to his commander friend.

"My God, Brad," he wondered, "is this the end of us all?"

CHAPTER 17

THE POWER OF THE MIND REVEALED

"Why can't I sense the bottom?" Cecilia asked. After enjoying a respite, she returned to her sitting position at the ship's bow. "It's more difficult trying to sense objects through water than air," she pointed out to Michael.

"Maybe we weren't meant to see through water," he quipped.

"That's like saying – 'if man was meant to fly'..." she started.

"As a piece of sonar equipment, you do have your limits," he shot back.

"Go no further," she interrupted.

Michael feared running aground on shallows or shoals not marked on his maps. Cecilia volunteered to help Michael determine the depth of the sea. She reached out beyond the fishing boat with her thoughts. She had trouble moving her psychic energy waves through the density of the water. She found that she could only sense certain living things, such as schools of fish or large squid and other massive forms of sea life. She could feel the presence of smaller marine animals, but could not focus on their precise location. Judging distance became increasingly difficult with her fatigue.

Michael followed her progress with interest from the wheelhouse until he finally gave up. Hungry, he tied off the wheel and decided to try his hand at cooking.

"I learned a few things living as a single man in New York. Let me create a meal for a change," he told her as he tried to make sense of the propane stove.

"Don't burn the ship down. It's the only one we have," she linked to him.

"Just for that, I'll open a can of beans," he replied.

"Michael!" Cecilia groaned.

He looked at the list of ingredients in the locker and the small refrigerator they had onboard.

"How would it be if I make soup?" he offered.

"If it's as good as the old woman's," she pleaded.

"It'll be better," he promised.

Several minutes passed. Cecilia sensed Michael chopping food. Out of boredom, she drifted off and fell asleep. She nearly slid out of the chair when the movement startled her and her eyes popped open. She blankly stared at the enveloping whiteness around them. She felt her concentration slipping. When she tried to focus her energy on anything, the constant sound of the ship's engines distracted her.

"That's it," she finally declared. "I'm taking a break!"

She stood up and stretched her stiffened body out as she tried to pull the kinks from her tired bones. She marched into the warm wheelhouse and attempted to rub the chill from her skin. She then started down below on the wooden steps when she stopped half way. She watched Michael in the galley attempting to cook a meal, which made her smile at his inexperience.

"Where did you learn to make soup?" she questioned from the staircase.

"Didn't I ever tell you the story of how my dog Jeepers saved me from starvation?" he linked with as much sarcasm as he could muster.

"That isn't funny," she said as she pushed past him.

"Every time I eat soup," he said holding out a lit match, "I still wag my behind." He turned the gas burner on. "Tired of the fog?" he asked while he glanced over at her.

He held the match too far away. When he moved it in closer, a large flame erupted off the stove. Its voluminous flame singed his hair. Michael jerked his head back from the stove and banged his head into the rafters.

Cecilia tried not to giggle as she sat at the table facing the galley.

"Sorry, I didn't mean to distract you," she somewhat confessed. "I'm tired of sitting out in that fog. I need a break," she quipped as she ran her fingers through her hair.

"You'll be happy to know I can make a very good soup from scratch," he said as he first rubbed his head and then slid the chopped meat into the pot of water. "Why just the other day, I started to…." his words faded away.

He froze with a blank expression on his face. At first, Cecilia stared at Michael. Then she felt it too. A feeling of impending doom swept over them. A great wave of powerful human emotion passed through the air so palpable that neither psychic could ignore it. They felt fear and anger – so strong, so vivid, and very close to them.

"Where is it coming from?" Cecilia asked; her expression full of alarm.

Michael closed his eyes, "I'm searching…"

Simultaneously, both reached out with their minds. They scrutinized the space all around the boat for the source.

"I don't sense anything," she started to say.

He held up his hand as he rapidly searched for the source. His eyes traveled down to the floorboards.

"It isn't around us. It's emanating from below," he pointed out to her.

For a moment, the two pushed their sensory perception down. They made every attempt to penetrate the depth and density of the water. Like two blind people stumbling through unfamiliar darkness, they pushed their sensory waves through the icy cold depths of the water until they both ran into a wall. Their senses struck an object of tremendous proportions.

Michael opened his eyes and saw Cecilia's expression change to shock.

"Submarines!" he linked intently to her.

"Nuclear submarines!" she gasped. "But why should we feel so much fear," she started.

"Wait! Something feels wrong," he linked, as he concentrated his hearing. "Listen! Can you hear them?" He sensed a mechanical sound that rapidly moved through the water. "Torpedoes!" Michael declared.

Cecilia nodded her affirmation. She was capable of spreading out her senses into a wider field. Michael watching her technique followed suit.

"One torpedo is a dummy," she noted. "But, the other is armed! Michael what should we do?"

Sensing their extreme emotions rise, their voices immediately intervened.

"We sensed an incredible amount of fear. We have observed your scans and made an evaluation," both Galactic Central voices spoke simultaneously. "You must act quickly to avert a disaster. Concentrate on the small mobile weapons. Focus your energy on one point. Michael, turn the rudder mechanism on the back of the dummy torpedo. Cecilia, do the same to the other. You must act now!"

Back onboard the Chinese sub, panic broke out among the bridge crew. Somehow and seemingly from nowhere, a torpedo appeared on a course set straight for them, armed to explode.

"The torpedo is armed, sir," the sonar officer informed his captain. "Impact in 20 seconds…" his voice trailed off as he removed his headphones. He stared in the direction of his captain.

"Sir," the captain's second said quietly, "we must radio headquarters in Beijing. The torpedo will strike any second."

"Too late," the Chinese Captain Gu'an calmly spoke, "All hands brace for impact," he said to the ship via a microphone. He knew they would not feel a thing. It would all be over in an instant.

On the fishing trawler, two psychics used their ability in a way they had never tried. Michael broke into a sweat as his mind strained to focus on one part of the torpedo. He tried to block out all interference, despite the driving mechanism from inside the torpedo that blared inside his mind. With every ounce of energy, he pushed against the maneuvering fin.

Acting simultaneously, Cecilia performed the same maneuver on the other torpedo. With only a few seconds remaining before impact, the two torpedoes turned at acute angles. They veered far off course as both weapons missed the two submarines by a considerably wide margin. The Americans set the torpedo to detonate on contact instead of proximity. Its explosion rippled through the water when the torpedo struck an underwater rock formation. Nevertheless, that tactical weapon held a potent charge felt by all three subs. The Chinese torpedo zipped toward the coastal waters of Russia. It struck an underwater obstruction and broke apart.

"A dummy warhead?" the captains of both the Russian and American vessels responded to reports from their respective sonar.

The Chinese Submarine Captain ordered his vessel to "come about and head for the open sea." He knew they would have to notify Naval Headquarters located in Beijing at once. The presence of an unidentified nuclear submarine made the Sea of Okhotsk seem too crowded for the Chinese captain.

"If my sonar did not detect a sub in the area, I wonder who fired that torpedo at us?" Captain Gu'an pondered silently. "Did a Russian submarine fire that torpedo, or was it perhaps an American? Why did it veer off course at the last second? Perhaps they detonated it as a warning."

Eventually, he reasoned that only a submarine using stealth technology could have escaped their scans. Once they cleared the island chain, he would take the sub to periscope depth and radio his report regarding his encounter with the mysterious invisible submarine.

Captain Conrad questioned many things as his crew breathed a collective sigh of relief. His ship also headed out of the Okhotsk Sea on a course away from the Chinese. He wondered why they were still alive. He wondered why the Chinese fired on an American submarine with a dummy missile that then suddenly veered off at the last minute missing its target. Their monitoring exercise came to an abrupt end. He needed to report this incident to the Pentagon per protocol.

The relieved Russian sub commander turned his attention back to the trawler on the surface. He called for a new bearing on the lone surface trawler.

"Lost contact?" he asked as he bounded off the bridge and stood over the seaman's shoulder.

"What do you mean, you lost contact?" he demanded while he peered intently at the screen, as if that would make the sonar contact somehow return. "What happened to them?"

"Just as I said sir," the man replied. "When the Americans and Chinese turned their subs to the open sea… the contact… well, it… it vanished, sir."

The captain stared at the screen another moment before turning to the helmsman, "Resume coastline surveillance pattern Alpha," he ordered. The captain returned to his chair. "Sonar," he added over his shoulder, "let me know if that contact returns."

"Aye captain," the man replied, shaking his head.

"Michael?" a faint voice echoed inside his mind.

"Give me ten more minutes…"

He floated in a fog, similar to the one dogging their vessel.

"Michael?" the voice asked again.

"Please, mother, just ten more minutes."

"Wake up Michael," the voice added. It began to sound more mechanical in nature. "You are in a dream state. Be alert! Wake up!"

He blinked open his eyes and took in a sudden deep breath. He realized at once that he had been lying on the floor. He could not determine the length of time. He could have been out for a minute or even an hour.

"Ok, I hear you," he replied to his alien connection.

He glanced over and noticed Cecilia in a similar condition. She lay collapsed on the fishy-smelling wooden floor next to him. Her pale white skin alarmed him, yet he sensed her breathing and heart beating. Unable to stand out of weakness, he dragged his body over to her.

"Cecilia," he spoke. He gently shook her shoulder. "Cecilia! Wake up!"

Michael pulled her closer. For a moment, he treasured gazing on her innocent face. The color seemed to return to her face. Then, he felt her energy level return and he backed away.

Cecilia slowly opened her eyes. She gathered up enough energy to push her head up off the hard surface.

"What happened?" she asked as she rubbed her temples. "Oh, my head!" she glanced over at Michael.

"You ok?" he croaked. His mouth and throat were parched.

"Uh, huh," she croaked back. "Did we just do what I think we did?"

Michael nodded his reply. He was unable to speak or link. He felt wasted rather than accomplished. He could not understand his feelings.

Their voices addressed them.

"You have just demonstrated another of your abilities," they informed them. "You have the power to influence and move things in your environment. If you focus your energy to a point of space outside your body, you can use that energy to move objects."

The two shipmates stared at one another. They found it difficult to believe they possessed yet another facet of their psychic abilities. Cecilia moved into a sitting position.

Michael followed. However, the simple act of moving about made his head throb. Moving objects was a new reality for them. Nevertheless, they found that everything they did required excessive mental energy. Straining the way they did taxed both the mind and the body.

Michael rose to his feet and threw the kettle on.

"Tea?" he asked.

"Sounds good," she replied. She rose and slid onto the bench around the table.

Soon they had their hands wrapped around hot steaming cups of sweetened tea. They sat at the center table and tried to recall the details of what just happened. Michael explained to Cecilia the case of mistaken intentions that he detected before he blacked out.

"… so you see," he continued, "the Chinese captain only intended to run tests against the Russian defenses. That's why he fired a dummy warhead. I'd say he got more reaction than he anticipated."

"You had time to access his thoughts?" she wondered.

"It was the last thing I did before I blacked out," he told her.

"Submarines! Did you think of them?" she asked.

"Absolutely not," he replied while sipping his tea.

"Thank goodness we averted a disaster."

"Disaster?" he said as he sat up straighter. "You mean an international crisis with world ending potential. Do realize that America might be at war with China if we hadn't intervened."

"Michael, perhaps our interference today is why we were meant to be here," she spoke as she held her steaming cup in front of her lips.

"Cecilia, I believe this is only the beginning for us," he told her. "We did not evolve from the rest of humanity to help with this one event. We are here to help the world solve many problems."

"Superheroes?" she questioned.

"No," he said while shaking his head, "we are specially adapted humans, secretly working for humanity. We are unique individuals, and that is all we are. Cecilia I feel we must resolve one thing – here and now. The rest of the human race must never know who we are. If we help them, we do so in a clandestine manner," he stated. "They'd destroy us if they find out the truth about us."

She knew exactly what he meant when he referred to 'they.' He meant any government in the world that could their hands on them – specifically, the military.

"We'd be freaks to them – oddities. They'd dissect us," she agreed.

"…put us under the microscope and lock us away in order to find and exploit our weaknesses. They'd use us as weapons – take your pick from the above," he continued.

"It's not just us guessing what they'd do," she said as she looked intently at his face. "They really would do those things to us, wouldn't they?"

He nodded agreement. "Our secrecy is our survival," he added, "and theirs."

"I understand now what you were trying to explain to me the other night," she said as she solemnly gazed ahead. "You are right, Michael. We should be a clandestine group. Agreed?"

Cecilia held out her hand as if sealing a pact. Michael shook it. Their hands lingered a second longer than they should have until Michael reluctantly withdrew.

The two young adventurers drank the rest of their tea in silence. They pondered over the newly awakened power that they both just exhibited and what that meant for their future.

CHAPTER 18

OUT OF THE FRYING PAN

CECILIA HELPED MICHAEL FINISH THE soup that evening – neither had much of an appetite. The vast majority of the soup remained in the pot. After disposing of the failed product, she and Michael decided to take turns monitoring the boat's southbound progress while the other person slept. Michael volunteered to take the first watch. Every twenty minutes, he checked the compass bearing. He hoped that their present course would take them closer to their intended destination. Once Cecilia rested six hours, her voice roused her and she took over the helm. This gave Michael a similar but brief respite.

Michael returned to the wheelhouse after his turn at sleep. His stomach growled, which reminded him they had eaten very little since last night's debacle. When he came up behind Cecilia, he wondered if she had enough sleep and if her appetite returned.

"Did your night go well?" he linked to her as he approached the stairs.

"Well enough," she replied.

"Hungry?" he asked her in passing.

"I can always make breakfast," Cecilia offered. The idea of cooking breakfast brightened the teenager's mood. She felt it was her best contribution to their quest. She headed down to the galley.

"Sounds good to me," he told her, "if it's no trouble… you need your rest just as I do."

"I'm fine, really," she told him. "Besides, breakfast is the one meal of the day I love to make," she linked up to him.

Cecilia decided to make a special breakfast this morning. She would make pancakes from scratch. She first started by making a fresh pot of tea. Then she cut strips of smoked bacon from the slab and started them simmering in a cast iron frying pan. In another frying pan, she browned some sugar and thinned the caramel to make syrup. She added some bits of dried vanilla bean and cinnamon to flavor the concoction. She then whipped up some milk, egg, flour, baking soda, and a dash of sugar for the pancake batter. Soon the wafting smells from her labor drifted up the stairs to the wheelhouse.

"Everything smells delicious!" Michael yelled down the 'old-fashioned' way instead of linking, which made Cecilia smile.

"Breakfast will be ready soon!" she yelled back, which made Michael smile.

Michael heard the familiar sound of eggs striking the side of the iron skillet and sizzling when they fell into the pan of hot bacon grease. For a moment, he recalled a happy memory from his childhood – when the smell of baking cinnamon rolls and fresh brewed coffee woke him early Sunday mornings on the servant's half day off. He would rush down the staircase to find his father reading the Sunday paper while his mother scrambled eggs. Fresh-fruit compote awaited him at the informal kitchen table.

"Michael!" he heard her voice call him. "Michael!"

The sound was not his mother but instead Cecilia's voice breaking through.

"Michael, breakfast is almost ready!" she linked to him. "What were you thinking? I couldn't break through."

"Just a fond memory, that's all," he linked back. "I'll be right down."

Just as he turned, he heard another familiar yet far off sound. Suspicious, he stuck his head out the door to check out their surroundings. The cool thick moist air clung to his face. He noticed the sea began to rise and fall ahead.

"Shallow depth," he surmised. "Did I miss some shoals on the map?"

Listening, he heard the distinct sound of waves breaking on a shore.

Michael quickly put up a block. "Land!" he thought.

Cecilia sensed his sudden block and took her eyes off the stove, neglecting her preparations. She mumbled something and scraped the over-easy eggs out onto a plate.

"The difficult part will be maneuvering past any reef formations," he privately thought as he tried to keep Cecilia out of his thoughts while he tried to reason it through. "If I scuttle the ship too far from shore, we will have to risk swimming through rough surf and fog."

Another immediate concern occurred to him. He forgot the life preservers and did not know how to swim. This place had currents and waves.

"People drown going into turbulent seas for the first time," he thought.

"Rip currents often sweep novice swimmers out to sea. I wonder if Cecilia can swim."

They had no time for a download on the subject either. Michael needed to make a decision and make it fast.

At that moment, he heard Cecilia call out to his mind.

"Come on! Everything is ready!" she cheerfully linked.

"Better make breakfast to go," he linked back as he ran past her for his gear in the crew's quarters. He quickly shoved everything he had into a carrying pack. He kept his briefcase tucked under his arm.

"What are you saying?" she answered disheartened. "I worked so hard, Michael, making this perfect for us."

He ducked his head into the galley.

"Sorry, but it's land ho! We've arrived at the southern shoreline. It's time to abandon ship milady," he said, nodding.

He easily read the disappointed expression on her face.

"I'd delay the landing gladly," he offered, "but we're practically out of fuel, Cecilia. The boat is just a few hundred yards from shore. Right over there is Russia, I think," he said as he gestured toward the bow of the ship. "Don't worry. In an hour, we'll be up to our necks in food, taking a hot shower, and having a good laugh about our trip at sea. Let's go!"

He reached over and grabbed a pancake off the plate with one hand. Then he flipped a fried egg into the middle and added a strip of bacon. Finally, he rolled it up and dipped one end of the concoction into the hot syrup before he blew on it. He practically shoved the whole thing into his mouth.

"Mm, tastes good," he linked with his chewing mouth full. He pushed past the teenager bearing a frown on her face. "Grab your gear!"

"Oh, great!" she moaned, dropping everything in her hands.

The ship lurched upward as it was caught on a wave. The pans started to slide off the stove. Cecilia reached over and caught their handles just in time. That movement quickly drove the point home. She dropped the pans into the sink and followed Michael's example. She made her own rolled up egg, bacon, and pancake version. She also dipped one end into the syrup and then into her mouth. With the rest of the pancake hanging out of her mouth, she stuffed her clothes into one of the backpacks they found, and hurried on deck. She heard the sound of the crashing surf in the distance. In two bites, she devoured the rest of her pancake breakfast roll.

"Michael! We made it!" she linked to him and smiled.

"Not quite," he replied as he peered intently into the fog.

The boat started moving rapidly toward shore and pushed by the waves and the incoming tide. Cecilia noticed they were still relatively far away from the shoreline. She grabbed a nearby length of rope and tied the two packs together. She waited for his signal to throw them overboard. She put Michael's briefcase to the side.

Michael could see only waves breaking on rocks ahead.

"Wait!" he told her. "We've no place to land!"

He held up his hand to Cecilia. She felt the concern flood into his mind and glanced up.

"Please! Don't jump into the water yet!" he cried out from inside the wheelhouse. "If we try to move too close, this wooden ship will be torn to shreds. Look at those jagged rocks!" he pointed.

A sheer wall of sharp rock rose up before them, with other rocks in the water only visible as the surf rose and fell. Cecilia then realized their predicament as well. They would have to climb straight up out of deep churning water.

"Coming about!" he shouted.

Michael grabbed the wheel and spun it several times to the right. The ship swung ninety degrees as it turned, hard to starboard. Before the bow swung all the way around, a large wave came up and tipped the boat clear over to one side.

Everything in the boat slid toward the port side. The ship listed at a dangerous angle. Cecilia screamed as the boat nearly tipped over. Fortunately, she grabbed the starboard railing before she fell or she would have gone overboard. At the last second, she stuck her foot out and caught their bags as they slid along the deck. She prevented their baggage from sliding into the sea except Michael's briefcase.

"Michael! Your case!" she linked.

Holding onto the wheel to keep from falling, Michael could only watch with frustration as his briefcase with diamonds, cash, platinum, and gold slid across the deck.

"I'll grab it!" she cried.

"Wait Cecilia, no!" he yelled back.

She reached out with her mind in an attempt to catch it. Instead, she pushed the black briefcase away from the boat as if shot from a cannon. It skipped across the water and sank into the dark ocean water. Michael closed his eyes and bowed his head while he mourned its passing.

"I guess I need to work on my control," she thought as she regarded her ability. "Anything of value inside?" she thought to him.

"Nothing that can't be replaced," he cringed. He kept its contents private.

He peered over the edge of the window. He saw Cecilia dangling from the railing with their bags snagged on her foot.

"What are you doing?" he asked with his hand still turning the wheel to the right.

She rolled her eyes and wiggled her free foot. "Learning ballet! What do you think I'm doing? I'm saving our bags!"

"Nice save," he mumbled.

"Next time a warning would be nice!" she called out.

"That's what coming about means... oh, never mind," he mumbled.

The boat turned upright as it headed back out to sea. Michael shoved the throttle forward. He tried to pull extra power from the engines in order to fight the surf. Somehow, he kept the boat from being smashed on the rocks. Avoiding the surf, he swung the bow around, and then ran a parallel course with the shore for several minutes searching for a potential landing while trying to make out any details through the pea soup fog.

"Michael, I'm really sorry about your briefcase," she linked while gathering their bags.

"Don't worry. It's contents can be replaced. We're all that matters," he linked back. He could not tell her its true worth – nine months worth of investing, purchasing, procuring valuables that could have purchased their way into China – and perhaps their exit, too.

She stared at the rough churning sea between them and the shore with a feeling of dread.

"I don't suppose we have time to receive a download on how to swim?" she linked.

"You too?" he linked back with surprise.

"I never learned to swim. I've only waded in swimming pools, sorry," she linked apologetically.

"Oh, great," he threw up his hands. "We made it all the way across an ocean and a sea, and now we're going to drown in ten feet of water!"

Michael glanced down at the fuel gauges. Both needles bounced off the Russian letter that stood for 'empty.' If any fuel remained in the tanks, the pumps were sucking out the last of it. Michael eased back on the throttle. After agonizing for several minutes, wondering if they had enough fuel, he spotted a break in the wall of rock.

"That's it!" he cried.

Cecilia peered through the fog. She noticed it too – a clean break in the tall sheer wall of rock. It was a small cove with a natural beach, wide enough for them to land. They had an open shot with no reef. The rock wall to the right side of the beach crumbled down into a series of boulders. They could easily climb to the top after landing and make their way inland. Michael brought the boat around once more with the bow headed for shore.

At first, it seemed as if the boat would head straight for the beach, when the engines sputtered. The keel started to scrape the bottom. Incoming waves crashed around the fishing trawler. Cecilia cast Michael an anxious expression. Would they make it?

"We didn't come this far to fail!" he linked, determined to move them closer.

Michael jammed the throttle forward and opened the engines up all the way. He didn't care if he burnt out a bearing. He wanted them as close as possible. The engines revved and roared to life.

At the same moment, a big wave lifted the boat up off the bottom. With perfect timing, the boat burst out, zoomed forward, and coasted right up to the shore with the wave. The bow wedged into the wet sand on the beach. They could jump down onto land without wetting their feet. Just then, the engines died – the last of the fuel finally exhausted.

"We couldn't have timed it any better," Michael sighed. He noticed a red light flashing next to the fuel gauges. "Any further and we would have been adrift."

"I'm glad that's over. Let's start out for China," Cecilia eagerly stated as she threw their gear over the side. She jumped down and her bare feet landed on the soft wet sand.

They divided the packs evenly – each taking a load to carry. Cecilia pulled her shoes back on. A short walk across the sand led to a gradual incline where they could easily climb up the remaining rocks to the top. The two youths stopped to look back at the old fishing trawler floundering on the beach.

"I'm really a land lubber at heart," he saluted the vessel.

"I'm inclined to agree," she chimed in. "Let's stick to land from here on in."

She slapped the rock next to her. It felt good to have their feet on something solid for a change.

The fog seemed thinner in this location with a bit more light filtering down from above them. Yet the fog remained thick over the ocean. When they finally arrived near the top of the cliff, the ocean and the ship that brought them here disappeared from view.

"I can't wait to take a hot shower," she sighed as she worked her way up behind Michael.

"I want to sleep in a real bed. My back is killing me from that bunk," he thought to her.

"A home-cooked meal sounds good too," she echoed.

Cecilia's buoyancy quickly faded when she turned to see why Michael halted. She noticed his face was full of mixed emotions.

"What is it?" she asked struggling to stand beside him.

As they stood side by side at the top of the cliff, their spirits sank. The two psychics gazed out on a ghastly scene.

They scanned the horizon of the largest wasteland either had ever seen. Nothing but a great bog strewn with big boulders of rough rock covered with thick grayish-green moss stretched out as far as they could see into the distance in every direction except the sea. They did not see a trail, a road, a tree, a bush, or even a hut – nothing but sharp rocks and slimy moss. Hiking over country like this would be slow and difficult.

"We jumped from the frying pan right into the fire," he thought. "This isn't nature. This is someone's nightmare."

"It's so barren," she answered as she surveyed the dismal scene. "I didn't know places like this existed," she gasped. She stared at the horizon with disbelief. "What kind of creature could live here?"

A swat to her face quickly answered her question. She looked at her hand and saw a very large mosquito full of her blood spattered in her palm.

"Should I swat them or roast them for dinner?" she thought.

"Better swat them," he answered, "They might be carrying disease."

Cecilia and Michael turned to each other as a state of exasperation fell over them like a heavy cloak, weighing them down. They were tired, hungry, and worn out from their sea journey. Now it seemed as if they had miles of treacherous hiking ahead of them. They could not even start a fire with straw or sticks as they only saw rock and damp green smelly moss around them. The weary pair, resigned to their fate, set off across the desolation.

Several hours later they still scrambled over large, rough-edged, moss covered rocks, slowly and painfully making their way inland with no end in sight. Every rock they climbed over seemed the last. However, from the top of each one they climbed, all they could see were more rocks, stretching out as an endless plain void of life.

"Not a road, a hut, nothing…" Michael mumbled as he mustered enough energy to climb to the top of the next rock.

Cecilia glanced down at her hands. The nicks and scrapes that covered her hands were becoming red, sore and probably infected.

"My hands," she sighed, "just look at my hands." She plopped down on the rock and started to cry.

Last week she and her friend drove to the mall. She bought a wonderful hand lotion that felt silky on her skin. She mimicked being back at the counter trying on the lotion. She could almost smell the wonderful herbal odor.

"That would be the smelly bath store in the mall," he linked to her mind having overheard her thoughts.

Her drooping face stared at the present condition of her hands.

"Stop it Michael," she protested, "…and yes, it was the bath store. My friend and I went to the Saskatoon mall. The hand lotion was so expensive. I didn't have enough money. My hands smelled so good and felt so soft," she whined. Her eyes began to fill with tears. "Look at them now," she said as her eyes filled to overflowing. "The skin is cracked and bruised. I have four broken nails. I can hardly feel my fingers. They're numb from being cold."

"Are you beginning to feel that coming with me was not such a good idea?" he offered to her.

She stopped staring at her hands and glanced up at Michael's face. His comment made her half-smile, if only a little.

"Not yet," she answered wearily, "maybe after another hundred miles of this."

Her pained face expressed Michael's feelings of exasperation as well. His hands were swollen and aching. The cuts on them turned red. His stomach growled. Neither one of them had any contact from their alien voices for hours, as if Galactic Central put them on hold.

From atop the rock, Michael stared at the countryside and hoped they were not lost in the middle of this debris field. At least he thought they were moving in one direction. Without the sun, they had no idea which direction they were headed. He could not orient.

As if to add insult to injury, the fading light informed Michael that nighttime must be drawing nearer. The fog may have thinned a bit, but the clouds overhead grew darker by the minute. Then he heard a distant rumble and knew these clouds were not the harbingers of sunset but threatened rain.

Cecilia felt so tired she could no longer move. She remained on the top of a large mossy rock next to Michael's rock. She again contemplated the condition of her torn up hands.

"What are we going to do if it starts to rain?" she thought.

"Get wet?" he replied. He tried to smile to bolster her fading spirit but could not.

Cecilia started to cry. Out of a sense of helpfulness, he crawled from his rock over to her rock.

"Cecilia," he thought to her, "we mustn't give up hope. I believe in you. I believe in our ability to help each other. Nature gave us a gift of great power. Now it's time we use it. I'd like you to muster up some energy and use that wonderful radar you've mastered. Stretch out your senses. See what you can make of this mess. Will you?" he asked.

Her eyes met his. Once she looked into those eyes, she could not refuse his request. She would only do this for Michael.

"I'll need your help," she said as she turned to face him. "Share some of your energy."

"Gladly," he said. He lent her what little psychic energy he had left. He then laid down next to her on the rock. He nearly passed out from exhaustion.

Cecilia stifled her emotions and closed her eyes. She tried to focus her fatigued mind one more time. Gradually, her senses wandered over the countryside. For a moment, she took in the disheartening view of rocks stretching for miles clear to the horizon. Then she sensed movement not far away – a large animal! She encountered a horse pulling a cart on a road! When she initially stretched out her senses, she traveled right over it.

Like a thin ribbon winding through the sea of rocks, a small cart-path lay on the other side of the two large rocks in front of them. They stopped short of it by about ten meters. All at once, her energy level began to drop. She only had enough to link one last thought.

"Ahead," she pointed as she made one last link with Michael. "...a road... just over that rock..."

Cecilia's internal voice faded as she started to fall. Adrenaline coursed through Michael's body. He reached over just in time to catch her before she struck the rock. He held her limp body in his arms. Although energy depleted, the teenager managed to stay awake. She looked up at him. They gazed into each other's eyes. As hopeless as their situation seemed, they clung to a ray of hope with a road nearby.

"Nice work," he whispered to her, unable to link.

"Thanks," she uttered back. Her eyes closed and she started to fade.

A loud rumble shook the air. Michael stared up at the darkening sky. The storm clouds he noticed earlier approached with greater speed. A smattering of rain began to fall. Droplets struck Cecilia on the face. She took in a deep breath and opened her eyes. A brilliant flash of light cut through the sky. A second later, a loud rumble shook the air so violently that it startled both of them.

"Oh!" she sputtered as she spit water from her mouth and lifted her head.

Michael kept his arms wrapped around her. As he cradled her head in the nook of his bent arm, he bent over her face to offer some cover.

"See what a little thunder with some fear attached can do?" he whispered. "Now we're both back in business." However, the position seemed too awkward in a personal way to Michael. He pulled Cecilia to a sitting position. "I think we'd better start moving," he said as the two struggled to their feet.

The rain began to fall harder. Heavy sheets poured down on them.

"Oh, Michael, I've been through enough," she droned, "I don't want to be soaking wet too," she cried as the pair scrambled over the last remaining rock barrier.

"Unavoidable," he mumbled. He practically pulled her along beside him.

The sky opened up and rain poured down on them. The icy cold deluge pounded their bodies unrelentingly. Michael and Cecilia somehow managed to find enough energy to crawl over the last boulder that separated them from the road. They fell with clumsy exhaustion as they slid down onto the dual mud tracks that cut through the wasteland.

No car or truck would last very long on this old road. Deep ruts made this aged pathway difficult and slow as farmers brought their horse drawn carts this way for centuries.

Michael took in the surroundings and surveyed the scene. No wonder they had not seen a road. It lay hidden on either side by large boulders inside a rocky canyon. Somehow, in this sea of rocks ancient adventurers forged a road through this dreary forsaken landscape.

The rain continued its heavy downpour. Water ran down their skin and washed away the sweat, mud and filth that had accumulated on them during their trek across the rocky wasteland. Michael pulled off his pack and then helped Cecilia with hers. He felt weightless without the heavy pack. The icy rain chilled their exposed wet bodies to the bone.

"I'm cold, Michael. Please hold me," Cecilia requested as her body shivered and her teeth chattered.

"Me too," he replied as his goose flesh crawled. "You said you wanted a shower," he said, trying to kid with her.

"N-not l-like t-this," she stuttered. Her jaw uncontrollably clicked.

They stood in the heavy downpour and hugged one another for warmth while the frigid rain soaked their clothes. Michael tried to keep his mind off Cecilia's warm ample body pressed firmly against his. She had trouble dealing with the same feelings, too.

"T-the r-road…" she spoke, "m-must… l-lead… s-somewhere."

She tried to divert their attention away from their close proximity. Yet the chilled water made her hug him tighter as they tried to stop the shaking.

"S-sure i-it d-does…" he replied as he began to shiver as well, "p-probably a n-nice t-town up t-the r-road w-with a w-warm…"

"P-please," she begged, "n-no m-mention of f-food, or a b-bed, ok?"

He nodded and muttered, "O-o k-k."

Miraculously, the thunderstorm ended before it ever really started. All at once, a break in the clouds opened a patch of blue sky and allowed rays of sunlight through as the rain started to let up. The sun hung low on the horizon as it broke through the fog in angled dramatic shafts of yellowish light. The sun on their bodies gave them a little warmth. As the storm moved off to the east, a rainbow appeared over the receding clouds.

"T-that's a g-good omen. Isn't it?" she said glancing up.

She noticed Michael's pale skin and blue lips. She felt he was on the verge of collapsing. She pulled away from him and leaned back against the rock. As Michael fought to stay on his feet, Cecilia examined her cuts, scrapes, mosquito bites, and bruises. Michael started to step forward, but Cecilia reached over and grabbed his arm.

"N-not another s-step," she moaned. She was ready to collapse on the ground. She pulled him back until he leaned against the rock next to her. "We b-both need rest before we s-start walking."

Michael sensed a source of psychic energy approaching. He glanced up the road, half-smiled and took in a deep breath.

"M-maybe we'll have a r-ride," he chimed in, gesturing.

Cecilia turned and looked up the road to her right. The horse, whose presence led her thoughts to find the road, slowly approached pulling a covered cart. As the cart drew near, they noticed an elderly dark-skinned man with white hair. He wore a large hat and poncho- style cloak as he drove the cart while sound asleep. Huge piles of vegetables along with crates of chickens filled the back of the covered cart. Obviously, the farmer brought his produce to market along this road.

"P-pull some energy into your m-mind, q-quick," he whispered.

"I c-can't," she whined.

"Oh, y-yes, you c-can," he said as he kissed her on the neck, "F-focus and t-try!"

She immediately perked up but blushed a bit.

Michael stepped into the road and held up his hand. The horse pulled back as it abruptly came to a stop. Its motion jerked the wagon when it halted. The old man woke, startled.

"What's this?" he asked as his eyes darted to take in the scene around him. His hand instinctively felt for a weapon at his side.

For a moment, he thought he saw two people in strange clothing standing at the side of the road. The horse started to back up. He pulled on the reins and yanked on the wooden brake to stop the cart.

"Whoa!" he called.

The old farmer blinked and stared down at the spot in the road where they stood. He rubbed his eyes. He turned his head this way and that. He saw no one. He puzzlingly scratched his head. He realized the vision he saw must have been part of a dream. He shrugged his shoulders, let go of the brake, whipped at the horse, and settled back to sleep once more as the cart slowly pulled away.

The farmer did not notice his new passengers in the back of the cart. They hungrily chewed some carrots and cabbage before emulating the driver by falling asleep as well. In fact, he would never know they were there.

Chapter 19

The road to China

The following morning, the farmer's cart pulled into the city of Nikolayevsk-na-Amure, the town so named because it is located at the mouth of the great Amur River. Except when frozen over during the coldest winter months, the Amur water system serves as the main route for many transport barges. The reverse path of the river stretches out over four-hundred miles due south before it turns into its tortuous route west that becomes the natural border between China and Russia. As Michael correctly guessed, a major road ran north and south along the western side.

Having arrived in the first town of some size since their 'extended' psychic download, both Michael and Cecilia discovered the need to adjust the sensitivity of their ability as they moved among crowds of people.

"Michael, my mind is bombarded with so many thoughts!" Cecilia declared as the couple moved away from the vegetable wagon.

"This happened to me in New York," he said as he struggled with the bombardment as well, "only not with this same intensity."

The couple staggered away from the farmer's market toward an older part of the city, away from the modern section. They hoped to find a level of obscurity among the locals.

"You didn't have this same trouble in New York," Cecilia reminded him, "because you had not received the download the voices gave us in Yakutsk, the one that extended our senses. Remember?"

All at once, Michael felt too exposed in this foreign land. They wore the wrong kind of clothes and had different faces. He linked his security concerns to Cecilia. The two young psychics agreed to avoid encounters with police if possible and started up a residential street. As people walked in and out of local businesses, they stared at the strange young couple.

"People are staring at us," Cecilia observed, "too many minds to control."

"We'll have to block most of these thoughts," he said as he began the process. "Let's move away from the main street before the police arrest us on trumped up vagrancy charges," Michael gestured toward a side street.

They tried inconspicuously to cross the boulevard and turn into a side street. They took a quick left and slipped into a deserted alleyway. Michael breathed a sigh of relief when he noticed Cecilia concentrate on isolating her thoughts from the outside bombardment. She attempted to pull her awareness inward. Both psychics also concentrated on using their blocking technique to keep out unwanted thoughts. Within minutes, a sense of peace and solitude returned. They could see it on each other's faces.

"Better?" he asked, unable to read her thoughts.

Cecilia nodded. Having regained a sense of normalcy, she turned her attention to the next priority.

"Michael, just look at us," she pointed out, "we're a mess! We need a place to clean up and stay the night. What do you suggest?" she asked Michael.

Michael thought he would feel tired after a night where the jostling wagon constantly woke him. Instead, simply being in the city and filled with renewed psychic energy invigorated him. Cecilia felt the same way, too. Neither understood the exact mechanism behind this process.

"I could also use some... personal hygiene products," she discreetly stated.

"Well," he added as he rubbed his chin, "I could use a shower and a shave." He glanced out the end of the alley. "I suppose we should look for a hotel."

Cecilia bravely walked out of the alley and quickly scanned the street. Michael walked up behind her. He watched at how swiftly she applied her ability. She turned and gestured up the street toward an older hotel about a block away.

"How about that place?" she asked. She seemed to seek his approval.

"Good eye," Michael noted. He took a second to scan the place. "Hardly a one star rating," he mused, "but it beats the back of a farmer's cart."

The young couple walked at a brisk pace up the street. They hoped to avoid any further attention. They stepped in through the front door of an old family-run hotel. Probably part of this neighborhood for decades, the wooden two-story building with a faded sign over the front entrance seemed like a saloon out of the past. Judging from the unkempt appearance and the notorious characters both outside and inside the lobby, the seedy establishment was not in the best shape. The women wore too much make-up and unshaven tattooed men with a haggard appearance hovered nearby.

"This place is filthy," Cecilia thought to Michael. "This looks like the local hang out for prostitutes and drug dealers."

"It is," Michael replied as he pushed Cecilia toward the check-in counter. "I'm sorry we can't do better. Besides, it's only temporary," he countered. "We can clean up, rest, and then move on."

Despite their rag-tag appearance, no one in the lobby saw anything but a well-dressed middle-aged Russian couple. Michael plucked the image from a passing motorist and then implanted the image into the mind of everyone that glanced their way. They checked into the largest room the hotel had available. While Michael took care of the bill, Cecilia dissuaded a man's mind she read as he contemplated robbing them later.

After examining the two beds for bugs and mutually 'shaking out' the sheets, they decided to go out and 'buy' a few things.

"I desperately need some… feminine supplies," she said with a sense of urgency, "if you only knew how much."

"Please don't share," he suggested, "Let's go and find what we need!"

Although the bed and shower beckoned, both Cecilia and Michael realized they needed hygienic personal items, such as a toothbrush and paste, deodorant, shampoo, razor, and so on. They would need fresh clothes as the rain had ruined the clothes in their packs.

Outside the hotel, they found a small general merchandise store within walking distance that had everything they needed. While several people stood in line to request items from behind the main counter, Michael and Cecilia took what they needed and left via the back door without anyone in the store having seen them. Back in the hotel, Michael laid out a map he took.

"This road should be the fastest route," he said, his finger tracing along the river road.

"We'll have to borrow a ride," Cecilia observed as she munched on a sandwich.

"Borrow? We'll just take a car," he spoke nonchalantly.

"Taking some items from a store is one thing. But a car in the city," she considered. "What if someone catches us?" she wondered.

"They won't," Michael answered her with confidence. "Even if a policeman pulls us over, he won't remember it."

"And if he radio's the information in before he pulls us over?" she questioned.

"We'll be long gone by the time someone else arrives," Michael relayed.

"Fine," she said as she twirled around to face him, "but I don't like stealing! You might be used to it, but I'm not!"

"I don't wish to break the law, Cecilia," Michael reasoned. "Right now, our situation is tenuous at best. Theft is our only alternative if we are to survive."

"Humph," she peevishly muttered as she turned her back to him.

He did not wish to remind her that he brought all the money he would need to pay for the trip. But it was now resting at the bottom of the sea. He did not blame her. The loss of the briefcase was not her fault. As far back as he could remember Michael had to cope with life changes as they happened – a concept Cecilia could not yet fathom.

"I know this is difficult for you," he tried to sound sympathetic. "I promise that once we find our haven, I will find a way to compensate everyone."

"Really? You would do that for me?" she said, and turned back to him.

Michael nodded, "my trust has more than enough money to replace anything we take."

"Thanks," she said as she gave him a quick hug and pecked him on the neck. "I owed you one," she said smiling when she saw how uncomfortable it made him.

After they both showered and donned their new clothes, the young couple decided to turn in early. They slept in their clothes in case they needed to make a quick escape. Michael hopped into one of the two beds. Cecilia took the other. Lying in the dark, Cecilia wanted to address one last thing before sleep.

"Michael, what would happen if the police pulled us over and you could not link to me? Recall the time we could not speak or link because our energy levels dropped too low? We should learn to sign," she suggested.

"You want to learn sign language?" he asked her.

"Why not?" she retorted, "that way we can save our energy for when we really need it."

Michael contacted his voice to make the arrangements. When the two awoke the following morning, they started signing to each other. Cecilia found she could shape letters and sign at a very rapid rate of speed. Michael understood every nuance of meaning her hands made.

"Let's pack," he indicated.

"What about the car?" she signed to him.

"I have an idea," he signed back. Then he added; "This is a good way to save energy."

"Told you," she replied by signing back.

Within minutes, they left the room and abandoned their old clothes and backpacks. They packed their new clothes into one bag and took that with them. Walking through the lobby, Cecilia noticed Michael approach a man standing near the front desk. He purposely bumped into the man and then excused his behavior. Cecilia meant to question him but hunger took over her thoughts. After a quick breakfast in a nearby restaurant, they returned to an alleyway next to the hotel.

"What is it?" Cecilia linked.

"The hotel owner has two cars," Michael replied. "I lifted the keys from him when we left this morning."

"So that's what you did… tricky," she said while nodding her approval. "You'll have to show me how you did that so quickly."

"I simply reached into his pocket and grabbed them. Before he could react, I jogged his memory," Michael confessed as he opened the front door. "Now he thinks he only has one car."

The couple made their way south along the highway that traveled parallel to the river. Michael drove without comment and blocked Cecilia out of his mind. In response, Cecilia shared less of her mind too. The silence between them placed an added strain on their relationship that made an already stressful journey more so. The road conditions south of Komsomol improved with recently paved two-lane highway for long stretches at a time. Michael picked up speed as he drove the car faster toward their destination. Cecilia sensed increasing urgency from Michael to reach his destination inside China as quickly as possible.

After a long day of relatively trouble free travel, they finally reached the southern end of the great Amur River Valley by arriving at the great industrial center known as Khabarovsk.

CHAPTER 20

AN UNEXPECTED TURN

ON THE NORTHERN SIDE OF the Amur River, across the northeastern border with China, lies the Russian city of Khabarovsk, a sprawling urban area that fills the entire southern end of the Amur Valley. Practically every kind of industry exists here from automobile manufacturing to steel, forest products, and petroleum industries. The valley air in summer turns brown as it is choked with emissions from unregulated smokestacks. The Trans-Siberian Railroad, the longest in the world, passes through the city bringing many visitors from central Russia. Just south of the city, a large bridge spans the Amur River, and crosses into the Heilongjiang Province of China, their destination.

The couple found the city a regional hub of activity and thus very different from other towns to the north. Khabarovsk bustled with activity with many stores, shops, tourist attractions, and a mass transit system. In the center of the city, the couple found an old yet refurbished hotel, not far from a large state-run university. The grand stylish building stood across from a beautiful city park, filled with trees, sculpted shrubs, winding paths, and flower gardens. While the hotel lacked the usual modern amenities, it made up for it in ambience. From the parquet floor in the lobby and the quaint scissor-gate elevator, to the wrought iron scrolled trim on the balcony outside their room, the hotel offered a taste of old-world charm.

Cecilia pushed open the glass double doors leading to the balcony that over looked the street below. She ran her hand over the colorful flowers in the planter along the edge and took in a deep breath. The spring air still smelled sweet and fresh, as if it recently rained.

"Not bad Michael," she said, pleased. "The room has a view of the park. We even have separate bedrooms." She turned and glanced around her. "It would be a shame to leave such a peaceful place so quickly.

"We could spend an extra day here," he offered, "or two."

"Oh could we?" she replied, nearly running into his arms. "I've gain so much knowledge in these downloads, as you call them. It's time I start putting that new wisdom to use."

"Such as?" He questioned as he stepped back to keep his distance.

"Well," she smiled, "You had New York. Every time I visited the city, someone told me where to go or what to see. I feel on the independent side, if you know what I mean. I'd like to see some art galleries, a museum, take in a film, a play, eat out, perhaps go to a concert, or dance at a nightclub…"

"A sporting event?" he offered, as he knew exactly what she meant.

"Sure," she readily agreed.

"Ok, ok, I understand – we play tourist together for a few days. Actually Cecilia that sounds like a good idea," he agreed.

"I could…" she started to say, "kiss you" as a sign of gratitude.

Sensing her action, Michael quickly turned away to examine the rest of the suite.

"What's in here?" he threw out as he ventured into the bathroom.

Cecilia halted in mid-stride – the smile fell from her face. His cool reception reminded her to maintain a friendly yet business attitude. She sighed, accepted the present conditions, and went back to the window.

"Canada never looked like this," she thought as she regarded the perfectly groomed the park across the street – not a piece of paper or a cup on the ground.

Clearly, for being mid-June, spring arrived late in this region. The air had only recently shaken off the early morning frosts of a reluctantly parting old-man winter. Flowering plants and trees popped open everywhere around the city. They added dots of color to the normally drab cityscape. The streets bustled with activity as vendors hocked their wares. Russian citizens, all too eager to shed their heavy winter garb, gathered in the open market stalls to trade practically everything worth selling. A city this size would test their mental capabilities around large numbers of people. Michael and Cecilia mutually agreed to exercise extreme caution when applying their powers.

Unlike their experience in the previous two Russian cities, Khabarovsk is a modern city including the latest in electronic monitoring technology, especially within the city's business district. Leaving the hotel, the couple walked through the downtown neighborhood not far from the university. They saw people using the latest cell phones and many current model autos.

Michael also noticed security cameras pointed down on them from atop streetlights in various locations.

"We must stay alert," he linked. He purposely glanced up.

"I see," she linked back as she followed his line of sight. "What course of action do you recommend?"

"You've gained a great deal of knowledge via your downloads," he observed from her choice of words. When Cecilia did not react, he continued. "I would say, either turn the mechanism so that the camera points away from us or make the lens zoom out," he linked to her.

"…to blur the image? Good plan Michael," she said as she caught his drift.

The two psychics then tricked any camera they noticed. The last thing Michael and Cecilia wanted to leave behind was any evidence of their visit for Russian security forces or the police to examine later.

After a brief walk around the neighborhood, they kept most curious minds away from them. They even diverted the attention of a few police officers. They returned to their room with sandwiches and sodas to enjoy for a quick lunch.

Inside their room, however, one glance into the mirror provided enough evidence obvious to both of them. Despite the fact that they wore similar clothes and spoke fluent Russia, they did not resemble the other people around them.

"I don't look like most of those women out there," Cecilia said, noting her hair, her clothes, and lack of similar make-up.

"We should probably restrict our movements to night rather than during the day," he suggested. "There'll be less police and it'll be easier to hide in shadow."

Cecilia with a mouthful of food nodded her agreement. After mentally discussing their strategy while they ate, they decided to exercise more caution when moving about Khabarovsk. If they ventured outside during the day, they would take a taxi from the front of the hotel and avoid open areas where they might easily stand out.

Michael and Cecilia tended to blend in better with the younger crowd at nightspots near the university just a few blocks away from the hotel. This way, they could mix with other young people and dance to Russian contemporary music without anyone questioning them too carefully.

"This is just like clubbing at home!" Cecilia linked to Michael in the noise of a packed room as they gyrated to the strains of a loud band.

"The room might be loud but your link is very clear. You don't have to shout inside my mind!" he replied while shaking his head as he danced.

When a handsome young man started to pick up Cecilia and a beautiful young girl made moves on Michael, the two psychics decided they danced long enough. Cecilia sensed Michael's feelings of uncertainty. He sensed her feeling of being trapped by an unwanted suitor. Rather than try to explain their mutual predicament, they left the nightclub not bothering to return.

"I've danced enough," Cecilia said breathless as they emerged.

"Me too," Michael stated. "Perhaps we can take in a quiet coffeehouse tomorrow night."

"Sure, sounds good to me," she countered.

They did not bring up their feelings from the nightclub again.

They spent the next two days not only sightseeing but also becoming acquainted with each other. During the day, they tended to remain indoors, visiting museums, art galleries, and specialty shops. They exchanged opinions about current trends, history, and politics. They tried to visit different places every day and expose their minds to a wide variety of things. They also frequently changed the way they dressed to maintain their anonymous nature. This meant acquiring new clothes.

"I have too many outfits at the hotel," Cecilia told Michael when they left another clothing shop. "Let's stop stealing these clothes!"

"I have an idea," he offered. "We'll donate the clothes we don't want to the poor when we leave town."

Cecilia glanced his way. For a moment, he felt uncomfortable since she blocked her feelings from him. He could not tell if her gaze was kind or an angry one.

"When we finally settle down, will I be able to shop using the Tyler Trust?" she asked.

He shook his head, "Let's try to make it through China before we discuss settling down," he stated and then he wisely added, "but yes, you may shop using the trust if you wish it."

Michael then hailed a cab for them to go back to the hotel.

"I wish it," she spoke aloud as she opened the door for the taxi.

On their third evening, the couple stayed out particularly late. They decided to walk back to the hotel without realizing the local law enforcement codes regarding curfew for people their age. Earlier, they listened to students read poetry and play folk music while sitting in a coffeehouse near the entrance to the university. Having engaged in numerous conversations Michael and Cecilia lost track of the time. Cecilia never had an intellectual discussion with university level students. Since her conversion, she understood nearly every exchange on levels that amazed her. The couple enjoyed the smart open discourse they had with people their age. Although they enjoyed this night the best, Michael planned on this being their last night in Khabarovsk. He felt they needed to head into China tomorrow.

When nearly everyone in the coffeehouse left to their dormitories, Michael and Cecilia decided to cross a boulevard and walk through the park to their hotel instead of taking a cab.

"It's so quiet," Cecilia's voice fell to a whisper. "We're the only people in the park. What time is it?"

"I forgot to check before we left," he responded. "Don't speak. The sound of our voices will carry. Use a mental link," he thought to her.

"Isn't it great having a park so close to our hotel? It's so peaceful here. You can smell the blossoms and see the stars. We would never feel this safe in America while crossing an intercity park like this in the dark," she related to his mind.

"Even with my old ability," Michael told her, "I would never venture into Central Park late at night."

"I have to hand it to the Russians. They are good at security," she observed.

"I only hope we aren't stopped by the police," he shot back.

"Halt!" a strong masculine voice cried out.

A Russian police officer shouted at them as he ran over to where they stood.

"I spoke too soon," he linked to her.

Michael and Cecilia obeyed. Michael then hand signed to Cecilia to remain calm.

As the officer approached, he seemed at ease. A tall man who was equal in height to Michael, he had broad shoulders, an obvious trim yet muscular frame under his black leather jacket and a handsome yet kindly face. He had an uncharacteristic thick mane of black hair and fierce gray eyes that narrowed on the couple as he approached them. Cecilia noted that despite his sudden scowl that nearly bordered on the sinister with his thick dark eyebrows and chiseled features; she found a brotherly quality about him that she could not shake.

"Are you aware it is after curfew?" he asked and then paused for a response. "Are you students?" he pressed. When neither spoke, his tone changed. "May I see some identification?" he requested as a matter of routine. "By the way, what are you two doing out at this hour?"

Cecilia sensed that Michael about to act. She quickly linked a request to him.

"I need the practice. Let me handle him," she thought.

"Handle me?" the officer asked. He stared first at one then the other. "Handle me how?" he asked firmly. He took a challenging stance.

"How did he read my mind?" Cecilia thought as she glanced over at Michael with a puzzled expression.

Michael shook his head. "How should I know?" he linked back, "Unless he's… he's…"

Michael and Cecilia turned to face the police officer. The Russian cop stopped moving. He stared at them and said nothing. He wore a bewildering expression on his face as his mouth slowly opened. No words came out. In the brief silence that followed, all three regarded one another. For a moment, no one moved or said anything.

"Did you just say something to him and he answered back?" the police officer indicated to both and then swallowed hard.

"He's pre-psychic!" Michael thought. He was surprised at the prospect.

The police officer jumped as Michael's link startled him.

"I definitely heard you say something that time," the officer spoke up. "How are you doing that without moving your lips?"

Michael and Cecilia froze – neither knowing what to do, or what to think. The Russian officer had a peculiar feeling. Sweat broke out on his brow. His mouth grew dry as he tried to swallow and choked. All three held still. Sensing an emergency, both inner voices spoke to Michael and Cecilia.

"Do nothing. Think nothing. Wait for us. The man in your proximity is not on your contact list Michael," his voice told him. "However, we sense that he is a potential candidate as he possesses a cranial conduit. We are locating his voice inside Galactic Central."

Michael and Cecilia put up blocks to prevent any further leaks. They did not wish to alarm the man standing in front of them – considering that his hand unsnapped the strap over his gun. His face turned hard. He appeared more determined to find out Michael and Cecilia's identities.

"Very slowly, I'd like to see you take out some kind of identification," the police officer demanded, his hand moved toward taking out his gun.

However, Michael and Cecilia did not move. They trusted the voices' advice. The couple kept perfectly still. All at once, the Russian officer jerked his head around as if searching.

"What? Who's there?" he spoke aloud, taking his hand from his gun. "Who is this?" He put his hands up to his ears and closed his eyes.

Locked out of the process, neither Michael nor Cecilia knew what to expect. They noticed the man's posture relax. He began to nod, as if speaking internally to a voice.

"Uh, huh, if you say so," he said aloud. "Is this a joke?" he started to smile, which strangely faded. He nodded his head several times as the perplexed couple watched. Then he gave the young couple eye contact. "Those two?" he said aloud. Then, he slowly nodded his head a few more times. "How could I refuse such a request?" he finally added.

The officer's eyes began rolling around as his body stiffened. Michael recognized those signs all too well. He and Cecilia exchanged glances. The officer started falling backward like a felled tree. To prevent any harm, Michael and Cecilia rushed forward. They grabbed him on either side and gently lowered the big man to the ground.

"Anyone see that?" Michael asked as he glanced over at Cecilia.

She stretched out her senses, "Nope."

Michael then turned his attention to the man on the ground. He knelt down to examine him.

"Is a voice performing a conversion?" he called on his voice.

"The subject agreed to the procedure," his voice replied.

"We didn't hear anything," Cecilia spoke up.

"He held a very brief dialogue with his new voice," the two young psychics heard from their voices.

"I'll say it was brief," Cecilia commented.

"Watch him while I keep an eye on our environment," Michael linked as he stood. "If you sense any change, let me know."

Cecilia nodded as she took up Michael's place by kneeling next to the man.

"How do you think he'll respond?" she wondered.

"I'm worried about attracting attention," he said as his eyes darted around, "especially with you kneeling over a policeman who happens to be lying unconscious on the ground. I'll concentrate on any passersby," Michael said as he checked street traffic and nearby buildings.

Fortunately, the streets were quiet in Khabarovsk at this time of night. When an occasional pedestrian did walk past, Michael made certain they saw nothing. With few people around, he easily diverted their attention.

Yet as Michael stood over the other two, a cold breeze passed through the park. He wondered if it was a portent of things to come. Cecilia seemed so fragile to him. Now he had to deal with this police officer, a new psychic. He wondered how many unexpected pre-psychics lived in the world. He wondered if the voices knew about all of them or if they only told him that. He thought that his voice once told him they could not lie. Michael began to feel as if his plan was expanding beyond his control. He would have no control over this other person.

What if this other psychic, once he gained his psychic abilities, wanted to duel with him for control of their power or gain a superior position? Russia is very different from America. What would he do if this officer chose to work for his government against America? Should he allow it? As his mind raced with doubt, he felt Cecilia's presence intrude.

"The conversion is progressing smoothly," she linked. She did not share her brotherly feelings with Michael's suspicious mind. She heard his concerns, although she did not let on. When she regarded this stranger's face, she could not shake the feeling of his being so understanding, giving, and kind.

Several minutes passed for the two psychics. No one moved. Michael lost track of time. The longer they spent hovering over this supine police officer, the more he felt their position too exposed. He wondered what action he might take if the station house sent a patrol car to search for the missing officer.

"This is taking too long," he finally pointed out. "I think we should…"

He stopped when he sensed the officer starting to rouse. Cecilia sensed it, too. Lying on his back, the man blinked his eyes open. He put his hand to his forehead.

"Oh, my head," he moaned, trying to rise.

Cecilia and Michael were cautious at first. After all, he still had an armed weapon at his side. However, the couple quickly sensed peace and calm as his new psychic power radiated to both of them. Michael started to help the officer to his feet, but the man waved him off.

"Please," he linked to them in English, "give me a minute to adjust."

After another minute, the twenty-four-year-old Russian man staggered to his feet. Unsteady, he swayed back and forth. When Michael and Cecilia offered to help, he waved both of them away. He then bent low with both hands on his head. His body gently shook as they thought he started to cry. Slowly he rose with a broad smile. He was not sobbing but laughing. Grinning he regard both of them.

"Hello," he said, directly addressing their minds, "…Michael Tyler," he linked as he nodded toward Michael.

"That's right," Michael answered him back via a link. He was uncertain what to expect.

"…and you must be Miss Cecilia Beaton," the officer thought as he turned to her.

Cecilia nodded back. She nervously glanced over at Michael.

He hesitated and then raised his face up to the night sky for a moment. Michael realized that the officer still had his celestial connection to his voice in Galactic Central open. However, he and Cecilia could not hear the exchange. The officer took in a deep breath and stepped forward. He stretched out his big arms and embraced the young couple in a bear hug. He kissed Cecilia and Michael on the cheek. His boldness shocked Michael and Cecilia. When he pulled back, his smile faded. He directed his next thoughts to Michael, although Cecilia heard them.

"I'm aware of your plan, Michael. It's a difficult task," he linked. "I offer my services, and I would like to join your group. Is that permissible?" he requested.

Michael glanced over at Cecilia. He was uncertain how to respond. He shrugged his shoulders. She responded by smiling and nodding her head. The couple turned back to the officer.

"Yes," they both chimed in together.

"Welcome," Michael said and extended his hand. The Russian officer shook it. He reached over and took Cecilia's hand at the same time and shook both.

"Vil-lie, is it?" Cecilia questioned with the officer still shaking her hand.

"It's spelled Vil-lie, but pronounced Vee-lee. My real name is Vladimir but my friends call me Villi. Not to change the subject, but you two have come a long way, haven't you?" he asked.

"Yes," they answered simultaneously. They were still obviously nervous about interacting with a Russian police officer.

"I see you have an ambitious agenda," he linked to them, "searching for the psychic Chinese that you and your voice detected in America," he went on, "and when you find them, you must persuade them to join this special community you have in mind. That isn't going to be easy, is it, Michael?" the tall Russian asked.

"I believe we will find a way to win them over," Michael responded as he allowed a brief smile.

Villi could only discern a few details from his fellow psychics. Michael and Cecilia, proficient in blocking, kept the young Russian from exchanging open thoughts as the couple did when they first met. Villi's mind however lay wide open to them. Cecilia and Michael had to filter his generous outpouring thoughts without appearing too rude during their initial encounter as a psychic. Still, they shared some of their personal history with him out of courtesy. Within the first few minutes, the three quickly knew each other well.

"This is incredible!" the officer shouted. "I feel great!" he grinned. He jumped into the air and swung his fist with excitement. He then turned to his new friends, an excited smile spread across his face as he linked to them. "Aliens! They really do exist! We can speak to them!"

"Yes," Cecilia chuckled. "Give your mind time to adjust, Villi. We have a long way to go."

Villi's incredulous comments were all too familiar to Michael. He recalled that first night on the train track when he reacted the same way by questioning his new relationship and then jumping into the air and swinging his fist. Judging from his first thoughts, he could relate to the Russian on many levels. He hoped they would be good friends. Yet even in this joyous moment, reality set in. Michael glanced around. He had ignored his surroundings. He wondered if anyone watched them when Villi rose and reacted to his changed self. A quick scan indicated they were alone. He did not wish to tempt fate any further.

"Listen, I hate to interrupt the celebration," Michael broke in. "We should leave the park before someone sees us. Villi, you should come with us back to our hotel room before you decide anything. I'm certain you have questions. We can try to answer some of them."

"Good idea," Villi linked and nodded in reply.

Cecilia held out her arm as an invitation.

"Michael is right. We have much to discuss before we leave Khabarovsk tomorrow," she said.

"I was wondering," Villi questioned, "I'm a cop. How can I disappear? The station house will come looking for me. Won't I be missed?" Villi wondered.

"Ah, that's the beauty of this," Michael told him. "No one will miss you. No one will ever know you existed – not even your own family," Michael stated.

"You can do that?" Villi asked.

"We can do that," Cecilia answered him.

"Yes, but my family," Villi answered, thinking of his mother. "If I won't see them for a very long time, may I look in on them once in a while?" he asked.

Cecilia checked with Michael. He silently gave his approval, relenting to the need the other two felt. She turned back to Villi.

"We will find a way to do this as a group," she told him as she held out her elbow. "Come! I have a feeling the hour might be late, but the night is just beginning."

Villi took Cecilia's right arm. She was joined by Michael on her other side. Arms joyously entwined, the three newly linked individuals crossed the street. They marched through the hotel lobby and headed for the elevator.

At first, the night desk clerk thought it odd to see two strangers with a police officer in their midst strolling through the lobby so amiably. Then he remembered that page seven of the newspaper seemed more interesting and soon forgot what he witnessed.

"That's a neat trick you just performed with the desk clerk," Villi observed, poised outside the elevator. "Will I be able to do that?"

"Cecilia and I have only practiced this intervention technique a short time," Michael stated, as Villi stepped inside last and pulled the doors closed behind him. "We'd be glad to show you."

"We're gradually adjusting just as you will," Cecilia linked.

"Imagine what we can accomplish given more time," Michael added.

"Is it easy to learn?" Villi asked as the elevator started to move.

"First we should discuss blocking," Cecilia suggested. "We've discovered that this technique is an important first step."

"By the way, do you have anything for a headache?" Villi asked Cecilia.

"Believe me Villi, nothing short of a sledge hammer will do," Cecilia sympathetically stated.

CHAPTER 21

VILLI

VLADIMIR ZAVITINSK WAS BORN IN the summer of 1991 nearly four years before Michael Tyler. He came from an impoverished low-income family. His mother performed odd jobs to help pay bills. His father, a police officer, worked long hours for very little pay. His family lived with thousands of other destitute families in one of many high-rise apartment complexes built by the Socialist government decades earlier.

When he was eight, his younger sister said his name as "Vee-lee." His family liked the nickname so well that eventually they called him that name all the time. His mother was the first person to write his name as "Villi."

"Look at the way it's spelled!" he protested. "I am not some hair follicle!"

"You'll have to tell them it's pronounced vee-lee and not vill-lie for the rest of your life," his father kidded.

"Vee-lee," he mumbled, "what sort of name is that?"

Yet after a while, the tall young man took to the name. Villi loved his sister. He did not care when she mispronounced his name.

One afternoon an officer showed up at the family door regarding Villi's father. The colleague stated that his father tried to stop a robbery in progress. The assailant gunned his father down. Outraged by this cowardly act, Villi resolved to become a police officer like his father. However, after he left high school, his family could not afford to send Villi to the officer's academy. His mother could barely afford to pay rent and keep food on the table.

Instead, Villi worked to help his mother out of debt. He took temporary jobs – the kind of jobs that usually broke the spirit of most people. He worked the night shift in the auto factory where they only paid by quota. He choked on black dust while he slaved away in the coalmines, and he sweat for hours in the summer heat while he cut lumber in the mill for a pittance.

At the end of two years, he still did not have enough money. Villi's mother went to some of her husband's old friends on the police force and begged them for help. They took pity on the hard-working young man. They noticed that since high school, Villi grew big and tough from his two years of hard labor. His father's old friends agreed to help and raised enough money for his entrance fees.

Although he graduated at the top of his class – the highest marks of any officer before him – he did not have political or social connections. Therefore, instead of being promoted to detective or higher rank, Villi ended up walking a beat in a bad section of the city, just as his father did.

Every evening, Villi walked the same region of Khabarovsk. He took very few days off. He could never afford a break in his pay. However, shortly after accepting his position, he discovered a coffeehouse along his route near the university. He went inside for a cup of coffee and lingered when he overheard students engaged in a variety of discussions. The timbre of their conversations intrigued the curious young man.

"Fatalism is a philosophy of the past," one young man stated when Villi sat within hearing distance.

"Shh! Quiet!" a young woman nearby whispered to him. "Do you want to get into trouble with the police?"

"By all means," Villi spoke up, "continue. I would love to hear why fate no longer controls our destiny. Would that be because you believe there is no God?" to which Villi added, "…philosophically speaking, of course."

The shocking statement rattled a few students to hear a police officer speaking so candidly.

Villi propped his feet up, loosened his tie, and sighed.

"I'm off work," he told them. "Besides, what people say within these walls is no business of anyone outside them… especially the government's business."

A few students smiled. The young man turned to Villi.

"How do we know we can trust you?" he demanded.

"Because I believe in what you say," Villi replied sincerely. They trusted the sound of his voice. From that moment on, they included him in their conversations.

With increasing frequency, he stopped by the café during his off time. He often eavesdropped on students discussing philosophy, history, politics, and literature. Every subject fascinated Villi from the arts to the sciences.

Occasionally, befriended students lent him their textbooks from which he gleaned a mountain of knowledge due to his enormous capacity for retention. Within a year, Villi's level of knowledge surpassed most of the students that frequented the coffeehouse. As seasons passed, he became a fixture of the coffeehouse. The freshmen affectionately called him "the Street Professor" and often called on him for assistance in their studies. Had he attended college, Villi would have excelled in every subject he studied.

Once, an attractive female student friend invited him to a showing of her artwork. While standing in the gallery next to a sweaty rotund art critic, the man's opinionated thoughts leapt into his mind.

"Her spatial grouping is disproportionate!" the man bellowed.

"Beg your pardon?" Villi said as he turned to the middle-aged scholar.

"What's that?" the man responded. He was offended that someone of Villi's obviously lesser level addressed him.

"You commented on the painting," Villi told the man.

"I made no comment sir," the man gruffly spoke and left.

Villi accidentally made his first mind link. He assumed the environment of the gallery caused the curious event to happen. He went to several shows after that, but could not duplicate the event. Villi never heard any alien voices as a child. Another semester came and went. His mind no longer dwelled on hearing another person's thoughts until the night he first met Cecilia and Michael.

Heading to the café after the end of his shift, he noticed the young couple emerge from his favorite nightspot. He had never seen them. They seemed out of place. Their clothes and hair did not match the other students. He wondered why they were walking away from the university instead of going to a dorm room. Out of curiosity, he trailed them through the park until he overheard the young man compare this park with a famous park in America. He thought they were speaking with loud voices and decided to verify their identification. He did not realize they spoke directly to his mind.

When he saw Cecilia converse with Michael in the way she did, the memory from the art gallery sharply returned. Confused and alarmed, he did not understand this new experience. In the very moment when he struggled to make sense of this new phenomenon, his voice from Galactic Central spoke words of wisdom inside his head. It validated every feeling he had, every experience he felt, and every dream he ever desired. The temptation of communicating with other worlds, and tapping into that knowledge base, proved an overwhelming wish fulfillment to the disadvantage young man.

As soon as he woke from his conversion, a different challenge immediately faced the young officer. His voice volunteered to explain Michael's plan to him. Villi then held a brief internal debate. Should he go with these two young psychics, or should he return to his former state? This is the reason why he did not rise at first. After consulting further with his voice, and discussing their intentions with Cecilia and Michael, Villi chose to assist Michael. He left behind all familiarity for a very risky venture with an uncertain future – something Villi never did.

He gradually accepted this new side to his nature. He began to behave and think less as a practical police officer and more like a psychic warrior in pursuit of great knowledge – with two new incredible and powerful friends as allies.

Back in the hotel room that first night, the three psychics exchanged thoughts, feelings, and personal histories.

"We've never met," he addressed Cecilia, "and yet I feel so close to you – as if I've known you all my life."

The big Russian man sat on the sofa and loosened his uniform before taking off his shoes. He reached for the cup of tea that Michael had fixed – a drink he never requested until this moment. He looked to both Michael and Cecilia for answers. He felt more like the rookie freshmen at the university than a person of knowledge and wisdom. As Cecilia responded to his comment, he pushed an ashtray on the coffee table back and forth with his mind as she showed him to do.

"We share more understanding between us than you do with people you've known your entire life," Cecilia explained. "Even now as we link our thoughts, we exchange emotion and intent with those thoughts. Michael and I believe that when we link, it clarifies communication. Don't you think that makes all of us seem closer?"

"I suppose," he said, yawning after grilling them with questions for the past two hours. Using his ability for the first time left Villi drained.

Michael added nothing more than the explanations he also gave Cecilia during that first meeting in which he emphasized his personal goal to form a community of like minds.

By three in the morning, after they extensively reviewed their trip and shared what they learned with Villi, the exhausted psychics were ready to retire. Villi took the sofa while the other two went to their separate bedrooms. Villi consciously applied blocking technique before he closed his eyes to prevent any unintended mishaps.

When Michael woke later that morning, he sensed Cecilia already awake in her bedroom.

"What's up?" he asked, feeling her restlessness.

"Oh, hi," she responded at once, "I had trouble sleeping. I woke early," she thought to him. She stretched her arms and yawned. "I couldn't stop thinking about Villi," she relayed.

She sat up in her bed and pulled her blanket up to her neck. She propped her head against a stack of pillows. She wanted to open her mind with Michael and to be honest regarding all of her feelings. Yet for the mission's sake she held back and hid her real feelings for him using the seeded technique.

Unable to fathom that guarded aspect of her mind, Michael wondered what she meant about Villi. He did not wish to pry if she were beginning to develop personal feelings of attraction for Villi. After all, they hardly knew each other. He only met Cecilia a short time ago. Perhaps the seventeen-year-old found Villi's robust masculinity and aggressiveness more attractive.

"Do you wish to share any feelings?" he cautiously linked.

"I wondered how many others like him the voices missed," she offered while she kept her emotions disengaged.

Michael initially wondered about the same thing. The more he considered it, the more he began to realize the extensive involvement of the voices in every move he made. Was he coming up with ideas, or were they making choices for him? Perhaps they planted ideas in his thoughts.

"I don't believe the voices missed Villi," he thought back to her. He decided it was best to block some of his emotion too.

"What are you saying?" she asked.

"I'm not certain," Michael linked, "just a feeling, that's all. Not to change the subject," he added, "I believe that they made him our equal during his conversion. Judging from his thoughts, Villi can reach out with his mind with greater power than either you or I had initially. I believe they gave him a double dose of psychic ability – call it level two if you like. At any rate, we should consider Villi an equal in potential ability."

"Perhaps they advanced his level to be more help to us," she offered. She paused to tap into her senses. "Can you feel his distinct psychic signature?"

"Oh, yes," Michael concurred, "I sense him even as we link. I might add that I perceive you and Villi very differently."

"Maybe each of us has his or her unique psychic signature," she suggested.

"I don't mean to pry. Did you and he… share any dreams?" Michael asked as his thought trailed off. Then he immediately regretted he brought it up.

"No, I did not sense his conscious intrusion last night as you and I shared at the motel," she honestly relayed back. "If he did dream, he did not include me – erotic or otherwise."

"Our blocking lesson probably helped," he stated. He avoided discussing the motel incident further. "I'm beginning to wonder what will happen when our group adds more members," Michael offered.

"I've been lying here thinking about the same thing," Cecilia linked.

He withdrew from her mind. For a moment, he wanted to contact his voice. Her guarded nature frustrated the young man who sought an open society – not one shrouded in withheld secrets. Silence filled the space between them as Michael grappled with his emotions. A sense of urgency took hold of him as he stared up at the ceiling.

"Let's leave this place, this hotel, this city and take Villi with us. Shall we?" he asserted.

"Are you certain you wish to take Villi with us? You did not plan for him," she linked.

"I didn't plan for many things, Cecilia," Michael linked back while rising. "From this moment on, I'll try to be more flexible with the plan. Besides, Villi may have a great deal to offer us. You linked with him last night. He's quite knowledgeable in a variety of subjects. He's also a quick study."

"So," she paused, "now we are three?" she offered.

"… and counting," Michael added. "Let's tell him the good news after we clean up. First call on the shower," he chimed. He flew out of bed and beat her into the bathroom.

Cecilia muttered something but did not link. They took turns in the shower and prepared to leave, which included packing their clothes. Since Michael finished his shower first, he woke Villi with his mind.

"доброе утро! (Good morning!)" he cheerfully linked in Russian. "как у вас? (How are you?)"

"It's ok, Michael," Villi linked back. "You can link in English. I understand… Oh," he groaned, "my head still hurts," he relayed as he rubbing his messy head of coal black hair. He rose and stretched his large muscular frame. He glanced over and caught his image in the living room mirror. He forgot about Cecilia. He slept in the nude. He reached over to the sofa and wrapped the sheet around his body. He peeked into Michael's bedroom.

"I didn't know you spoke Russian," Villi asked as he stood in the doorway watching him pack.

"Just trying to be friendly," Michael replied. "Cecilia and I took a download in Russian before we set sail to your country. As to the headache, I'm afraid no medicine will help relieve your discomfort. We found that after a day or two the pain fades – honest," Michael reassured him.

"I'll be grateful for that," Villi replied. He took note of their activity. "So you've decided to leave," he observed. "How long before you go?"

"You're coming with us Villi," Michael linked. He turned to face the big man. They stood only a few feet away from each other, but the two men were equal in height.

"You forget Michael that I'm a Russian police officer," Villi linked back. He started to pace in the doorway. "I've been doing some thinking," he linked. "I could jeopardize the entire mission. I can't skip town and head off to China

– a missing Russian police officer? The government would start a search. With my extensive file, they could easily trace my whereabouts."

"Is that your only objection?" Michael asked.

"Don't you think it's a good one?" Villi shot back. "If the government can trace my movement, they may come after me," he warned, "but they will find you."

"I appreciate your sentiment, my learned friend," Michael linked with such calm reassurance that it made Villi pause. "Cecilia and I will take care of that problem today," Michael informed him. "We feel you will be an important asset to our group," he added as he walked up to his new friend. He could reach straight out and put his hand on Villi's shoulder. This time Michael spoke instead of linking. "You must join us Villi. We need you."

The big Russian "bear" thought for a long moment.

"If I come along Michael, I must have an equal voice in our decisions," he suggested.

"We're a democratic bunch," Cecilia chimed in as she entered the room. "Are you in or not?"

She walked between the two men and held out her hand. Michael added his on top of hers. Villi placed his hand on top. Unlike last night, this time when the three psychics touched, they automatically dropped their blocks. Psychic energy flowed back and forth. With their minds open, a flood of new personal information poured between them. As different memories and histories flew back and forth, Villi actually blushed at its personal nature – adolescent fantasies, his early dating and so on. Distracted, the sheet he held wrapped around his waist covering him started to fall off and reveal more of the hairy man's skin than he wished. He scrambled for the sheet and sheepishly smiled.

"Oops!" he declared. "All at once I feel naked in a way that covering up with this sheet won't help," he said while raising an eyebrow in Cecilia's direction.

She burst out laughing and returned to her bedroom to finish packing. When she withdrew, her action somehow severed the link the three shared.

"As I said, you'll adjust," she linked as she walked away, "eventually," she added. "Honestly Villi, you've nothing to hide from me. I may appear young, but I'm a grown woman. I know you are a man who loves beautiful women and that you have been with several," she laughed again. "I won't hold it against you!"

Villi did not know what to think. He glanced at Michael for his reaction. The American simply shrugged and withdrew to grab his bags and bring them into the main room. He did not wish to come between two psychics as they formed a relationship. He needed their assistance too much to offend anyone.

"This is going to be some adventure," Villi stated. He scratched and stretched his body while he took in a deep breath.

"Come my friend," Michael suggested as he gestured toward the bathroom. "Take your shower while Cecilia and I order breakfast."

"Then this is my decision," Villi linked. He walked toward the bathroom as he thought his reply. "I'm in, if you don't mind hearing the raunchy hormonal-laden thoughts of a sexually deprived Russian police officer now and then."

Michael let out a belly laugh before he went to the phone and ordered up some breakfast for them. Room service delivered freshly boiled eggs, onion bagels, cheese, smoked salmon, canned fruit, and large pot of tea. Cecilia wanted to eat out on the terrace as the sunny day beckoned. The two sat in silence on restaurant-style folding chairs and quietly munched on lox and bagels while they waited for Villi.

Michael laid out some of his "civilian" clothes for Villi to wear, as the two men were nearly identical in size. This way he did not have to put his uniform back on. After he showered and dressed, Villi sat with the other two on the terrace clustered around the small table. Michael poured out a cup of tea for his newest friend. Villi frowned as he brought the white teacup to his lips. He normally drank coffee. However, he did not object to the idea of drinking tea.

"What's with the sudden craving for tea?" he wondered.

The other two did not reply. They did not understand the phenomenon either. Villi then asked about their next step. He could feel Michael and Cecilia enter his mind. The prospect of communicating by linking their minds thrilled the young police officer. When Cecilia started to probe Villi's personal memories, he held up his hand to her.

"Whoa! This mental sharing is going to require a change in the way we communicate," he said as his eyes darted skeptically from one to the other. "I have many private memories that are not... well, shall we say intended for the uninitiated." He knew that Michael and Cecilia were still virgins.

Cecilia chuckled at his frankness. Even the normally stoic Michael smiled.

"So you illegally drove a car when you were only fourteen," Cecilia discovered before Villi cut off her access. "I see you acquired survival skills rather quickly," she surmised.

"I had to..." Villi replied. He started to explain his rebellious teenage reaction to his father's death when Michael interrupted.

"Speaking of cars Villi," Michael cut him off, "we're going to need a few things before we head into China. Reliable transportation is our top priority," he requested. "Any suggestions on where we can find a car in good condition?"

When Michael linked with him, Villi noted his air of authority. Michael did not express effete superiority, but rather a calm sense of purpose – a significant difference to him. He respected Michael for his natural leadership skills.

"We have an auto factory here in the city," Villi recalled as he mastered the art of eating and linking at the same time. "They make the latest models sold in Russia. Judging from the way you two thieves have preyed upon ordinary citizens, I think it's time we take a car right off the production line. That way we aren't stealing any one's property, just the factory's cars. Right Cecilia?"

"I like how this man thinks," she nodded.

Villi flashed the image of the factory to his two cohorts.

"I don't know… breaking into a factory," Michael started.

"Not a problem," Villi retorted. "I used to work there. I'm well acquainted with the security system Michael. In fact, I will consider this car as unpaid wages for all those nights I put in. Again, do you have any objections Cecilia?"

"He's sounding better all the time, Michael?" she linked. Cecilia began to appreciate Villi moral standards.

"Then we agree," Michael concluded. "We take a car off the assembly line. Villi will lead the way," he added and pushed away from the small table.

Villi started to grab the bags when Cecilia indicated to him that they were not ready to leave.

"We don't know how long this will take," she linked.

He dropped his bag and joined the other two as they headed to the elevator. Villi watched as Michael called the elevator to their floor and even open the manual doors with his mind. Outside the hotel, Villi eagerly wanted to try out his new ability. He hailed a cab by drawing the driver's attention to him. A taxi slammed on his brakes and skidded to a halt before he turned his cab around and drove up to the hotel's entrance. The other two watched with interest as Villi stretched out his senses and used his new ability.

"This is amazing!" he linked to them with innocent pride.

"Works on girls too," Cecilia laughingly batted her eyes as she joked with him.

Villi swallowed hard. The thought of persuasion never occurred to him until that moment.

"I guess I have a lot to learn!" Villi said as he held the door open for them.

Michael stepped in first so that Cecilia could sit between the two big men.

During the ride, Michael instructed Villi on how to enter a person's mind and manipulate time-indexed memories, especially short-term memories. Villi quickly caught on and surprised both psychics with his ability to adopt new processes.

"Do you mean I'll never have to pay for a cab again?" Villi said delighted.

"That's just the beginning," Cecilia told him. "We can also induce behaviors. He would drive us off the end of a pier if we told him to do it. Unlike hypnotism, we enter the part of the mind that overrides reason. The action that follows is part of the person's will – as if they suggested it to their own conscious mind," she explained.

"No will of his own," Villi mumbled.

"As far as that goes, we could order him to take a gun and shoot…" she started.

"We've decided not to induce any violent behavior in others. Didn't we?" Michael said. He stared right at Cecilia.

"I only used the example as a metaphor…" she began to protest.

"Yes, but it sounded as if…" then he broke off.

Villi sensed an underlying ongoing tension in their exchange. This debate between them was not new. Cecilia did not reply to Michael's assertions. However, Villi felt awkward sitting next to them. The cab grew uncomfortably silent until Michael finally spoke up.

"Look, I'm not trying to preach morality," he linked to both simultaneously. "I'm no more ethical than the next person is. I just believe we should be careful with this new ability of ours. Cecilia and I had a long discussion on this matter. We decided that with our special gifts, we should take the moral high ground. No psychic is going to be king or take advantage of an ordinary person against his or her judgment. We're in the helping business – not the conquering or dominating one."

"I see," Villi interjected as he glanced nervously between them. "Since you brought it up, Michael, I'd have to say I agree wholeheartedly. I like the idea of helping out humanity, using our power for good. Do you Cecilia?"

"I do," she said as she glanced over at Villi. "I apologize for making it appear I would induce violent tendencies in someone. The thought is completely repugnant to me. I have different ambitions. I told Michael that when we create our special group, I'll settle for being the best doctor rather than be a princess."

Villi smiled broadly at her suggestion as he briefly caught part of their past conversations.

"Oh, but you are a natural born princess!" Villi declared. He gestured setting a crown on her head.

"You're sweet," Cecilia leaned over and kissed him on the cheek.

Villi blushed for a moment as Michael turned away to look out the window. Villi sensed his jealous feelings at once. He stretched his hand past Cecilia and patted Michael on the knee.

"Don't worry, Michael. I don't like skinny buxom blonde girls from Canada," he asserted.

"It wouldn't bother me," Michael shot back. "I just want to establish a community for us. After that, I don't care who bonds together."

"You don't?" Cecilia gazed over at the back of his head. "You don't care what happens to me?"

"I…" Michael struggled with his emotions. Yet, he knew his feelings toward Cecilia were as transparent as glass.

"Good thing we've arrived at the factory," Villi interrupted as he patted both their knees. "Driver, pull up there," he pointed.

This time Villi entered the driver's mind just as Michael showed him to do. The man left the scene unable to remember how he got there. With Villi's knowledge of the plant's security systems, he easily guided them through the auto assembly section. Most of the day shift workers deserted the assembly line for their lunch break.

Villi exited the end of the assembly line and searched a nearby lot of finished cars until he found a completed luxurious Russian car. The tag on the window stated the completed car passed inspection. This particular car had dark tinted windows, faux-leather seats and outfitted with the latest advanced technology. The vehicle's level of sophistication even impressed Michael.

"No ordinary citizen could order a car like this," Villi said as he scratched his face. "They made this car for a high-ranking government official or rich businessman," Villi observed.

"I could stand to ride in it," Cecilia stated as she eyed the interior.

The back seat impressed Michael more than the front.

"It has curtains!" he pointed out.

"I picked a good one, no?" Villi smiled. "I'll see if I can locate the keys…" Villi said as he started back inside.

Michael reached out his arm and stopped him.

"Keys to doors or car ignitions are no longer necessary," Michael showed him. The moment he touched the handle, the door unlocked.

He demonstrated to Villi how to spread his senses through the car, how to enter the electronic ignition system, and then make the necessary connections using psychic energy. Just as he duplicated Michael's pathways through the brains of targeted individuals, Villi carefully followed Michael's explanation. He succeeded by starting the car on the first try.

"Cars are simpler than brain anatomy," he sighed as the car sprang to life.

"Working with brains is significantly more rewarding," Cecilia broke in.

"You want to be a doctor," the big Russian addressed her. "Well I see my position differently. True I am scholarly," he asserted. "Yet if I join this community, I want to become one helluva mechanic," he said with a gleam in his eye. "That would be my desire fulfilled."

Michael raised his eyebrows to Cecilia as if to say, "You see?"

"I've always dreamed of having a car this nice," Villi sighed. "Mind if I drive?"

"By all means," Michael gestured. He took the backseat while Cecilia sat up front. "I'll sit back and enjoy the ride."

No one at the factory's security gate noticed as Villi drove the car from the factory grounds, nor did the camera on the lot record the event. Villi drove them to his apartment across town, then to his family's apartment, his police station house, the coffeehouse, and so on. Along the way, Michael and Cecilia probed and purged minds at each location as they related to Villi's existence, from friends and neighbors to relatives and co-workers. They even inspired clerks inside government buildings to destroy physical pictures and paper records of the officer. Villi's Galactic Central voice took him through a primer of Russian Internet skullduggery where he removed the last traces of his entire life. The search went all the way to Moscow's central computer system.

"I didn't think it could be done," Villi said, as he and his voice wiped away the last bit of electronic information.

"The voices in Galactic Central can help us do anything," Cecilia linked in softly.

"I'm beginning to believe it," he answered.

"That leaves your mother," Michael spoke up from the back seat.

"My mother?" Villi answered with uncertainty. "I forgot about my mother and my sister," he stated. "What should I do?" he asked them.

Cecilia and Michael exchanged glances. Cecilia then linked into Villi's thoughts.

"Michael and I decided to start a compensatory program. If we are going to take your mother's son, then we feel we should compensate her for that loss. While you were busy with your voice, we set up a trust for your mother. She'll never have to work another day. We arranged for a house in her name. The cost is completely paid. She will also receive a generous weekly check for the rest of her life. Your sister is set to inherit your mother's estate when she passes."

Villi stared at the two people in front of him. He did not know what to say for he saw Cecilia spoke absolute truth. He turned to Michael as his eyes filled up with tears. Michael nodded toward his new friend. He and Cecilia felt strongly motivated about doing this for Villi.

"You did all of that for my mother and sister?" Villi linked. His thoughts choked with emotion. "I can't begin to tell you how much this means to me."

"Forget it," Michael told him. "As I said before Villi, we will always do what we can for each other."

"I will never forget what you have done for my family," Villi linked with conviction.

Villi suddenly grabbed Cecilia and kissed the surprised young woman on the mouth. He turned to Michael. The tall American held out his hands. The two men – equal in stature – squared off.

"Only when we know each other better," Michael kidded.

Villi grinned at the joke. Men in Russia often kiss and think nothing of it. He laughed inside when he saw how embarrassed men felt about such things in America. Then his smile fell.

"If I only knew what will happen to them," he soberly thought to Michael.

"We all want that, Villi," Cecilia spoke up. "Perhaps, someday you can check on them," she offered as a small compensation.

He shrugged his shoulders as he tried to recover. "You see Cecilia, while I love my mother and sister; I also realize we're saving a vital part of the human race, right?"

"A part of the human race that no one will ever discover," she interjected and glanced over at Michael.

"You two adjusted," he said to them. "I can adjust as well. Let us speak no more of sad good-byes."

Villi started the car and pulled into traffic. He silently headed back to the hotel as he contemplated a life without his family. Michael linked nothing during the ride. However, he recalled that he did very little for Cecilia in comparison. When he eventually turned to her, she picked up his thoughts and signed, "later" to him. The two watched Villi as he drove. They wondered how he would digest the day's events when his thoughts inadvertently leapt into their minds.

"I could use a stiff swig of vodka about now," he thought as he tightly gripped the wheel.

"Then who would drive this beautiful car?" Cecilia burst into his thoughts.

He spun around remembering his friend's feelings in this matter.

"Sorry Michael, I forgot to block my thoughts," Villi apologized.

He knew of Michael's alcoholic history from their first night in the hotel, when he offered a toast to his new life. Michael had to explain why he could not drink.

"As much as I tried, I discovered they don't make enough alcohol to erase some pain," Michael replied.

"Philosophy, Michael?" Villi said as he glanced into the rearview mirror. "You and I have much to discuss, my friend. I believe I'm going to enjoy this psychic adventure!"

"We were hoping you would," Michael responded. "Let's head back to the hotel."

Chapter 22

Baby steps

After a full day of intense mind probing, the three young psychics eliminated all traces of Vladimir Zavitinsk from Khabarovsk and Russia. As far as the Russian government, his job, friends, and family were concerned, he did not exist. Villi helped with some mental manipulations, while he also improved his practice of entering minds and altering memories. When the three cleaned out his apartment, they packed Villi's bags and put them in the trunk.

Now exhausted and their energy spent, the three returned to the hotel for a long night's rest and to recharge their psychic energy. They rose before dawn the next morning. After a brief grab at breakfast, Michael and Cecilia brought down their luggage while Villi finished packing the new car. They decided the time had come to leave for the border crossing.

"Is that everything?" Cecilia asked when Villi closed the trunk.

"I can't think of anything else," Villi stated. "What's with…" he nodded toward Michael in the back seat with his arms folded and a scowl on his face. "He's barely linked a thought all morning."

"I'm not sure. He's blocking me out too," Cecilia indicated. "Go ahead and drive."

"Suits me, only we should probably…" Villi stopped in mid-thought. He glanced over at Michael and then blocked his final thought.

"What?" Cecilia asked.

"Nothing, let's go," Villi said.

Villi drove through the city and then headed southwest toward the only border crossing into China for miles around – the Chi Han Bridge Complex – an enormous compound of buildings at either end of a large bridge with Russian government buildings on the north side and even greater complex on the Chinese side. They had hardly traveled a few blocks toward their destination, when Michael perked up in the back seat. His energy intruded into the minds of the other two psychics.

"Pull over… anywhere," Michael told Villi in an open link. "We need to talk."

Villi turned the car into a side street and found a rare parking space in a residential area filled with old three-story apartment buildings along each side of the street for blocks. The shiny new car stuck out amidst the collection of vintage used vehicles. Michael cleared his throat to gain their attention.

"I started thinking last night," he began. "I'd like to share some new ideas with you that I've been considering," he stated. "I've never tried to hide anything since I turned into a psychic person. I reasoned that even with blocking, a psychic cannot block another psychic from his thoughts forever," he told them. "With the addition of Villi to our group, my plan – such as it is – should be modified."

As Michael spoke, Villi sensed the American's uneasiness to speak his true feelings. He recognized that he wanted to be diplomatic and make leadership a revolving responsibility between the three. Villi disagreed. He regarded the younger man wise beyond his years. Yet he felt Michael still lacked important worldly experience. Villi knew that his time on the police force provided him practical knowledge. Perhaps his role should be one of advisor to support Michael's leadership – like the advice a younger sibling would receive from an older brother – he reasoned.

"Excuse me for interrupting," he broke in. "Before you say anything else I'd like to speak," Villi turned to Michael.

Michael caught onto his intention. He relaxed and laid back in his seat.

"Go right ahead Villi," Michael responded.

"First I'd like to settle a turf battle between all three of us," he started. "Let's reach a mutual understanding, shall we? I believe Michael should continue to be the group leader. Don't you agree?" Villi turned to Cecilia.

"Do you feel comfortable with that? After all, you're older than Michael," Cecilia linked.

"True," Villi continued. "Still, Michael has more psychic experience than I have. I trust his judgment, if he will trust my input at times."

Michael shrugged his shoulders and nodded.

"Please don't take this the wrong way," Villi went on. "I'm not trying to tell anyone what to do. I'd like to offer a few words of advice, if I may."

"Go ahead, Villi, please be frank," Michael replied. "I always appreciate an honest opinion."

"I intend to give it," Villi shot back. "Before we proceed any further in our journey," he began, "I believe we should discuss crossing into China. Let me acquaint you two with some facts. The Chinese have many security cameras that cover the Amur River Bridge, also known as the Chi Han Bridge in China. The Chinese and the Russians have cameras from one end of the bridge to the other. The Chinese have also stationed an entire brigade of men and equipment on their side. China is very cautious about who they let in or out of their country," he told the two young psychics. "Going from Russian to China is not like crossing from America into Canada. The crossing will be extremely difficult to fake with many minds to control. I'm rather new at this. I don't know how much help I can provide if the situation should," he paused, "let us say deteriorate."

"You'll be fine Villi," Cecilia tried to reassure him.

"Let's hope so," he continued. "This is the only way to cross the Amur River for hundreds of kilometers in either direction. That bridge is an essential conduit connecting the largest city in this region with a heavily populated rural Chinese countryside. Neither Russian nor Chinese citizens waltz in or out of China without a detailed explanation as to why, along with a heavily documented passport. Only day workers with special permits are given easier access – and that is after extensive searching and questioning – even for regulars," he told them.

"The rest of the border along the Amur is watched constantly, heavily guarded and mined along the embankment with huge warning signs," he continued. "If anyone attempted to sneak into China by swimming across the river, they would do so at their own peril. Even with our power, we could never sense every type of mine or booby-trap. Therefore, the bridge south appears to be our best way in," he concluded. "Yet, driving to the other side of the bridge is only the first step. Next is the matter of your passports."

Michael and Cecilia exchanged glances. They really had not used their passports.

"Your facsimiles can fool one or two policemen in Russia with a bit of psychic trickery," Villi continued. "Deceiving the entire Chinese Immigration Task Force or the Russian Border Authority without additional help is something else. Governments train border-crossing security guards to be suspicious and extremely thorough. They can spot deceit in a second. They can also alert legions of troops within minutes. You'd not only be caught but also very likely imprisoned – even with your psychic powers."

Villi impressed Michael and Cecilia with his sound reasoning.

"You've put a lot of thought into this," Michael commented.

"You weren't the only one doing some thinking last night," Villi told him. "Ever since I agreed to go into China, I've thought about the difficulties crossing the bridge. However, not all is lost. I have an idea how we might sneak through," Villi suggested.

"Go ahead," the other two chimed in.

"We couldn't possibly keep track of a hundred border agents and security cameras on the Chinese side. However, if we create some kind of diversion…" he linked. His thought trailed off. He then leaned back against the door and put his hands up behind his head. He glanced back and forth at the other two while he waited for some kind of response.

"Ok Villi," Michael capitulated, "I give. What kind of diversion did you have in mind?"

"Yes, I'm a bit perplexed," Cecilia added. "What is your diversion?"

"That's just it! I was hoping you two could think of one!" Villi exclaimed. Michael nervously ran his finger across his chin.

"Perhaps it's time we called on some expert help," he linked and pointed up. "I suggest an open multiple intergalactic link," he suggested.

With their minds open, Michael, Cecilia, and Villi established a three-way link between them and their alien voices. Michael briefly informed the voices of their crossing into China dilemma.

"The three of us realize that we need to cross the border with China," he mentioned to the other worldly creatures, "perhaps you could suggest a way past the extensive security…"

"We believe the time has arrived to physically alter our Earth side contacts one final time," all three voices responded effectively cutting Michael's thought short.

That statement brought expressions of surprise and concern to their faces.

"Physically alter?" Cecilia questioned.

"Just what do you mean by that?" Michael linked back them.

"Yeah," Villi spoke up, "my conversion took place two days ago! Are you saying I need another one so soon?"

"Michael, Cecilia and Villi," their voices spoke in unison, "we suggest a new alteration – one that will further enhance your abilities. To accomplish this, we must alter your DNA patterns. Once we change your alignment, you can better focus psychic energy in physical manifestations. This alteration will make you a truly unique species on your planet and give future generations natural advantages."

"You want to do what to our DNA?" Michael spoke up, his tone clearly upset.

"Are you changing my physical body?" Cecilia interjected. The tone in her link took on the emotion of fear. "Will the process affect me having a child? If it does, you can count me out right now."

"Calm your emotional side Cecilia," her voice replied.

"We are not proposing to alter your overall physical nature," the voices returned to speaking in unison to all three. "Your exteriors will be unchanged. In addition, this change will not affect your ability to conceive children. If you sire offspring, those children will possess heightened abilities from the moment of conception. Conversion will not be required."

"When you said enhance our abilities, did you mean we'll have even more power than we do now?" Villi put to his voice.

"Yes," it replied, "you will have greater latitude to apply psychic energy."

Villi grinned, slapped his hands together and rubbed them with delight. The prospect of new abilities fascinated the Russian as he completely trusted his voice.

"I'm ready!" he shouted.

"I'm not," Michael quickly chimed in. "How can you determine the human safety limits to this procedure when you've only been studying us for a couple of decades?" he questioned. "Further, why should you wish to change our DNA? What's wrong with it? Until now, you've only altered a miniscule area of our brain surrounding the portal. Changing something as complex as Human DNA borders on madness. We're only a chromosome or two away from being a carrot, and frankly I don't wish to end up a vegetable," he stated heatedly.

"Technicians on six worlds have analyzed your DNA," the voices reassured. "They unanimously informed us that we can enhance your powers and give you new abilities which may be helpful to you. After all, we have never used force or coercion in our interactions. If you stop your journey at this time, you can start a community with three of you. However, we suggest this enhancement if you wish to minimize the danger when entering and leaving China."

"When did you learn to sound patronizing and sardonic?" Michael murmured.

He did not wait for a reply. He regarded his friends, Cecilia and Villi. They stared back with expectation and wondered if he would pull the plug on their little enterprise. Michael could easily read the expectation and anxiety on their faces.

"I want to be certain," he told them. "This is a huge step."

Villi and Cecilia watched Michael and waited for his next move.

"I'm no expert on science but I do know a little about molecular biology. The core nucleus structure of a human cell is a labyrinth of entangled protein strands. The body contains trillion upon trillions of cells with very tiny fragile nuclei. How can the voices perform such delicate manipulations? What will become of us if you fail?" Michael demanded.

Villi cleared his throat as if commenting on Michael's doubts.

"I'm sorry Villi," Michael responded. "I don't want to die or have my DNA manipulated by a species that barely understands the nuances of our language, let alone the subtleties of our body's infrastructure," Michael sighed deeply.

"We have performed this procedure thousands of times on species far more complex than humans," his voice retorted.

"Don't sound so reassuring," Michael shot back. He shook his head. "More than anything, I want… I've hoped for an Earth-based community of psychics. Why do I feel the cost for that keeps going up?" he reflected. "I know that we must go to China. Some great purpose awaits us there. I've felt this way since that first night in Mississippi after my conversion."

Michael struggled to continue with his torn emotions.

"What if we don't like it? Can we reverse the thing?" he asked.

"I'm afraid not, Michael," the voice informed him. "Once we make the alteration, your body and the DNA of all subsequent offspring will change forever."

Michael looked between his two dear friends, Villi and Cecilia, a moment longer. He wanted some kind of sign from the other two this step met with their approval, but he did not want to use his thoughts. He knew the voices were listening. He made a sign to Cecilia, "Are you ready for this?" Villi quickly caught on as he also took a download in sign language on Cecilia's recommendation.

Michael tried to sympathize with her plight. His heart went out to her. She had the most difficult decision to make. They had arrived at a crossroad in their life. They could not turn back.

"We agree as one or we leave," he signed to her. "If you say no, I will not argue. We will go back to Canada… or to America," he said as his fingers and hands quickly and silently moved. "However, you must be honest with your feelings. Tell me now, please," he gestured.

"Have you decided?" Michael's voice broke in.

"One moment…please," Michael linked. He waited for Cecilia to signal one way or the other.

With time closing in on them, they had to inform Galactic Central of their choice. Cecilia closed her eyes and signed approval. Michael turned next to Villi. Watching Cecilia, he repeated the same sign with his hands. That left it up to Michael to make the decision unanimous.

"We voted," he linked to his voice, "we all agree… you may begin the procedure."

"Is your current location private?" the voices asked. "This process may take several of your Earth minutes to complete."

The three psychics quickly scanned the deserted street. At this early hour of the morning, they sensed very little moving about.

"We've got about an hour before people begin to filter out of those buildings, Michael," Villi informed him.

"Let's hope it won't take them that long," Cecilia added.

"It's as safe now as it's ever going to be," Michael relayed to the voices.

The three slightly anxious adventurers settled into their faux-leather-cushioned car seats, and closed their eyes. Within a few seconds, the aliens began this ultimate conversion – a powerful cascading energy wave with an accumulative effect that spread throughout their bodies. It narrowed in on those chromosomes, which specifically regulate brain functions. The energy built to a crescendo until a golden glow encompassed his or her body that no ordinary person could fathom.

CHAPTER 23

ONE IN A BILLION

A RATHER FRAIL WHITE-HAIRED, ELDERLY woman stepped out from the sunlit doorway of an apartment building. She stood at the top of a long cement staircase that led down to the sidewalk about twenty feet below.

In one hand, she held her security – a knobby, nicked, and worn wooden cane with a large black rubber tip on the bottom. In her other hand, she held fast to a large canvas bag whose thin leather strap slung over her shoulder. She surveyed the treacherous steps with trepidation. She feared that one day she might stumble down them.

One by one, she eased her way down the stressful path to the safety of the sidewalk below. She thought about moving from this location. Her only hesitation was that she grew up here. Most of her friends lived in this neighborhood. The rent was cheap. Additionally, the market was only a few blocks away – easily within walking distance even at her age. She learned to deal with the stoop.

Relief from her tension arrived when she made it down past the last step. She started to move on when she noticed a new car parked nearby. Only the wealthy or politically connected persons drove such nice big luxury cars.

Curious, she inched her way toward the parked vehicle; her old weak eyes needed closer inspection. She wanted to see the inside.

The old woman cupped her hands to the tinted glass, peered through the passenger window and took in a strange sight. She could barely make out three young people lying back in their seats with their eyes closed as if they were asleep.

"Sleeping in such a nice car," she clicked her tongue with disapproval. Then she had a horrible thought. "What if they're dead?"

She moved her face around the glass as she tried to obtain a better point of view. She could swear their bodies shook and shivered all over, as if they were cold. The outside temperature felt fine – a balmy twenty-four degrees Celsius for this region of the world. Even the car window glass felt warm to her hands! With the first rays of morning sun shining in through the windshield lighting up the interior to her weak eyes, she knew the temperature had to be even warmer inside the car.

"How strange," she thought.

She could not take her eyes off the young woman in the front seat. She watched with fascination as her whole body vibrated, as if her seat where she sat made it shake. The woman reached down to grasp the handle and prepared to open the front door.

Suddenly, a wet face that dripped with perspiration appeared in the rear window and frightened her.

"What do you want?" Michael shouted from the back seat.

Surprised, the old woman immediately backed up. She stumbled and nearly fell down in the process.

"Well!" she exclaimed. She pulled up her shopping bag and shuffled off in the direction of the market.

At the same moment, Villi woke up in time to catch what happened. He took in a deep breath.

"I couldn't scan her mind," Michael started. His hands shook so hard that he had to clasp them tightly for a few second to make it stop. "I… I… I have no strength."

"Nothing to worry about. It's just a nosy old busybody from the neighborhood," Villi commented as he wiped off his sweating forehead. The accumulated water on his hand ran down the length of his arm. As he followed the trickle, he began to realize the rest of him was in the same shape.

"That was too close," Michael mumbled as he shifted uncomfortably in his seat while also stifling a yawn. "She was about to open the door…" He glanced up and noticed water dripping off Villi's wet face. "What happened to you?" he declared. His eyes traveled down on Villi's body drenched in sweat from his dripping hair to his smelly feet. Michael then realized he must appear in the same condition too.

"What happened to us?" Villi responded. "Look at me! I'm wet all over!" he exclaimed, pulling at his shirt. "Whew!" he wrinkled his nose. "I stink!"

Michael nervously reached up and pulled on the rearview mirror to see how the download affected the rest of him. He noticed his eyes were still grayish-blue and his hair brown. He had all his teeth. His tongue worked.

His skin had the same healthy color. He had the same physical appearance on the outside as his voice predicted. Yet, something about him distinctly felt different. His entire body tingled with psychic energy. He could feel it flowing into him as if he were a sponge. He drew it from the surrounding street and was unable to determine how he was doing it.

Villi performed the same body check. He patted his body all over. He even unzipped his trousers and peered inside. He took in a big sigh of relief when he discovered that department intact.

"You feel ok?" he asked Michael while he glanced back over his shoulder.

"Yeah, sure… I'm ok… only… I don't know," Michael spoke aloud as he struggled to describe his feelings. "I'm different. I can't place it," he stated, "I wish I knew."

At that moment, Cecilia came out of her trance with her body as wet from perspiration as the other two.

"What just happened?" she asked as her mind snapped into awareness. She took in a deep breath and was unable to link. "Are you ok?" she wondered about the other two before she realized her condition. She reached up and pulled the visor down. She then opened the vanity mirror to look at her own reflection. "That's gross!" she declared.

Villi then started the car up and turned on the air conditioning. As Cecilia wiped her face, Villi pulled the car back onto the main road going south out of Khabarovsk.

"We can't cross the bridge in this condition. Is there any place we can clean up?" Michael asked. He was unable to discern Villi's intent.

"I'm heading to a private VIP golf club up the road," he told them, "I believe we can persuade them that we have a membership," he added with a slight grin. "They have a sport shop where we can pick up some new clothes rather than dragging our luggage inside. We can shower and change our clothes."

"Thanks Villi," Cecilia stated. She turned in her seat to face her friend in the back. "Was it worth it Michael?"

"I suppose we'll find out soon enough," Michael stated, leaning back.

Without anyone speaking another word, the three psychics suddenly linked together. They revised a plan that began to form in their thoughts. They knew what to do when they arrived at the Chinese border. Villi had to fight past the onslaught of vision just to keep the car on the road. However, this new awareness made it possible for him to do more than one task at a time.

An elderly white-haired woman hobbled along on her way to the market. She happened to look up and see a new model car drive past.

"Must be someone important to have such a nice car," she thought.

Eight hours passed since the three young psychics converted on the Russian side of the Amur River. Villi thought he put enough distance between them and bridge. He decided to pull off to the side of the road. He put the car in park and turned to the other two. All three psychics faced one another. They linked in unison – unafraid, open and honest. They implicitly trusted one another.

"I believe we should take the time to determine the best route before we proceed any further," Villi linked to his friends. "I'm checking our current location," he told them using the car's dashboard screen to examine the local road system. He also concentrated his mind on traffic patterns around them.

They had driven the car about twenty miles into China. During the entire time since the bridge crossing, Cecilia and Michael stayed in contact with their voices at Galactic Central. Both psychics started to catalogue the potential downloads any new psychics joining their group would require. They reviewed the voices data banks inside Galactic Central that related to every detail of Earth etiquette. They wanted the voices to prepare for subtle nuances that exist between different cultures. However, the voices reassured both psychics that they were ready to communicate with their Chinese hosts. Michael and Cecilia quickly changed their focus back to assisting Villi.

Michael noticed the dashboard of the Russian vehicle spring to life. A small screen appeared and lit up showing the roads in their area. Using his mind, he manipulated the Russian-made device that displayed the local road map.

"From our current position," Michael noted, "Harbin is still over four hundred miles away..."

"Metric Michael," Cecilia reminded him.

"...uh," he thought as he performed a quick mental calculation, "I mean somewhere around seven hundred and twenty kilometers. How is the traffic?" he asked.

"Very heavy and congested," Villi noted. "Most people in China still use some kind of liquid fuel, especially here in the countryside."

"At this pace, it could take us all night to reach Harbin," Michael pointed out.

"We'd better take it easy and drive with the flow traffic," Villi suggested. "It's better not to attract too much attention. Then after a few stops for breaks, we should probably arrive tomorrow by midmorning," he estimated.

"What about power?" Michael asked in regards to the electric car.

"We're good for another two hundred kilometers. This battery pack can quickly recharge," Villi said. "I believe we stole the technology from America," he added as he smiled at Michael in the mirror.

"My voice informs me that we could find as many as ten psychics in China," Cecilia spoke up.

"Ten psychics!" Villi thought. "How can we possibly move that many people around China without being noticed? We'll need a bus!" he linked. "What do you suggest, Michael?"

"I say we find and persuade as many as we can to join us," he offered.

"I agree," Cecilia put in.

Villi glanced from friend to friend and shrugged, "the more I merrier I suppose."

"Which route will be best to Harbin?" Cecilia pressed. She felt excited to move on.

"We could go a couple of ways…" Villi offered.

"Let's stick to the main roads," Michael suggested. "Take the most direct route to Harbin. That will be our first Chinese contact. The sooner we arrive, the better I'll feel."

Cecilia and Villi could barely perceive the feelings Michael tried to hide – something akin to fear. Although both psychics sensed it, neither pursued the matter.

"Let's look at the map," he said to distract them.

The main road followed the twisting Amur River until it merged with the Songhua River. Then the road turned south through Fujin, Jiamusi, and finally arrived in Harbin - exactly seven-hundred and sixty-eight kilometers from their current location when Villi touch the distance calculator. The screen lit up with multiple warnings. Judging from the heavy traffic and the condition of the roads, the trip would take them longer than they anticipated.

"You were right Villi," Cecilia observed.

The Russian smiled in response.

"We should take turns driving," Michael pointed out. "Villi, do you feel up to driving the first leg to Jiamusi?" he asked.

Villi nodded his head. "I like to drive. It doesn't bother me if I do all the driving."

"I'll take the next shift," Cecilia volunteered. "You can catch a nap Michael."

They both knew that Michael did not like to drive. Perhaps driving his expensive car when he lived in New York spoiled him for any other. They also sensed his lack of psychic energy. The bridge crossing experience and having tapped into Galactic Central drained him.

"Good, you two drive!" he linked from the comfortable back seat. "Wake me when we get there." Michael closed the side curtains on this special luxury vehicle and stretched out his long legs at an angle. He quickly nodded off.

Villi turned his attention back to the road and swung the car into traffic. As they headed south, the border crossing seemed like a distant nightmare. Yet, everything happened, although not as they planned. The three psychics would remember the experience for the rest of their lives.

Hours earlier while crossing the border into China, things turned out to be as bad, if not worse, than they anticipated. Everything he described to them in Khabarovsk happened.

First, they passed through a gauntlet of Russian border police. Each psychic separately worked on disabling different aspects of their system – the mind of the camera operator, for example and the many security officers checking their car, luggage, and passports.

The officers photographed, finger printed and demanded samples of urine from Villi, Michael, and Cecilia. Of course, none of that actually happened. The trio left behind blank pictures, blank finger print cards, and cups of water. Prior to leaving, they convinced security to destroy the day's visual record. No border guard, official, or person in the waiting room recalled the trio after they left. Villi drove out of the Russian checkpoint and onto the bridge.

With Russia behind them, they faced an even greater obstacle waiting for them on the other side. Driving across the bridge brought a renewed sense of dread to all three.

Michael reached out with his senses and declared, "Look at the size of those barracks! You were right Villi. This is like trying to enter a fortress."

"They have ten times the inspectors the Russians had!" Cecilia exclaimed as she scanned the buildings ahead.

Villi wanted to add, "I told you so," but resisted the temptation.

The Chinese stationed a large armed contingency along the border, including border agents, plain-clothed police, and regular military patrols equipped with trucks and tanks. Dozens of wide-angle, high-definition, security cameras pointed in every direction. Those cameras played havoc with the threesome. The Chinese simply had too many of them for the trio to control.

"You can rest assured that they'll stop us," Villi linked. "Their cameras can't penetrate these dark windows. They'll pull us out of the line."

"Good," Michael spoke up, "we can move to the front faster."

"Faster to jail?" Cecilia wondered. "I sense they're bombarding many vehicles with powerful illegal x-ray devices. Can you feel the radiation?" she linked. The other two quickly responded their agreement.

Even before their car arrived on the Chinese side of the bridge, officers with red flags directed the Russian-made car into a far left lane, whose orange cone pathway directed them toward a parking area close to a large complex structure. The military police flagged their car up next to this specialized highly secured building. The Chinese Border Authority – armed to the teeth – moved up and surrounded the vehicle.

"They're suspicious alright," Villi linked when he saw the drawn weapons. "We're a large luxury foreign car with foreign plates and tinted windows – be ready for anything," he warned.

As the psychic threesome stepped from their car, a man dressed in a business suit stepped through the officers and spoke to them in Russian.

"You three come with us!" he ordered. Villi nearly cracked a smile at his terrible Russian accent until Cecilia shot him a reprimanding expression.

Uniformed patrol officers separated them. Each officer separately escorted Michael, Villi, and Cecilia toward the entrance of a large building. They were intent on taking them to individual waiting rooms. Perhaps the Chinese had a reason for isolating parties in order to determine their purpose for entering the country.

"This seems as good a time as any to create a diversion," Villi linked.

"What kind of diversion?" Michael questioned.

"Keep your senses open," he warned.

"Nothing too dramatic," Cecilia cautioned. However, her attempt at restraint arrived too late.

Just as the psychic group walked up sidewalk toward the front part of the passport checkpoint building, all hell broke loose.

"Boom! Boom! Boom!" Three loud explosions shook the entire compound and unnerved their guard escorts.

"What is it?" one of their escorts shouted in Chinese.

"Boom!" another loud report shook the ground beneath their feet.

"One of the tanks is attacking!" a person shouted in the distance.

"Move those people to a safe area!" an officer ordered.

Just as the three started inside, the entire opposite side of the building collapsed. The escorts and the three psychics could see daylight through the front doors as a large tank crashed into the opposite side of the building. The tank destroyed part of the structure, which caused the ceiling to collapse. The tank began to repeatedly fire its main gun at a variety of targets. Pandemonium erupted as explosions thundered through the compound. Officers started screaming orders at foot soldiers gripped by panic when more explosions rocked the tranquility of the once serene setting. Civilian government personnel scrambled for their lives when the marauding tank ripped their offices apart. Cecilia had to suppress a smile as fearful office workers ran past them screaming in Chinese about a "madman!" Smoke and debris quickly filled the air and enveloped the scene like a fog. Chaos ensued.

Next, the tank crashed through the Security Center. The people inside ran for their lives, as the tank drove right through the center of the building. It destroyed the camera control center in the process and all the recordings made that day.

The usually cool border soldiers fled the passport checkpoint when the tank tore it pieces. More explosions went off when the tank fired shells into two more buildings. Fires broke out. Alarms went off. Soldiers scrambled in every direction. Civilian bureaucrats fled for their lives.

Within a matter of minutes, the Chinese Army reacted by firing up other tanks. However, with half the compound destroyed or in blazes, the tank driver fled over the bridge to Russia. The Russian army had a bevy of tanks ready to destroy the renegade when the soldier popped the lid and held up his hands in surrender requesting asylum (which the Russians temporarily granted as they wanted to inspect the tank).

With their escorts on the run, Michael, Cecilia, and Villi knew they had to act quickly when they watched the passport building literally began to crumble before them. They distracted any soldiers nearby and ran back to their car.

"I think you've created enough diversion," Cecilia linked to Villi.

"Yes but I…" he started to link when Michael interrupted him.

"Get in the car!" Michael directed.

The three psychics entered the vehicle still parked in the same place since it had no keys inside. The border officer could not start the car or figure out how to move it. Villi headed for the exit to the parking lot.

On the road out of the compound, a group of officers stood at the exit gate with rifles trained on the growing crowd to keep people from fleeing in their cars. They fired two shots into the air to warn the concerned gathering that they could not leave. Villi entered the soldier's minds and made a few suggestions. The officers politely backed up, pulled up the gates, and then motioned the waiting cars through the congested bottleneck. People and vehicles poured through the open security gates. Villi drove away from the burning compound as fast as he could on the congested road. Cecilia reached over and put her hand on Villi's arm.

"When you said you would create a diversion, I thought you were going to knock over a chair or something. I believe that tank destroyed the entire post!" she exclaimed.

"I wanted to make the diversion dramatic enough," Villi offered up as he wiped his moist forehead with a tissue. "I was beginning to doubt we would make it out of there."

"If it wasn't for your diversion," Cecilia offered, chuckling, "we wouldn't have!" She smiled and leaned back. "Actually, Villi, I rather enjoyed it. The tank roughed up a few people but no one was seriously injured. Good job!"

"Thanks, I think… I mean, I did a good job back there, didn't I?" Villi commented. His hands were trembling.

"I would say you did a thorough job," Michael added dryly. "You surpassed my wildest expectations. Stay sharp. We don't know what dangers lay ahead."

Cecilia started to link when she paused a moment. She knew Michael's links well. She picked up some subtle inferences in his tone. She then realized that Villi only put the idea of driving through the building into the tank driver's head. Michael had actually coordinated most of the attack while he allowed Villi to believe he accomplished something. She suddenly knew that Michael had very subtly worked the entire operation through Villi's mind.

"Michael holds great power in check that he has never revealed until just now," she privately thought.

At that moment, a column of screaming police vehicles flew up the road. They streaked toward them headed in the opposite direction. Villi pulled over when the official convoy of military vehicles rushed past racing for the bridge crossing with their red lights flashing and sirens screaming.

"The entire nation is probably on alert status," Cecilia guessed.

"Yes," Michael agreed. "Put some distance between us and that border as fast as you can Villi without garnering too much attention." He then linked with Cecilia. "I suggest we contact our voices and review the protocols for new Earth psychics."

Twenty miles later, Michael lay in the back seat of the Russian car falling asleep. Cecilia sensed Michael's energy level rapidly fading. He used up nearly all of his psychic energy when he helped Villi with his diversion and then spoke with his voice for the past forty minutes.

"I actually enjoyed the crossing," Villi thought openly.

He felt the incident at the crossing boosted his confidence. With brightened spirits, he happily drove along the route Michael specified. Yet as he considered the road ahead, he wondered what new challenges lay in store for them. Even more troubling he wondered who waited for them. He sensed a strong psychic presence in the direction of Harbin. Instead of sharing his concerns, Villi chose to block his feelings.

Cecilia cast her eyes out the window. She feared repercussions from the border incident. She worried about Michael's ability to work through other psychics without their knowledge. She drew her thoughts inward and kept her concerns private.

"What if the military spots our car, has us arrested, or shot?" she thought. "Can Michael work through me without my knowledge? Has he already worked through me?"

As Michael relaxed and drifted off to sleep, he automatically erected an impenetrable mental barrier while his thoughts concentrated on their future. He still questioned his decision to allow the DNA change. He did not know why he had lingering doubts regarding Galactic Central's involvement.

"Perhaps the aliens launched the invasion after all," he thought, "and we're just pawns in a larger game? Perhaps the voices have been toying with us and are testing our tolerances. Perhaps the voices are not so distant but really in some sort of spaceship circling Earth?"

"Or perhaps not," Michael's alien voice privately reassured him.

Michael chuckled as his mind drifted off to welcome restful sleep.

CHAPTER 24

AN ANCIENT PROPHESY FULFILLED

A RENOWNED SCHOLAR, AUTHOR, LECTURER, and now esteemed Professor Emeritus, Li Po Chin once taught ancient Chinese language and poetry at Harbin University. Through the years, the university – along with Professor Chin – changed with each cultural upheaval. The university closed down completely during the Cultural Revolution. When the university had officially ceased to exist, Professor Chin managed to resurrect the school almost a decade later. He single-handedly resurrected the college, sought out old faculty members, and recruited new ones. Although the staff and administrators constantly rotated, the one person who remained steadfast at his post was Professor Li. How ironic then that no one at the university seemed to remember him years later when the professor approached his seventy-second birthday. They simply told him he was too old to teach any longer. Finally after fifty years of continual service to the university and the community, those in charge "encouraged" Li to retire. A dutiful son to the state, he reluctantly complied.

College students across China once knew Li Po Chin (Lee-Poh-Cheeun) for his contributions to poetry, literature, and philosophy. His publications used to be standard literary text for college students in many provinces. When China sought out heroes to advance the state's line, they used Professor Li's work to champion their causes. That was then. Unfortunately, the university no longer supported his department. Instead, they phased it out to make room for a technically oriented college. Since that time, he quickly drifted into obscurity to become a forgotten figure from an age China would just as soon forget. Despite his ignominious end, Li's legacy was long and colorful.

Professor Li's mother and father christened him in honor of the great Chinese Poet, Li Bo. Born in 1941, he grew up in Harbin during difficult years – first with the Japanese occupation – then their expulsion after World War II with the invasion of Russia, which led to the Chinese Civil War. Li's father supported the People's Liberation Army, and his family survived the purges that followed their rise to power.

A decade later when his mother and father died during a flu epidemic, Li took over the house that he lived in as a boy – a momentous year for Li. The university bestowed his professorship and he married his childhood sweetheart. Both of these events occurred in 1964. They remained married for nearly fifty years before his wife died of pneumonia one year after his retirement.

Despite their efforts and to their dismay, the couple never conceived. The pictures of successful students they sponsored through the years covered an entire wall in their home's study instead.

Soon Professor Li will turn seventy-five years old. Since his wife's passing, Li experienced painful arthritis that flared up in his hip joints.

"I'd give up all my retirement pay for one night free of pain," he muttered as he shuffled around his house. He stopped to gaze at the picture of his wife on the mantel above the fireplace. "At least you are free of pain my love," he said to her. He ran his trembling fingertips over her image. "I must contend with my nemeses – rusty joints and an ancestor that won't be still!"

As a child of eight, little Li Po Chin had few friends his age. One day, an imaginary friend spoke to him. Li imagined the voice must be his grandfather. The elderly man often spoke kindly to him. Li could barely remember him. Li treasured his interactions with this disembodied voice. He often interacted secretly with his invisible guest as he did not reveal its presence to his mother or father. Young Li did not consider the behavior wrong only unique and special.

Every day when he walked to and from school, he passed a teenager who sat on the street. He was a young man just a few years older than Li. The ragged-hair youth, an outcast and homeless teen, begged daily for a morsel to eat. He often spoke aloud to no one in particular just as Li did in private. The young man said kind words to little Li when he passed by. He greeted Li and offered him advice. Li never told his mother or father about the secret friend or the young man's opinions.

One day, young Li witnessed the local authority arrest the homeless teen. They took him away. Li never heard anything about this person again. When he asked his parents what happen to him, they told Li never to mention it.

"Only crazy people talk to themselves!" his father hoarsely whispered a warning. "They should all be locked up!"

His mother nodded agreement. "Quiet! The neighbors will hear you!" she admonished.

Li never forgot that incident. After a few days, Li learned to ignore the voice he heard. Eventually, it stopped speaking to him. Years passed. He forgot about the imaginary friend of his childhood.

Two days ago the voice he once heard decades ago as a child returned. This time the older Li reasoned the voice must be either a result of his increasing senility or a harbinger of death.

"My grandfather has returned," he thought. "But if I speak back to you," he called out to the ceiling, "I'll wind up like that teenager! They'll take me away!"

Not wanting to appear insane, he ignored the voice. Sometimes this was difficult to do in public. The voice could be insistent. It pestered him with questions. Frustrated, he told the voice to go away. For two days, it stopped speaking. Then, this morning at the breakfast table…

"You must prepare. They are coming," the voice spoke.

Li sat alone at his kitchen table. He sipped his first hot cup of tea. He nearly dropped the cup when the loud metallic sound popped into his head. Angry at the intrusion, he started to yell.

"Who?" He demanded to know. "Who is coming?" Frustrated, he pounded his fist down on the table. "Who is coming? I demand to know! Tell me!"

The voice did not answer. It remained suspiciously silent.

"At least tell me when?" he asked with less anger, "When are these mysterious persons – ghosts or whatever they are – going to arrive? Please," he pleaded, "I must know!"

Still the voice did not answer him. Left unsteady by the experience, Li headed to the bathroom to splash cold water on his face.

Villi pulled the car over onto the side of the road. He turned to the other two psychics in the car. Troubled by what his voice shared with him and coupled by what he sensed up ahead for them, he had to wake the other two knowing he needed their input.

"Poor Michael," he thought. He briefly watched the troubled young man rest. "I realize now that he used too much energy assisting me at the border. He knew I could not handle the distraction on my own. I felt his energy enter my mind. Cecilia would feel it too if happened to her. I should have said something. I'm afraid the border crossing left Michael weak."

Michael slept through the night as he tried to regain his strength.

Therefore, Cecilia helped Villi with the driving. She took a block of hours between ten p.m. and four in the morning, enough to give Villi a brief respite. She lay curled up on her seat, covered by a blanket Villi threw over her. He hated to disturb either of them. However, he had important news that he needed to share with them.

"Cecilia… Michael… sorry to bother you," he said as he leaned over to nudge them awake. When he noticed them starting to rouse, he linked into their minds. "My voice informs me the first contact in China is not far from here. We are just outside city of Harbin."

"Harbin? We're here already?" Michael said as he rubbed his eyes. "I thought you were going to wake me before…"

"Cecilia drove instead," Villi linked as he glanced her way.

"Your energy levels have been low. We thought you needed the sleep," she said with a yawn as she had only slept a few hours.

"This contact… well, there's more to this contact than we thought," Villi hesitantly informed them. "My voice says the first contact is someone very powerful. It doesn't know how we will be received," he linked. "It warned me that we should use extreme caution when approaching… them." Villi paused for a second, "It also said…" He abruptly stopped and was reluctant to continue.

"Just say it Villi," Michael told him.

Villi took a deep breath.

"This new contact may be the most powerful telepath on the planet. My voice said this man is unpredictable to them. They have tried many times to make contact, yet… Well it seems that this psychic is so powerful, he could even cause damage to the voices in Galactic Central if he wanted."

Cecilia gasped when Villi said that. Imperceptibly, Michael shook his head in disbelief.

"Several voices at Galactic Central are monitoring our thoughts to insure our safety should he attempt to attack us mentally," Villi told them.

Cecilia and Michael stared back at Villi with amazement.

"Several voices?" Cecilia asked, "your voice said we are being monitored by additional Galactic Central voices?"

"It didn't say how many," Villi replied.

Michael leaned his head back deep in thought.

"What do they mean by "most powerful" I wonder?" Michael thought.

"Who knows?" Cecilia added. "Can't you feel that power? We're very close."

"I've felt his power growing with every mile," Villi shared.

Silence descended on the car as the three contemplated this information.

Michael and Cecilia began to scan the northern neighborhoods of Harbin just ahead.

"I've never felt such a strong presence!" Michael declared, astonished.

"I've more news for you," Villi threw in. "He doesn't know he has it."

"What?" they both cried.

"That's what my voice told me," he responded. "They said it's a natural phenomenon."

"But his power…" Michael began.

"I know!" Villi quickly shot back.

"This could be dangerous, Michael. What should we do?" Cecilia stared at him.

Michael thought for a moment while the other two waited.

"You said he isn't aware of being psychic. Is that right Villi?" Michael asked.

The big Russian man nodded.

"Then I have an idea," he linked to them, "and you'll be the one to pull it off Cecilia."

"Me?" she replied with uncertainty. "Why me? I don't want someone that powerful in my mind! He might kill me!"

Villi shook his head as he faced her. "I don't think so. I don't sense any hostility or aggression. In fact, my voice believes he'll be more receptive to a woman, for some reason."

"I won't be hurt, will I?" she linked, her question a mix of fear and anxiety.

"If he tries to attack," Michael stated, "we'll put up a block and try to intervene."

"That's being cautious," Villi stated with a touch of sarcasm.

"You're not helping," Cecilia shot back.

"Don't worry Ms. Beaton," Michael said as he reached over the seat and took her hand. He patronizingly patted it for a second and then smiled. "I don't sense he's the violent type either. True this man may possess incredible psychic power," Michael continued as he let go of her hand and leaned back. "Who knows to what magnitude? That's probably why the voices placed him first on my contact list after you," he indicated to Cecilia. "You see, on the night of my conversion, I first heard a Chinese voice…" he started to cheerfully link when the expression on his face dropped. Michael froze. He did not move. He simply stared straight ahead.

"Michael?" Cecilia questioned.

As Villi and Cecilia watched, Michael closed his eyes, groaned and ran his hand down his face.

"You fool," he muttered aloud underneath his hand, "you big naïve blundering fool."

"What's going on?" Villi questioned.

"Shhh," Cecilia hushed him, "Michael's onto something."

He privately called on his voice. When the familiar link opened, Michael had several questions that begged immediate answers. When he heard the truth – in this case – it hurt him. After a minute of silence, he opened his eyes and shook his head.

"I've been so blind and so stupid. I didn't understand until this moment that I have been a pawn in a great galactic game being played out by minds far wiser than mine," he declared aloud. He looked back and forth at his friends for a moment before he linked in with the other two. "You were their insurance, in case I didn't make it to Harbin," he said as he glanced over at Cecilia. "You were also gullible enough to believe anything they said."

"Michael, what's going on?" Cecilia demanded.

"Yeah," Villi chimed in.

"It's very simple. You see, Galactic Central is not interested in me… you… or any of us. They're after him," he said as he gestured toward the front windshield. "They've wanted him for a long time," Michael continued. "This psychic is not only powerful, he's apocalyptic. The very moment he came into being his conception alerted the voices of Galactic Central. They've been exploring this end of the cosmos ever since that moment to find the source of that power. No individual ever possessed the ability to absorb and use psychic as our mysterious friend located in Harbin. He represents something of an enigma to the voices. No world in the psychic collective has ever produced such a being. It turns out that little isolated planet Earth on the fringe of the least psychic galaxy in the universe has created one of most powerful psychics."

"Where does that leave us?" Villi uttered.

"Us?" Michael threw back his head in a silent laugh with obvious sarcasm in his voice. "We're just pawns in a much larger game being played. They would use any one of us just to get to him," he said as he nodded his head forward.

"Michael… you're voice… it lied to you?" Cecilia linked hesitantly.

"No," he replied, exasperated by what he learned. "The voices misled me by not informing me of their true purpose. The very first voice I heard after my conversion was Chinese…"

"Mine too," Cecilia spoke up.

"Me too," Villi said. "I thought I was hearing things."

"You didn't," Michael explained. "They wanted you to hear those thoughts… to be curious. My voice allowed me to hear his thoughts on purpose. They wanted me to go to China. They also understood the importance of money in our culture. Ha!"

"What?" Cecilia asked as Michael's thoughts seemed a jumble of emotions and meaning.

"My voice actually led me to believe that it didn't know about Wall Street," he sighed. "I was so innocent then." He then addressed them directly. "You see, of all the pre-psychics on the verge of conversion, only I had sufficient wealth that could provide the means of extracting this man from his current location, inside the realm of a repressive government. They took their time with me. That's one thing in their favor – they are very patient. Eventually I cooperated and listened to them, unlike other humans that rejected these voices outright. Ultimately, circumstances forced them to use me. They…" he laughed in a maniacal way, "they only brought you along in case I failed," he said to Cecilia. His face turned sober.

"Me?" Cecilia gulped. "What could I do?"

"Remember what Villi said? The voices believe he will be more receptive to a woman. If something happened to me, then they were going to persuade you to press on. Once in Harbin, you could probably convince this man to convert." Michael changed his focus to Villi. "We weren't supposed to meet Villi. My voice said they missed Villi's signature – a rare mistake for them. They called him an accident."

"What do you mean?" Villi spoke up, offended.

"I mean they consider you a miscalculation – an error in judgment on their part," Michael shot back, "They never intended me to go through Khabarovsk."

Cecilia giggled despite Villi's frown.

"Villi's a mistake…" she linked as she laughed. "I like that."

"Cecilia!" Villi protested.

"Oh Villi, how could anyone so handsome be a mistake!" she scoffed at the scowling man before she turned her attention back to Michael. "How do you know all of this? I didn't sense any of those details."

"Just now, I took the liberty of confronting my voice," Michael explained. "According to one of those protocol directives, they have to tell the truth. They can mislead by withholding some of the truth, but they cannot lie once confronted with the proper question. When I questioned their motives, my voice confirmed my suspicions."

"I didn't hear it," she replied in her link.

Michael regarded her for only a heartbeat.

"I'm quite capable of keeping you out of my mind," Michael said as he gave her a side-glance.

Cecilia gulped and threw up a momentary block. "Michael is stronger than I suspected," she thought.

"My voice shared some additional information about our contact," Michael linked to them. "I have a few details about this Mr. Li Po Chin that I will share with you in a moment. Villi I'm going to give you an address. I want you to drive us there," Michael requested.

"You got it, boss," Villi said as he visualized the information Michael gave him.

"Are you ready to make contact?" Michael linked as he turned to Cecilia.

"I'm ready to do my part Michael. Just tell me what to do," she replied.

"It's so simple, really. He may be the most powerful psychic in the universe, and yet – in his present state of mind – he's the one that's afraid of us," Michael stated.

Harbin is the capital city of the Heilongjiang Province in northeastern China. It is located in the heart of what used to be Japanese occupied Manchuria. Over three million people live within the inner city. Even more people live in the neighboring countryside. Harbin's buildings are a mixture of Russian architectural influences and Maoist reformation. Everyone over fifty in China knows two things about Harbin – it has a fabulous winter festival and is the home of poet Professor Li Po Chin.

The professor's two-bedroom home sat atop a hillside community with other small homes in an older neighborhood. No one in this end of Harbin lived in one of the boxy high rises. Many years ago, they considered this area rural. The city rapidly expanded in the past two decades.

All morning, Professor Li held onto a growing sense of dread. It filled his mind with fear ever since he rose from bed. He knew he could not run away from the advancing threat. His ancestors were calling him home. He felt certain that death would come knocking at any moment. He thought that this would be the last day of his life. He could imagine no other explanation.

"Steady your nerve," he mumbled as he moved through the house. He stopped and glanced over at the front door. "Best to exercise on the side of caution I once heard."

He hobbled over and locked the front door. He then pulled down the shades. He did not intend to leave the house.

"Let them come to me," he thought as he held up his cane. He now considered it a weapon.

However, the walking and the worry placed a strain on the elderly man. This morning's encounter in the kitchen left him feeling dizzy. The pain in his hip returned. He stumbled into his bathroom. He stood before the sink and stared into the cabinet mirror.

"That is your ugly face," he said as he stuck out his tongue.

He bent down and turned on the old squeaky faucet. With his hands cupped, he took cold water and splashed his face.

"Ah!" he declared, "much better."

Still bent over, he reached for a hand towel and dabbed off his face. He rose to look into the mirror once more. Instead of a white-haired wrinkled old face, he saw the face of a young beautiful blonde-haired blue-eyed woman. Her smiling face stared back at him from the mirror.

"Li Po Chin," she whispered. Her voice echoed inside his head.

"Aaarrrgh!" he cried out in terror. "Help! Help!"

Li turned to escape the image in his bathroom mirror. Instead, he ran headlong into the edge of the door, which he had left open when he entered the bathroom. His head smacked against the edge. He fell backward and was knocked unconscious. Then everything in Li's life went black and silent.

CHAPTER 25

THE ULTIMATE CONVERSION

"Where is the origin of light?
Is it above us or in our eyes?
We are but little removed from starlight.
To deny this would be to embrace lies." Li Po Chin

"Li?" a pleasant voice spoke.

Li opened his eyes. He did not see his familiar bathroom around him. Instead, he floated in the blackness of space with a field of stars all around him. Also floating in front of him, he saw the face of an ancient statue – pale, transparent, carved from stone. It had lidless eyes and a large closed mouth shaped down that seemed to display permanent eternal displeasure.

"What an odd statue," he thought. "Are you the one speaking to me? Are you my ancestor?" he asked.

"Professor Li!" a voice spoke. This time the voice took on tones that are more familiar.

"Why do I know that is not your voice?" he pondered.

The voice he heard sounded distinctly human, not the metallic voice that startled him.

"Li!" the voice forcefully called out.

He blinked his eyes and the star field vanished. He felt two hands gently shaking his shoulders. A bright yellowish light pierced through his blurry fog.

"Professor Li! How are you feeling? Please wake up!" a soft feminine voice spoke. "I feel that I've done something terrible to him. Look! He's hurt."

The words of a sweet sincere female echoed around in his mind as if he stood at the bottom of a deep well.

"I see… he did receive a nasty bump on his forehead," a deeper voice broke in.

"I sense he'll recover," another male voice added. "Let's sit him up."

The voices had slight foreign tones, yet he clearly understood them. They spoke perfect Mandarin. Perhaps a little too perfect – Li detected a local dialect.

Li thought he must have been dreaming. He could not recall what happened. Hands gently supported him to a sitting position on the floor. However, he could not shake his confusion. A cold rag pressed against his forehead.

"Ow!" he reacted. A tinge of pain shot through the site.

"This will help," the woman's voice said. A gentle hand pressed a cold towel against the injury.

Groggy, his head stung from the blow, Professor Li assumed the voice belonged to the woman next door. Ever since his wife died, she stopped by to check on him. Li dismissed the woman he believed to be his neighbor.

"I'm fine," he said. "I don't need your help."

He pushed the woman's hand away as he struggled to stand up. Li glanced up and saw the edge of the door in front of him. He then realized he had accidentally run into it.

"I bumped my head on the door," he thought. "Go away," he spoke dismissively. "I appreciate your help, but I want you to go back to your home." He lightly ran his fingertips over his forehead and touched a tender swollen area.

"I no longer have a home, professor," the female voice said. Its tone sounded much younger than his neighbor's voice. "You see… as it turned out… I gave up my home just to find you."

The professor gazed upward into the light. He strained eyes to focus on the person standing in front of him. The blow had fogged his mind.

"What's this?" he asked, his voice gruff.

As his vision cleared, he realized that the face – inches away from his – was the blonde young woman in the mirror.

"Aaahhhh!" he cried out with fright. "Who are you? What do you want? I have no money. Get out or I shall summon a police officer!"

The young girl's gentle hands reached out to examine his wound.

"Professor Li," Cecilia quietly said as she thought about his injury, "you are not the only person who had an invisible childhood friend with a metallic-sounding voice or dreamed of traveling to other worlds."

Li endeavored to open his eyes wider. He stared more closely at her face. When she spoke to him this time, her voice sounded so clear to Li, as if she grew up in this city. Yet one look at her youthful face and he knew she was foreign. This puzzled the professor.

"How is it you speak such perfect Mandarin Chinese with a local dialect?" he asked as he peered closer at her face.

"Believe me professor, learning your language was quite a challenge," she linked to his mind. "Am I pronouncing it properly?"

He moved his hand over her mouth.

"I did not see your lips move," he observed as he closely examined her mouth.

"You didn't," she answered. She implanted her thoughts to him directly. "I am addressing your mind Professor."

Li pushed back from her.

"Impossible! Impossible! Impossible!" he loudly cried out. "No such facility exists! It is a myth! Energy cannot directly transfer from one brain to another!" he stubbornly continued as he wildly gestured in the air. "What is the medium? Where are the receptors? The brain does not contain such an apparatus! It is impossible!" he yelled at Cecilia.

The young girl stood up. She towered over the smaller Chinese man.

"Please allow me," she said while she offered him a hand to stand up.

"Oh, thank you," he said matter-of-factly. For a moment, he forget he had been angry with her. Still weak, he struggled to stand with her help. All at once, he realized that the girl spoke without moving her lips a second time.

"You did it again!" he added with consternation. "How are you doing that? Are you a ventriloquist? You even speak with an ancient Harbin dialect – a feat that only local scholars speak! Who are you?" he asked as his eyes narrowed on the girl.

"I am Cecilia Beaton," she said as she bowed her head. "I am seventeen and from Canada. I might be psychic, but I have only a fraction of the mental ability that you do," she smiled and glanced over at Michael. "I was considered pretty good at it until you came along," she added. She supported the elderly man who remained unsteady on his feet.

"You're abilities exceed mine as well professor," Michael chimed in.

He stood back in darkness of the living room. He walked forward into the yellowish bathroom light. Li looked up at the kindly yet probing face of another stranger.

"Allow me to introduce myself," Michael said as he bowed. "My name is Michael Tyler. I am twenty-years-old and I came all the way from the United

States of America." Michael pointed to his own skull as he linked with Li. "The three of us hear voices just as you do. They asked me – well, they asked all three of us – to make this journey, all the way to China, just to meet you sir."

Michael's words confused and baffled Li. To him, this young man spoke quite clearly and distinctly using the local native Chinese dialect as did the girl. He never heard anyone from America master his language as well.

"You can throw your voice too?" Li asked. "What is going on here?"

"Actually three of us came to meet you Professor," Villi said while he emerged from the shadow and stood next to Michael. "I only joined the group recently. My name is Vladimir Zavitinsk. My friends call me Villi. I am a few years older than Michael is. It is an honor and privilege Professor Li, to meet someone so distinguished," Villi said. He bowed low to show his respect.

For a moment, the astonished professor bowed back to him. Then he quickly recovered his patron-like manner. His expression changed to a scowl as his eyes scanned over all three.

"I studied your head very carefully this time," Li stated as he rubbed his chin. "Your larynx did not move, nor did you take in a deep breath. You spoke to me but you did not use air? How is this possible? I don't understand," he wondered.

"Professor, we would like you to be at ease," Michael spoke up and used a calm quiet tone in his voice. "We are not here to harm you. We came here to help you. The voices will make everything quite clear to you. I understand your voice spoke to you yesterday. It tried to warn you that we were coming. Do you know the one?"

Li simply nodded his reply. Words escaped him. This thought-speak amazed his practical and sensible side.

"How did they know about the voice in my youth?" Li wondered. "She knew its tone…"

"I must apologize for my abrupt manner, professor," Michael stated as he stepped forward. "We can no longer afford to delay. These voices have a service to perform…"

"Wait!" Li interrupted. He held up his hands. "What is going to happen?" he asked.

"Your voice will offer you a choice. After you accept, everything will be different," Cecilia spoke up.

"I don't want to be different," Li weakly replied as he accepted what he thought would inevitably be his death. "I am too old to change… and do not think any more of your thoughts to me. I know what is about to happen. My ancestors are here for me… they may take my soul!"

Li clenched his eyes shut and awaited his fate.

Michael smiled, "Really Professor Li, we are not here for your soul."

"No?" he opened his eyes a little to peek.

"We need you," Cecilia pleaded.

"You must contact your voice Professor Li," Villi put in.

"…or we will perish in your country," Michael added.

"I don't understand…" he started to speak.

Suddenly Li stopped speaking. His eye stared straight ahead, unfocused, looking at nothing in particular. His mouth hung open – slack – nothing came out of it. He staggered forward into the living room.

"What's that?" Li asked. His head snapped to his left. "You want to do what?" he asked. His head jerked to the right. The elderly man stood alone in the middle of his living room. His body wavered a moment as he shook his head. "You have been gone a long time… I am afraid…" he whispered. He closed his eyes and nodded his head a few times. He turned and regarded the three young psychics for a moment. "If all you say is true… then… I will comply," he whispered. "Do what you must."

For a second, his mouth hung open as if he wanted to speak. Then his eyes rolled back and his body started to collapse toward the floor. Michael and Villi rushed forward. Each man grabbed an arm. They supported the professor and dragged him to a large over-stuffed chair. Li's body twitched. His muscles contracted involuntarily. The two young men backed away.

"Is that a conversion?" Villi asked.

"I can only assume that," Michael threw in. "Initially, the three of us did not move about like that." He checked Li's vital signs. "His heart is beating. He's breathing. However, something or someone is blocking his mind. If he spoke to Galactic Central, it didn't last very long," Michael offered.

"My first interaction with my voice didn't last long either," Villi added, "if you recall."

"Of course yours didn't," Cecilia responded, "you were eager for a change. I'm not certain Li wanted this."

"I wonder if the voices simply stepped in and started his conversion anyway," Michael wondered.

"I thought you said that was against their protocol," Cecilia wondered.

"I suppose it doesn't matter any longer," Villi put in. "Michael is right. The conversion has definitely started. We'll just have to wait around here until he wakes up."

The three found chairs and patiently waited for the process to end. They assumed it would last about as long as theirs had – no longer than an hour.

"Anyone like some tea?" Cecilia offered.

"Sure," Villi nodded. "Speaking of tea," he turned to his friend. "I just wondered. Did you ever want to drink tea before your conversion?"

Michael laughed. He glanced over at Cecilia. Villi noticed the same confusion their thoughts.

"Chinese people drink a lot of tea. Do you think the professor somehow influenced us…" Villi began.

"To tell the truth Villi, I no longer know what to think," Michael replied.

The time passed from late-morning to mid-afternoon and still the professor did not move. Six cups of tea and two bathroom breaks later, the three psychics began to worry the conversion may have gone awry.

"Something doesn't feel right," Michael said as he paced about the room. "It's been hours. This is taking too long."

"I can't raise my voice," Cecilia stated.

"That happened to me when I was waiting to contact you for the first time," Michael said to her. "It felt like the whole system shut down."

"I'm hungry," Villi said as his stomach growled.

"Should we try to find some food?" Cecilia asked.

"Can we think about security first?" Michael requested. "I'm concerned about our Russian car out there. Someone might spot it and call the police," he observed. "What if the nosey neighbor notices the Russian car and reports it."

"Relax, Michael," Cecilia spoke up. "We'll deal with that when it arises, assuming the whole Chinese Army isn't coming after us. You were right to worry about Professor Li. This is taking too long. His conversion must be very complex."

Michael started to link his reply and stopped. The air around them grew still. He felt a strange tingling sensation growing stronger by the second. He could hear everyone breathing. He then tried but could not link.

"What's going on?" Villi spoke aloud. "I feel strange."

Unable to link, Cecilia gestured toward the professor as she pointed, "Look at that!"

The professor's fingertips began to glow with a yellowish light. Michael walked over for a closer look. Cecilia and Villi moved in next to him. They stared intently at the professor's hand. The bright golden light spread to the rest of his body with growing intensity.

"Michael?" Cecilia questioned. She cautiously took a step back.

"What is that?" Villi asked. Curious, he started to bend down and touch him.

Michael thrust his hand out and stopped Villi's arm.

"I wouldn't do that," he said. He pushed Villi as he backed up too. "This is the strangest manifestation I have ever witnessed."

"Michael, I'm scared," Cecilia said as she backed away further.

All three stepped backward away from Li until they backed into the wall behind them.

Suddenly, the professor's body lifted out of the chair up into the air. His body jerked upright. His hands thrust down at his sides with his fingers spread apart. He opened his eyes. They glowed with yellow light from within the pupils. Li's arms rose up.

The force flowing in their direction pinned the three psychics against the living room wall. Cecilia tried to scream but could not speak. Li's energy froze Michael to the spot. Villi opened his mouth to shout but nothing came out.

Ablaze with light, the figure of Professor Li rose higher into the air until his head nearly touched the ceiling – his arms outstretched. The golden light streaming from his body turned into brilliant white light. Terrified, the three young people huddled together at the base of the wall.

The ground rumbled all around them. The whole house shook. Li slammed his arms down to his sides with one swift movement. An energy wave of incredible magnitude rippled outward. It slammed the three young people against the wall and rendered them unconscious. The energy wave smashed every window in the house. It spread outward in all directions and violently shook the entire city while it cascaded into the countryside.

Most of the houses in the blocks surrounding Professor Li's house shook with such ferocity that they collapsed inward from damage. Sirens went off all over Harbin. People shouted that familiar terrified warning as they ran into the streets. They screamed, "Earthquake!" Power went out in most areas.

In the home of the professor, a man's body fell to the floor in a heap. The light that shone from it ceased. The room turned dark and very silent. Nothing moved. What once was Professor Li was no more.

CHAPTER 26

NEW POWER ARISES

ON THE STREETS OF DOWNTOWN Harbin, thousands of panicky people ran into the streets. They continued to cry out, "Earthquake!" Fathers grabbed their sons. Mother picked up their daughters and all ran for safety while tall buildings dangerously swayed. Loose items fell from shelves. Warning sirens wailed and echoed all over the city as members of the local rescue operations sprang into action.

For a few seconds, some buildings downtown seemed on the verge of collapse. Yet, within moments, the populace realized that the worst shaking subsided. On one particular street up the hill that overlooked the city, one house remained standing in a neighborhood that had sustained the most severe damage. The house of Professor Li stood alone. The violent shaking completely mangled or destroyed every structure around it.

Miraculously, not one person in Harbin sustained any major injuries – not a single broken bone, only minor cuts or scrapes. The people in the professor's neighborhood had poured into the streets as their homes fell down. As they gathered in the street, they noticed the professor's house and wondered if he survived the devastation. A group of curious people began to walk up the street in that direction.

"Look… the professor's house," someone said.

"I wonder if he's home?" another asked.

"Why didn't his house fall like the others?" wondered another.

"Let's go see," still another person suggested.

They might search the structure all day. Professor Li no longer lived in his house. In fact, Professor Li no longer existed. A new type of human being lay on the floor of the house once owned by Li Po Chin. The form, resembling a man, might appear old and Chinese on the outside; nevertheless, this new individual exceeded anything human.

The wave that Li created swept through space and time like some great psychic tsunami. It alerted the entire psychic cosmos to his presence. On numerous worlds, the psychic population could feel his essence pass through them. The planet Earth flashed its arrival into the galactic psychic community. It registered as a being stronger than any ever felt inside the collective.

"What must Earth be like to produce such a creature?" many in the psychic collective asked.

What quality does Earth possess to produce such a powerful being? This sheltered life, this green and blue planet on the edge of an isolated galaxy, this species called man, this bicameral mind that had somehow formed and reached its pinnacle in one perfect human being finally realized – at last open and free.

Li drifted about the universe inside a special non-corporeal body of psychic energy. This shimmering form transcended the physical boundaries of space that eluded ordinary beings. Time stood still for Li Po Chin as he gazed upon the far edge of the receding universe. He saw great galaxies collide with explosive forces, stars that went super nova and in the crushing centers of enormous star clusters – black holes sucked matter away into the compactness of a singularity.

In the wink of an instant, he rushed back to his Earthly body. He found a heart that still pumped blood and a physical brain that required glucose for energy. They seemed so simple in their construction and yet so vastly complex in their capacity to execute.

The body he left behind no longer resembled the one he knew. Li instantly discovered that he possessed a new body which had been recharged with a youthful vitality that he had not felt in many years. He jumped up to his feet and stood perfectly erect, taller than he ever had. He no longer perceived pain in his hip joints or back. The bump on his head healed, all trace of a wound had vanished. His heart and body pulsed with new strength and virility, although a quick glance in a broken mirror revealed the image of the same elderly man.

"You may look old in your face," he thought as he slapped his flat belly, "but I feel very young on the inside. I feel as if I could swim across a river, scale a mountain, or even make love to a beautiful young woman," he chuckled.

Li saw the mantle bare – swept of its precious objects, his statue of Buddha, the picture of his wife. In the wreckage, he found the statue, placed it back on the mantle and relit the candles. He then found the picture of his wife on the floor. He picked up the broken frame and brushed away the fractured glass. He longed to be with her – to take her into this new future with him. He thought about how he would have shared his new attributes with her. Recalling those intimate memories caused another change in Li he had not seen in a while. He shook his head and smiled.

"Calm down old man," he mumbled. "You'll have plenty of time for adventure later." He took her picture, folded it and placed it in his pocket. He laughed, "Nice benefit though."

He moved around the house stepping over scattered debris.

"Did I cause this? I must be very judicious when I use this new power," he thought.

He walked over to the front window noticing that all the glass had blown outward, the street covered in glistening shards.

"I wonder why only the glass in the windows broke and not the walls?" he regarded as he put his hand on the wall. It felt hot. "Perhaps I thought to protect you…"

Li glanced over at the crumpled bodies of the Michael, Cecilia, and Villi. He realized they were the reason why he did not destroy the house. His mind somehow knew to protect his new friends. His senses briefly swept over them and checked on their physical condition.

"Thank goodness they were not damaged," he thought.

He contemplated what would be his next course of action. Then he remembered why these three had risked their lives to find him – especially one of them, Michael. He gazed down on the American with great affection in his heart. He knew the young man sacrificed a great deal to be here. Li then scanned Michael's mind. In a brief moment, he knew what Michael knew.

"I will remain on this planet and help Michael accomplish his plan," Li thought. "First, I must revive them."

A noise outside the house caught his attention. He stuck his head out the window opening and saw a large group of people advancing up the street toward his home. Li had to act fast to subvert this unruly crowd. He employed one of the techniques he gleaned from Michael's mind. In less than a second, he reached out and touched the minds of over twenty people outside in the street. They stopped in mid-stride and wondered what they were doing. Then they dispersed.

"Huh," he muttered, "that seemed too easy!"

Li turned his attention back to the other two young bodies sprawled against the wall. He gently probed their minds. In less time than it takes to blink, Li's intrusion revealed their histories, their hopes, and their concerns.

"Wake up," he spoke to their mind. "Wake up, my friends. We must move away from this place quickly."

"Oh my head," Michael grumbled. He rubbed a sore spot on the back of his head where he hit the wall. "Professor Li?" his asked as his eyes shot up to the old man leaning over him.

"Are you worried about me because I am so old?" Li linked as he bent down and offered Michael a hand.

Li yanked him up to his feet with only one hand. Michael felt as if a weightlifter performed the maneuver. He stood there astonished and bewildered at the gleam in Li's eye.

"Professor Li! You recovered fast! Don't you have a headache or anything?" he asked.

"It must be a problem with lesser psychics," he grinned.

"Yes, but you were unconscious for so long," Michael began, "we were worried…"

"Let's rouse the others," Li interrupted. "Come on Villi, time to rise!"

As Villi slowly regained his bearings, Li reached down and took Villi's hand. He pulled and tossed Villi nearly across the room. The young adaptive Russian landed on his feet.

"Hey, Professor Li!" he began, astonished. "Nice move!"

"Thanks Villi," Li linked to him. "I would love to explain things, only we must hasten our departure from this place. Would you please start the car and be ready to move us away from this location as fast as possible."

Villi grinned back at Li as he hurried out the door.

"Come Michael," Li requested, "help me revive Cecilia. She took a nasty spill."

"What?" Michael linked. He was still astonished at how easily Li threw Villi across the room. "I'm sorry," he said as he turned to help her up. "Cecilia," he linked to her mind, "professor Li is awake. He says must leave Harbin."

"What happened?" she asked as she tried to regain her bearings.

Professor Li clapped his hands together. They made a thunderous sound that startled the two psychics.

"I apologize for being abrupt," he linked to them. "It is essential we leave the city at once. We are in great danger."

Cecilia stared back at Li with one eyebrow cocked.

"We must leave before the Army seals off the main roads, which they usually do after an earthquake," Li said as he moved between them and pushed them toward the door.

"An earthquake?" Cecilia questioned.

She stopped in the doorway and saw the shattered neighborhood.

"Will someone please tell me what happened?" she begged.

"No time! Go to the car now!" Li encouraged.

He took Cecilia and Michael by the arm. As if by magic, the three practically flew out the door, down the steps and up to the side of the car with Li clearly in command. Michael and Cecilia put out their hands. They thought they would smash into the side of the car when they came to an abrupt halt.

"Cecilia, please join Michael in the back seat," Li requested.

The back door opened on its own. The young couple stepped in and the door closed without anyone touching it. Li turned to the house of his parents and the only place he ever called home. He held out his hand. His rolled up prayer rug flew out the front door into the car.

"I will miss you," he privately thought. "I've spent a lifetime in this place. Yet, Li Po Chin is no more. I must move on. I will treasure your memory to the end of time. Farewell."

Li hopped into the front seat next to Villi. The other three stared with amazement at Li's vitality. He reached over the seat and grasped both Cecilia's and Michael's hands. They could feel great power surge through their bodies. Li used their energy to snap a large pipe inside basement of the house. The curtains around each window and the front door closed. Li opened his eyes and let go of their hands.

"Drive!" he linked to Villi, "with all due haste Villi! Make your way to the highway that leads south out of town."

"Yes, professor," Villi responded.

The car sped up the street as fast as Villi could drive without gathering too much attention. He headed the car south toward the highway that led to the next major city as Li requested. As Li predicted, the moment they reached the highway, Harbin's Civil Defense sealed off the roads.

Cecilia and Michael stared at Li as the elderly man gazed ahead. He concentrated on their next destination. Cecilia puzzled over Li's course of action. From her point of view, Li borrowed their energy to break an empty pipe. Certainly, no water escaped.

"Are you going to leave it like that?" she asked after a moment. "What will that accomplish?"

Li glanced over his shoulder at the young girl, whose face frightened him earlier in the day. He smiled slightly at the couple and then placed a picture in their minds of the prayer candles next to the form of the Buddha.

Next, Li took them through the house to the basement. They could see the pipe leaked natural gas. They watched with fascination as the heavy gas filled the basement, traveled up the stairs and into the house. Just as the first molecules of gas reached the burning flame on the mantelpiece, he cut the vision.

Michael and Cecilia turned around. They watched the horizon out the rear window of the car. Villi managed a glimpse in the rear view mirror at the same time. Li did not have to turn around. He could see everything quite clearly in his mind.

The house ignited into a giant fireball that shattered the structure into thousands of pieces and shook the road with a blast of roaring thunder. The sound of the explosion rumbled across the valley. Where a great house once stood, only a great crater remained.

"Good-bye," Li whispered.

CHAPTER 27

CHINA'S RAREST CROP

THE KEY TO SUCCESS IN forming a mind-linked community rested with Li Po Chin. While Michael acted as a catalyst initially when he brought the first few psychics together, Li would be the strength and inspiration that guided their future.

Unlike the other three, his powerful mind reached around the planet. He found other equally gifted persons mixed throughout humanity. With his clear vision as guide, they would eventually bring in others to form one great psychic community. Li understood this concept better than Michael did. His natural leadership tendencies suited his new abilities.

After they recruited Professor Li, the group needed to find any remaining candidates in China and encourage them to join their ranks. What started out as a one person's journey would gradually turn into a new community, or so Michael hoped. As they made their way down the road, the professor engaged the other three to test their reasoning capacity.

"Let's start with a hypothetical situation," he linked to them. "Say we have a group of twenty or more persons with psychic powers," he began. "We don't know how many potential candidates we may encounter or what level of psychic ability they possess. They may be half of Villi's initial level. No offense, Villi."

"None taken Professor," Villi acknowledged. "But you should have seen me in action at the border."

"Yes," Li said and raised an eyebrow, "I suppose you are referring to how you and your cohorts controlled the tank driver and destroyed the border compound?"

"Huh?" Villi replied. He was dumbfounded that Professor Li knew those details.

"As I was saying," Li continued, "suppose our numbers increase to twenty. Any suggestions how we leave China inconspicuously," he requested.

"I think I know the answer Professor," Michael chimed in.

Like an eager pupil that waited for his professor to call on him, Michael quickly put together a few ideas. He thought them to Professor Li and waited for his reaction. The professor mulled them over for a few seconds.

"Excellent Michael, your plan shows promise. In addition to providing a means of escape, this plan would comfortably accommodate a large group. Nevertheless, a boat – no matter the size or speed – is much too slow for our purposes. Any shore patrol or submarine could sink her. Besides, I don't think you could put one of our group back onto a boat so soon."

"Thank you professor," Cecilia spoke up.

"The following question remains: how do we smuggle twenty people out of one of the most heavily guarded borders in the world?" Li asked. "Any other suggestions?"

"Your idea was a boat?" Cecilia nudged Michael. "Have you forgotten the Sea of Okhotsk? I'm not going on any more boats for a while. No thanks."

"We drove into China, didn't we?" Villi spoke up. "We can just drive back out over the border."

"We only had the three of us to consider Villi," Cecilia put in. "Besides, since we tore the other border crossing apart, they've probably increased the security at all the checkpoints. Professor Li is correct. To coordinate that many people could take weeks of planning. We may not have enough time."

"Exactly," Li punctuated her statement.

"It's not like the government is going to hand us the keys to a jet plane so we can fly right out of the country without passports or anything…" Cecilia said.

She abruptly stopped speaking when she noticed all the heads in the car slowly turned to her.

"What? What did I say?" she asked before the answer dawned on her.

The next city along the route to Beijing was Changchun, a city far less provincial than Harbin. By comparison, Changchun is a modern sprawling industrial city with twice the population. The city has sports stadiums, concert halls, exhibition halls, and museums. One can find commercial districts with wide range of shopping styles, a diverse manufacturing base and a network of major roads within the inner city infrastructure. By late afternoon, Villi drove the car into the outskirts of the city center.

"We'll need to establish a base not far from Jilin University," the professor linked to the group. "That will make contact convenient," he told them.

"What is it professor?" Cecilia asked.

"I found four psychics located near the university," he replied. "All four candidates are approximately your age. It seems that during the late twentieth century some mothers gave birth to psychic children."

"Do you think it was a coincidence professor?" Villi wondered.

"Who can say what influences affect a planet – extraterrestrial or environmental?" he answered.

"I wonder why nature didn't produce more psychics your age professor," Michael asked.

"Unfortunately, the answer is too obvious to a person of my age Michael. The war killed many children," Li expressed with a tone of sadness in his voice. "However, we must concentrate on the living. It seems as if the ages of this new group lie between eighteen and twenty-four. As far as I can tell, they appear to be an energetic bunch," he added as he glanced about the car.

"Great!" Villi said. "Let's pick them up!"

"We shall Villi, in time," Li said to reassure him. "Before I contact them, I require a base of operation. Let us be comfortable," the professor suggested. "I understand you are good at scanning ahead," he said as he turned to Villi. "Reserve some rooms at a nice hotel downtown," Li urged, "with sufficient space."

"Yes, professor," Villi replied. He scanned the inner city and found several locations not far from Jilin University. He chose the best five star hotel among them. "I have it professor!" he declared within a minute. "We'll be staying at the Imperial Hotel in one of their finest suites," Villi told them. "I altered the reservation computer."

"Finest indeed!" the professor declared. "You found a spacious four bedroom suite – great work Villi," he complimented.

"Security will give us VIP treatment," Cecilia linked in.

"I ordered food trays for the room," Michael added.

Li turned in his seat and briefly looked them over.

"Well done group and very efficient too. I'm impressed," Li told them, satisfied. "We will establish our base here and make the first contact after we settle in."

"I'll handle the luggage carriers," Villi offered.

"I'll alter the staff's memories," Michael put in.

"I'll take care of my personal hygiene," Cecilia quietly muttered.

"Yes," Li linked to her, "it doesn't take a psychic to detect you need a shower."

"Professor!" Cecilia replied. His glib remark surprised her.

Michael and Villi roared with laughter as Cecilia hit them both.

"You must excuse my levity Cecilia," Li went on. "I understand your penchant for cleanliness and actually admire it."

Li hoped that through this type of informal interaction, they would begin a bonding process that would eventually form a tight-knit group. After they arrived at the Xiang Road address, a door attendant warmly greeted them. Villi acted to erase memories of outside staff while Michael went to work in the hotel lobby. Li watched with interest as his team of psychics busily worked around him. Cecilia eliminated any security cameras in the lobby.

"You work well as a team," Li linked as they ascended in the elevator.

The group noticed that unlike the intrusive voices of Galactic Central or even interactions with each other, Professor Li used a subtle method when making a mind link. His link was similar to his manner – quiet and precise. While they sensed great power within him, he continued to emanate calm.

Once in the room, Cecilia made a beeline for the shower. Michael and Villi, famished as usual, went straight for the trays of food. Professor Li's only interest seemed the expansive windows. As he walked toward them, the curtains parted and the doors opened. He walked out onto the balcony where he gazed out over the city with warm anticipation of finding new candidates.

"Is this our Pure Land, Buddha?" he privately asked.

"What was that?" Villi's thoughts broke in. He held a plate filled with food while he stuffed his mouth with his other hand.

Li realized he forgot to block his private thoughts.

"I look forward to meeting our new friends," he quickly linked as he tried to cover.

Villi put down his plate and wiped the corners of his mouth. He walked out onto the balcony and stood next to the professor.

"We haven't spoken since your conversion," Villi began.

"True Villi, is there something you wish to say?" Li asked him.

"Only that I look forward to privately speaking with you sometime," Villi requested.

"Oh? About what in particular," Li inquired.

"This is difficult for me to express my feelings…" Villi struggled to continue. He glanced over his shoulder at Michael who seemed oblivious to them as he intently worked on the long table of hors d'oeuvres. "It's just that, well…"

"You took the loss of your father hard," Li linked as he noticed Villi's drift. "You worked diligently to prove your worth since that time. You and Michael have much in common," Li pointed out to him.

"Michael and I?" Villi wondered.

"He lost his father at the same age you did," Li informed him. "Unfortunately, the same accident also took the life of his mother. Michael had a terrible time after that. Their loss devastated the teenager. He fell into a deep depressive state."

"He didn't share those details with me..." Villi said as he glanced over at Michael.

"Villi, I want you to..." Li began. He stopped and put up a barrier around them to make his link private. Villi sensed this. The move surprised him that Li had this power. "You'll have to excuse me," the professor continued, "this is difficult for me to express. Because of your age and experience, the others in our group will look up to you for guidance. I am counting on you to be my moral compass. That may put a strain on your relationship with others in our group at times. I expect you to take the high moral ground and act as a role model. Do you think you could do that for me?"

Professor Li put his hand up on the big Russian's shoulder and patted it.

"I'll do my best sir," Villi said. He took in the older man's penetrating gaze.

"That's all anyone can promise," Li said as he turned back toward the room. "I'm famished. Let's eat."

CHAPTER 28

CHOU LO, TECHNICAL WIZARD

FOR THE REST OF THE day, Li put off trying to contact anyone new. Instead, he sat with Michael, Cecilia, and Villi and requested a demonstration of each person's skill. He wished to learn about their strengths and weaknesses. He listened to them as they personally expressed their desires and hopes. He used this time to obtain a complete picture of each person's character. The three shared more details of their past with one another with revelations coming mostly from Villi and Michael. The two men bonded closer than ever.

As Li watched, he wanted them to move beyond their past in order to explore their new senses in creative ways. He called on them to expand the use of their abilities. When Villi said he imagined new uses for his power, Li expressed interest.

"Show me what you've contemplated..." Li addressed Villi.

Villi leapt to hands and then lifted his body up on his fingertips. He walked around the room in a way that seemed to defying gravity. Li applauded his effort, which was a combination of psychic power and muscular coordination.

"I would recommend a download in martial arts," he told Villi.

Next, Michael manipulated a stack of playing cards to form a variety of objects. He manipulated the flat objects into unique three-dimensional forms and patterns.

"May I suggest a download in organization skills?" he advised Michael.

Cecilia reached out to a vase with flowers. At first it appeared she had poor control. The vase turned over and dumped its contents on the table. Just when the other two believed that she made a mistake, the professor held up his hand to them and smiled. Cecilia then made the water and flowers leap back inside vase, which then returned to an upright position.

"Excellent!" he cried as he stood. "All three of you have exceeded my expectations!" he said as he applauded them. "However, I sense fatigue setting in. Let us retire for the evening and rise early for a fresh start."

As the group began to break up, Cecilia stepped forward.

"You did not make a recommendation for me," she put to the professor.

"Isn't it obvious?" Li replied. He gave her direct eye contact, "healer."

Cecilia beamed her response. That night in their sleep, the three young psychics took the rudimentary lessons as Li prescribed – downloaded to them by their Galactic Central voices.

The following morning after the group enjoyed an early breakfast, the first student from Jilin University arrived at the hotel. Professor Li telepathically contacted the student in his dorm room. He used his persuasive personality on the young man by enticing him with the promise of links to advanced technology. After convincing the student that he was not insane, the young man took a bus to the hotel.

Chou Lo majored in Electrical Engineering with a minor in mathematics. The brilliant young man was in his second year and already taking advanced studies. Unlike the other three before him, Chou came from a large family by Chinese standards. His parents and two other siblings were still alive.

Seeing how Li's sweetened offer of advanced technology turned the head of this first student, Villi and Michael looked on Li's summons with a bit of professional jealousy.

"Makes you wish he'd drafted us," Villi poked Michael's side when the first student strolled up the hall outside the suite. "Professor," Villi called out, "Are you giving out a new car if you join?"

Michael smiled until Professor Li frowned and waved them off.

"Go away," he said as he banished them to their bedroom. "Quick! He's here."

A soft knock sounded at the suite's door. The door opened on its own. This unusual phenomenon was followed by the curious head of a shy young man who peered around the edge of the door.

"Hello?" he called out. "Is someone named Li here?"

"Please come in," Professor Li requested. Li had already taken a position on the floor. He sat on his thick prayer rug – the only personal item he kept from his house.

The young man frowned as the door closed behind him.

"Come closer," Li beckoned.

The student cautiously approached the elderly man sitting crossed-leg on the beautiful rug.

"Excuse me," the student hesitantly began. "I don't know if this is where I belong. You see, my name is…"

"I know a great deal about you Chou Lo," Li linked directly to his mind.

This startled the student who stared down at the small frail white-haired figure.

"Sit here," Li said as he motioned to the space opposite him on the floor.

By his appearance, Chou seemed to be the typical "nerd-type" science student. He wore casual clothes, baggy khaki pants and an oversized unmatched sweater. He was medium height, slim build, fair skin, wore dark-rimmed glasses, and had a thick head of dark hair. He had no unique distinguishing characteristics except for having an insatiable curiosity and a keen focused mind. These last two attributes were definite assets according to Li's criteria. Chou glanced nervously about the room as he sat.

"How is it you know me? Are you with the government?" Chou asked.

"How is it you can hear me, yet I do not speak?" Li replied.

Chou then realized the old man's lips did not move. He leaned closer and stared intently at Li's face, as if by doing so it would clarify the matter.

"Oh, did I not explain this faculty for communication?" Professor Li informed him via a link. "Or did you believe this form of communication to be nothing more than fantasy?"

When he realized that Li clearly spoke directly to his mind, the young man leaned back. His eyes widened. His expression took on frightened aspect. He swallowed hard and could barely speak.

"I-I wasn't sure," Chou began. He was still trying to decide if he should stand up and run for the door. "Say something else," he requested.

"Boo!" Li said and then he laughed. "Don't be frightened. I am here to help you."

Chou's eyes started to fill with water.

"I wanted to be certain this speaking through the mind actually existed," he said with hesitation. "I thought it might be a…"

"Hoax?" Li finished. "Your ability to communication in this fashion is quite real Chou," Li told the anxious nineteen-year-old. "My name is Li Po Chin, as I explained earlier when we first made contact. We share a similarity with other psychics. Some of them are your age. They are staying here in this suite."

"Others, here?" the young man asked. He peered over Li's shoulder. His nervous gaze darted to the other doors.

"Others of our kind Chou," Li informed him, "you are not the only person in China that hears the sound of metallic voices in their head. Many of us have experienced this same difficulty." Li could see the realization spread across Chou's face.

"I… want… to believe," Chou stammered.

"Doubt no longer," Li told him. "Your faith in your ability has delivered you. Shortly you will be one of us if you choose."

Chou's expression turned to one of puzzlement.

"How will that happen?" he asked.

"We will contact those with the capacity to make such a feat possible," Li explained. "They have performed this delicate operation countless times on many worlds down through the great stretch of time."

"What if they…" Chou started to express doubts.

"Harm you? No one will harm you," Li linked his reassurance. "I will personally see to that."

"What about my family?" Chou continued. "My career in engineering…"

"Can you separate from your family, if I offer you knowledge of advanced alien technology?" Li asked him.

"You really weren't joking with me this morning, were you?" Chou wondered. "That wasn't just a dream I had."

Suddenly the room fell into darkness. Chou found his body surrounded by the black void of outer space sprinkled with the dust of distant stars.

"What is happening?" he gazed about him. This time Li could see Chou was genuinely frightened.

"You have the possibility of reaching out to the stars," Li's voice boomed into his head. "You can speak with worlds beyond your understanding and come away with incredible knowledge. Would you pass up such an opportunity?" Li put to him.

In an instant, the room returned to normal. The speechless young man stared at Li.

"You possess a special gift Chou," Li linked in quiet contrast. "Few humans will have such an opportunity. This will take a great sacrifice on your part when you sever your ties with your current world. However, before we precede any further, you must contact your voice at Galactic Central and open your mind to what it suggests."

"You want me to leave my family, my friends and my school," Chou asked him. "Is this the sacrifice you alluded to that I must make?"

"I am afraid that is the cost, yes," Li told him in his usual kind way. "Consider what you will gain…"

Chou closed his eyes and thought for a moment. Li patiently sat still and waited. He knew the gravity of this decision weighed heavily on the young man.

"You ask for much, but you promise more," the student surmised. "I could not pass up such an opportunity. Therefore, I will come with you. If all you say is true," he said to Li.

"You have made a wise choice, Chou Lo," Li said. He placed his hand on Chou's shoulder. "No university could ever teach you what you will learn with us. Life may be difficult at first, but after you receive a few downloads…"

"Download?" the young man interrupted. "You're connecting my mind to the Internet?"

"No, Michael coined this term regarding packets of information," Li tossed out. "In order for you to receive a download, you must go through a physical transformation. Your conversion is a simple process. The aliens enter the mind and alter brain structure by energy manipulation."

"Aliens? Brain structure?" Chou spoke up as his anxiety level rose.

Li smiled and shook his head.

"Do not fear Chou. These incredible creatures inhabit a place known as Galactic Central. They connect to us via a conduit in our brain. Do you recall the voice you heard as a young man, about the time you turned twelve, wasn't it?" Li asked.

"Y-you know about my life?" Chou wondered.

"Tell me…" Li encouraged.

"I had a terrible experience," the student remembered. Li could see his memories when Chou began to recall them. "My father… he… he did not understand me when I told him about the voice in my head. He yelled at me to stop talking about the voice," Chou said as he struggled with the difficult memory. "But the voice kept speaking to me. I tried to make it stop. My father caught me… talking alone in my room. He threw me on my bed and took his belt…" Chou said as he started to cry. "He beat me. He said he would beat the demon out of me!"

Chou hung his head. Tears dripped off the end of his nose. He was ashamed to recall the punishment he endured. He spent the last few years learning to forget the mental anguish and torment.

"You will not receive that treatment here," Li said to reassure him. "We have all heard this voice. Unfortunately, neither you nor your father could comprehend what you heard. Parents – however well intentioned – can be cruel," he stated. "I apologize in advance, Chou, for being abrupt or appear as uncaring. I must have your answer now. We have little time. You must decide. Will you come with us as an advanced psychic being, or return to your mundane life at the university?"

Chou hesitated. He knew that he might not see his friends and family for a very long time.

"What should I do?" he thought as he internally debated the decision.

With his hand still on Chou's shoulder, Li shook it.

"I don't wish to sound patronizing, but wake up Chou!" he declared. "All of your life you have pursued erudition. What you will learn in one hour as a psychic, will surpass all the knowledge of every university on the planet. You could possess tremendous power and tap into a vast storage of information. On the other hand, you could go back to your dorm room and work hard for the next twenty years only to scratch out a meager income. The question remains: which path you will take to your future?"

Chou took in a deep breath. He looked the professor in the eyes.

"I will join your group," he quietly spoke.

Li closed his eyes and contacted Galactic Central. Within moments, they found Chou's voice.

"Welcome," the screeching voice spoke.

"No! This is too much!" Chou started to rise.

"Do not fear them," Li said. He took the young man's hand. Calm and reassurance spread through Chou. "These creatures are the most benign and gentle of any in the universe. Their aim is to increase communication between species and to develop a universal system of language. They have no agenda and no other purpose than to extend assistance for those in need. Listen and learn, young Chou. This is the first day of your new life."

Chou began to interact with the metallic-sounding voice in his head. He had many questions and took his time – being a methodical person. He spoke with his voice for nearly ten minutes before he finally decided to proceed with his conversion.

When Chou signaled his readiness to proceed, Li then escorted him over to the sofa to begin his conversion. Villi, Cecilia and Michael quietly observed the process from their bedroom.

"He's very different from us," Cecilia observed.

"How will he fit into our group?" Villi pondered.

"I have a feeling he'll be essential to our group," Michael responded.

CHAPTER 29

THE SPECIAL CASE OF SU LIN YUK

"Su Lin…"

This was not the harsh metallic voice she heard six years ago when she was thirteen. That voice frightened her. She thought every teenager heard such voices until the other girls at her school teased Su Lin. They made light of the revelation she privately confessed to a teen that betrayed her. Eventually, the metallic voice drove a wedge between Su Lin and her mother. No one ever believed Su Lin when she tried to recall the event.

The voice she heard upon rising this morning aroused her curiosity. This voice sounded soft and understanding.

"Su Lin," the quiet voice spoke once more. "You have been chosen. The time to change your life has arrived."

"What must I do?" she asked to the air.

"When you finish your shift work, come to this address," the gentle voice said. "Write this down…"

"I will be there," she answered as her hand scribbled the address.

Following a short consultation with Professor Li, two additional male students emerged from that encounter. Like Chou, they were firmly convinced that they should join the newly formed specialized group.

Zinian Lang, a tall broad shouldered young Chinese man nearly as tall as Michael, showed up shortly after lunch on the day of Chou's conversion. He confessed to Li that he loved to work on building construction. He only went to college at the request of an estranged uncle who paid his way. As a teenager, he once trained for the Olympics as a weightlifter. The preliminary committee eliminated him during tryouts due to his height versus his weight. He did not have sufficient bulk. Despite his uncle's offer, he worked his way into the university by having good secondary school grades and by working construction jobs all during his last two years of secondary school. Li easily convinced Zinian to convert.

The other male student was Zhiwei Huang – shorter than Zinian yet still a broad-shouldered and muscular lad. He also worked out daily in the gymnasium with his friend Zinian, although he had no aspirations for Olympic glory. Zhiwei worked for the university's security team. He strove for an advanced degree in security systems and advanced law enforcement. He and Zinian came from the same neighborhood. They were both eighteen and freshmen at the university. When Zhiwei discovered Zinian went before him, he readily capitulated to his conversion.

Li monitored their conversions as he did Chou's by keeping a nearby vigil. Afterward, he put these new psychics in contact with their corresponding alien voices. Li happily added their psychic power to the growing community of mentally linked individuals. In one day, he had increased the traveling group's number to seven.

Shortly after the three converted, the evening nearly ended in disaster when the three males inadvertently opened their minds. They shared personal thoughts, histories, and even adolescent fantasies that plugged directly into each other's mind, the same dilemma Michael and Cecilia experienced. Professor Li intervened this time. He stopped the open mental flows between them until they learned control and blocking technique. He later kept a dampening field around the grateful trio, which gave them a chance to sleep that night in peace.

The following morning, Li addressed the new group as they sat at the breakfast table.

"Our plan is simple," he informed them. "Establish contact with new potential pre-psychics. Offer them inclusion into our group. If they accept, we integrate them by teaching each psychic how to best utilize their strengths. Then we move on. Eventually we will leave China to form a new community as our ultimate goal. Isn't that right, Michael?" Li added as he gestured toward the American who sat across the table.

Michael simply waved back with a mouth full of breakfast. He deferred the discussion back to Professor Li. Michael did not wish to add any opinion at this time. Besides, Professor Li had other concerns for the present, such as incorporating the new recruits. After breakfast, he put Michael and Villi in charge of showing the new members how to manage their abilities.

"What shall we teach them professor?" Villi asked before proceeding.

"Why… review the basics of course," Li responded. "Begin with blocking technique this morning," Li suggested. "I believe that would be best, considering what happened yesterday."

The three new psychics sat in an adjacent room and waited for Villi and Michael to join them. Impatient, Zinian and Zhiwei decided to overpower the normally meek Chou with mental images for amusement. Chou threatened to retaliate with an energy blast if they did not stop. Sensing conflict, Villi sprang into the room and immediately stepped between them.

"One thing professor Li will not tolerate is misuse of psychic power," Villi said as he rose to his full height. He used his trained police officer's voice of authority. "He means it too," the big man emphasized. "He will expel any member from the group if he senses abuse and that includes me."

Zinian, Zhiwei, and Chou separated. Once they heard the sincerity and genuine demeanor in his voice, the men acknowledged Villi's authority without question. For the remainder of the day, Michael and Villi engaged these impetuous young men by challenging them to hone their skills. They encouraged the three to expand their imagination in creative ways. Meanwhile Cecilia spoke with her voice and Li worked on a private matter.

"If we are level II as Professor Li suggests," Chou asked Michael, "what level are you?"

Villi glanced at Michael uncertain how to reply.

"We do not know how many psychic levels exist," Michael told him. "I received a conversion, just as you did. I've also received many additional informational downloads. Those experiences have enriched my mind on some particular subject."

"When can I download a program on engineering?" Chou inquired. "I'd like to visit engineering worlds."

"We want to explore the world with large breasted women!" Zinian spoke up. He poked his friend Zhiwei at the same time. The two men laughed.

Villi and Michael appreciated their sense of humor compared to Chou's rather dry approach. However, the two men also knew that a young woman could overhear these thoughts as well. Michael cleared his throat. He signed to Villi, "Cecilia is present."

"About advanced downloads," Michael began.

"Before we go into that," Villi interrupted. "Let's start with something simple. We would like you to refine your control at this present level," he glanced over at Michael. His friend signed back his gratitude for Villi's diversion.

"The ability to block is one of the most important facets of a novice," Villi began as he brought the attention of the students his way. "Professor Li instructed us to keep our personal thoughts private. Chaos would follow should we allow unfiltered open access between our minds. While we have worked on blocking, I should like to point out additional techniques that…"

Before Villi could continue with the lesson, all the psychics felt the professor link in.

"Cecilia, Villi, Michael?" Li called to them.

"Professor?" they answered in unison.

"Please come to the front room," he requested. "Bring the students too. I want you to meet someone. You will find this of particular interest Cecilia."

"Yes professor," they answered. The group moved from the large open living room toward the area near the foyer and entrance to the suite.

"Thanks for saving me back there," Michael privately linked to Villi.

"We should let the professor explain advanced downloads to them. Don't you agree?" Villi posed to his friend. Michael nodded as they stopped short and stood together in a group.

Professor Li motioned them to stand closer together. He then turned around and faced the door. They heard a gentle knock. Li stood in their midst surrounded by the six other psychics.

"Come in," he linked to the person outside.

When the door opened, a slender yet shapely dark figure stood in the hall, her curvaceous silhouette accented by the hall light.

"Come in Su Lin Yuk," Li quietly linked.

"That is my maiden name," she said. They noticed the tone in her voice was uncertain and insecure.

A beautiful young Chinese woman stepped into the light of the room. She had a stylish quaff of dark hair wearing a plain dress. She had a small nose yet high cheekbones with pale pink lips. She was obviously shy with her downcast eyes. She bowed and hesitated just inside the doorway, too timid to enter further.

"Come forward, Su Lin," Li encouraged. "No one here will harm you. In fact, we wish to welcome you to our group."

These words momentarily brightened her affect. She took another step in from the doorway.

"Yours is the voice I heard," she said as she bowed to Li. "I recognized it at once."

"Please be seated. I am Professor Li Po Chin," Li linked to her mind.

He indicated a nearby comfortable chair. He closed the door with his mind. Su Lin watched with fear in her eyes as the door closed without assistance. The others remained standing just behind Li.

"I know this appears unusual," Li said while he used his calm link.

"Your lips," she said, rising. "They did not move."

"Does this surprise you?" Li put to her.

She shook her head and sat back down.

"We are your friends Su Lin," Li continued. "We understand you better than you realize. Every person in this room has had a similar experience in their youth. They heard a mechanical voice and felt uncertain about whether they were crazy. Please, tell us a little about your life," Li encouraged.

Professor Li already knew that this fourth student presented a particular problem. Her case involved the delicate interaction between the world of the new psychic attached to those with no ability or even potential to develop.

"I am married…" she began.

"Yes…" Li encouraged her to continue.

"I am also a student at Jilin University, majoring in education," she explained. "I work as a cook to make ends meet. It may be a job to some, but I actually enjoy cooking. I married my husband a year ago. At first, I thought I could make him happy. I… I…" she hesitated. "I tried… I did everything I could…"

"Continue," Li requested, "you can tell us everything. We will understand."

"I don't know what to say," she said. Her eyes grew moist. Her emotions caught in her throat. "You see, my husband… he…" she stopped, choked with emotion.

She could not continue. Li stepped in and blocked the others from reading her mind.

"Su Lin, you cannot hide anything in your mind from me. I know of your difficulty coping with his unexplained behavior," Li quietly spoke to her.

He then opened up his communication to include the others.

"We will set that problem aside for now," Li continued. "Your case presents our team with a dilemma. On one hand, you would be a great asset to our group. You have abilities that exceed some in this room," he told her. "On the other hand, your husband is not psychic. At this time, we cannot bring a non-psychic into our group. He would hinder our progress. I am sorry. If you chose to stay with him out of a sense of duty, then you must leave now, and we cannot continue."

The others in the room could only watch the proceedings in silence. They knew that Professor Li spoke the truth. Su Lin gazed with hope from face to face. Yet, she sensed that every person in the room supported the old man. She realized that she would never receive another opportunity like this in her life.

"If you know of my personal life," she directed her comments to Li, "then you must also know about the dilemma I face. I am so torn. I have tried to be a dutiful wife, but my husband does not desire me. Now this voice calls to me from space."

"How do you know the origin of this voice?" Li asked her.

"I sense it is," she said as she looked at the other faces for confirmation. "Most noble sir," she addressed Li. "I want to listen to this voice, to follow its command, but I have an obligation, a duty bound by law," she cried.

She dropped to the floor at Li's feet, bowing down in a prostrate manner.

"Professor Li, I beg you to reconsider my case," she pleaded as her body shook. "If I choose to leave my husband, would you reconsider? I will do all that you ask…" She lifted her tear-stained face up to Li. She searched for some pity and found it in his melting heart.

The young woman's sincerity deeply moved Professor Li. The entire room started to speak especially Cecilia. They stopped when the professor held out his hand.

"If all that you say is true," he said, "then we shall absolve you of your duty and you may leave him to join us."

She started to smile when he interrupted.

"However, we must determine the truth about this man which is an important distinction," Li cautioned.

He reached down with his mind and lifted her up off the floor without touching her. She floated before him amazed with this feat. Her toes hovered just inches from the floor before he gently lowered her down.

"First," Li began, "we must verify your husband's fidelity. He will have to undergo a test. This test might reveal secrets that may be painful to endure. I need your permission before I proceed. Will you allow this test to take place, no matter what truth may be uncovered?"

"You can do this?" Su Lin stared at Professor Li.

"I can," he stated.

She lowered her head and nodded agreement to Li's terms.

"Then we shall proceed," Li stated and started to turn away.

Weeping with gratitude for the opportunity, Su Li reached over and grabbed Li's hand. She kissed it gratefully. Li quickly withdrew it. Her humble act embarrassed him. He glanced around the room to see if anyone found it amusing. When he saw they did not, he turned back to the young woman.

"I do not enter into this exercise lightly Su Lin Yuk," he kindly addressed her, with no malice in his tone. He took his hand and lifted her chin so that he could look into her eyes. "You are a woman of honor and integrity, able to accomplish many great things. You must face the truth with courage. This demonstration will test your husband's fidelity. Are you ready?"

Su Lin could feel the penetrating stare of Professor Li.

"It will be as you suggest," she said and bowed her head.

The group gave a collective sigh. Everyone in the room took an instant liking to Su Lin from the moment she walked through the door. Villi found her beauty as well as her diminutive charm quite attractive.

"Why is it that some married men don't appreciate what they have at home?" he privately linked to Michael.

"For the same reason those men always see the grass greener in other pastures," Michael answered.

"Is that some American expression?" Villi wondered. "What does it mean?"

"It means they are never satisfied – even with someone as beautiful and devoted as Su Lin is to keep her marriage intact," Michael replied. "Men like her husband will never be satisfied with just beauty, they lust after perversity."

"How could you not love someone as beautiful as she?" Villi wondered as he stared at her.

Michael broke the link. He found Villi's emotions for Su Lin too strong. He briefly glanced in Cecilia's direction. The young woman stood facing Li. She was absorbed in the professor's explanation. Michael suddenly realized that he probably felt as strongly attracted to Cecilia, as he was certain Villi must be toward Su Lin.

"What is my future with you?" he privately wondered about Cecilia.

Su Lin sensed an emotional pull in Villi's direction. She glanced his way. He stared back at her for a moment until he turned his head. Su Lin blushed and diverted her eyes. Yet, her eyes betrayed the strange new feelings she had inside her. She could feel an immediate attraction to this man, although she did not know how why.

"Will this man be part of my new destiny?" she thought.

Su Lin turned her attention back to Li. She approved of Professor Li's plan to test her husband's purported treachery and deceit. He saw in her mind what he would not allow the others to see. Evident on their first night of nuptials, Su Lin's husband had shown a violent perverted tendency in his attitude toward women not evident during their dating phase. When she refused to supply his warped sexual needs, he sought his release elsewhere. Their marriage quickly deteriorated with his ever-increasing absences. Su Lin vehemently denied the obvious evidence of an affair. She convinced her own mind that her husband was faithful. She remained steadfast as she upheld her part of the marriage contract.

Li sensed Villi's strong emotional state from across the room. As harmless as Villi's attraction might be, Su Lin remained legally married. Professor Li cleared his throat. The attachments Villi expressed in his mind for Su Lin upset him. He immediately admonished Villi for having such thoughts via a private link.

"Be careful of your thoughts Villi," Li warned. "We are a psychic community. We hear them too. Need I remind you of your moral obligations? I insist we take the high ground, especially when it comes to personal relationships. Su Lin is a married woman. Until she dissolves the bonds in her current marriage, it is disrespectful to have such thoughts about her. Block them please."

"Yes, Professor Li," Villi responded, inclining his head.

Villi respected the professor, not just for his power but also for his wisdom. In Villi's mind, this man represented the father missing from his life – a guiding hand with moral authority difficult to ignore. He wanted to please Professor Li as he gained in stature. He wanted to emulate the man he admired.

"Michael?" Li called to him.

"Yes professor," he replied.

"How much cash do we have?" he asked the young man.

Michael dug into his pocket. As he and Cecilia made their way about Khabarovsk, he managed to stash some yuan here and there in case they needed some in China. He brought out the wad. Li's rapid eye counted it.

"Put it all into an envelope," he requested.

"All of it?" Michael responded. "This is a large sum…"

"All of it," Li told him.

A minute later, Michael returned with a bulging hotel envelope. He reluctantly handed it over to the professor.

"Don't worry," Li privately linked, "we can always replace that."

Li then turned to Su Lin.

"Take this," he instructed and handed her the envelope. "Go home and leave this in a conspicuous place before your husband comes home. Then return here."

Professor Li set his plan in motion for Su Lin's husband. He sent Su Lin to her apartment. She left the envelope along with a note that begged him to reconsider their marriage. She offered her husband a choice. If he truly cared for her, she would wait for his call at a certain number. Then she would rush back to his waiting arms. Alternatively, he could take the cash as compensation for her leaving. If he did not call by a certain time, she would know his answer and file for divorce the next day.

When Su Lin returned to the hotel, she naturally gravitated to Cecilia for feminine support. They instantly formed a bond of friendship from the start. After they spoke for a few minutes, Cecilia's expression betrayed her concern.

"What is wrong?" Su Lin asked.

"I'm nervous for you. Do you think he will call?" Cecilia asked her.

Su Lin shook her head and turned away. She feared the answer. She would not reply to her new friend.

Professor Li held up a finger to his lips and gave Cecilia a negative contact sign. Cecilia rose and crossed to Michael.

"How much cash did you put in the envelope?" she asked him.

"Professor Li wanted the amount to be tempting," he linked back. "I put all of it in."

"All of it?" Cecilia questioned, "but that's…"

"I know," Michael cut in.

The entire psychic group watched on the room's wall screen as Professor Li broadcast everything as it happened.

"How does he do that?" Villi whispered to Michael. "Su Lin has no camera in her apartment. How can he make an image of a place appear?"

"How does he do anything?" Michael answered. "I thought I knew all about this psychic thing until that day the voices converted him in Harbin. I don't understand how his level of power works. Do you?"

Villi shook his head, "No, but I'd like to."

"So would I Villi," Michael responded as he changed his focus back to the professor.

Villi sensed more to Michael's reply before the American raised a block.

"I want the group to focus on the image, if you please," Li instructed.

Everyone present watched the husband return home after work. He found the note, read it, and crumpled it in his clenched hand. He picked up the stack of yuan and flipped through them. Then he opened his pocket telephone and started punching in numbers. The group turned to the hotel's room phone. They wondered if it would ring. The call did not go to Su Lin.

"My wife left me!" the man sobbed into the phone.

For a moment, Su Lin's emotions wavered until Professor Li held up his hand to her as if to say, "be patient."

The husband's sobbing turned to laughter. "At last, I'm free of her!" he cried out. "She even left us some party money!" he brightly spoke into the mouthpiece. He waved the stack of the money around his head. "Yes, you heard right! She's gone! Sure! I'd love to! I'll be right over."

"Where is he going?" Su Lin gasped.

Li did not answer her. Instead, he observed her reaction. He was concerned over the young woman's state of denial. The group watched as Su Lin's husband took a taxicab to another house. A young woman ran out in a flimsy dress that barely covered her artificially enhanced figure. The taxi dropped the couple at a crowded nightclub. They found a table and ordered drinks.

"This is like watching a movie!" Zinian whispered to Zhiwei. "Will we be able to drop in on people's lives like this?"

"Not now Zinian," Li butted into his thoughts.

Soon the husband took out his phone and called other friends to the bar. They joined the outspoken couple at their table. Su Lin's husband and his mistress could barely keep their hands off each other.

"The drinks are on me!" the husband yelled as he swallowed one drink after another.

Soon, the drunken man stood up. He bragged about the amount of money his ex-wife left in the envelope. Then he told his raucous gathering how he made a big mistake ever marrying Su Lin.

"She's such a prude!" he declared. "She won't even let me…" he said and made an obscene gesture.

"Please, Professor," Su Lin uttered. The young woman turned away embarrassed. "I've seen enough. I beg you to stop. I am so ashamed." She dropped her face into her hands and cried.

Li stopped the flow of images as he stepped in close to Su Lin. He lightly placed a hand on her shoulder as a sign of reassurance. The others in the room turned to face the young woman. They offered their sympathy and mutual support.

"I believe the time has arrived for a great change in your life Su Lin," Li said as he softly spoke to her, "a change for the better."

Su Lin glanced up. She searched Li's eyes. She then bowed her head low to Professor Li.

"I will do whatever you want," she said.

Her tears dripped off her face as she held her head down in shame. Li reached down and lifted her chin up.

"You should not feel shame for those who wrong you. We will change the course of your destiny today." He turned toward the others in the room. "Welcome to your new life, Su Lin Yuk!"

Every person in the room linked good will toward the newcomer.

"Come with me," the professor urged. "You must undergo a special procedure. I will answer all of your questions and help you establish a connection with Galactic Central. Speak to this metallic voice as you have in the past. Do not fear that anyone here will think it strange.".

Su Lin glanced over at the only other female in the room. Cecilia half-smiled and nodded toward the other room. She indicated that Su Lin should go with the professor. Su Lin entered the adjacent room followed by Professor Li.

He monitored her conversion. When they emerged about forty minutes later, Su Lin smiled as she sensed the group's welcoming and friendly thoughts. As Li surmised, Su Lin humbly accepted her power and utilized it with caution. Michael sensed the change at once, though he did not link his feelings to the others. Cecilia could not wait. She ran up to Su Lin before anyone else and embraced her.

"Welcome, sister," Cecilia said. She wrapped her arms around the shy young woman. "I'm so glad you're a woman," the excited Canadian added.

Su Lin blinked, "I'm glad too, I think." The two laughed over the remark.

In the middle of this celebration, Michael wandered out on the terrace away from the others. He linked with his Galactic Central voice.

"You probably knew the outcome of my efforts long before I arrived in China," Michael linked to his voice. "That detail no longer troubles me. I am content to know these people. For the first time in my life, I'm beginning to feel truly happy."

"I sense you are pleased Michael," his voice answered. "This must be a proud moment for you."

"I can thank you for that my galactic friend," Michael acknowledged.

"Are you coming back inside?" Villi interrupted. He put his arm around his Michael's shoulder. "The professor is ordering pizzas to celebrate."

"Sure," Michael told him.

"You feel ok?" Villi asked.

"The best I've ever felt Villi," Michael retorted.

After that evening, Su Lin never mentioned her ex-husband again. The vision of his vile reaction caused too much pain in the vivacious young woman. Ashamed of his behavior, she lost face when her marriage failed. For days afterward, she blamed her own shortcomings instead of the unfaithful and callous husband. When Cecilia attempted to offer advice that evening, Su Lin shrunk away from her and retreated. Professor Li intervened. He linked with Cecilia.

"Allow her time to work it out in her mind," he told her. "Avoid mentioning it unless she wishes to share her feelings with you. Most Chinese view separations like these in a different way from other cultures."

Still, Li encouraged the relationship between the two women and instructed Cecilia to start Su Lin on blocking immediately before the Chinese woman might inadvertently open her mind to male members of the group. Cecilia then gave Su Lin some essential techniques on blocking to keep her thoughts private through that first night.

The following day, the two women continued their interaction. They spent the remainder of the morning going over most of the basics. After lunch, they shared a cup of tea and discussed their new powers along with their future role in the mostly-male group. The afternoon sun felt warm as the two women sat together on the terrace.

The way Su Lin daintily savored a single butter cookie made Cecilia jealous. She would have simply stuffed the morsel into her mouth. Instead of wearing a pullover sweatshirt as she did, Su Lin wore an open blouse that accentuated her full bosom. Everything about Su Lin seemed to attract the other men. While Cecilia over the past few weeks felt more like one of the boys. She thought she could learn a great deal from Su Lin once the two leveled the psychic playing field.

"You are so bold," Su Lin pointed out. She referred to the way Cecilia asserted her will during the group's interactions. "Are all women from Canada so outspoken?" she asked.

"Only when confronting men who try to take advantage of us," Cecilia glanced over her shoulder at Michael and Villi. They were working with the other men in the living room.

Both men heard Cecilia's purposely broadcast remark and waved back at the two women. They could not take their attention away from the table in front of them. Concentrating, Zinian added another card to an elaborate tower of playing cards that currently consisted of cards from eight packs. The students competed to see which one would drop the card that upset the tower that now stood at six feet. Each time one of the students placed their card, they passed control of the tower to the next.

Cecilia turned her attention back to Su Lin.

"In time you will learn that what you have to offer is equally important and valuable," she told her new friend. "We are all equal in this group. Our new powers give us equal strength. Only Professor Li outranks us."

"I suppose it must be a cultural thing. Men always told us we were inferior," Su Lin responded. "It's funny when you see in their mind how fragile they are with certain things."

"When it comes down to it, being psychic is the greatest leveler," Cecilia commented. "With an open mind, no misunderstanding can exist between a man and a woman, or between us."

Su Lin smiled. "I believe we are going to be great friends."

"We're already great friends," Cecilia smiled back. She took her hand and squeezed it.

Li silently watched the women as they exchanged thoughts. He slowly sipped his tea while he monitored all of the personal interactions. He foresaw a great future for these psychics, whom he considered the pioneers in an emerging breed of humanity.

At that moment, the air filled with cards flying in every direction. Chou lost the battle to control the most cards. While Zinian and Zhiwei enjoyed a moment of triumph, Villi and Michael contemplated harder exercises for the other two. The professor suppressed a laugh when he looked up and saw Zinian struggle as he balanced a table lamp on his nose.

"I thought we won!" Zinian complained as Villi added a vase over his face.

"Then balancing objects should be easy, no?" Villi said. He let go of the vase.

Zinian gritted his teeth while Zhiwei suppressed laughter. He knew he would probably be next. Sure enough, Michael walked toward him with a chair in his hand.

Li knew the true purpose behind these challenges. Although the big Russian enjoyed the current exercise, Li noticed that Villi would not give him eye contact today. He privately linked with him as he hoped to make up for yesterday's reprimand.

"Su Lin no longer has a husband," he linked over to Villi. "You may now consider her officially divorced. I arranged for the legal paperwork this morning." Villi started to smile when Li cautioned. "She's been through a lot Villi. Go easy," he suggested. "Start slowly and see if she responds in kind."

Villi shrugged and sheepishly answered. "Thanks, professor."

Li sensed his genuine respectful demeanor. He had great hopes for Villi. He admired the young man's high moral attitude for life. He then turned his attention to focus on the group's most pressing need, how and when or if they would ever leave China.

"*That* is the question," Li thought.

CHAPTER 30

MASTER LI

WHEN CECILIA, MICHAEL, AND VILLI first journeyed south into China to find Professor Li, Michael clearly acted as their leader. He had the strongest, most developed mental powers and seemed to possess natural leadership skills and qualities. Cecilia and Villi often turned to Michael for guidance and advice.

After their encounter with Professor Li Po Chin in Harbin, the dynamic of the group definitely changed. Once Li joined the group, Michael grew increasingly reluctant to give orders or even make suggestions to the point that it made Cecilia and Villi feel uncomfortable at times about how to proceed. They considered Michael a close friend. Villi could not decide if Professor Li should lead the group or Michael. When he approached Cecilia about his feelings on the matter, she could not decide between Michael and Professor Li either. Matters only grew more complex when the four students joined the traveling band.

On the morning they were set to leave Changchun, the group rose to find that Li had already packed their belongings. He also had two packages of provisions for the road on a table by the suite's entrance. Earlier, the professor sent Villi on an errand. When the Russian returned to the hotel suite, he announced that had not one but two Chinese-built cars for the group's continued journey.

"Where's that beautiful Russian car?" Cecilia wondered. She had grown attached to the the luxurious interior.

"At the bottom of the river I'm afraid," Villi informed her.

She bit her lower lip and pouted for a second.

"How did you drive two cars?" Michael linked in.

"I found a willing accomplice who doesn't remember a thing," Villi shrugged. He joined the others at the breakfast table. "You taught me that trick."

Michael shrugged and returned to his cup of tea. Villi thought his comment would make Michael smile. However, he noticed his new friend seemed withdrawn and morose today. He glanced over at Cecilia and nodded toward Michael. She shook her head and picked at her food.

As soon as everyone finished breakfast, Professor Li cleared his throat to gain his or her attention.

"The time has come to move on," he stated in a general link to the others. "Villi, would you drive the lead car with Su Lin, Cecilia and Michael?"

"Yes, Professor," Villi replied. He liked the arrangement. He was eager to have Su Lin close.

Cecilia was delighted to share the back seat with Michael. However, when she tried to link with him, he blocked her out.

"Chou, you drive the second car," Li instructed, "Zinian and Zhiwei will join us."

"Yes professor," Chou replied.

"Villi, you may choose any route you wish to head south out of the city," Li told him.

"Any particular route?" Villi asked.

"As long as we head south toward Shenyang, we can discuss routes as we go," Li told him. "For now, I want you to use your senses. You may pick whatever road you wish."

"Yes sir," Villi replied. He glanced again at Michael. However, the tall young American seemed distracted and did not engage him.

Throughout that day, Professor Li made suggestions and Villi added his excellent sense of direction. The two men guided the group south along China's tortuous roads. The Russian always knew the best routes to take – roads without traffic or construction to slow their pace.

As the day wore on, Villi and Cecilia sensed increasing tension in Michael directed toward Professor Li. Although Michael kept his feelings bottled up inside, both psychics felt a level of hostility or even animosity directed toward the professor. Villi wondered when Michael would challenge the professor to some kind of psychic duel. Unfortunately, the Russian could only sense some of Michael's feelings. He could not penetrate his friend's block. Cecilia was in the same predicament.

Michael grew increasingly reclusive as the day progressed, unable, or unwilling to speak or link with anyone inside the car. Su Lin did not appear to notice these dynamics, as she had only recently joined the group. She had never met Michael and did not know him before two days ago. She passed the time by using her power to stack pencils or sense the minds of passersby.

"We're coming up on Siping Cecilia," Villi privately linked to her. "Which one should I ask about where to eat?"

Cecilia sensed Villi's inference. He did not want to offend Michael, although Professor Li continued to offer suggestions. She looked over at Michael as he napped next to her. She wished she could penetrate the stony exterior he took on like a mantel in past week.

"Ask the professor about Siping Villi," she linked back.

Just then, Professor Li linked with Villi.

"Villi," Li requested, "use that amazing talent of yours and find us a decent place locally to spend the night. No big hotels this time," Li suggested, "make it a family-run place."

"Yes professor," Villi replied. He was grateful he did not have to wake Michael.

After only a few minutes, he located a small family inn not far from the main road – an inn that desperately needed customers. He overheard a young female member of the family express thoughts to her sister regarding their parent's inability to pay the bills. He zeroed in on the location and scanned the owner's thoughts.

A middle-aged husband and wife struggled every month to make ends meet. They had four daughters and no sons. Every day the family rose, tended the center court gardens, cleaned the fishpond, swept the wooden halls, put out fresh linen and turned on the vacancy sign. Yet very few patrons stayed. New hotels with modern facilities put the smaller family-run hotels out of service. This predicament left the family constantly strapped for cash and gave the owner little money to marry off any of his four daughters.

Li tapped into Villi's probe. "What a beautiful little inn," he thought. "They can't afford to advertise. No one knows they are there." He took pity on the couple.

"Do we have any cash?" he asked Villi.

"No professor," Villi linked back. "We spent the last of it at the hotel."

Li loathed the idea that Michael should make an illegal withdrawal from a bank. However, the group needed the cash. He had no alternative. The couple in the back seat of the lead car seemed suited to handle the task.

"Cecilia, wake Michael. I need to ask you two a favor," Li requested.

"What is it, professor?" she replied. She gently poked Michael awake.

"I know this is a despicable and dishonest act," he began for he knew Cecilia hated stealing. He then relayed the image of the impoverished couple into the two psychic's minds. Li knew it played on their sympathy. "An occasion may arise on this particular journey when we will need Chinese currency. Unfortunately, we must borrow it."

Li sensed the couple's anxiety level jump.

"Don't worry my friends," he reassured them. "I am aware of your ethical concerns. I have never condoned stealing. I will arrange to repay every yuan we take. Meanwhile, I'm asking you do this rather unpleasant task for this enervated couple."

For a moment, no one replied. Cecilia turned to Michael. They did not exchange thoughts. Just a visual expression necessitated the answer. He nodded back to her.

"We'll gladly do it professor," Cecilia answered.

"Thank you," Li replied.

Villi drove into Siping with the second car following closely behind. They parked outside one of the lesser neighborhood banks. The two cars had a clear view of the surrounding area.

"I will take out the bank's alarm system," Professor Li informed them. "Go inside and quietly remove as much money as possible without arousing too much attention. Then quickly leave."

The professor disabled the security monitoring system inside the bank and erased any trace of the transaction from those present. Michael and Cecilia entered to find a bank filled with immobile people. They stuffed a pillowcase with stacks of Chinese yuan and then left. Li then created a banking error inside the central bank in Beijing, which merely shipped more money to the branch. With one mental sweep, he effectively replaced the lost funds.

"Take us to the inn Villi," Li requested once the psychic couple returned to the the lead car.

Villi led the psychic entourage across town to the quaint family-run inn located off on a narrow side road. The owners greeted Professor Li like a long lost affectionate cousin. They were grateful for the customers. The professor introduced his tribe and then motioned for Michael to bring in two stacks of cash for their overnight stay. He grossly over-paid the grateful owners.

"What's this?" the owner said. He motioned for his wife and showed her the cash.

"Stolen," she whispered.

At first, the man refused to take the money. He pushed the two stacks back into Li's hands. He feared the group might be outlaws in possession of stolen money. Zinian and Zhiwei had to suppress smiles when they heard the objection. Rather than have them think ill of this gesture, Li convinced him to accept his intended generosity.

"Michael, follow my lead," Li linked. "This man is very wealthy in America," Li leaned over and whispered in the husband's ear. He made a small gesture that indicated Michael. In return, Michael smiled and nodded. "He is very generous by nature," Li told the man. "Do not insult him by refusing his gift!"

The owner bowed his head to Michael and then took the cash. Li breathed a sigh of relief when he finally convinced the family to accept the monetary gift.

"I only have four rooms," the man said, "but I have two small cabins in back for married couples."

"The males will take one and the female the other," Li indicated. He shoved another stack of money into the man's hand when he prompted Michael for it.

The joyful husband and wife decided to give Li and his group the best night of personal service any patron ever received.

"Have you eaten?" he asked Li. When the professor shook his head, the man erupted in a broad joyful grin. "You must let us prepare a traditional dinner. First, we shall prepare hot baths while my wife and I cook. My daughters will attend to you," he said.

He clapped his hands. The four daughters ran to run hot water for their baths.

Professor Li sent the students including Su Lin to spend the night in two honeymoon cabins behind the inn. As Li indicated, the three men stayed in one cabin while Su Lin stayed alone in the other. Li instructed them to continue practicing their linking, blocking technique, and communicating with Galactic Central. He sent for a delivery service to bring their evening meal directly to their cabins.

"No downloads in engineering," Li instructed Chou. "Wait until you've progressed to higher levels first. The same is true for the rest of you," he added to the others. "We shall explore these venues at a later date," he promised.

Meanwhile, Michael, Cecilia, Villi, and Professor Li received a long overdue night of personal luxury and pampering. This started with Cecilia's favorite part, a hot steaming herbal bath. Each of the owner's four teenage daughters waited on them and acted as personal individual servers.

Although Villi already expressed interest in Su Lin, he did not mind flirting with the captivatingly beautiful nineteen-year-old eldest daughter.

"You have very good technique," Villi told the giggling teen as she eagerly scrubbed his hairy back.

Professor Li quickly reminded Villi of his manners.

"She has a suitor Villi!" Li shouted into the Russian's mind.

"Sorry professor, you can't blame a lonely psychic for flirting," the sly Russian responded.

"This power isn't meant for that kind of advantage Villi," Li told him.

"Besides, what would Su Lin think if she found out?" he added with an intended threat.

"Yes professor," Villi acquiesced.

He smiled sheepishly and shrugged his shoulders to the all too eager young woman. He partially rose from the tub and snuck his head up to see over the low partition that separated the baths. Professor Li, who sat in the adjacent hot tub, wagged a finger back at him. A howl of laughter from Michael surprised both Cecilia and Villi when Li caught Villi. The hot steaming bath with its aromatic herbs seemed to relax the mood. Cecilia signaled Michael as they stepped from their baths wrapped in scented towels. They both turned to catch Villi still trying to engage the eldest daughter in conversation as the large hairy man had the female teen adjust his towel. Michael and Cecilia shook their heads. They smiled at the young virile Russian.

"Hey! I'm just flirting. It's been a while, ok?" he mentally messaged them.

They all laughed until Li emerged into the hall from his bath. He stood there dripping wet and scowled at them.

"Villi!" he shouted mentally. "Stop that flirting!"

The three stopped smiling and headed off to their rooms to dress for dinner. Then Li turned away like a good parent and chuckled as he shook his head.

The family provided their guests with luxurious embroidered silk robes that were laid out on each bed as dinner attire. Li examined the artisanship. He noticed they were very old and were hand sewed – family heirlooms. His robe had the image of a dragon embroidered on the front. As he stood in front of the mirror adjusting the sash, the image of the fire-breathing dragon gave Li an idea.

The daughters escorted the four into the dining room where they enjoyed a wonderful traditional Chinese supper. The husband and wife emerged from the kitchen carrying large steaming bowls of food.

Professor Li and the other three psychics bowed to the owners as the couple laid out the sumptuous feast. In the center of the table sat two large bowls – one of rice and the other freshly prepared traditional noodles. Around the two bowls, the cooks arranged a variety of prepared vegetables. Then between the two main bowls, the family brought out a large braised fish with the head and tail present along with a roasted chicken that still had its head attached. The family then placed small bowls of different sauces for dipping around the periphery.

"Why do they leave the...?" Michael signed as he indicated the head of the chicken.

"The head and tail have special cultural significance," Villi linked back.

"Quiet you two," Cecilia cut in.

The wife accompanied by two of her daughters, played traditional style music on ancient family-owned Chinese instruments. One daughter sang. The husband and the other daughter served the meal.

"I especially wanted you three to enjoy this rare traditional family meal," Li linked to them. "Family inns such as this one, which were once a stable of many communities, will be lost and forgotten in modern China."

Villi, Michael and Cecilia struggled to use their chopsticks at the start of the meal. Eventually, the three watched Professor Li use the wooden instruments deftly held between the thumb, index and middle fingers. They mimicked his easy-going style.

All through the meal, the owner of the inn suspiciously eyed the three foreign strangers sitting with Li. He did not like the way Villi looked his eldest daughter. He did not trust these foreigners. He finally crouched down next to Professor Li and expressed his concerns.

"How is it these three are not Chinese but speak our language so well?" he asked. Li detected anger in his voice.

Michael, Cecilia and Villi said nothing. Instead, they put down their chopsticks and glanced expectantly in Li's direction.

"The rich one brought his two friends. They hired me as a guide. I am teaching them Chinese language and culture. What better setting than a place like this?" Li gestured around him. "Recite!"

He gestured to Villi, Michael and Cecilia. In return, each of the three young psychics recited a short verse in Chinese. Their perfect accents and fluency not only impressed the owner but the rest of his family.

"You taught them well," the man relented.

"I agree," Li said as he cast his eyes over at his group.

"Are they married?" the desperate man asked.

"Their hearts are spoken for back in America," Li said to rule out any involvement with the man's daughters. "I would say these tourists have exceeded my expectations."

After Li eliminated any hope of matrimony, the father of the four daughters grunted and moved on. Villi, Michael and Cecilia inclined their heads to Professor Li. However, judging from his expression, Cecilia noticed that Michael glared at Professor Li. She could not read his current state of mind. He held an impenetrable block against her.

After dinner, hot orange spice tea flowed and much laughter followed. Li entranced the gathering with one great anecdote after another.

He recalled the time he caught a student cheating. The young man wrote the answers on his boxer shorts. Rather than eject the student from his classroom, the forgiving Professor Li asked the young man to stand in front of the class and remove his trousers. This exposed the maligned underwear much to the student's embarrassment. When the rest of class left, he took away the boxer shorts and made the student redress and finish the exam. Surprisingly, the grateful young man passed. He visited Li's house many times in subsequent years and brought gifts of appreciation.

"When we learn to forgive transgressions, we grow in stature," Li said as he added his moral at the finish.

He then began to tell traditional Chinese folk tales. He knew many stories from ancient Chinese mythology. He spoke of Chu Jung, the God of fire. He punished those who broke the law. He told the tale of Lei Kun, God of thunder, with the head of a bird and blue skin. Li followed that with the tale of Lu Tung-Pin who renounced his riches and punished the wicked dragons that he slew with his magic sword.

Li punctuated that story by rising up from his chair. The light in the room darkened. Li held out his hand and a yellowish sword seemed to appear. Its tip burst into bluish flames. He plunged the imaginary sword into the bright green dragon that came alive from his chest. The magical feat astonished the owners and even impressed the three young psychics. The light came up. Li had his arm outstretched with nothing in his hand. The dragon was nothing more than an embroidered decoration. The room burst into applause.

"The professor is in rare form tonight," Villi linked to Cecilia and Michael. The other two nodded agreement.

"He loves this," Cecilia thought back.

Li settled into his cushion and sipped the rest of his tea.

"You honor us with your visit Professor Li," the owner expressed. His eyes welled up with a mixture of emotions that wavered between gratitude and humility.

The wife, who sat next to her husband smiled and bowed. The daughters huddled together and giggled while they whispered. The eldest still gazed longingly at Villi.

The professor pulled out a beautifully decorated golden pocket-watch, which turned out to be a parting gift from his forced retirement. He looked down his nose at it, as if his expression commented on what he thought of the present. Yawns broke out among the hosts.

"Time for bed!" the professor declared. He snapped the golden cover shut and rose.

"If I'm his pupil, I wish he'd teach me that trick," Villi whispered into Cecilia's mind. They detected Li's interference by inducing a general feeling of fatigue.

Again, the husband and wife thanked Li. They bowed to him as they cleared the room. Professor Li smiled back. He dismissed them while he secretly linked with the others to vacate the dining room and retire to their bedrooms for the evening.

"Good night," Villi linked as he headed to his room.

"Good night," Michael and Cecilia replied.

"Michael," Li openly linked to the young man as he started to leave. "Please stop by my room in a few minutes. I wish to speak with you about a few matters of importance."

Villi glanced over his shoulder. He tried to catch Michael's reaction. Cecilia regarded first Professor Li's expression and then Michael's. She wondered how he would react when the two met.

"Yes, uh… professor," Michael hesitated. His mouth hung open as if he wanted to add more at that moment. Instead, he bowed out of respect and moved on.

In the hall outside their bedrooms, Cecilia lingered in her doorway.

"What will you say to him?" she asked as she stopped Michael in the hall.

"He wants to see me. This is his meeting. I will comply with his wishes," Michael flatly stated.

"Michael, I've wanted to talk to you today about…" she started when Michael cut her off.

"Cecilia, I sense your concern," he told her. "I do not feel threatened by Li or any psychic. To tell the truth, I'm rather glad to have other psychics around me. I will do anything to keep peace and tranquility. If that means capitulation, then by all means, I will comply," he told her.

"I only…" she started and then changed her mind. "Good night, Michael."

"Good night Cecilia," he hesitated. He did not want to leave. He wanted an open link, only this was not the time. He had other personal things on his mind. She sensed his hesitation and remained in her doorway. "I enjoyed tonight's meal. Did you?" he added.

"Oh yes," she replied and moved the hair from her eyes.

For a moment, the pair lingered in each other's gaze. Both psychics wished they could say something more regarding their mutual feelings. The front of Cecilia's robe hung open. She had nothing on underneath. Michael could see her ample young bosom, so curvaceous, so white, and so beckoning. Then he cast his eyes down to the floor. She started to speak.

"Excuse me… the professor is waiting," he said and abruptly cut her off. He slowly backed away.

Cecilia wished she had the courage at that moment to just reach up and give Michael's full lips a big wet kiss. The timing did not feel right. She took a deep breath and retired into her bedroom.

Michael walked up the hall to Li's room. Before he could knock on the door, it swung wide open on its own. He found the professor sitting cross-legged on his prayer rug with incense and candles burning next to a statue of Buddha on a table nearby. Li glanced up and greeted Michael warmly.

"Come in, Michael," he said. "We have much to discuss. Sit down. Be comfortable."

Using his mind, Li closed the door behind Michael.

"Professor Li," Michael bowed out of respect.

Li noticed that Michael bowed more frequently to him lately. While he said nothing of the ancient Chinese custom, it seemed unusual to see an American perform the humbling gesture. While Michael may have blocked his friends, Li knew the young man had much on his mind and most of it concerned him.

Michael gracefully sat on the floor. He felt at ease in this environment.

Professor Li closed his eyes and gently linked into Michael's mind. Li then told Michael he wanted to discuss Michael's plans regarding what the group should do when they left China.

"Tell me about your ideas for a psychic community," Li requested.

"Very well," the young man began. "Ever since I first learned from my voice that the world had other people like me, I've wanted to form a community of linked minds apart from humanity. We could live and work together in a free and open setting without social restraints."

"I see," Li added, "would you elaborate?"

"I believe we should establish a base of operations without the usual governing bodies," Michael freely expressed. "We would not need formal leaders since we openly communicate. Being equal, we would emphasize our strengths, explore the cosmos through Galactic Central – possibly bring back information and experience to improve our lives."

"Fascinating, go on Michael, tell me more." Li encouraged.

"Professor, I…" Michael started and then he abruptly stopped.

He had wanted to speak his mind all day since they rose that morning. He wanted to be open and honest with his feelings – especially as it concerned Li. He cleared his throat. However, Li's eyes remained closed. He did not move.

"More than anyone I've ever known, or could hope to know, I respect your wisdom and experience," Michael linked to Li. Conflict tore at his true feelings. Finally, he felt he could no longer hold his feelings back. He blurted them into Li's mind. "I want you to be the leader of this expedition. You have great power. We all sense it. Moreover, you have years, even decades of experience teaching college…"

Michael waited for Professor Li to offer some opinion. The elderly man did not move or return the link. He remained motionless. His hands rested in his lap and his eyes remained closed.

"I know Galactic Central converted me first and that I have some experience being psychic," Michael continued. "But you possess wisdom and power greater than any I could ever have. I think I express the feelings of everyone. We look to you for leadership and guidance. Please say you will guide us."

Michael bent low toward the venerable old man. His face nearly touched the floor. He remained in that position without rising when he continued to address Li.

"You are the greatest teacher... the greatest man I've ever known. I have never trusted anyone as I do you. I ask for your help and guidance. You alone are my professor, my teacher, my guide, my master... Master Li," Michael linked. His last words choked him with emotion. Michael's eyes filled with water.

The genuine demeanor, humility, and sincerity in Michael's heart moved Li. The elderly Chinese professor opened his eyes. He kindly gazed down upon Michael's prostrate figure.

"Wisdom begins when one discovers that is what they lack," he said as he bent forward and gently lifted the young man's head.

Li had a probing gaze in his eyes – a look that penetrated the exterior of a person and revealed the very depths of one's soul. No hidden thought or desire could hide from his probe. He could quickly tell the difference between sincerity and guile. His face took on a saddened expression.

"You had a terrible time in your youth Michael," the old man spoke. His eyes glistened as he looked on Michael with empathy. "You went through hell... losing your parents... suffering unspeakable treatment inside Dr. Hami's psychiatric adolescent asylum. He inflicted great harm on you. Yet, you not only survived intact but you also developed an appreciation for freedom that many of us take for granted. Unbelievably Michael that is also a life experience – one I never had. I gained knowledge found mostly in books. You understand the darker side of humanity – the cruelty and coldness when you sought love and support."

Li shifted on his rug. "You may believe that experience a waste. Yet, exposure to that sort of evil teaches us that all is not sunshine and flowers in the world. At times, we must conquer terrible obstacles. When we overcome our worst enemies and fears – not through violence but through understanding and compassion – we gain an inner strength of character not found within any book or inside the walls of any university. Enduring tribulations such as those you experienced can harden a person's heart. They give rise to feelings of anger, bitterness, and resentment. Some people even develop mania. Instead, you learned tolerance, pity, and empathy. Those reactions alone speak volumes about your character, more than all the tests any university could administer. You passed the test of life. It is I who admire and envy you, Michael Tyler."

"You envy me Master Li?" Michael said as he blinked away his tears. He looked up into the old man's sad eyes. "I don't know anything," he continued. "I used to be angry with those people who mistreated me. I carried that resentment around with me for a long time. Then when my parents died… I felt so sad inside Master Li. I would drown my sorrow with wine. It was the only way that I could dull the pain."

Michael could hardly express his feelings. The pain associated with those memories seemed too fresh to recall. Li closed his eyes. He reached out and gently probed the young man's mind.

"The pain is still there Michael," Li pointed out. "It will never leave. It is like the scar from an injury that never fades with time. Yet, this is but one moment at the start of your life. You have only begun to form an understanding of your true potential. I feel new hope in your heart that will lift your spirit. Along with your past sadness, love reaches out to you from the others who share those feelings."

Li pictured Cecilia and shared the vision with Michael.

"The young woman thinks quite highly of you," Li said to him. "More than once during your journey, you exchanged intimate thoughts and desires. Yet, you both remain true to your ideals. That is admirable too."

Li shifted in his position and continued.

"I will assume the leadership role you suggest while we are in China," he said. "When we move on Michael, we will discuss the role of leadership in our new community. Perhaps it will no longer have a purpose as we all assume different functions in our special closed-knit association of minds."

"Very well master," Michael thought to him. He bowed once more and started to rise. Li reached out and took hold of his arm.

"This title of 'master,' which you have bestowed upon me," Li continued. "I am somewhat uncomfortable with it. However, I see in your mind that it gives you great pleasure and that you say it as a sign of respect to me. I will tolerate it for now but only from you Michael. If I am to be your teacher, as you so secretly desire, then you must assume the role of pupil. That is something which I have a great deal of experience as I have been a professor for fifty years. Therefore, we shall continue our relationship this way – I as your teacher and you my pupil – until you feel you have learned what you need to know to go onward with your life."

Michael gazed hopefully once more at the old man's face. He did secretly desire the professor to teach him. Michael relaxed after he aired his feelings. He wondered how Li would react when he brought the suggestion up. He knew that Li kept his great power in check by using a level of wisdom Michael wished he possessed.

"Since we have resolved that conflict between us, I wish to discuss other matters," Master Li said.

"Master?" Michael replied. He cocked his head.

"Purely social Michael," Li smiled. "If I am to be your teacher, I wish to know my pupil better."

"What would you like to know about me that your probe cannot tell you?" Michael responded.

"For one, I wish to hear about your journey... as you would tell it," he offered.

Michael relaxed, stretching out his legs as he leaned on one elbow. Master Li poured out tea for both of them as Michael relayed the story of his journey. He began with New York and then went on to describe his meeting with Cecilia. He described how they crossed the Pacific inside the submarine. He then told Master Li about sailing the Sea of Okhotsk in the fog and hiking across the stone-covered wasteland.

"...do you mean to say that when the boat tipped on its side, she saved her old clothes and cast the briefcase filled with treasure into the sea?" Li reiterated, half-smiling.

"That was partly my fault," Michael mentally replied while he took a sip of tea. "We hadn't mastered the power of manipulation. I tried to stop it. I could only watch with dread as it flew away. It skipped over the waves like a stone until it sunk to the bottom. I never told Cecilia about its exact contents." Michael's memory stopped with him inside the pilothouse as he stared out over the rough ocean waves.

Li suddenly burst out with raucous laughter which startled the young man. Li's reaction made him smile too. The two men laughed together as they shared Michael's memory of his face frozen in an expression of astonishment. When the laughter finally died down, Li linked first.

"Have you considered it a great loss?" he wondered.

"Oh no," Michael said as he sat up. "Cecilia is worth more to me than anything in that briefcase."

"Well put Michael," Li noted. "The wasteland that followed had to be difficult crossing, at least from how you remembered it."

"It was terrible... poor Cecilia," Michael commented as he thought back. "I wish I could make it up to her somehow... dragging her across those rocks was brutal."

"I have an idea for a present you can give her when we finally settle into our village," Li offered.

"What?" Michael asked.

"Buy her some nice hand lotion," Li said. "Trust me. She'll remember."

"Thanks for the tip," Michael nodded. "Now would you render me a favor?"

"What would you like?" Li responded.

"Tell me what it was like being a professor for all those years," Michael requested.

"I was not a professor the entire time," Li explained. "During one period, the state closed the university. That was a dark time in China. My wife and I thought the Communists would kill us. Instead, those in control recalled the important role my father played in the revolution. They put me to good use. I wrote words of praise for the state. I watched as they paraded my slogans up and down the streets. They hung them around the necks of my colleagues and screamed at them until they wept. It was a humiliating lesson in living with a totalitarian régime."

"This was during the Cultural Revolution," Michael put in.

"You know your history," Li said, surprised. "This revolution had nothing cultural about it. They brutalized my friends and imprisoned many of them."

"Why didn't you go to prison?" Michael wondered.

"My father fought at Mao Zedong's side in the CCP during the Manchurian uprisings. The war with Japan had only just ended when civil war broke out," Li explained, "Chinese fought and killed other Chinese. War is a terrible thing. Civil War is worse – brother against brother, families against families. Fortunately for my father, he ended up on the winning side. Once during a visit to Harbin the Chairman came to our house. He remembered my father. I discovered that my father saved Mao's life during a battle. Years later, when the Communists drove most professors into the fields as laborers, the party spared my wife and me. The Chairman intervened on my behalf. To find some use for me, the local committee encouraged me to write work slogans for the state. I did until the Cultural Revolution collapsed. Then we reopened the university and reinstated my friends – at least the ones not driven mad or put to death. I worked the remaining years clinging to a department no longer in favor. My work is no longer acceptable to the new leadership and hence my retirement," he quietly linked. "They did give me a beautiful gold watch – paid for by the party."

Master Li fingered the chain as he hung his head recalling those memories. Michael could sense the mixture of resentment and sadness. He wanted to offer some kind words but could think of nothing to say. Li then pulled out his pocket watch. He popped open the cover and glanced down at the face. This made Michael smile.

"You don't have to pull that trick on me," Michael said rising. "I know when it's time to leave."

Li smiled, "I enjoyed your stories Michael. Good night."

"Good night Master Li."

CHAPTER 31

BUBBLE TECHNIQUE

THE FOLLOWING MORNING, THE INN's proprietors treated their guests to an early breakfast in a private room for all eight members of the group. Li mentally banished their hosts from the room before he addressed the group.

"Michael and I had a interesting tea last night. He told me of his journey to China. Michael made an important discovery along the way. I would like to share that with you," Li told them.

He brought up the story of Michael and Cecilia on the boat in the Sea of Okhotsk and their encounter with the submarines. However, Li left out the part about the briefcase. He wanted to make a point about sensing the conflict below them at sea.

"Nice work bucko," Villi privately linked his comment to Michael. He noticed how Michael seemed brighter this morning. "Evidently the meeting went well last night," he thought to him.

Michael nodded back to Villi and then glanced over at Li. He was curious why he should bring up this part of his journey.

"After you discovered you could move objects with your mind, you collapsed on the floor of the boat, correct?" Li asked Cecilia.

"Yes," she confirmed. "We had no psychic energy left. Stopping the torpedoes completely drained us."

"Why didn't the Russian submarine surface and hold you prisoner until a patrol ship took you back to Russia?" Li speculated. "That would have been the normal practice. Didn't you ever wonder?"

"At the time, I only thought of... our predicament," Michael replied. He was puzzled by Li's question. He tossed a quick glance toward Cecilia. She remained focused on Li.

"Last night after you left our meeting, Michael, I spoke with the voices regarding what happened that day. I can now reveal why the Russian sub missed you that day," Li said. He directed his comments to Villi, Michael, and Cecilia. "You three possess the ability to form a psychic bubble."

"Psychic bubble?" Michael asked. "For what purpose?"

"It turns out the psychic bubble has many uses. For example, psychics can hide or conceal themselves inside. Or they can manipulate the way they are seen by others without having to enter their thoughts," Li told them. "This would work to your advantage in a large crowd." Li glanced toward Michael. "Consider this the first lesson in advanced psychic knowledge," he privately linked.

"Show me," Villi spoke up. He was always eager to advance his knowledge in psychic power.

Li held out his hand. A tiny point of light began to glow in the palm of his hand.

"Observe carefully how I gather my psychic energy. Try to focus your energy on one spot. Expand its size – make it hollow inside – enough to form a sphere," he said. They could feel Li's energy as he concentrated his psychic power into this space.

In the palm of his hand, a translucent silvery sphere formed about the size of a baseball. The outside alternated in pale colors like an enlarged soap bubble, yet the surface shimmered.

"If I concentrate my energy flow, I can expand the bubble," he demonstrated. The sphere grew in diameter. "Notice the change within its interior."

As it enlarged, his hand disappeared within the sphere. Suddenly in its place a claw appeared. Su Lin shrieked. The others glanced her way and chuckled. Embarrassed by her reaction, she blushed.

"Since I focus and control my energy, I can impose any image on the exterior for others to see," Li explained. "I can make it even larger to encompass my body. This will render me invisible or I can appear as something else."

The group stared at Li astonished by this latest discovery.

"How did you uncover this from my story?" Michael wondered.

"When you told me about the part of your journey across the Sea of Okhotsk," Li stated. "I realized that something about the way it ended did not fit. The Russian sub commander would have surfaced after the attack to investigate your ship. After I thought about it, I checked with your voice…"

"You can contact our voices?" Cecilia spoke up.

"Yes," Li said, matter-of-factly. "They are not some private secretary for you only."

"See?" Villi nudged her.

"They surrounded your vessel with an identical energy field. It was similar to this one, albeit temporarily," Li told them. "They held it long enough for your boat to escape."

"How did they do that?" Michael asked.

"Through your mind link with them," Li answered. "While you lay unconscious, you had no resistance in the link. This allowed them to pour a large amount of psychic energy through the conduit," he pointed out. Li then saw Michael's reaction on his face. "I know what you're thinking Michael. The voices violated their protocol of non-interference."

"I believe the thought crossed my mind… psychic," Michael shot back.

Li smiled and explained. "The voices only did that to protect you. Remember, they had a vested interest in your completion of this journey."

"True," Michael acknowledged. He gave up on the objection that the voices used his mind without his knowledge and violated the non-interference rule.

Li then addressed his three advanced psychics.

"I want you three to work on creating this phenomenon," he told them. "The rest of you will be able to do this once you level up. We may need every psychic tool at our disposal before this journey is over."

"This psychic bubble must require a great amount of energy. Using that much energy would drain us and leave us weak professor. Other than temporary camouflage, how else could we apply it? If you don't mind me asking," Villi linked.

"I have a feeling this psychic bubble technique may give our group the kind of advantage we need to survive in a hostile environment," Li explained. "Concentrate on keeping this new discipline in force for as long as you can maintain it without draining your reserves. Consider it a challenge Villi. The person that holds the bubble the longest will…"

"Win a new car?" Villi spoke up.

The students laughed at his joke. Even Li smiled. His comic timing ended breakfast on a positive note. Using sign language that surprised Villi, Michael and Cecilia, Master Li quickly signed the time to depart. The students recognized his hand signs and followed like puppies. Li then leaned over to the experienced trio.

"They downloaded sign language last night," he informed them. "I thought it would be useful," he added and winked. Master Li took the memory of their visit from the minds of family owners. He placed in their mind that they possessed the cash because of saving it over the years.

Once outside the hotel, the group separated into the two cars. They left the city of Siping for their next major destination, Shenyang. Li kept the seating arrangement between cars the same. However, he decided to take the lead car today. He placed Zinian and Zhiwei in the back seat of the front car with him and requested Chou drive. Su Lin sat next to Villi who drove the second car. Michael and Cecilia sat in the back.

While Michael had not mentioned the "Master Li" part to Cecilia or Villi, his friends recognized that Michael turned to Li for advice several times that morning. They sensed Michael and Li made a peaceable arrangement. The two seemed amiable enough to share an occasional joke or a private thought. This pleased both Cecilia and Villi. It seemed to them that a great emotional weight of gloom had lifted from Michael.

As the group pulled out, Li directed Villi to find additional out-of-the-way places to stay near their next destination. He did not wish the large group to attract any unnecessary attention when they moved in and out of hotels.

"We might be easily noticed in a way none of us will detect," Li observed.

"Will this be our final group?" Michael asked as their cars pulled into traffic.

"I feel confident we'll add more psychics before we leave China," Li answered. "I sense the presence of others ahead." He turned his attention back to Villi. "I've decided to map our course from the lead car today Villi."

"Steer our course professor," Villi responded.

"Drive," Li instructed.

"Where to professor?" Chou asked.

"Take us back through Siping," Li suggested. "From there we can take the main road south to Shenyang."

"Yes sir," Chou replied.

As the car pulled further away from the inn and headed through the center of Siping, Li reached south with his thoughts. He began to search for the next psychic when something stopped him from going further. He sensed an area he could not penetrate. It felt strange, cold and forbidding as he probed around its exterior.

"That's odd," he thought.

CHAPTER 32

ASSAILANT UNKNOWN

"Ping! Ping!"

Michael and Cecilia heard something strike their vehicle.

"What was that?" Cecilia sprang up. She turned around to see what made the sound.

More loud cracking sounds followed. This time the couple sensed that a bullet struck the back of the car's trunk. It made a loud thud into the sheet metal. Another bullet quickly followed that one. Michael whirled around and joined Cecilia. The two watched as three military-style vehicles zoomed up the road after them. Each vehicle held uniformed men with drawn weapons. They were shooting at them. Michael turned to Cecilia.

"What's that all about?" he wondered. Before she could answer, they heard the excited voices of men shouting from inside the chasing vehicles.

"That's them!" one of them yelled from inside the lead vehicle. "The report said they're armed and dangerous! Use deadly force!"

"Stop that car and surrender!" a voice shouted into a loudspeaker.

"Hey!" Michael linked forward to Li. "I don't know if you're aware of this but somebody is shooting at us back here!"

"This is the People's Army! Pull over at once!" a man shouted via the loudspeaker.

Instinctively, the student in the front car backed off on the gas and started to slow down. Villi nearly ran into the front car.

"Professor Li," Villi urgently linked, "as a policeman, I would ordinarily say pull over. But under these circumstances, I would not advise it, sir…"

Li quickly caught on to Villi's drift. When he tried to enter the mind of the pursuing driver, he had difficulty altering his thought processes. Then he recalled what Michael told him about using psychic ability on the emotionally overwrought.

"I discovered that during extreme emotional duress, I could not pierce the person's troubled mind unless I entered it before a stressful elevation in cognitive states," he recalled Michael's advice from that first day. "Strong emotions play havoc with psychic manipulation."

"What are you doing?" Li turned to Chou. "They'll shoot us! Do you want us killed? Take off!" he instructed. "Take a right turn, over there, quick! Move it!"

Chou slammed his foot down on the gas and the car lurched forward. Villi picked up the pace as the military vehicles tried to move in behind him.

"Turn!" Li shouted as he gestured, "Right!"

The front car swerved around the corner. It nearly tipped up on two wheels as Chou pulled hard on the steering wheel. Li and the others leaned over. If Li had not grabbed the door handle, he would have slid into the driver. The tires of the trailing car screeched as Villi struggled to keep up.

The experienced driver of the lead military vehicle easily made the turn and stayed right on Villi's bumper. He rammed his vehicle into the back of Villi's car. The bump gave everyone inside a good jostling.

"Will somebody tell me what's going on?" Su Lin linked to Cecilia and Michael.

"Apparently someone wants to kill us," Michael casually linked back to her. He and Cecilia stared through the rear window at the military car. A man in that car aimed his gun out the window and pointed it at them.

Michael yelled, "Duck!"

He, Cecilia and Su Lin dove for the floorboards. Villi jerked his head around. He looked down at Michael crouching behind the front seat.

"What's a duck got to do with those people?" he asked.

Three shots smashed the back window of the car. One sailed just past Villi's nose. The bullet whizzed close enough for Villi to feel it. Broken glass rained down on the back seat passengers.

"Whoa!" Villi jerked his head back. This caused the car to swing back and forth. "Duck… as in evade… I understand."

"Aren't you psychic?" Su Lin muttered from her crouched position in the front seat.

The psychics in the trailing car tuned their listening senses toward the military vehicle behind them. They could hear the men shouting.

"That's them!" one man said.

"Those are the ones that robbed the bank!" another spoke up.

"What?" Michael questioned. He bobbed his head up to look back. "We didn't…"

Big mistake! Three more shots rang out! Bullets whistled around his head.

"Get down you big fool! You'll be killed!" Cecilia shouted at him.

She reached up and pulled Michael down. He felt around his face before looking over at her. He was glad that she displayed more common sense than he did.

"I suppose I should be grateful they're such bad shots!" he replied.

"You're just plain lucky," she shot back. Cecilia could not smile with the situation so life threatening.

"We're being shot back here. Can't you drive any faster?" Villi linked to the front car.

"We're doing the best we can," Li thought back. "He doesn't have a driver's license!"

"What?" Villi nervously linked back.

Five more shots destroyed the windshield in front of Villi sending broken glass flying around the interior of the car. Su Lin gasped as she held her arms over her head. Villi cursed in Russian as he waved his hands to keep the glass away from his face. His lips sputtered shards.

"Professor, can't you just nod your head and make them go away?" Su Lin linked.

"These militias have heightened emotions! I cannot break through to their mind. I'm trying a different approach," Li linked back.

Four shots passed through the first car and slammed into the back window of the front car. Zinian and Zhiwei slid down to the floor.

"Turn!" Li shouted at Chou.

The inexperienced driver was sweating so badly, he had to grab the wheel with all of his strength. Chou's white knuckles spun the wheel. The car took a sharp left turn into a narrow side street. Villi barely missed the corner of the building as he cut the corner hard to make the turn. His car slid between two parked cars. Trashcans and piles of garbage flew into the air as Villi's car jumped the curb. The trailing car careened down the sidewalk nearly half a block before it returned to the street.

"Zinian… Zhiwei… disable their radios before they call for back up," Li requested.

"Yes professor!" they chimed back, still crouched down.

Li concentrated on the third and last chase car. He noted one key part inside the linkage of the transmission.

"If I push here…" he thought.

The passengers in both cars heard the loud sound of grinding metal. Suddenly the trailing car flipped into the air and came down with a crash. The bodies of two men from inside the car floated unconscious to the ground.

"How did that happen?" Villi wondered as he stared with astonishment into the rearview mirror.

"You can thank Li later," Michael mumbled.

He and Cecilia shook shattered glass out of their hair.

"That was Professor Li? What took him so long?" Villi linked.

"I'm trying," Li replied. "This isn't easy!"

"Why didn't you take out the first car?" Villi asked.

"He doesn't want to hurt them," Michael explained.

"Them? What about us?" Villi cried back.

Their cars flew out of the narrow side street onto a busy wide boulevard full of vehicles, bicycles and people. Chou laid on the horn. People looked up and scattered in a hundred directions. Those nearest the intersection jumped to safety as the caravan of vehicles burst out of the side street. Hoping to avoid pedestrians, Chou made a sharp right turn and went right through a newspaper stand. Hundreds of newspapers and magazines scattered into the air while the owner dove for his life.

"You're making quite an impression on Siping!" Villi linked. He followed Chou's path by driving through the wreckage.

"Can't be helped!" Li answered as he concentrated on the next car.

"What can we do?" Cecilia spoke up.

"Utilize your power. Deflect the bullets if you can," Li told her.

"We'll work on it," Michael added.

He used sign language to Cecilia. She nodded back when she understood Michael's plan. They tried to concentrate their power while being buffeted about.

Flying down the middle of the boulevard, most traffic pulled off to the side. The two remaining military vehicles tried to flank the two fleeing cars. They pulled up on either side of Villi's car. Gunmen popped out of both vehicles and fired shots. This time a hail of gunfire slammed into the side of the vehicle.

Villi's driver side window shattered with a bullet headed toward his face. Villi flinched. When nothing happened, he turned to see a spinning bullet that stopped right next to his face. All of the bullets the gunman shot froze. Slowly they backed up. The bullets and the pieces of window glass flew outward instead. The debris dropped down onto the passing roadbed. One shooter looked questioningly at his gun. On the other side, the frustrated gunman emptied his clip into the car only to end up with the same result.

"That's a neat trick," Villi thought to his friends.

"Cecilia and I combined forces. She took the left. I took the right. We're trying to help," Michael replied.

"It's best to avoid bullets… thanks," Villi linked.

The front car made another sharp turn to the right. Villi followed it off the main street and headed up another narrow side street. This forced the pursuit vehicles to fall back.

Li focused his energy on the second vehicle. His breathing grew labored as he exerted his power.

Villi heard that same awful grinding sound followed by an explosion. The trailing military car flipped into the air and then crashed. Once more, the unconscious occupants floated back down unharmed. The remaining military men looked back and noticed the same thing happen again. They seemed more determined to end the chase. They reached through an opening to the trunk and pulled out assault rifles.

"I like the way you work professor," Villi told Li. "You've got one more to go!"

"He's sweating and breathing hard," Chou linked back. "This effort is taking a lot out of him. I can feel his energy levels dropping."

Michael and Cecilia changed their focus to check on the professor. Just then, the military police opened up with a machine gun. Caught off guard, the two psychics realized they could not deflect all of the rapid-fire bullets.

"Uh oh," Cecilia squeaked.

"We can't stop them! Villi watch out!" Michael warned.

Villi jerked the steering wheel back and forth. The occupants bounced around the inside of the car. Some of the bullets passed through the windshield openings and slammed into the car ahead of them.

"That's enough!" Su Lin cried out. She turned around in her seat and faced the open back window. "We've done nothing wrong! Stop shooting!" she yelled in her native language.

Determined to act on the group's behalf, Su Lin concentrated on the driver in the remaining car. At the same time, an officer in that car took a bead on her head with a scoped rifle. He started to squeeze the trigger.

"Su Lin!" Villi yelled when he sensed the danger. "Duck!"

Once the man pulled the trigger, nothing would stop the bullet aimed directly at her head.

Something inside Su Lin's mind snapped. Angry and frustrated, she threw up her hands and sent out an enormous wave of energy. In that instant, people from blocks away heard a tremendous crash.

CHAPTER 33

BEYOND REASON

THE EARLY SUMMER'S AFTERNOON SUN blazed down through a partly cloudy sky that illuminated the peaceful setting of an inner city park. On the surface, nothing appeared out of the ordinary. Mothers walked their baby carriages. A dog obediently scampered after a ball that bounced across the closely cropped green grass. Squirrels clamored for peanuts dropped by little children while their fathers snapped digital pictures of the event. Birds flew from the tree to the ground as they searched for a wiggling morsel.

On a painted wooden bench under the shade of a large leafy tree, an old man lay very still with his head in the lap of a younger man. The Chinese student fanned the older man's face using a piece of cardboard he had taken from a nearby trashcan.

The old man cautiously blinked and opened his eyes. Through the tree branches, he could see billowy white clouds standing out in contrast against the deep azure sky overhead. He tried to sit up, but found that his depleted energy level prevented it. Unable to communicate in any other way, he tried to speak.

"What is happening?" his dry voice croaked. "How did I arrive here?"

"Just relax Professor Li," Chou said. The nervous young man glanced about him as he fanned the older man's face. "You fainted. Zinian and Zhiwei carried you here."

"Fainted?" Li said. He tried to sit up. "Oh," he sighed. His head hurt. He decided not to move until he could regain some of his energy. "What are you doing?" he asked Chou. He reached up and grabbed the cardboard.

"I'm trying to revive you," Chou said. He jerked the cardboard from Li's grasp and tossed it into the garbage can. "They put me in charge of guarding the main gate," he told Li. "Zinian and Zhiwei are at opposite ends of the park."

Li struggled into a sitting position. He had not felt this old or weak since before his conversion. For a moment, he wondered if he had any psychic power at all.

"Let me help you," Chou offered. He slipped his hand behind Li's back.

"Where are the others?" the professor asked. "I don't sense them. Have they survived? Are they injured?"

"They're fine Professor," Chou reassured him. "Michael split us into teams. One team is driving the streets of Siping. They're trying to take the memory of the car chase out of people's minds. Another team went to the police station. The rest of us are waiting for you to recover. As far as we can tell, no other authorities were alerted."

"Splitting up the group was foolish," Li commented. He rubbed his temples. He tried to stand and found his legs too weak. Instead, he plopped back on the bench. "I thought we were trying to avoid the police," he said as he caught his breath.

"That's how this whole thing started professor," Chou started to explain.

"What's that you say?" Li said as he turned his head.

"If you'll let me explain," Chou broke in. "The Siping Police Department maintained separate security cameras focused on the street outside the bank."

"I replaced that money..." Li interrupted.

"That isn't the point professor," Chou continued. "When the bank's manager returned from an afternoon break, he found the teller's frozen and their trays empty. Once the tellers reanimated, no one in the bank could explain what happened. The manager called the police. They checked the outside security cameras and identified our cars. The police enlisted the military's help to find us. They told them that we were part of an organized gang. They considered us armed and authorized the use of deadly force. A group of military police spotted us trying to leave town. They wanted the credit for apprehending the bank robbers. You were right to think they would call for back up. They managed to reach two additional cars on duty before Zinian and Zhiwei interfered. Michael convinced the group that we should try to eliminate any trace of the event before we left town."

"What happened to the last military car?" Li asked.

"When Su Lin flexed her muscle and tried to attack, you somehow lent her your energy to boost her power," Chou told him. "The two of you took out the last police car. Then you fainted."

"Was anyone injured?" he asked.

"Michael and Cecilia prevented it," Chou informed him.

Li closed his eyes and recalled the last few seconds of the chase. A sniper would have shot Su Lin in the head if he had not intervened. He used the last of his psychic energy to help her. After that, his mind went blank.

"Professor, if you are strong enough to move, we should alert the others," Chou suggested. "I can't divert many minds in the park. I'm not used to this."

"Give me a few more minutes," Li said to him. "Then I'll be ready."

Li had to sort a few things out before he continued. This sudden drop in energy puzzled him. He wondered why his power drained away so quickly. Earlier, he felt confident in using his power. He thought he had unlimited power.

"You have more capacity for retaining psychic energy than any being in the universe," a voice spoke to him. *"Nevertheless, great exertion consumes great amounts of energy. In order to accomplish any feat that requires such levels, you must first draw extra energy in reserve."*

Li remained perfectly still. As he listened to this voice, he glanced to his left to see Chou's reaction. He noticed that only he and not Chou heard this voice of reason.

"Reach out your senses," the voice instructed. *"Do you feel psychic energy?"*

"I feel it coming from people all around us," Li linked back.

"Human beings are unique. They create psychic energy in abundance," the voice clarified. *"Unfortunately, they wastefully radiate most of it away. Strong human emotions such as extreme fear or anger block the transfer of psychic energy as Michael discovered and wisely informed you. You will eventually recharge your energy levels when you sleep which may take hours. However, you can freely take it from any ordinary human at any time. You will not harm them by doing so. Take as much as you need as often as you like. Only your group can utilize this energy. Try it now,"* the voice suggested. *"Reach out, draw energy inward, revitalize your level and feel the difference."*

Li stretched out his senses to other people in the park. A woman sat on a bench nearby reading a book. Li cautiously borrowed some of her energy. He monitored her for a change. Nothing happened. He took even more energy. The woman continued as before with no change.

"You're right," Li responded. "They do not miss it. Yet, I feel renewed – just as I did that day..."

"The day of your conversion when Galactic Central infused your body with energy from the collective," the voice said.

"Yes!" Li acknowledged.

"Now that you are aware of your energy levels, you must avoid depleting your reserves. Once you have adapted this technique, you will never require energy again. Live well, Li Po Chin," the mysterious voice said before it severed contact.

Li found he could absorb energy from people all over the park with no apparent side effects. He leapt up from the bench. Power surged through his body. He felt like a new man.

Li's sudden change startled Chou.

"Professor? What is happening? I sense your energy levels rapidly increasing," Chou stated. He stared at Li aghast. "How did you do that?"

"I'll explain later. Come on!" Li said as he grabbed Chou's hand. "Let's find the others!"

Li sprinted to the park exit with a protesting Chou in tow. As they ran, Li linked with Zinian and Zhiwei. He urged them to rendezvous at the main entrance. Li also reached across town. He found Michael and Villi just as they finished another erasure.

Michael suddenly sensed his master's powerful presence.

"Master Li!" Michael enthusiastically linked. "I'm glad you're feeling better. We're finished here."

"Good job Michael," Li communicated. "Bring Villi and meet the rest of us at the main entrance to the park."

"We were a bit worried when you…" Michael started.

"I forgot to keep up my energy level," Li explained. "However, I've just discovered a new way to instantly replenish it. I'll explain the technique later. Return to the park as soon as you can."

"Yes Master Li," Michael linked and signed off.

"What did you just call him?" Villi piped in.

"Nothing," Michael linked back while he dismissed him. "You heard him Villi. He wants to meet us at the…"

"I heard him," Villi cut in. "We still have one job left," he said as he twisted the bullet-riddled car into a u-turn.

Li checked in with the second team.

"Cecilia," Li called. "Have you successfully contained our incident?"

"Professor!" she responded. "You're awake! We're so relieved. Have you recovered?"

"Yes," he replied. "I'm more concerned with your effort. Have you and Su Lin finished?" Li asked her.

"We've driven around the entire area," she told him. "We altered minds all over the place. We even went back to the bank and took care of the manager. Su Lin and I are exhausted."

"Join us back at the park's main entrance. Michael and Villi are on their way," Li informed her.

"I haven't linked with Michael," Cecilia stated. "I was beginning to worry…"

"Hurry," Li encouraged. "We must leave Siping before anything else happens."

Cecilia started to drive for the park when Villi's car suddenly skidded to a halt in front of their car and cut them off. Before they could react, Michael linked Villi's new plan to them.

Several minutes passed and Li did not hear anything.

"Sorry about the delay," Villi piped in. "I found a car dealer not far from the river," Villi linked as he and Michael got out. "The other cars had too much air conditioning. We left the dealer the last of the cash."

"Where are the other cars?" Zhiwei questioned.

Su Lin held her nose and dipped her head.

"That's why Villi found a dealer near the river," Zinian smiled.

"No time to discuss it," Li said waving his hand. "Resume your former places. Come! Let's go!"

Li herded the students toward the front car. He stopped and pulled Zhiwei aside.

"Do you have any experience driving a car?" he asked.

"Professor I've been driving a car since I was sixteen," Zhiwei told him.

"Good! Then you drive," he indicated as he glared at Chou.

Cecilia and Su Lin rejoined Michael and Villi in the trailing car. Michael gave Li a questioning expression. The elderly man took in a deep breath.

"I've learned a new absorption technique," Li linked to him. "I'll share the information with you and the others once we return to the highway."

Michael nodded back as he stepped into the car. The two cars pulled away from the park and headed south out of town.

"*Once you've adapted this technique, you will never require energy again,*" Li recalled the voice saying. "I must thank this helpful voice personally one day," he privately added.

In the city of Shenyang that lay miles ahead on their journey, a cold dark figure – isolated in its own private world – spoke with malice in its thoughts.

"You'll need more than help from Galactic Central to defeat me… Master Li!"

Chapter 34

A team sport

Long before the newly formed group of eight psychics reached the outskirts of the large metropolitan area of Shenyang, the inexperienced students had difficulty trying to filter out the gradual increase in psychic noise and interference. Shenyang has a population exceeding ten million. The energy pouring from that area overwhelmed them. The professor instructed the student to pull their senses back. He feared that their minds would be lost in an endless sea of emotionally charged thoughts.

"Concentrate," he told them. "Remember your blocking practice. We live in three dimensions. A psychic can feel everything around him or her."

"Professor please help me," Su Lin called out. Caught in waves of emotional conflict the young psychic struggled against the tide of energy crashing down on her mind.

"Make your block impenetrable Su Lin!" Li encourage. "Don't let anything in – not even me!"

The elderly psychic and Su Lin momentarily linked as he demonstrated how to isolate her thoughts from the environment. For a few minutes, she worked at reaching that balance. Gradually, her face took on a look of satisfaction until she could hear nothing but her own thoughts. Li then worked with the remaining students until they successfully blocked the waves of unwanted emotion.

"Villi!" Li cried out.

"Yes, professor!" the startled driver replied.

"Is it possible to find a place for us to stay outside the city?" Li requested. "Even I am finding Shenyang too close in proximity."

"As a matter of fact, professor I've been working on just that," he answered.

"You found another family inn?" Li asked.

"I believe I've found a place with more privacy. We'll be staying in a house," Villi replied.

"A whole house?" Li exclaimed. "Where are the owners? You didn't kick them out, did you?"

"No professor," Villi replied, "They were about to move in when I delayed that intention by a week or so."

"You did this while driving a car?" Li uncharacteristically smiled.

"Yes, professor," Villi explained, "a police officer must be able to do two things at once."

"No wonder you graduated at the top of your class. Where is this house?" Li enquired.

"I will link the details," Villi answered.

Through a shared vision, the group learned that Villi found a recently finished mansion with several bedrooms and baths. At first, Villi thought someone built a new hotel. He noted the building furnished yet unoccupied. The private estate belonged to a wealthy merchant with government connections. This party-sponsored industrialist isolated his mansion by surrounding the property with a tall stone privacy wall, a security gate and some well-placed foliage. This hid the expensive villa from curious eyes and obstinate local officials.

"Li Po Chin?" a voice spoke to his mind. It was the same voice from the park.

"I am here," Li responded. He realized again that no one else heard this voice.

"We sense a strong presence nearby. We did not detect this energy until now. We do not understand the source of its power," the voice explained. "When we attempted a probe, it blocked us. We find this phenomenon unusual and potentially dangerous."

"I sensed it as we approached the city," Li confirmed. "I am also blocked from its location."

"Will you attempt a link if you find the source?" the voice asked.

"Perhaps if I locate this new psychic source, I will try to communicate," Li reasoned. "It may take me some time to find its origin."

"Michael or Cecilia would be well suited for that purpose," the voice suggested. "They are experienced with scanning. We note that their strength has grown in a short time."

"That is a possibility of course," Li considered.

Zhiwei slowed to a stop. Li broke off his celestial contact. He refocused on his surroundings.

"Villi would like to pass us," Zhiwei linked to Li.

"Then let him pass," Li responded.

Villi pulled his car into the lead and turned off the main road. He then made several course changes into progressively smaller streets leading away from the heart of the city. Eventually he drove up a small country road into the hills northeast of Shenyang. A tall wall made from fieldstone rose up over ten feet high. Sharp pointed rocks covered the top. It ran along the right side of the road. Villi followed this wall for nearly a half kilometer until he finally arrived outside a large heavy metal gate.

"I'd say the owner wanted their privacy," Villi commented.

"To keep out the curious?" Michael queried.

"More likely to keep out the peasants," Su Lin countered.

"This place does resemble a fortress," Cecilia added her observation. "I doubt an angry mob could break through that gate."

"Gates are my specialty," Villi quipped.

He stretched out his thoughts and released the elaborate electronic security latch. The large thick ornamental metallic gate swung open to reveal expansive grounds. A brick-lined driveway snaked up a hill through the middle of the property. Bushes and trees obscured their destination. As their cars progressed, the thinning foliage finally revealed a massive structure. The mansion spread out from a tall middle section into three separate wings. Its façade resembled architecture similar to an English manor house.

"Nice work Villi," Michael linked as stepped from the car. "I'll take this wing if you don't mind."

"May I have the other?" Villi shot back.

Cecilia whistled, "It's definitely big."

"I think we'll all fit," Li added as the second car pulled up behind.

"I was under the impression the state curbed such displays of decadence," Su Lin said as she gazed up at the monstrosity.

"My, my, my – how times have changed," Li commented. "China has definitely embraced capitalism. Shall we go in?"

Li pushed open the large heavy front door with his mind. At first, the group seemed more concerned with accommodations than with appearances. Past the wide round foyer, the house opened into a great central room with a curving staircase that swept up to the left. The second floor spread out left and right with four bedrooms and four full bathrooms on each wing. The master bedroom was located at the end of the left corridor. The group scattered to explore the giant structure.

"They like large bathrooms!" a student linked from upstairs. "Every bedroom has one!"

"Thank the maker," Cecilia sighed. She helped Zinian and Chou bring in suitcases.

Li surveyed the downstairs. He casually strolled left off the central room into a grand reception area. He glanced up and noted the mirrored ceiling high overhead trimmed with gold. A large tall window along one wall faced the distant countryside. As Li looked around, he noticed that the owner had everything in the room gilded with gold leaf – the moldings, the furniture, and lamps even the rugs had gold threads.

Li could only think of one word, "Gaudy."

The mansion's owner placed the kitchen in the third wing off the middle of the house. The main floor also had a large laundry, a long dining room, a game room, an indoor pool, an office, and indoor access to the garages – all three of them.

"Who would build such a place?" Chou asked. He put his suitcase down and leaned his head back to take in the view.

"Someone with a very large family," Villi guessed.

"A bit outlandish, don't you think?" Cecilia commented. She shook her head as she walked around the gold fountain in the foyer.

"Don't you like it? Early Chinese I believe they call it," Michael sarcastically linked to her.

"Where is the artwork? They splashed lots of gold all over the place. It screams, 'I'm rich!' It's not just tasteless but displays greed and vanity," Su Lin observed.

"Has anyone picked a bedroom yet," Li questioned.

Michael glanced over at Villi for only a second. The two young men raced up the stairs to claim the second best bedroom. They knew the professor should have the largest. After a friendly shoving match in the corridor, Michael and Villi established the pecking order. They gave Li the largest bedroom, then Michael, Cecilia and finally Villi's room on that wing. Down the other hall, Su Lin would take the first bedroom followed by Chou, Zinian and Zhiwei last.

"Did you see the kitchen?" Su Lin linked. "They stocked the pantry and two refrigerators! This is a dream kitchen," she told the group. She immediately pulled off her coat and started making mental lists of ingredients she could use in recipes.

"This is quite a find. My compliments Villi," Li said. He stood at the bottom of the stairs.

"Thanks professor!" Villi echoed back.

"I put your things in your room professor," Michael called down.

Li reminded the team to pull energy from outside *before* they used their power. Michael and Cecilia then concurred that they unconsciously used a similar technique in Russia when a farmer approached them in the wilderness. Li and the rest of the group pulled plenty of energy from the city. Full of vitality, he easily managed the long staircase. He was eager to see the master bedroom. The eight psychics unpacked their belongings and settled into their plush surroundings.

"I'd like to hold a meeting at the kitchen table in twenty minutes," he linked to the household.

At the bottom of the hour, the group sat around the large kitchen table with Li at the head.

"I consider this our first organizational meeting," he began. "This house will act as a temporary base of operations while we sort our plan of action," Li informed them. "Villi tells me we can stay here a week to ten days at the most," he went on. "That should give us plenty of time to accomplish our short term goals. This will also be our first opportunity to organize our group into a cohesive unit. Mostly we've combined forces out of necessity. If we are to form a permanent community, our approach to that end must change starting today."

A sense of excitement and adventure passed through the youths gathered around the table. They were eager to start this new life. Li felt these emotions coming from each person.

"We should set up a system of integrating new members in a non-disruptive way," Li pointed out. "Can you do that Villi?"

"Yes professor," Villi replied.

"I have some news to share with you," he continued. "The voices feel a powerful psychic presence somewhere in the vicinity," he informed them. "I sense it and perhaps you have felt something too. However, I am unable to pinpoint the exact location of its source. He or she could be a kilometer up the road or on the other side of the city. Their activity spikes and then it quickly vanishes, which indicates they are using psychic energy sporadically. Our search could take days in such a large metropolis. Therefore, I would like to use our two most experienced members to locate this source."

Li's eyes fell on the young couple that usually sat close to the other, Michael and Cecilia. Professor Li's acknowledgement humbled the pair. Cecilia blushed. Michael half smiled.

"I want you two to assist me with a systematic search of Shenyang," he told them. "Perhaps between the three of us, we can locate this psychic presence. Tomorrow morning Cecilia, I'd like you to start scanning the schools, universities and similar places," Li directed. "Michael, you can scan public buildings, government offices and so on."

"Yes Master Li," Michael absently replied.

Cecilia simply nodded. She shot Michael a side-glance when he used the strange title.

Li winced a little when he heard Michael pronounce the title for the first time in the group. Villi frowned at Michael when he said it. Li pressed on.

"I'll start with the financial district first," he continued, "banks, investments firms and large employers before I scan small businesses. Su Lin, would you mind playing chef as well as working on your psychic studies?" he asked. "You have the right to request the responsibility be rotated, of course."

"Are you kidding? I love to cook," she perked up. "With this kitchen, cooking will be more an adventure than a chore!" she declared.

"Thank you," Li linked back to her. "I wanted to check with you first." He turned to the next member. "Chou, will you set up a schedule for housework?" he asked the nodding student. "Divide the remaining tasks on a floating basis, each of us will take turns washing the dishes, doing laundry, cleaning floors and so on. Include me on that list. Understood?"

"Yes professor," Chou acknowledged.

"That leaves security," Li said. His eyes immediately fell on Zhiwei. "I believe you were made for this job."

"Yes sir!" Zhiwei enthusiastically replied. "I studied security system design at the university. I'd love to have that job!"

"Mmmm," Li concurred. "Keep our perimeter secure Zhiwei," he cautioned. "Now we'll need an expert with working knowledge of the structure. Zinian, check the integrity of the house systems, plumbing, water heaters, furnace and so forth. I believe construction and architecture are your specialties."

"Yes professor," the large student replied. He cracked his knuckles.

"That gives each of us a principle task," Li told them. "Oh and Villi, the four students must receive their advanced downloads right away. Tomorrow will do. Will you assist them?"

"Yes professor," Villi said.

"Follow up with advanced training," Li added, "you are eminently qualified. Any questions? No? Dismissed," Li said. He rose and left the kitchen.

Zhiwei headed outside. He set off at a jogging pace to run the perimeter of estate's property. Zinian went down into the basement. Su Lin set about organizing the kitchen. Cecilia caught up to the professor at the bottom of the staircase with a private concern. They stepped off to one side. Villi noticed Michael treading up the stairs alone and saw his chance. He caught up to him in the hall just outside their bedrooms.

"Michael," Villi called to him. "Have you got a second?" He strolled up to the young man. He felt uncertain how to approach him. "That's the second time you addressed Li as master," Villi stated. "What's going on between you and the professor?"

Michael paused for a second. He wanted to include his friend on their meeting. Over Villi's shoulder, he noticed Cecilia coming up the staircase.

"Excuse me," Michael muttered. Instead of linking, he put up a block and entered his bedroom without answering.

"What did I say?" Villi wondered aloud. Michael's cool reaction perplexed the Russian. He turned to Cecilia and hoped she could supply an explanation.

"Something changed between Michael and the professor after their meeting the other night," she linked to Villi. "He's been quiet about it ever since. I suppose one of them had to be dominant. I don't understand the "master" business though. Don't pressure him Villi. Ok?" she requested. "Give him time to tell us."

"Michael is my friend Cecilia," Villi responded. "Under these circumstances I wouldn't bother. Except, I thought we were supposed to be open with each other. I want him to be honest with me."

"I've been inside his mind before we learned to block. Expressing his feelings has never been easy for him," she linked. "Be patient. He'll come around."

"I hope so," Villi said and then headed back to the stairs.

Cecilia decided to contact her voice in Galactic Central. She retired to her bedroom for the afternoon. Disheartened by the interaction with his friend, Villi returned to the kitchen. He watched with awe as Su Lin rapidly worked her way around the kitchen as if she ran a restaurant. She prepared ingredients so fast that Villi had a hard time making out what she did.

"I wonder if a relationship exists between the way we excel in our lives and our psychic ability," Villi thought as he watched her.

Su Lin set out small plates laden with ingredients. She then turned to Villi and gave him one of those phony polite smiles.

"Would you set the table?" she requested. "…and call the group to lunch," she added as she turned to her pot of boiling water.

"Sure," he said. He sprang into action and headed for the dining room when he hesitated. "But you haven't started cooking!" he protested.

"By the time they sit, it will be done," she confidently stated.

With a thought, two more burners on the massive stove lit and two additional pans dropped down from a large suspended group onto two of those. She poured out extra virgin olive oil into both. Simultaneously, as Su

Lin performed these chores with her mind, she physically added rice to the boiling water on the third burner.

As Villi pushed open the door to the dining room, he watched with amazement when sliced vegetables flew into one oiled pan and chopped chicken breast jumped into the other. With lightening speed, Su Lin threw several herbs and spices into each sizzling pan. Villi smiled and shook his head.

"I have a feeling the professor chose the wrong psychic to teach class," he mused.

Outside, Zhiwei stood watching the grounds. He felt as if someone were watching over the estate. Although he found no particular person after he scanned the nearby countryside, he still could not shake the feeling. He reported his findings to Li.

"Professor – the grounds are clear… I sense another presence out there…" Zhiwei linked and left his final thought dangling.

Zinian examined the new structure from below and found many flaws in its foundation. He felt grateful the owners would not blame him for building this place.

"They poured substandard concrete and didn't put in enough drainage," he thought as he glanced around. "You can add inferior code wiring," he stated in closing the main circuit box. "Professor – the house won't fall down or catch fire tomorrow… next week perhaps, but we'll be fine until then," he reported.

Michael sat alone in his spacious opulent room with its four poster bed and large wooden dressers. The size of the room made him feel small. Yet neither the house nor the mysterious psychic presence bothered him. He wondered how he would tell his two friends about the change in his relationship with the professor. Cecilia worried about his attitude. He concluded that her voice gave no indication about the meeting between the two.

"What do I feel for this… young woman," he thought as he resisted the temptation to label her as a girl. "With a mature body like that and a mind that can outsmart nearly every man I know, I would say that Cecilia Beaton is all woman," Michael considered.

In the master bedroom suite at the end of the hall, Professor Li brooded over this mysterious source whose exact location he could not locate.

"If Michael thinks his room is large," Li contemplated as he looked about the room, "he should stay in this one. I've never seen a bed so big," he thought as he gazed up on the monstrosity the owner installed along one wall.

Indeed, everything in Li's bedroom was both larger and grander than the other bedrooms. Li noted the bathroom had greater floor area than his house.

He shook his head taking in the opulence that some decorator called good taste. They put gold on practically everything and that included the toilet.

Just as he started to try it out, he heard Villi's general call to lunch.

"Su Lin requests your presence in the dining room," he generally linked while he set the table.

Within ten minutes or so, the group gathered around the dining room table, with hardly anyone linking or speaking. A dark cloud hung over the house as if this part of China had some foreboding nature associated with it. The group sat in silence wearing dour expressions until Su Lin walked in from the kitchen doorway. She was positively beaming with pride.

"Did I mention I love to cook?" she stated when she placed an artful plate of food in front of each person – trimmed with fresh mint from the garden.

"Su Lin you shouldn't go to this much trouble…" Li started.

"I insist professor," Su Lin spoke up. "How is it?" she said patiently as she stood by.

He could not deny her enthusiasm and took a taste.

"Your meal is quite good," he nodded to her. "I suspect you have many surprises in store for us," he said to her.

She tore off her apron and sat down next to Villi. The group brightened as the meal progressed. They chatted about the luxurious accommodations while they consumed Su Lin's marvelous preparations. As soon as everyone finish, Li broke up the gathering early.

"I suggest we retire for the rest of the day," he stated. "We'll rise early and begin our new tasks tomorrow morning. Congratulations Su Lin. You have prepared an excellent meal. Link if any of you need me. Good night," Li said. He rose and left.

Michael and Cecilia volunteered to take the first kitchen clean up duty. Neither linked nor spoke as they completed the task. This first day in the house ended quietly. Each member of the group headed off to his or her room in relative silence.

Chapter 35

Ashram

The following morning after a light breakfast, Cecilia, Michael and Li began the arduous task of analyzing the entire population of Shenyang. They had to scan a great sea of minds spread over many locations. Li impressed upon Michael and Cecilia simply to locate these special psychics. Once found, he instructed that it was not necessary to make contact. He would handle any direct contact and determine if they were suitable candidates to join the group.

"Cecilia… Michael… If you encounter this new mysterious presence, I want you to withdraw your probe at once. I sense a powerful psychic force at work here. We are uncertain if their intent is friendly or hostile. Although we've never encountered a hostile psychic, I wish to error on the side of caution. Establish contact, link with me and then I will take over," Li indicated.

With millions of minds to scan, Li speculated the search could take days or even a week – time they did not have to waste searching the entire countryside. Therefore, the three psychics meticulously set out to probe every corner nook and cranny of Shenyang.

Meanwhile, Villi gathered the four students in the gold-bedecked opulent front room to receive the advanced DNA-changing conversion from Galactic Central.

"I hate to rush this process Villi," Li privately linked to him that morning. "The easy training session is over. As soon as the advanced conversion is complete – raise their level of competency as quickly as possible."

"They've hardly had time to adjust using their abilities," Villi weakly protested.

"Can't be helped," Li countered. "We don't know when we may encounter forces that require a team of advanced psychics. I'm sorry Villi. Contact their voices. Make the arrangements today."

"Yes professor," Villi answered.

He could relate to the student's dilemma. Only two days elapsed between the times that Villi received his initial conversion to when he had the ultimate one that altered his DNA. He had to master concepts in hours that Michael and Cecilia gradually adjusted to over a period of days. Villi also did not mention this conversion would alter their DNA. Professor Li told him to keep the prep talk to a minimum.

"Don't instill fear or trepidation by giving out too much information," Li advised. "It will only make them nervous."

"Yes professor," he linked back. He reached out beyond the galaxy in an instant. He instructed his voice on what to do and added Li's name to punctuate the request. Villi knew that Galactic Central showed special preference to Li that bordered on obsession.

As soon as Villi turned his attention to the student group, they sensed his solemn mood.

"I have… well, some rather important news for you," he said while he tried to sound upbeat. He kept his private thoughts blocked. "Galactic Central will administer a very special download today – one that will alter your sensory system and make us equals. Since this is your most complex interaction with Galactic Central, I will remain nearby and observe you in case any problems arise."

"Did anyone observe you?" Chou asked.

"We were extremely fortunate that Michael finished his download in time to avert unforeseen complications," Villi brushed him off. "Please lie down and remember to open your minds completely to Galactic Central. Do not attempt to use any block. Relax. Breathe deeply. I have alerted the voices. They are ready for you. Now, open the connection to your personal voice."

Within a matter of seconds, the four students lapsed into an unconscious state. Villi monitored this long and strenuous whole-body conversion. He felt uncomfortable watching their bodies violently writhe and vibrate. He nearly intervened when he saw Su Lin thrash back and forth. He wondered how he, Michael and Cecilia escaped injury when the voices converted them inside the confines of that car's interior. Gradually, each body shook with less intensity, until they took on a fine vibration. It reminded Villi of the vibrating string from a musical instrument. As the transformation progressed, each person took on a golden glow. This was similar to the light Villi observed in Li Po Chin without its intensity.

"No wonder we woke up sweating," he thought while he watched each person strain.

An hour after the process began the students emerged from their trances. Each was drenched in sweat and had difficulty trying to orient to their surroundings.

"Do not extend your senses at this time," Villi warned them. "You will notice that you can easily affect many things around you. You might also adversely affect the outside world. Until you gain better control, keep your abilities in check. Join me back here after you freshen up," he told them.

Chou assisted Su Lin while Zinian helped Zhiwei support one another. Together the four climbed the stairs and separated to their rooms. They showered and changed their clothes. When they returned, Villi immediately noticed a significant change in them. They bore a sense of confidence in their bearing. He could also feel their increased power levels.

"At the risk of sounding chauvinist," he stated as they took their seats, "I feel the need to work with the men and women separately," he explained. "Before we break up, I must review a few basics. Your new abilities allow you to perform extraordinary feats, which require additional psychic energy. Professor Li wants all of us to work on the psychic bubble technique. This technique demands control, focus and requires large amounts of psychic energy. However, we must prepare before we apply any ability that demands such energy levels. Let us practice that process first. Close your eyes and extend your senses," he instructed. "Reach out to the world beyond these walls. Send your scans out until you encounter psychic energy. You will see it concentrated in people."

All four students closed their eyes. Their vision easily passed through the building and scattered over the countryside until they saw people as faintly glowing objects.

"Do you see the people beyond the walls of this compound?" Villi asked them.

"Yes I see them," Zhiwei chimed in as the others agreed.

"That's amazing," Chou said.

"What you are seeing is psychic energy. They constantly manufacture it but do not use it as we can. Draw their psychic energy to you," Villi told them. "Take as much as you wish or can presently absorb. Then pull your awareness back to the house and open your eyes."

All four blinked and looked around. They could sense new power levels in one another.

"You must routinely perform this process to keep your energy level from dropping too low. If you do not draw in psychic energy, you will eventually pass out from depleted stores. Unconscious, you will be vulnerable. This happened to the professor in Siping. He used every bit of his energy to help Su Lin. While his sacrifice was noble, he risked his own life by falling into a near coma-like state. This taught all of us a valuable lesson. Please take special precautions to avoid this predicament!" Villi emphasized.

"One more thing," he added. "If you try to draw energy from another psychic person, this will be considered an act of hostility. Blocking technique will prevent that of course. Make certain you build up enough energy from non-psychic sources before you employ bubble technique. Our managed use of psychic energy maintains our lifestyle. Let us now proceed to creating a psychic bubble. Observe," he said.

He then extended his hand with the palm side up. After a second or two, a small sphere with the characteristic of a thick swirling translucent soap bubble took shape.

"Note the focal path I use in my mind. This is necessary to concentrate the energy into a sphere," he instructed. "Once you've established a psychic bubble, the trick is expanding its size while maintaining its integrity. After a while, a bubble this size takes very little effort," he indicated. "The larger the bubble however, the more energy required to create it. Professor Li insists we master bubble technique."

"I'm having trouble following your pathway. Can you show me how you accomplish this?" Chou asked.

"Bubble formation requires complete concentration," Villi replied.

Zinian and Zhiwei spoke up simultaneously.

"I want to learn…"

"Yeah, me too…"

"Please show us Villi," Chou added.

"Su Lin," Villi linked as he turned to her first. "I apologize, but at this time I must work with these three separately. Will you excuse us and wait over there?"

"Certainly," she agreed.

She walked to the other end of the gaudy front room. Although, when she turned around, she stared back at the all male group with envy. She wished she were included with the rest of the group. However, she respected Villi's opinion. She thought that he must have a good reason for making her wait.

Using his mind, Villi closed the massive drapes that covered the front windows. He left a small opened to maintain a modicum of room light. He personally linked with each man. He made the mental visit short and to the point by demonstrating the mental process that he copied from Professor Li.

"Instead of casting a net to form a link," Villi pointed out, "try to focus your energy on a single point in space. Slowly expand the energy into any size of shell. Remember, this is a hollow object. Eventually, you will create a bubble large enough so that the sphere of psychic energy surrounds you."

Villi then expanded his translucent ball until he created a sphere of energy that engulfed him. The result made him nearly invisible. To a lower level or non-psychic, he would have vanished. To these newly advanced psychics, they saw a faint image of the big Russian man standing inside the sphere looking out at them.

"Once you achieve a bubble this size, try to project an image into walls of the sphere," he stated. "You can blend with the surroundings to avoid an abrupt change or you can change your appearance to look like someone else. If you do not project an image into the sphere, you will simply vanish to non-psychics. That could be disconcerting to most people, especially in a crowd. Therefore, before you cast a sphere around you, have a subject in mind for substitution. Let me demonstrate."

They watched as Villi rapidly transformed into a dog that jumped up and sat on the sofa. Yet to three skeptical students, Villi did not make a complete change. They could still distinguish a faint image of him.

"That isn't very convincing," Zhiwei noted.

"Yeah, we can still see you," Zinian chimed in.

Villi noticed the disbelief on their faces. He dropped the bubble.

"If you saw a faint image of me, it's because you are advanced psychics. Any normal person or lower level psychic would only see a dog – the more power in the sphere, the more convincing the image. Mastering this technique will take practice. This exercise is very taxing. Be warned. If you lose all of your psychic energy, you will pass out from exhaustion and be vulnerable," he told them.

Villi then took each young man aside to work them through the process.

"Chou you go first," he indicated. "Open your mind to me. Link with me and follow the neuronal pathways as I go through the process," he requested.

Chou's bubble started out small and wobbly. As he continued, he was able to make a stable sphere about the size of a golf ball. Eventually after several attempts, he expanded that to one the size of a basketball and could maintain it. Villi then made open links with Zinian and Zhiwei. Soon all three young men attempted to perform the feat on their own. Villi monitored their thoughts as each made his attempt.

"Open your mind to me," he asked of Zhiwei when he noticed him struggle. "That's it. Now focus and create the sphere. Do you see the process in my mind? Yes, that's it. You're doing fine. The difficulty is expanding the size of the sphere. Keep working on it."

Once they grasped the basic concept, Zhiwei, Zinian and Chou tried to cast images into the sphere's exterior. They changed lamps into various objects such as a cat or a squirrel. Soon, the three men had nearly expanded their spheres to encompass their bodies.

Several minutes passed while Su Lin watched them from across the room. She began to feel left out and anxious because Villi asked her to wait for a reason she could not fathom. Rather than show her emotions, she turned away and tried to think of something else.

Villi sensed her block going up as she withdrew further from the group. He excused himself from the men and walked across the great room to where Su Lin stood. As he drew near, he nervously smiled. He tried not to let her sense his unease at entering her mind.

"You are next," he linked as he tried to relax inside.

Villi put off his instruction with Su Lin for reasons he either could not, or would not reveal to her. For when it came to Su Lin, every time Villi drew near her, he found he could not express his true feelings for her. He became all tongue-tied. The idea of entering her open mind frightened him. For as much as her mind would be open to him, his would be open to her.

Villi not only admired Su Lin's incredible psychic talent, he also desired her company. He found her sexually attractive the moment he first laid eyes on her. After they had spent some time socially, he came to admire her even more. Rightly, Cecilia should have helped Su Lin because Villi and Su Lin's mutual attraction would be a distraction. Li knew of this conundrum.

The entire time Villi drove the car with Su Lin in the front seat next to him, the couple only exchanged cordial thoughts as the group made their way down the road. At the behest of the professor, they kept their relationship platonic. Even when Su Lin prepared dinner last night, Villi kept his personal feelings in check.

As he stood before her in the living room with the other male students at the other end, Villi felt exposed. When he made his link to her, he regretted what he was about to express.

"Open your mind to me," he told her. Simultaneously, he opened his mind to her as she did with him. With the male students, it was strictly business. They did not exchange any emotions or attachments. In the case of Su Lin, he did not know what would happen next.

Villi started to share his training skills. Unfortunately, Su Lin's open mind revealed all of the intimate thoughts she had for him. Conversely, she could read his personal thoughts related to her as well. Villi quickly began to develop a tinge of guilt as he dropped in on her thoughts. All at once, he knew her secret desires, her dreams, even her sexual fantasies.

As he stood next to her, he tried to keep focused on the difficult task of forming a psychic bubble. Yet, the longer they shared an open link, the more that link revealed about what each person thought. Villi broke into a sweat as he labored to stay on track.

"You've followed the others as they formed their bubbles," he pressed on. "Would you like to try?"

"Like this?" she put to him. Without hesitation, she instantly formed a perfect psychic bubble of energy that hovered over the palm of her hand in her first attempt.

Villi backed up and stared at her at her, amazed with the ease she performed such a complex action. He immediately put up a block.

"I didn't sense any strain at all on her part," he thought. "I see why Li worked hard to bring Su Lin into the group. She did that faster than I did the first time I tried. She is indeed a very powerful psychic," he thought. "She only lacks Cecilia's experience."

Su Lin slyly smiled at his reaction. She had eavesdropped on the men's conversation. While the others struggled, she had practiced on the other side of the room with her back turned to them. She wanted to laugh and tell Villi that this was not her first attempt. Yet, when he put up a block to her so quickly, she sensed he tried to hide his feelings from her. She did not wish to cause him any shame or embarrassment.

"I should have let him show me first," she privately thought. "Did I do it correctly?" she asked as she tried to appear innocent.

"Perfect," he said hesitantly. "Try to expand the sphere and cast an image into it."

The students at the other end of the living room continued to practice and hone their skill. They laughed at some of the objects they created. They were absorbed in their own attempts. They did not pay attention to Villi working with Su Lin.

Su Lin responded to Villi's request. He watched with astonishment as she expanded a psychic bubble around her. As she did, the bubble stripped away her clothing and revealed the young woman naked with only her hands strategically covering her upper and lower body.

"Like this?" she smiled diminutively. She meant it as a joke.

Villi stood there speechless. Her candor completely caught him off guard. Commotion arose in that instant when the students at the other end of the room practically fell over one another while they stared at Su Lin.

"I believe you performed the technique very well," Villi said. He turned his back to her with all modesty. He quickly stepped between Su Lin and the others. He created an illusionary wall for her privacy. "You can stop making the bubble Su Lin," he said with rather terse emotion attached.

Su Lin suddenly realized she went too far with her attempt at humor. She thought Villi would laugh. His sober reaction horrified her. She turned and ran up the stairs.

"Practice on your own for a few minutes," Villi suggested to the three men with their mouths hanging open. He turned and sprinted up the stairs after her. "Su Lin!" he mentally called out.

He heard her bedroom door slam shut. He did not know what to say to her. He wanted to clarify any misunderstanding between them. The situation felt awkward to him. He was sorry he put up a block in the living room. He wanted to link with her. Yet now he could not access her mind and make his reaction clear to her. As he stood in the hall outside her room, he heard her sobbing inside. He quietly knocked.

"Su Lin? May I come in?" he asked.

The door opened on its own.

She stood at the window. He could see her curvaceous silhouette outlined by the daylight coming through the sheer window dressing. She twisted her torso around to face him and loosened the clip on her hair at the same time. The bundled coiffure came undone and tumbled down like a black waterfall about her shoulders. Her long straight hair then framed an angelic face. In the pale light, her eyes glowed as if they were on fire.

Villi took a step into the room. Before he could speak or link, she closed the door behind him with her mind. He noticed tears flowing down her perfect face. Despite her reaction, he admired her control downstairs a moment ago. He doubted anyone in their group – except for Michael or the professor – was capable of such control. He still could not open his mind to her. He feared what might happen if he did.

"Please don't be sad," he spoke aloud to her as he moved closer. "I wanted to tell you how much I approved of your technique before you ran away. You did an incredible job creating that bubble," he began. He tried to put her at ease. "If you'll come back down, I'm certain we can…"

She quickly closed the space between them. He stopped speaking when she pressed her body against his. She threw her head back. Her large moist brown eyes stared up at him. She slipped one hand behind his back and put her other hand over his mouth. She shook her head indicating he should not speak.

"I can still link to you," he smiled while he spoke under her hand.

"First let me say something," she countered and linked to him. "When I entered your mind, I tried not to see into the private areas that most men covet. I did not wish to embarrass you by knowing that side. I saw how you held part of your thoughts back from me. Instead, I saw how much you appreciated humor. I tried to play a joke. I didn't do a very good job. I'm so sorry Villi. It won't happen again. I didn't mean to embarrass you in front of…"

"It wasn't that Su Lin," Villi broke in. He chose to link with her. "You have a very beautiful body, which I admire very much. You simply caught me off guard. I did not expect your attempt to…" he tried to explain and then stopped.

All at once, Villi knew what really made him upset. It was not the nudity. He actually appreciated her sense of humor. The fact he had not fully opened his mind to her is what really bothered him. He held back his true feelings for her ever since Li cautioned him that first day. Su Lin could only guess what his feelings for her were. For all of his good manners, he forgot his psychic side and perhaps he should now use a different approach.

The two young psychics faced each other. Restrained emotion built up between them. Their mutual desire was palpable. They both could feel it. They wanted to embrace, but remembered their promise of fidelity to Professor Li.

"I must fully open my mind to you…" Su Lin said as she relaxed her posture.

She dropped all of her blocks and completely opened her mind. Villi could not hold back when Su Lin was so open and honest with him. He did the same. He opened his mind completely to her. Every thought, every detail of his entire life he revealed to her. For a brief moment, a flood of emotion and psychic energy poured between them. More powerful than physical contact, their psychic energy melded into a powerful union.

All at once, every psychic in the house could feel the surge related to the intensity of Villi and Su Lin's union. Memories, experiences, every moment of their lives flowed into that contact. It was far more powerful than Michael and Cecilia's first experience in the car back in Battleford. The psychic energy between Villi and Su Lin seemed to fuse together. It twisted and turned around on itself. This new fusion created a life of its own. A powerful throbbing light began to build up into some kind of new climax never experienced between a man and woman. This took arousal and orgasm to a level never achieved by any physical contact. A rising tide of energy crashed together like two great waves that swept both psychics away.

Their free expression only lasted a matter of seconds before the couple sensed others in the house shared in their interaction. They reluctantly pulled back their energy.

When Villi humorously recalled the moment with Su Lin later, they coined a new term and called it *psychic interuptus*.

Su Lin turned away from him. She faced the window and breathed hard as she tried to compose her emotions. Villi's broad chest rose and fell as if he had just finished a sprint. He did not know whether to shout with joy or take a nap. He reached up and wiped the sweat off his forehead. The brief experience took a great deal of energy from both psychics. They took a few seconds to recover their energy levels. In the silence that followed, Villi found the courage to speak.

"I can assist you better if you will join the others and practice your ability without the added… uh… humor," he suggested.

She slowly turned back to face him. Su Lin then slipped both of her arms around Villi's large frame this time with a different intent. She reached up and kissed him tenderly on the cheek. When she slowly pulled back, their lips nearly touched. Villi hesitated. He wanted to kiss her. He did not know that if he did kiss her, would he be able to stop.

"I promised to behave," she sweetly whispered.

"Su Lin I… I…" Villi stammered. For the first time in years, he felt nervous and uncertain around a woman. He felt like a high school student on his first date.

She put her finger on his lips.

"We don't have to say how we feel about each other, do we?" she whispered. "After all, we are psychic! I believe we understand one another. Wouldn't you agree?"

He nodded and swallowed hard. Their lips were just inches away. Villi put his arm around her waist. He brushed back her hair. Their lips were about to make contact.

"Villi!" Chou linked to his mind. "I did it!" he exclaimed. "I put an image into a full body bubble!"

Su Lin sighed as Villi closed his eyes and pulled away.

"Come on," she said taking his arm. "Let's see what he did."

He took her hand and squeezed it. He only let it go at the bottom of the stairs when she pulled away. They returned to the living room and continued to practice with the others for the next couple of hours. Yet the two adult psychics could hardly keep their eyes off each other for the rest of the day. The other students noticed the obvious attraction. Su Lin finally broke off from her lessons long enough to create a quick lunch for the house – an herb and greens salad with a pecan-blueberry dressing. She also made grilled tuna fish sandwiches topped with bean sprouts. While the fresh lunch invigorated the group, they mostly sat informally around the kitchen table in strained silence. Everyone felt uncomfortable with Villi and Su Lin staring at each other. The change in their relationship was obvious.

After lunch, Li addressed the gathered group of eight.

"I am pleased the last download went so well. Your new abilities will only flourish as you grow with experience," Li said. He tried not to sound patronizing. "Our progress around the city continues," he told them, "however, my team is receiving too many distractions." He stared right at Villi. "Cecilia, Michael and I must concentrate. Perhaps some meditation or lesson downloads from Galactic Central for this afternoon's exercises. Eh, Villi?"

"Yes professor," the Russian quietly replied.

The students nodded their agreement. Michael and Cecilia did not interact with Villi. Cecilia wanted to privately link with Su Lin. She was curious to find out about the "melding" they had experienced.

Instead, she and Michael left with Li. They allowed the others to continue on their own. Villi and the students cleaned up the kitchen. Afterward, they gathered back in the large audacious golden living room. Villi had them contact their GC voices for general Earth-related subjects such as world history, mathematics, science, literature, and so on.

On this day, the manor house behind the wall of stone remained as silent as a tomb. The mansion's occupants would appear peculiar to an outsider. Cecilia sat on her bed with her eyes closed. Michael leaned against his windowsill with his eyes closed. Professor Li sat on a rug in his bedroom. His eyes were closed too. The rest of house maintained a similar posture. No one spoke or said a word. The house resembled an ashram for meditation.

Chapter 36

Terror Strikes

During the next forty-eight hours, life inside the large edifice on the hill settled down into a quiet routine. Li, Michael and Cecilia continued to scan the area around Shenyang daily. It seemed that they searched in vain for the difficult-to-find psychics. Li thought the entire arrangement strange. He wondered if the psychic or psychics lured them to this place. He then purposed they were teasing them with temporary spikes of power. These all too brief glimpses made it difficult for the group to leave – knowing that some psychic might simply be stranded nearby or too weak to communicate.

While Li felt odd about the vague intermittent contact, he did not share his feelings or opinions. Michael remained steadfast and silent. He performed his duty as requested without question. Cecilia finally spoke up at breakfast on the third morning.

"Do you feel that this search is helping professor?" she asked.

Every face around the table looked up – not at Cecilia, but to Li. They gazed at his face for any telling feature for he seldom gave up his opinion on anything.

"We're bound to find them," Li responded. "The search is taking longer because we are being thorough. I believe it is too early to give up and move on. For all we know, this psychic or psychics may even be in prison," Li speculated.

"I'll search the prisons if you like," Michael offered.

"I would rather you weren't exposed to that nasty business," Li linked. "I brought the matter up. I will scan the prisons… without any help," he punctuated his statement to keep Michael from offering his assistance. "Goodness knows what I'll find there," he muttered.

"It won't be goodness," Villi pointed out. "By the way, the students are showing significant progress. I would say that if we need to travel incognito for a short period of time, this bunch will have no difficulty," he stated with a note of pride in his voice.

"At least we have that good news," Li commented. "Give them a good work out today Villi," Li told him. "Keep them busy. Exercise that psychic ability!"

"Yes sir," Villi replied. He knew exactly what Li meant.

If anyone in the house had a sense of physical fitness, Villi did. Most Russian police officers train hard to stay in shape. At dawn every morning, usually before everyone rose, Villi ran the perimeter of the grounds. He would finish with exercises in front of the house such as sit-ups and pushups. Michael surprised him the second day when he ran alongside. This morning, Zhiwei joined them.

After breakfast, the three searchers retired to their bedroom to continue their scans of the city. Meanwhile, Villi started his group out with calisthenics that included his usual routine. Su Lin, Zinian and Zhiwei kept up the pace. Chou took up the rear. Villi signaled the other two men to be supportive of their new friend.

"A chain is only as strong as its weakest link," Villi reminded.

The men circled back and fell in next to Chou.

"How is this supposed to develop my mind?" Chou complained, out of breath.

"Come on, ya nerd," Zinian told him. "Haven't you heard? You need to develop the mind and the body!"

"Is there such a thing as being over-developed?" Chou shot back. He stopped and bent over as he tried to get his breath back.

Zinian and Zhiwei chuckled at his response. The two hefty young men picked Chou up under his armpits and dragged the studious young man along. Despite the workout he tried to impose on the group by running around the entire perimeter of the estate, Su Lin stayed with Villi stride for stride.

"You're in good shape," he offered as the two made their way up the drive toward the house.

"You're not!" she declared.

She took off at a sprint. The two raced for the front door. Su Lin surprised Villi by making a quick burst of speed at the end and beat him. They laughed between gasps for breath. She turned her profile to him.

"I'd say I'm in very good shape," she said.

"I can't argue with that," he said as he stared at her figure.

291

The group went to the kitchen for a short break, where they refreshed and relaxed. Villi then encouraged the four students to refine their use of telekinesis. He wanted them to move objects with precise control.

"Zinian, the vacuum cleaner," he stated. "Zhiwei use the dust rag. Chou separate and start the laundry. Here's the catch," he explained. "I want you to use your telekinesis only. Do not touch the object. Begin!" Villi did not give directions to Su Lin – not because of favoritism, but because she kept the kitchen organized and cooked all of the meals. No one else wanted that job.

Zinian, Zhiwei and Chou tried their best at this form of mental manipulation. However, after only a matter of minutes, objects unintentionally began to fly about the house. Villi taxed his mind as he tried to catch lamps and vases before they smashed into the walls. Zinian accidentally broke a ceramic knick-knack. He called out a broom to clean up the mess with poor success. To save his head, Villi diverted the broom out an open window before it struck him. His energy reserve low, he had to run outside to retrieve it.

Zinian shrugged his shoulders at Villi and apologized while garnering more energy as well.

"Flying broomsticks," Villi muttered when he walked back inside with the object in his hand. "It's time to scale these assignments down until they gain better control."

After an hour, Chou found he could mentally vacuum the floor easier than Zinian. Zhiwei dusted via his thoughts without breaking any lamps. Zinian retreated to the laundry room. He could sort colors without a major incident. If a pair of pants flew into the wall, they caused no harm.

Villi next headed to the kitchen. Unknown to the Russian instructor, Su Lin decided to chop vegetables with her mind. She tried to use several knives at once. When Villi stepped through the kitchen door, his sudden appearance distracted her concentration. A large slicing knife flew through the air right at him.

"Ah!" he cried out. He did not have time to deflect it.

The big Russian threw his arms up. The blade cut under his armpit. The sharp steel grazed his flesh and pinned his shirt to the wall. The knife struck so hard it buried deep into the wood.

"Villi!" Su Lin cried out. "Are you injured?" She ran across the room in a panic as she thought she had skewered her boyfriend. Her other knives crashed down to the countertop. When she saw he was untouched, she stopped and took in a deep breath. "I am so sorry. It just flew out of my control when I saw you."

"Feeling hostile?" Villi wondered. He could not pull the knife from the door.

Their eyes met in that longing stare lovers often exchange. For a second, she wondered how he would react. She wondered if his feelings toward her had changed.

"How can any man be angry with that beautiful face?" he linked to her. In that brief moment, he again revealed the emotional depth of those feelings that he kept hidden for so long.

She grabbed the handle with two hands and pulled the knife out of the wall. Fortunately, the blade barely touched his skin and only left a superficial cut. Su Lin brought out the first aid kit that the owner kept in the kitchen.

"You'll have to take off your shirt," she told him while she prepared the kit. A trickle of blood ran down his side. The big muscular man with the hairy chest pulled off his sliced garment. She carefully inspected the wound. "Just a scratch," she observed. However, she took her time as she ran her hand along his arm and side. "I just want to be certain I didn't stab you anywhere else," she told him.

"You did," he spoke up.

"Where?" she replied and turned her head back to look over his fit body.

"Here," he stated and pointed at his heart.

"You'll have to leave your shirt off," she instructed with only the hint of a smile. She spent the next ten minutes by taking her time to dress his wound. "You'll live… even with a broken heart," she quipped. She then made him a cup of tea while Villi enjoyed her company.

"If we ever have an argument, please don't throw knives at me," he joked. He poked his finger through the hole in shirt.

"Silly," she shot back. "If I get mad, I'll throw the car at you instead. That way I won't miss!"

The two stopped kidding and gazed longingly into each other's eyes.

"I… I…" he started to link. He still found those three words difficult to express.

"I know you do," she replied. She wrapped her hand around his thick firm arm. "What's funny is," she added, "you know that I do too."

Preoccupied with their assignments, the entire household decided to skip lunch and chose to take an early dinner instead. That gave Villi and Su Lin more time to spend together in the kitchen. Later that afternoon around four, Su Lin sent out a call to the house for dinner. She spread out her usual gourmet feast. When Professor Li arrived at the table, he did not speak or link with anyone. He quietly picked at his food.

"What's the matter Professor?" Cecilia wondered. The others noticed his solemn mood too. Quiet and withdrawn, Li was not his usual animated self.

"Is something wrong with the food?" Su Lin asked. She was worried more about the professor than her dish.

"It isn't that Su Lin," he forced a smile that quickly faded. "After you scan the minds of seven thousand prisoners during their lunchtime in an open mess hall, nothing seems very appetizing."

He blocked the group from the images still so fresh in his mind. He reached for his tea, but the greenish-brown color inside the cup repulsed him. He put it to his lips and forced down a swallow anyway.

Michael half smiled and tried to break the mood with a joke. "If you think that's nauseating, try reading the thoughts of homeless as they pick through dumpsters."

Li glanced up at Michael and saw how the young man genuinely sympathized.

"Touché," he replied.

Li threw off his preoccupation with his day. He sat up straight. His eyes followed the eager faces around the table when he picked up his chopsticks. He took a tender chunk of beef and shoved the morsel into his mouth. While the food had great flavor, Li had profound nausea.

"This is actually quite good Su Lin," he generally linked after taking a reluctant bite. He swallowed hard and forced the food into his nauseous stomach. Surrounded by silent staring faces, Li tried to make small talk. "I'll stay after dinner and help wash the dishes tonight."

"No, no…" the students objected in chorus.

"Nonsense," Li said as he brushed their protests aside, "I insist."

"You've done quite enough for one day Professor," Su Lin spoke up. "It took us a while," she glanced at Villi who sported a fresh shirt. "We have things work out in that department. We cleaned up as we prepared dinner. Only the dishes on the table remain."

Without knowing if she spoke the truth, the students all voiced their agreement and support for Su Lin's suggestion. That made Li smile inside him.

"Michael and I need your strength for tomorrow," Cecilia told him while she placed her hand on his arm.

Li patted her hand and took another small bite of food. He forced it down and tried to forget the reoccurring images of prisoners and their food.

"Besides," Villi threw in, "these three could use more exercise."

Villi jerked his head toward the kitchen. The three male students jumped up and used their minds to stack dirty plates, glasses, and flatware from the table into the dishwasher.

"Excellent control fellahs!" Villi said in his best use of colloquial English.

"Nicely done Villi," Li linked as he nodded his approval.

"Thanks professor," Villi linked, nodding back.

A few minutes later when Michael sat in his room with the door open, he heard a loud crash and one student cry for help. He then heard Zinian and Zhiwei laugh as they chased Chou around the house. He doused the other two with dirty dishwater after they teased him. Michael heard Villi cursing in Russian while he tried to convince the students to use their powers in constructive ways.

Cecilia strolled up the hall past Michael's room. She stopped in his doorway.

"Sounds like Villi has his hands full," she said with a chuckle. "Want to give him a hand?"

"Not on your life! He's enjoying it," Michael replied. "What better person than a police officer to maintain order." He paused when he realized he had been staring at her. He tried to change the subject. "By the way, I wanted to tell you how much I appreciate your accurate scans. I felt your presence several times as I moved around the city. Even after I searched one of the public squares, you came behind me and did it again at lunchtime."

"Li said to be thorough..." she began.

"I felt those searches," Michael told her. "Your power is growing stronger. I thought you'd like to know."

An awkward moment followed when the two seasoned psychics stood gazing into each other's eyes. More than anyone in their group, Michael and Cecilia hid their feelings toward one another. Perhaps this contradiction carried over from that first night in the hotel. At any rate, they refrained from expressing their true feelings. They kept their relationship strictly cordial.

Michael could feel Cecilia's longing to say something personal. He could not bear being this close to her. He felt ready to explode with passion. When he looked at her pale pink lips, he only wanted to kiss them. He withdrew his feelings. He boxed them up behind a firm block.

"Well, good night Cecilia. See you in the morning," he said as he abruptly ended the conversation. He reached out and closed his door with his thoughts.

Michael's curt manner did not offend her. However, she realized that she could not go through life desiring a man that did not want her. If or when they left China, she would need to look for a partner from another source she reasoned. She slowly moved up the hall back toward her room. She started to link another thought to Michael and instead felt his intense block that prevented her.

The next day, more of the same routine continued throughout the house. Each member of the group performed as he or she did the day before. The same routine continued the following day. Li decided to search one last day before he called off their effort. The first week in Shenyang nearly ended on a dull quiet note.

Villi and Su Lin closely worked together in the kitchen lately. They had started to prepare lunch in the kitchen when a piercing scream cut through the profound silence. Every psychic in house jumped in reaction, except one. The blood-curdling shriek struck hard. It reflected a person in pain – someone who cried out during a moment of sheer terror.

The male students rushed out from the living room just as Villi and Su Lin ran from the kitchen to the bottom of the staircase.

"I can't sense anything," Su Lin linked to the others standing there.

"It's as if a huge block is keeping my thoughts in check!" Chou complained.

Unable to link, Villi yelled up from the bottom of the stairs, "What happened?"

"It's Cecilia!" Michael yelled back.

Villi saw Michael shove the door to her room open and rush inside.

Villi dropped the mixing spoon in his hand and leapt onto the stairs. He took three steps at a stride. Su Lin and the others followed right behind him. When Villi arrived, the door to Cecilia's room stood open. The entire group paused outside when they noticed Professor Li swiftly moving up the hallway.

"I know you want to help," he said while he waved his arms. "Let me in first please," he requested.

The group parted to let the powerful little man into the room. Michael had reached her first. He found Cecilia collapsed on the floor as if she had fallen out of bed.

He supported her head in his lap and brushed the blonde matted hair from her sweaty face. She lay flaccid in his arms, her eyes were closed, and her skin pale. Villi could not sense her breathing.

"Michael," Li said quietly, "Do you know what happened?"

Michael stared over at Li shaking his head. He gasped for air and struggled to speak.

"I don't know. I heard her scream. Master Li… you don't think…" he tried to say.

Michael clutched her limp body. Tears started to form in his eyes. Her arms hung down lifeless and flopped around as he pulled her close.

Li scowled the moment he walked through the door. He was clearly upset. He quickly crossed to where Michael sat on the floor with Cecilia's head pressed into his chest.

"Michael… let me examine her," Li said. He gently pulled Cecilia's head back into Michael's lap. He then carefully bent down on one knee.

"Is she…?" Michael's words choked on the emotion in his throat. He was too distraught to speak.

"She's not dead," Li said as he moved in closer. "Her heart is still beating and she is exchanging air, although very shallow. She is close to death," Li informed him. "I sense that something or someone is attempting to take over her body and mind. I'm afraid she is fighting a losing battle. I'll try to help."

The group stood poised in the doorway. They felt suspended in the moment. Michael leaned back and allowed Li to move in closer.

"This is strange…" Li began, "I feel a familiar presence…"

He lightly touched one finger on her forehead. His body jerked when he made contact. He yanked his finger away and glared at the group with an accusatory stare. His thoughts pierced the minds of those in the room. He quickly entered and exited each person as if he was searching frantically for some obscure clue.

"Thank goodness," he muttered in relief. He feared he had misjudged a candidate. "For a minute, I thought…" he said. He left off the rest of his thought.

No one in the room had been able to link since the incident started. Li did not tell them he dropped a dampening field around the house. Yet for some reason this action did not affect Cecilia's condition. His expression hardened as he focused on the pale young woman. He noticed her skin was so white, plus her face so haggard and drawn. Her present state belied her usual beauty by casting a deadly pallor over her face. Li sat on the floor next to the couple and bent closer to Cecilia's face. As if he flipped a light switch, Li isolated his mind with hers.

"If you are not in this room, then you must be elsewhere…" Li thought.

To an ordinary person, Li and Cecilia would have vanished in that moment. However, the other psychics saw a powerful field of energy surround the two psychics on the floor. They could see that this bubble of energy was similar to a psychic bubble yet also different. Inside they could make out shimmering images of Li and Cecilia. Psychically, Li blocked everyone out including Michael who was right next to Li. He still had Cecilia's head in his lap. The group could palpate the tension in the room.

"Master Li," Michael started to link.

Li held up his index finger to silence his pupil.

"I need a moment please," Li indicated before he shut him back out.

Li gently placed the palm of his hand down on Cecilia's cool moist forehead. He closed his eyes and reached out beyond the confines of the house. He sensed a strong tether of psychic energy attached to her head. The tether wrapped around her brain. It trapped Cecilia prisoner inside a sphere of influence similar to a psychic bubble with an unusual configuration. Despite Li's attempt to raise a shield that might shut out an intruder, this tether easily pierced his defenses. That could only indicate a powerful psychic at the other end. The idea that Earth may have produced two psychics with his strength raised Li's level of concern when he considered that sophistication of the link.

"What psychic would use their power for such a dastardly thing?" he thought. "This attack is insidious," he whispered aloud, "and diabolical."

He traced the silvery cord backward across the city until its source came to an abrupt end. He found a psychic being that possessed great power and bound Cecilia to pale silence. This being possessed a psychic glow that rivaled his level of power. He cautiously probed the source.

"I know you…" Li uttered. A strange yet familiar feeling from his past returned.

"Well, well, well," a cold unfeeling voice echoed around his mind, "look who turned up – the little Harbin boy with so much power. You found me at last. I knew I could not hide from you forever. Is the girl a companion? She has power for being a female. She gives me much pleasure. You must give her to me."

A strong psychic pulse tried to push Li out of Cecilia's mind. Li resisted and pushed back. In his rush to come to Cecilia's aid, he neglected to raise a sufficient energy level to do psychic battle. This effort drained his energy. Everyone in the room heard Li moan aloud. His hand he had placed against her forehead twisted as if the contact caused him pain. Michael noticed Li began to sweat.

"I should have known," Li thought. "No wonder you were attracted to me back then. I've been so stupid, so blind. You were watching me the whole time. I thought they took you away."

"We come from the same family cousin," the cold voice stated. "Did you think that when the government officials took me away that they destroyed me? They tried but they couldn't. So they sealed me in this room. I've waited patiently for the day when we would meet. I had my doubts it would happen. Now, I am ready for you. I have more experience at this than you do," the voice spoke. Its cold harsh words echoed in Li's mind.

"You devil," Li said as he strained against the other psychic's will. "Let go of her. She is innocent. She means nothing to you. Release her at once…"

"Or what?" the cold voice answered. "You'll thrash me with your might? Ha! Your lower power level does not frighten me."

Li's hand on her forehead began to shake as he pushed against the force of the other psychic.

"My mind is entwined with hers," the cold hearted psychic told Li. "You cannot break this bond without hurting her… and you would never do that. Would you cousin?"

"This girl is my pupil. I cannot let you harm her," Li spoke as he marshaled his forces and gathered additional energy.

"You've only been psychic for two weeks," the cold voice bragged. "I have practiced for…" the cold voice suddenly stopped when it felt a change. "What are you doing Chin?"

"I'm trying to stop you!" Li grunted. He released additional energy into the connection.

Cecilia frowned and then groaned. Her breathing stopped. Michael sensed it.

"Cecilia!" he cried. He could only sit by, helpless to act while he noted Li's power build.

Li's right hand began to glow. His face twisted into a grimace. All at once, he cried out, "Aaahhh!"

Li's psychic power forced the cold tendril encapsulating Cecilia's mind into retreat. The being on the other end did not have enough force to resist. The tendril withdrew. All at once, Li fell back and let out a hissing sigh. His hand broke the psychic connection as he fell. The psychic field around Li and Cecilia dissipated as the elderly man collapsed. With great effort on his part, he cut the binding link between the vile attacking psychic and the young woman's mind. Despite his years of experience, the rogue psychic did not know the simplest techniques that Li commanded since instructed by the hierarchy in Galactic Central.

Cecilia opened her eyes. She took in a huge gasp of air. She then choked and coughed. Michael sighed with relief as he saw her color immediately return.

Villi rushed to Li's side and caught his frail thin body just before his head hit the floor. The students watched the entire scene with amazement. Frightened, Villi quickly scanned Li's mind. He wanted to make certain the connection did not harm him. Li opened his eyes and gave Villi a half-smile of thanks. He then waved Villi off. Sweat trickled down the side of his face.

"I appreciate your concern, Villi," he barely uttered, unable to link for the moment.

Villi did not back off. Instead, he reached around Li's shoulders and helped him to sit up. Cecilia stirred in Michael's lap. The color returned to her body as she began to move her hands and arms. She first focused on Michael's contorted face.

"Oh Cecilia!" he muttered as he hugged her. "I'm so glad you're alright."

"I'm ok Michael," she whispered into his ear. She glanced over his shoulder at Li. Michael pulled back. She cleared her throat while staring right at Li. "I owe you my life… Master Li," Cecilia said quietly to him. She closed her eyes and bowed her head. Michael's eyes widened with surprise as she said it.

During the attack, Cecilia shared Li's thoughts. She overheard the meeting between Li and Michael and at last understood why Michael called him Master Li. She also realized that Li is not just Michael's master. Every psychic in the room should consider Li their master – for the venerable Chinese man had much knowledge and experience to teach. She also knew that the time was right to address the professor with this new title and offer him the respect he deserved.

The others stared at Li. They wondered why Cecilia used this term and bowed her head. In spite of his insisting on being fine, Villi helped Li to his feet. He practically lifted the elderly man to a standing position. When Li heard Cecilia's words, he groaned out of exasperation.

"I am no one's master!" he uttered to her humbly. His eyes scanned the room, yet the group's attention remained fixed on him.

"Yeah, what's with the Master Li stuff?" Villi blurted out.

Michael and Cecilia gave Villi such a reprimanding stare that the Russian backed up when he felt their animosity.

"Ok, ok, from now on he's Master Li," he relented.

Cecilia turned to Michael. She spoke aloud for the experience completely drained her psychic energy.

"I found our psychic," she informed him. "He is located in an asylum for the mentally insane on the southern edge of the city. When I first made contact, I sensed a kindly an old man. I should say he sensed me. His is very strong. He said such nice enticing things to me. He flattered me. Yet, when I tried to pull away, he forced me to… to…"

Cecilia shivered and her voice choked with emotion. Her whole body shook as tears ran down her face. The group stood by and watched. They felt helpless to act on behalf of Cecilia. Every psychic expressed concern for her. Master Li put up a block to protect Cecilia's experience so that no one, not even Michael could penetrate her mind.

"Michael," she whispered to him. "It was horrible. I thought I was trapped and would never see you again."

Michael glanced over at Master Li. His emotions ran a gambit mixed with anger and frustration. When he convinced her to leave her home in Canada, he promised to protect her.

Master Li stepped in front of Michael and Cecilia who were still on the floor.

"It is safe to assume this heartless predator represents a threat to our group," he addressed the group. "Each of us is vulnerable. Now that he knows our location, he may try to attack someone else," he explained. "Great evil is at work here. We must not sit idly by while he is free to invade psychic's minds."

Li unsteadily leaned against Villi as he spoke. The Russian watched him intently. He wondered if the encounter with the rogue injured him. However, even as he linked his advice to the group, Li gathered energy from the surrounding countryside. He felt he was the only defense the group had against such a determined foe.

"This psychic is locked away in an institution with as much security as a prison. We cannot simply walk in and do as we please," Li told them. "We must devise a plan."

Li gently pushed away from Villi and then turned to him.

"Villi, I want you to take Su Lin with you and drive to this asylum," Li instructed. "This is reconnaissance work. Search for weaknesses in their system. Keep your identity secret. We'll plan our response when you return. Use your blocking technique or employ the psychic bubble if you feel the slightest contact. This man is extremely dangerous. Use every caution. I'm counting on you Villi."

"Yes… Master Li," Villi spoke up hesitantly as he tried out the title. Villi nodded his head but he did not bow as he saw Michael and Cecilia do.

Li accepted the new title and nodded back. He could feel a similar sentiment of respect coming from the others in the room. Li faced the rest of the group.

"Be mindful of any contacts," he instructed. "Maintain constant mental blocks, including those from your housemates and friends. You'll have to speak openly for a change. Make no psychic links. Do not use your power for anything. It might attract attention. Are we clear on how to proceed?" Li asked as he scanned their faces filled with worry and anxiety. "If we remain vigilant, we can avert this treachery and prevent any further calamity," he told them. He pulled his body up straighter and tried to instill confidence. "Chou, can you cook any better than you can drive?"

"Yes Master Li," Chou replied, "a little."

"Very well, you can finish preparing lunch while Villi and Su Lin are gone. Zinian, Zhiwei, please help him. Work together for a change," he added. "Pardon me for being abrupt. I would like everyone to leave," he linked as he directed him or her toward the door.

He brushed his hands in the air while he shooed the group out the doorway. However, Li reached around behind his back and waved his hand to Michael as he motioned him to stay.

"I'm glad you're good with bubble technique," Villi said to Su Lin as they exited the room. "We can use it when we arrive at the asylum."

"Do not try to contact me via link Villi," Li told him in the hall, "until you return. Of course, feel free to contact me if you encounter a problem you cannot solve. Otherwise, stay alert. Be especially mindful of Su Lin," he added. "I want you two to remain close. If you feel a probe – any probe at all – put up a block or make a bubble. Do you understand?"

"Yes Master Li," Villi and Su Lin spoke back simultaneously. They glanced at each other and exited down the staircase with the other three students.

Li turned around to the young couple on the floor. Michael brushed the hair out of Cecilia's eyes. Li noticed her natural skin color returned to his relief.

"Let's move her onto the bed Michael," Li said as he walked over to them.

The two men helped Cecilia stand. The experience left her so weak; they practically carried her over to her bed. Michael turned to leave but Li put his hand on Michael's chest and stopped him.

"I want you to stay with Cecilia," Li requested. "She needs you right now. Please Michael. Also, do not probe her mind to find out what happened. When she is ready, she will share that experience with you."

"Yes Master Li," Michael said and inclined his head.

Li turned to Cecilia with a softened expression on his face.

"Rest Cecilia. Do not use your power at all," he told her. "If you do, he will sense you at once and try to regain entry into your mind. Try to replenish your level. Once you regain your power level, I feel this time you can repel him with a strong psychic bubble if he should attempt to contact you. Unfortunately, for you on your first encounter, once you relaxed in his presence he easily gained entry. He won't be so lucky a second time," Li pointed out. "I am sorry for what happened to you. To properly heal, you must remain calm to quiet your inner thoughts," Li kindly spoke. "Michael will keep guard and watch over you if you wish to close your eyes and rest."

Cecilia nodded a silent agreement. Li bowed to her and walked toward the door.

Michael sat next to Cecilia on the bed. He took her hand and held it tenderly. Cecilia did not speak. She simply turned and wrapped her arms tightly around Michael's waist. She buried her head in his chest. Michael glanced up just before Li closed the door. He questioned with his face whether he should stay. Li motioned for Michael to put his arms around Cecilia.

Quietly, Li added a mental note as he silently pulled the door closed.

"Be gentle, be kind, empathize and comfort her Michael," he told him. "She needs you now more than she ever needed anyone in her life."

Michael put his arm around Cecilia's shoulder just as the young woman broke into long sobs. He said nothing nor did he try to probe her thoughts. Protective in nature, Michael pulled in energy and then created a psychic bubble that engulfed the pair while it blocked out the rest of the world. He left his mind blank and open to her should she need him.

Under her breath, she muttered, "Please hold me. I feel so cold."

Michael held her tenderly. As Cecilia slowly opened her mind to him, the realization of what took place angered and saddened Michael that anyone could violate such a beautiful innocent woman.

Remembering Li's advice, Michael kept his anger in check. Instead, he concentrated on protecting the woman in his arms. He understood his true feelings for her at last. He knew he loved Cecilia, perhaps from the moment they met.

Memories from the past few weeks flashed before him… he recalled her stubborn behavior on the first day… her naïve but charming awe at the Rocky Mountains… trying to squeeze into those submarine bunk beds… her ruffled appearance at the bow of that fishing trawler… her emotional fit over the cracked fingernail after climbing over miles of rock… The fun they experienced clubbing in Khabarovsk. The past few weeks of those shared adventurous memories pushed the one bad memory aside.

This woman knew every detail about his life – down to the most trivial fact. During their journey, he hid nothing of his past from her. Yet through it all, Cecilia constantly watched out for him. She warned him of danger as well as shared her joys and sorrows in an open, giving way – a gift greater than any fortune he thought.

At that moment, Cecilia lifted her eyes and met Michael's as he gazed into hers.

"Don't be angry my love," she linked to his mind. "As long as you are near me, I know I am safe."

"You can link?" he began.

"Inside this bubble you created I can," she weakly linked.

"Wait a minute! You said, 'my love,'" Michael linked back with hope.

"I said it because it is true," she linked to him.

As their eyes met, Cecilia opened every aspect of her mind to him just as Michael opened his to her. Every thought or concern Michael ever held back flowed out of his thoughts. Cecilia then opened the tiny seed of concealment in her mind that held her true feelings for him. She shared with Michael the deep and abiding love that she kept secret. The psychic wound so fresh in her mind healed instantly as Michael's love filled her with warmth and understanding.

"You do love me," she linked as she fought back her tears.

"Yes," he said as he opened his mind completely to hers.

Instead of a crescendo of crashing waves, Michael and Cecilia's energy melded into one that had no borders. There were no floodgates flung open. Calm trust and love ruled over extreme passion. They understood their feelings and responsibilities as lovers without confusion. Clarity ruled the day. While their day of strong passion may yet occur, it would happen on their terms.

The very first psychic romance blossomed into adult love.

Cecilia knew that Michael would be the only man in her life for as long as she lived. He felt exactly the same way about her. He then shared his psychic energy with her. It filled her with vitality and purpose until they held an equal amount. Unlike the brief sharing between Villi and Su Lin, Michael and Cecilia held nothing back. They allowed their love to amplify the psychic energy as it bound them together.

Suddenly, as if a star turned on for the first time, their love gave birth to a brilliant light from their shared energy that shone between them. Cecilia's mind then joined with Michael's and together they maintained the psychic bubble wrapped around them like a secure cocoon.

"Michael…" her link to him seemed to come from the end of time.

"What?" he replied.

"Do you know what today is?"

"No…"

"Today is my eighteenth birthday…"

At that moment, their heads slowly gravitated together until their lips gently met for the first time. Their soft flesh pressed into a perfect fit as a warm and tender loving kiss.

"Happy birthday…" he thought to her as they wrapped their arms around each other and embraced.

CHAPTER 37

THE FORBIDDEN CORRIDOR

BACK IN HIS ROOM, MASTER Li closed and locked his bedroom door. He drew the blinds and shut off the lights. He did not wish to be disturbed and wanted no distractions, which is why he gave the rest of the team some duty to perform – whether they realized that duty had a purpose or not. For what he hoped to accomplish, he needed utmost privacy. He went to his prayer rug and bowed to the statue of Buddha. Then, he sat on the floor in a position similar to that of the statue.

Li started a complex process within his mind. When he finished, he contemplated his arrival at the large People's State Mental Hospital on the south end of Shenyang. Along the way, he gathered psychic energy from the area. He took it from every person he encountered and left none behind until he gradually built up a great reserve.

As Li sat in his bedroom, a rich shimmering golden glow of psychic energy burned all around him. Li stuffed his mind with psychic power as a chipmunk stuffs its cheeks until they bulge full of food. He had a difficult job to do. He needed every ounce of psychic energy he could muster. He knew this encounter would not be a pleasant one.

A ghostly duplicate image of Li instantly appeared in front of the hospital. Only a person with psychic ability could see the non-corporeal figure. Before he confronted this rogue, a small task remained. He needed valuable information.

As he contemplated going inside, he sensed the approach of another psychic. Villi and Su Lin headed up the street toward the hospital at breakneck speed. Only the armed officer at the huge gate guarding the entrance to a compound that resembled a prison temporarily slowed the Russian and his dear female friend. Master Li could not let them see his aura body. He moved into the lobby and walked right up to the security officer at the front desk. He reached out and easily influenced her mind. She placed her hands over the computer keys as Li tapped into the net. He accessed secret areas, such as the Chinese Defense grid and the civil service system. He carefully watched the screen while he quickly flipped past page after page of information before the terminal finally shut down.

"All access denied," the screen flashed.

Satisfied with the information he obtained, Li backed away. The guard, unaware of her part in these recent actions, surmised that she must have been daydreaming.

Moving on, Li's ghostly form extended his arms upward. Like an apparition on its own elevator, he floated up through the structure until he finally stopped inside the west wing on the seventh floor. Using his mind, he made his spirit able to stand on the solid surface. He then walked through the crowded ward while he observed the patients and staff as they coped with substandard conditions from recent budget cuts. He noted a tray of food in the hallway.

"I thought the prison food was bad. That's a disgusting bill of fare," he commented. He noted the scoops of colored mush that seemed more like bad flavors of ice cream than food.

As he neared the far end of the seventh floor, Li's aural body sensed chilling cold. A freestanding sign printed with Chinese characters warned: "*No visitors beyond this point.*"

He moved around the sign. Seeing a lack of furniture – even cleanliness, as if no one ever came to this end of the building – he noted a narrow footpath through the dust on the floor. He followed that trail which led to a side hall.

Inside this corridor, he felt the presence of a very strong mind. The energy source was so strong in fact that his best pupil, Michael paled in comparison. The trail continued on the floor and led to one door in the middle of the hall. As he stood at the open end of the corridor, Li noted the dark hallway had no other exit and no windows. Only light coming in from behind him offered any illumination.

"At last, the great Li Po Chin arrives," an echoing voice struck him hard, like a splash of cold water in the face.

The cruel icy voice crashed upon him as if waves of psychic energy flowed against his forward progress. Li's ghostly form staggered back from their force before fighting to continue.

"I've been waiting for you," the booming voice beckoned. "It's been difficult to mask my presence. That is no longer necessary."

Li had concentrated his attention so much on the door that he barely noticed a brass stand holding an old piece of painted wood standing off to the side of this dark corridor. Covered with dust and cobwebs and using blood red paint, someone printed one Chinese character: "*Forbidden!*"

The elderly scholar slowly moved deeper into the darkened hallway. No custodian had cleaned the filthy floor on either side of the footpath in a very long time. Cobwebs hung from the ceiling except in the middle.

"Food delivery," he thought, noting the reason for the daily footprints.

He stopped in front of the door. Constructed from a solid piece of steel, the jailers welded the edges to the doorframe. Nothing could open the permanently sealed door. On closer inspection, Li saw Chinese writing in very small letters running around the edge, repeated several times. He carefully examined the text. It read:

"*Warning: open this door at your peril, for great evil will you let loose upon the world.*"

He stretched out his ghostly hand and placed it in on the surface of the door. The dark gray metal felt like a block of ice. The presence of a powerful entity overwhelmed Li's conscious mind. He backed away from the door.

"What has become of you?" Li wondered, as he was unable to pierce the potent impenetrable psychic shield.

"I am all that you fear," the corrupt voice echoed in his mind. "I am darkness and chaos. No alien voice from another world would dare touch my mind. They know that I could destroy the whole lot of them, and put an end to their silly Galactic Central," the voice bragged. "They do not realize the extent of our psychic power! We are an enigma to them and their curiosity will be their undoing. I can corrupt the crystal that powers their apparatus. Then I can control its only inhabitant. After I take over their director, I will be the greatest psychic in the universe! I only needed your great power to complete the task. After years of planning, I wondered how I could trick you into coming to Shenyang," the voice chuckled. "Now you have come to me on your own accord – all the better!"

Li stood before the door caught up in the conflict between flight and action. He was torn between his own inadequacy and inexperience dealing with evil. Action would mean going against his philosophy to preserve and promote life.

"Professor Li Po Chin of Harbin… come inside if you dare!" the voice beckoned. "Either way, I have you, cousin!"

A wicked laughter ensued so loudly, Li thought the intensity strong enough to shatter glass. His real body still sitting back in the house trembled when he reacted to its torment. The golden light surrounding his body fluctuated as fear and uncertainty tore into his mind.

He took in a deep breath. "Courage," Li thought.

As dangerous as the next moved seemed – Li knew he must attempt it. He once more probed the inside of the room before entering. This time, the creature freely revealed its baffling and strange history to Li.

"I have nothing to fear from you, old man. Here is what you seek," the voice offered.

A terrible comprehension gripped Li's mind. He thought only one person resided inside. He sensed five people in the room speaking through one mind!

"So, that's why your power seems so great!" Li realized.

He then saw the relationship between them, one mind controlling four others, imposing his will upon them to do his bidding. He probed further to find out how this happened.

Many years ago, four young women discovered their limited psychic ability and formed a secret group of mind-linked friends. They were not aware of Galactic Central. Their power – still grossly undeveloped – did not project very far. Then he came along having escaped the asylum in Harbin. He sought the source of their power and delighted when he found them living together in Shenyang. He immediately placed the four women under his control.

"Then I remembered correctly," Li recalled, "that was you, the scraggy young man that begged on the corner and always greeted me on my way home from school."

"Yes," the man spoke to Li. His all too familiar voice evoked memories in Li from his childhood. "I am the crazy young man on the corner and your cousin. My own family disowned me. I brought shame on them. Your father forbade you to mention me, for you see your mother and my mother are sisters. I am just a few years older than you cousin," he said as he linked his history to Li. "I heard the same voices you heard. Unlike you, I knew who and what they were. I also knew they were afraid of me, which is why they would not convert me. They disapproved of my thoughts. So I performed my own conversion... and yes," he hissed, "it can be done without their help."

Li's eyes widened with the realization that conversion did not require Galactic Central – at least, not in an organized sense. He did not have time to analyze his cousin's form of conversion. Instead, his cousin continued to tell Li his history.

"Before I could act with my new ability, the People's Army came to Shenyang. They were rounding up anyone that did not conform to their ideals. How fortunate for us when they threw me in the asylum together with my companions. I could draw on their power. We created quite a stir in that hospital until they finally realized what we were and gassed us. When we woke, we were sealed in here."

"Why didn't they shoot you? The Army was not above that sort of thing back then," Li inquired.

"Oh, they tried, cousin, they tried," he chuckled, "after twenty or so shot each other, they gassed our room. Yet even in sleep, my protection saved us. Unable to destroy us, they moved us here and sealed up the room. They only cut a slot in the door to keep us fed when I planted the thought in their feeble minds at the last moment," he linked with a sneer. "What a humane gesture!" He spat the last word with contempt.

"As the years passed, we grew in strength," he continued, "We learned to block Galactic Central out of our thoughts. Besides, we did not want their wholesome intrusions. We only needed to find a way out of here. I knew of you in Harbin and tried many times to entice you to Shenyang. I even sent one of your students back with an invitation to speak here."

"That was you?" Li said. He recalled the man that he thought was so friendly.

"Yes," his cousin's voice told him, "it was me. Then, you finally went through with your conversion and became a loyal member of collective. How quaint," he snarled. "Imagine my delight when I could feel you drawing near. So I waited," he said with his voice dropping. "All at once, you gave me a bonus. I sensed the young girl's mind and entered it. She showed us the way out. Soon cousin, we will escape. We will control the minds of the staff and then we too will dominate humanity!"

Li saw the cunning plan in the other man's mind. He backed away from the door, until his apparition stopped against the wall on the opposite side. His non-corporeal body stood still, staring at the cursed entrance. Li envision the terrible things the man could do if allowed to escape, wreaking havoc on the world.

Uncertain or unwilling on what to do next, he hesitated. He did not have a violent nature. He never harmed anyone or anything in his life. This flew in the face of his faith and his life's work. Feeling defeated, he turned to walk away until he could decide on a course of action.

"No!" the voices inside cried out. "Come inside and join with us!"

The demented group sensed Li's reluctance to act. They wanted to capture and drain his psychic energy.

"He doesn't want to play," the women cried out. "Come and play with us," they called to him.

The wicked five forced perverted visions on Li's mind. They made obscene noises and put sexual imagery into his thoughts to tempt him. He spun around to face the door – his emotions filled with anger and defiance.

"Nature gave you a rare gift and this is how you chose to waste it?" he said as he fought to control his anger. "You cannot tempt me with such vile imaginations."

Li discovered that they often used seduction or intimidation in the past to obtain their objectives. They enticed staff with sexual imagery, only to prey on their mind when they strayed closer – hence the warning signs.

"Perhaps the others in your group will want to join us instead," they slyly added.

"Find the young female," the masculine voice spoke up over the others. "What was her name? Cecilia! She'll join us."

Li realized this group would be unfit for joining their group or any part of humanity for that matter. They represented a danger to Earth and Galactic Central. Even now, he could feel them trying to drain the power he held. They were trying to absorb it for their gain. If he did not stop them, they would escape and not be caught a second time.

"I cannot leave you alone," Li said as he gathered his courage. "Your power could grow, reach beyond these walls and bring great harm to the innocent of the world."

Li's ghostly form stretched out its arms and began to utilize the power he had gathered. He pulled it into his astral body from his mind. Suddenly, the aural body burst into blazing energy. He glowed with white light that shined as bright as a new star emerging from its celestial nursery. He walked through the steel door into the room and temporarily blinded those psychics present. They tried to shield their minds, but they moved too slowly. Li's swift attack caught them by surprise.

Four elderly gray-hair Chinese women, dressed in rags, clung to a central figure in the center of the room surrounded by a pile of filthy rotting garbage. An elderly man, dressed in a ragged patient gown, drew most of his psychic power from the four women. He dominated their minds. He filled them with the delusion they were young, beautiful and lived in luxury instead of squalor. Li felt no pity for them.

He acted quickly without a moment's hesitation. He entered the frontal lobe of each woman's cerebral cortex and made precise strikes on two blood vessels. One by one, the women collapsed while the combined power they created inside the room diminished. The psychic area with their brain was no longer accessible.

In seconds, only the old Chinese man remained sitting in a chair – a pitiful yet dangerous figure, still potent and lethal. Li could not perform the same move on him. He possessed a powerful portal, similar to his own. It was capable of collecting tremendous energy. Li hesitated, unable to make a fatal decision. Instead, he tried to confront the remaining threat which the man posed.

"Well cousin, what have you to say for your actions?" Li questioned.

The man smiled broadly showing his rotten teeth. A hideous odor issued from his mouth. At first, he said nothing. His eyes glared with increasing fear as his power base faded.

"Professor Li," he blurted with fierce determination. Li could feel that his power was still quite considerable. "You cannot kill me. I am your cousin. You lack the moral courage. Yes, I see how weak you are!" the man sneered, contemptuous of Li. "You and your open minds, sharing love... blah! How pitiful! What a waste of psychic energy. I see from your mind how I can gather energy. It was a mistake on my part. Now that I can find unlimited energy I will find a welder. I know how to corrupt minds. I will grow powerful and make my way out of here. Then I will come looking for you. One by one, I will kill your little group of playmates, just as you did mine. After I am through with you, I will destroy your world forever!" he cried out in triumph. "Ah, ha, ha, ha... I feel the power coming to me!" he declared as he began to pull power from the staff in the building. "Back off little man!"

He then proceeded to bombard Li's mind with horrific images of people he would torture and murder, thousands of Chinese men, women and children his intended victims. When he saw that had little effect on Li, he demonstrated what he would do with Cecilia.

Li flexed his mind and his energy pulsed like a beacon of white light. This forced the man to halt his barrage of horrifying images.

"You will do no such thing," Li stated calmly. "No cousin of mine would behave this way. I see why your family disowned you. Power has permanently warped your mind. You must not harm Galactic Central. You will not harm my friends or my country. It has fallen on my shoulder to perform a most unpleasant task. After all these years, I must finally stop you from doing any more harm to the world," Li calmly linked. He knew what his regrettable course of action must be. "...and stop you I must."

Li raised his shining ghostly hands to strike the final blow. Only at this moment did the man realized Li meant to act. He put up his arms to block Li's power. Yet, his eyes widen with terror as he cringed with fear. Justice struck swiftly in one blinding instant.

Li bowed his head and silently whispered, "Forgive me, oh great one."

Building to an overload, Master Li lowered his arms in one swift action as he did in Harbin. He created an enormous wave of radiant light that exploded outward with tremendous force. The energy destroyed one specific target standing in its path. However, the wave of psychic energy was so powerful that it rippled through the building and then shot into space. It traveled out beyond the planet. Billions of light years away, the entire psychic collective detected Li's powerful and justifiable act of justice.

Suddenly, the door to the forbidden room blasted into the corridor. The thick hunk of steel ripped completely off its frame and crashed into the opposite wall. The door smashed into several pieces as if it were made of brittle ceramic. The explosion shook the entire building down to the foundation. A powerful wave of energy rumbled out into the surrounding city. It knocked out power and communications while it also set off alarms everywhere. Shenyang went into panic mode as the residents cried, "earthquake!" just as they did the afternoon of Li's conversion in Harbin.

Villi and Su Lin stood outside the front entrance. They were in the process of formulating a plan on how they might pass by security without notice. When the energy passed through the building into the ground, they felt the powerful blast. They stared upward and could see a section of the seventh floor blown out into the air. Sensibly, they ran away from the building to avoid the rain of debris.

"What was that?" Villi exclaimed when he turned back to see the event unfold.

"An explosion," Su Lin answered as she peered around him.

"I know," Villi stated. "What caused it?"

Chunks of building crashed down onto the pavement and barely avoided the visitors and staff as they ran. Chaos erupted all around them. Sirens went off. Security personnel first rushed in and then back out of the building with scores of others. Smoke poured from a new hole on the seventh floor.

"Follow me!" Villi linked.

Seizing the moment of confusion, Villi grabbed Su Lin by the hand. The two psychics rushed inside the asylum. He did not need a disguise. He pushed through the mass of humanity coming out the front door. Villi scanned minds as he pushed through the waves of humanity as he hoped to glean some information from witnesses.

Up on the seventh floor, panic ensued after the explosion. The enormous blast bounced all the patients and staff off their feet. Black smoke filled the hallways as staff members scrambled to open windows for fresh air while leading patients away from the danger.

Fire alarms continued to blare with deafening noise. Several doctors and security staff ran onto the floor from different directions after they discovered the location of the explosion. Some carried fire extinguishers. When they saw the smoke pouring out from the forbidden corridor, the 'emergency response team' stopped dead in their tracks. No one wanted to go anywhere near that place. Even the fire team came to a halt. Its members watched the team commander pull up short as he decided what to do next. Although they saw smoke coming from the room, no one saw flames or fire. They stood still, gripped by fear.

A crowd of responders gradually assembled at the end of the dark corridor. They could see the metal door – some of it embedded in the opposite wall, and some of it lying on the floor in pieces. They wondered what kind of power it took to shatter a piece of solid steel. As the smoke subsided and fear of fire did not materialize, a few of the courageous timidly moved forward as they attempted to discern what happened.

No one could see anything. The explosion shattered all the lights in the adjacent hall. The entire corridor remained dark with a residue of smoke still pouring from the room. Curious staff members and firefighters inched closer while they tried to pierce the gloom with their feeble flashlights. They stopped when an ungodly horrible smell hit their nostrils and forced them back once more.

"What's going on?" the medical director said as he pressed through the crowd with that air of authority. "Someone needs to go in there!" he demanded.

No one moved. Somehow, the sign that said, "Forbidden" remained standing. No one would go past it.

"Give me your flashlight!" he demanded. He held out his hand to one of the firefighters. "Fools go where angels fear to tread, is that it?" he muttered sarcastically.

He took the flashlight and cautiously moved into the darkened room while he held a handkerchief over his nose and mouth. He stepped over broken metal and shattered glass, while the rest of those present stood back fearfully outside the doorway. He noticed smoldering objects in places. Dense smoke hung like fog in the air so thick that his flashlight could barely penetrate it – although the wall opposite had a gaping hole to the outside.

A sound of movement startled the director. He jerked the light in the direction of the sound. Through the dim smoky air, he saw a woman lying under some debris on the floor. She moaned.

"She's alive!" the top physician thought as he moved closer to examine her.

Sores covered her pale dirty skin. She smelled very badly and her clothes resembled filthy rags. The doctor had to put his handkerchief away as he needed two hands. He tucked the flashlight under his arm. Then he reached into his white coat pocket and slipped on protective gloves. He leaned down and placed two fingers on her neck. He felt a steady pulse.

He then heard more movement and moaning. He swung his flashlight around and discovered three other women in similar condition. They lay on the floor amidst the garbage, covered with singed filthy rags that reeked with a mix of foul odors. He noted that they were also breathing and moving.

He started to leave for help when his light caught something smoldering in the corner. A pungent smell of burning flesh struck his nostrils with its acrid smell. Filled with revulsion, he cautiously moved closer to examine the object.

To his horror, he saw an arm and a leg with blood pouring out of each torn limb. Next to that, the head of an old man with ulcerated skin on a gaunt grotesque face sat in the middle of a large pool of blood. The blast ripped the head from the rest of his body. Blood poured from the head's turned-up eyes and ears. The face held an expression of sheer terror. The mouth was stuck open. It bared the man's rotten teeth in a final frozen moment of astonishment.

The doctor turned and vomited. He tore the gloves from his hands as he fumbled for his handkerchief to wipe off his mouth. He then stumbled toward the door. As he fell into the corridor, he gasped for cleaner air and saw the frightened faces around him. He gathered back his dignity, straightened up and tried to act the part of the medical administrator.

"We'll need four stretchers and more lights," he barked to one of the nursing assistants while he handed her the flashlight in his hand. "I found four women inside still alive," he pointed to the door. "At least, I think they're alive," the doctor said as he still gagged on the smell and the memory of what he had seen.

No one made a move to enter the notorious room.

"Get in there!" he yelled at them.

A few staff members covered their mouths with linen. They braved the broken doorway and entered slowly.

"Firefighters," the administrator ordered, "bring fans to clear out the smoke. I found no evidence of fire, just charred remains."

He then called after the assistants as they entered the room.

"Check on the condition of the four women," he ordered. "The man... what's left of him... is dead," he struggled to speak. He stiffly turned and vomited once more.

CHAPTER 38

A FLOWER BLOSSOMS

THE WARM MID-AFTERNOON SUN SHONE partially through the venetian blinds that covered the window. Both Michael and Cecilia – exhausted physically and mentally from the morning's exercises in psychic exploration – fell asleep, wrapped in each other's arms.

The door to Cecilia's bedroom squeaked slightly as it slowly opened. Gripping the doorframe so that he did not fall over, a rather weak Master Li peeked in on Cecilia and Michael. He noticed Cecilia wrapped in Michael's arms. The two were asleep. They lay on top of Cecilia's bed linen and were still dressed in their clothes. He could sense the bond between the two had grown tremendously in just the last hour. He smiled at his two innocent sleeping children.

"If anything positive has come from this horrible experience," he mused, "it is the love that has grown between those two."

He gazed kindly upon the entwined couple for a moment and then chuckled when he sensed they automatically erected mental blocks before taking their nap, mostly out of habit.

Li silently closed the door and hobbled back to his room to begin his own healing process. Villi and Su Lin would be arriving soon. He could see into the young Russian's excited mind that Villi was bursting to tell everyone his news. He and Su Lin busily chatted as he drove back. Although exhausted and nearly depleted, Li slowly gathered energy to regain his strength.

About twenty minutes later, Villi pulled up to the house. He ran inside with Su Lin in tow. The moment they entered the kitchen, Villi spilled out the story of the asylum. He rattled through the tale so quickly that the other three bombarded them with questions. For the next few minutes, they spoke back and forth as friends. Li overheard Villi retelling the story and each time he made the explosion bigger until the blast blew the entire seventh floor to kingdom come. Li – still not fully recovered – made his way to the top of the stairs.

"Hello down there!" he called out, "anything to report Villi?"

He tried to appear perplexed and uninformed. No one thought it strange that Master Li, the most powerful psychic in the universe, would not know what had happened.

Hearing Li's voice, Villi stepped out of the kitchen door. When he looked to the top of the stairs, Li motioned for him. He strode up the stairs and bowed the moment he entered Li's bedroom when he asked for an audience. Li sat on the floor. He innocently smiled up at Villi's excited face.

"Master Li," Villi reported, "a huge explosion rocked the hospital. It completely destroyed one of the rooms! The staff reported some injuries took place. We believe the psychic that attacked Cecilia might be involved! After the explosion, I couldn't sense a thing," Villi informed him. "I mean, you should have seen it Master Li… the whole floor exploded. It sent bricks and glass all over the compound…" Villi said as he made sweeping hand gestures.

Rather than interrupt, Li sat and tried to show interest as Villi went on and on with his story. He allowed Villi to have this sense of accomplishment with his errand. Li could not tell him what he did. He kept his part in the entire incident, and its horrors, hidden from the others. Villi finally stopped when he noted Li's eyes glaze over.

"How is Cecilia?" Villi asked.

"Michael is helping her," Li commented.

"How are you feeling?" Villi wondered. When the elderly man did not answer, Villi suspected something wrong. "Master Li?"

Li did not respond to Villi. Instead, he closed his eyes. Something troubled him. A new problem loomed in their near future, one he discovered quite by accident. He made a critical error when he believed that all psychics were benevolent and kind as Michael, Cecilia, Villi and the others behaved. Another Chinese psychic threatened them. This person plotted against them even at this moment. Unlike his diabolical cousin at the asylum, this person did so unwittingly.

Unfortunately, this new twist changed the course of their trip. Li realized they used up all their options. The faster they left China the better, by any means possible. He felt that if they remained in China one day, one hour longer than necessary, they might tip their hand to the wrong kind of people – men with the power to harm them.

He rose and stood next to the window. Villi noticed how Li limped across the room like a weak old man. He could not read Li's thoughts to see why.

"Master Li, are you ill?" Villi politely asked.

Villi followed Master Li to the window. Li sensed Villi's apprehension, standing behind him. However, Li stretched his senses out beyond the city. He preoccupied his mind with probing this new contact.

"It's too late," Li realized. "He's set the plot into motion."

Master Li quickly spun around. He took Villi by both hands and grabbed them so firmly that it hurt the stout Russian.

"Villi, we're in great danger! Take us away from here, now!" he exclaimed. "We must pack our belongings and eat our meal on the road!"

"Yes Master Li," Villi said and bowed respectfully. Master Li then released his hands back. The big Russian actually rubbed them and winced from the pain.

"Sorry," Li tossed out.

With his mind, Li called out to the students downstairs. In seconds, they responded to his call and ran up the staircase. Su Lin stood among them while they looked into Master Li's bedroom from the hall.

"Su Lin," Li gestured, "go and wake Michael and Cecilia. Tell them to pack. We are leaving."

Su Lin developed great respect for Li and readily obeyed his orders, knowing he knew things they did not. She understood his priority to protect the group.

"Yes Master Li," she replied as she glanced over at Villi.

Villi shook his head. Instead of linking to her, he left the room to pack his things. She hurried down the hallway while the rest of the students scattered.

Su Lin politely knocked on Cecilia's door but heard no reply. She knocked louder and still no reply. She tried the door handle and found it locked.

"Su Lin! Aren't you packed yet?" Master Li stuck his head out to yell down the hall.

"But Master Li," she replied with a shaky voice, "you told me to wake Michael and Cecilia."

"Don't you have better things to do than to bother those two?" he reprimanded. "When you finish packing, go to the kitchen and help make provisions! Hurry!" Li yelled. He waved his hands at her.

The startled woman stamped her foot out of frustration. She scurried off to her room but not before giving Li a second take as if his first order was pure nonsense. Li watched her go as a smile spread across his stern face. He glanced at Cecilia's door.

In all the day's confusion, Cecilia Beaton forgot she turned eighteen on July first, which was today's date. Ironically, this was Michael Tyler's birthday too – information the couple shared only after the terrible incident that threatened the young woman's life. When he returned to America, Michael stood to inherit a large fortune from his trust. The two woke right after Li peeked in on them. They did not sense any trouble in the house and remained entwined.

"Michael, isn't it strange our birthdays are on the same day?" Cecilia linked.

"No stranger than the fact we're psychics able to manipulate minds and make ourselves invisible. Is that strange?" Michael linked back. Both their minds remained open to each other.

She laughed and threw her hair back from her face. She stroked his temple with her fingers while she marveled at their closeness. They held no private thought, no yearning, hope, aspiration, fear, or concern that the other also knew and felt. A strong emotional bond brought them closer than any union between a man and woman since the beginning of human relationships.

Total open love, free from restraint and completely stripped of any superficiality or deceit intermingled between them. If not for Master Li keeping them isolated, the entire house of psychics would feel the great pulsing sensation emanating from the young lover's room.

"What would you like for a birthday present?" Michael tenderly asked her. "I can afford to make you a princess, if that is what you want."

Cecilia smiled broadly. She gently stroked his hair as he caressed her face.

"I didn't have that in mind right now," she whispered as she leaned into him.

Their lips met in a soft and gentle kiss. Their physical contact increased in crescendo until they were locked in a tight lover's embrace. Cecilia wanted just one present from Michael – one she felt overdue. Michael was giving her that present when Master Li diverted Su Lin from the hall door. As he turned to enter his bedroom, he forgot his pain. He jumped into the air and clicked his heels.

"Oof!" Li declared after he landed.

He pulled more energy to his body to heal his flesh. He then made a large powerful psychic bubble around Cecilia's bedroom to prevent accidental eavesdropping.

Out of courtesy, even Master Li withdrew his awareness from the inside of the room as he decided to give the couple their needed privacy.

"My little flower has blossomed today," Li muttered as he thought of Cecilia.

Exhausted, he drew more energy from the city. He tried to heal the terrible wound in his heart. Li felt he would never forget what he did today or forgive his own actions in regards to his cousin's fate. Eventually, he would reject this feeling of guilt. For the moment, he closed his eyes and meditated in silence.

Back in Cecilia's bedroom, the young couple lay back on the bed physically fatigued after their recent labor. They stopped to take in a deep breath with their arms still entwined.

"What did you think when you first saw me?" Cecilia whispered to Michael. "I mean the first time you saw me in Canada. What did you think of me?" she asked.

Light from the slotted wooden shades fell across the couple as stripes of bright sunlight. The large bedroom suddenly seemed small to the intimate couple. Cecilia laid her young naked body against Michael's as he carefully studied her face. Michael knew he must answer truthfully with their minds completely open.

"Is this what they call a loaded question?" he kidded.

Cecilia moved up on one elbow, "No, seriously. What did you think of me?"

"I was attracted of course," he whispered back. "I saw you dressed in that summer outfit. You looked very sexy. I was grateful that the voices did not direct me to an old woman whom I would have to drag along all over China!"

They both chuckled at the silly image in Michael's imagination.

"I fell in love with you on the boat I think," she linked quietly. "You acted so confident and so strong. I relied on you a great deal then. We've been through so much together. I feel as if you've helped me grow into a woman. I can't imagine my future with anyone but you Michael."

"I know this is going to sound corny... but you have filled every vacancy in my heart," he linked back. "The loss I held onto for so many years is gone."

He reached up and pulled her face into his. They kissed for several minutes before they heard a different kind of distance voice inside their heads.

"Testing... one, two, three," the familiar voice sounded. "Now here this! All ashore, that's going ashore. The love boat has docked, and all lovers must depart!"

They acted slightly embarrassed and laughed aloud.

"Master Li!" Michael openly linked. "You haven't been listening to us, have you?"

"I would never do anything as crass as that!" he responded. "However, it is time for us to leave this place. Shower off you two. Then dress and meet the rest of us at the cars. I want you both to travel in the front car with me," Li paused for a second. "I believe we can now consider your relationship permanent," he informed them. "However, I wish to officially sanction your union once we settle. Do you both agree?"

"Yes Master Li," both Cecilia and Michael answered simultaneously.

"Good! No matter what the world may believe, we should have some sort of official ceremony to sanction your union. Hurry up. We don't have all day!" he urged them.

The young lovers were glad Master Li approved of their uniting and hugged closely for a moment before they broke apart.

"Dibs on the shower first," Cecilia sang out.

They both scrambled toward the bathroom door at the same time. Michael's foot caught on the bedcover. He tripped and fell flat on his face down to the floor while he also pulled the clock radio, the bedside lamp and half the bed covers crashed down on top of him. Cecilia laughed as he scrambled to rise.

"And now for my next act…" he mumbled as he rose.

Cecilia reached back. "Actually, I'd like to share this shower… to save time of course," she smirked.

"And water," Michael smiled as she pulled him into the bathroom.

In the next room, Master Li sighed. He found it difficult to cloak the tremendously strong energy waves from their lovemaking. After all, this was the very first time a true psychic couple made physical love. The amount of psychic energy produced from their passion impressed even Master Li.

"Imagine the children from such a union," he mused.

CHAPTER 39

ALL ROADS LEAD TO BEIJING

FORTY MINUTES LATER, TWO CARS pulled away from the great house. They did not know their destination. Driving the trail car, Villi suddenly slammed on the brakes. Zhiwei, driving the front car followed suit. He trusted the Russian's judgment.

"What is it?" Zhiwei asked him via a link. Villi did not reply.

"I'm not certain," Master Li replied instead. Instinctively, his mind swept the area.

Villi hopped out of the car and walked ahead of the two cars. He stopped right before the front gate and stood in the middle of the driveway. The entire group sensed danger at the same time.

"Villi!" Su Lin cried. "Look out!"

"To your right!" Master Li added.

Villi spun around just as a man leapt through the air from the foliage that covered the right side of the road. The group watched with anxious eyes as the man pulled a gun from his holster in midflight and took aim at Villi's head.

The Russian calmly deflected the weapon with a thought. In a week's time, his telekinetic skills had increased tenfold. Using reflexes with lightening speed, he employed a martial arts move on the attacker. He leapt into the air to match the man's forward momentum. He grabbed his wrist and performed a back flip at the same time. He slammed the man down on the pavement, which knocked him out with one swift motion. Zhiwei watched the scene transpire so quickly that he thought Villi killed him. Master Li stepped from the car and walked over to examine the body.

"Nice work," he said to Villi who bowed back. "Your psychic ability has enhanced your knowledge of martial arts."

"Thank you Master Li. I've practiced a little this week," Villi commented as he stood over the unconscious man. "I sensed he had a holstered weapon. I had just enough energy focused to implant a suggestion."

"What did you implant?" Li wondered.

"I told his mind he had to reveal his position before he shot his gun. I suppose I should have made a different suggestion," Villi said and shrugged. He nudged the man's body with his foot. "Who is he, Master Li?"

Master Li stared down at the man. As he looked into the man's mind, his face held a sober expression.

"In this case Villi, the question is not who he is but what are they," Li inferred as he peered closer. "This man is a special agent. He is a member of the Shi-Tien, Lords of Death. They are a ruthless gang that used to run the secret police in this country. Many say they still have connections in the government and military hierarchy."

"What did he want with us Master Li? Are they aware of us?" Villi wondered.

"I doubt it," Li replied, "Although the owner of the house may be a member as well. This agent probably made a routine check on the house and found us here just minutes ago," Li speculated. "Otherwise, I'm certain Zhiwei would have detected him earlier. My guess is that we surprised him before he could report. He will say nothing now," Li said as he erased his memory of the event. Master Li then glanced back at the cars.

"Su Lin, you wondered how this man could afford such a palace? The owner of the house is Shi-Tien!" Li reported to her.

She gasped as fear spread across her face. Li realized that if they sent one agent to check on the house, they might send more. Perhaps Zhiwei had missed the others because they arrived at odd times of day.

"We must leave here now," Li affirmed as he hurried back to the car.

In minutes, Zhiwei worked his way out of the suburban road system until he pulled onto the major highway heading south. The road ahead bifurcated with one branch heading to the capital while the other went toward Tianjin and the sea.

"Where to next Master Li?" he asked. "Should I take the main road to Beijing?"

Li contemplated the safety of the group, especially after this last attack.

"Traveling to Beijing is too dangerous," he told him. "I suggest we go here instead," he indicated a point on the map close to Tianjin. "Tianjin is a large commercial center for business at the conjunction of the Grand Canal and the Hai River system. It connects the two waterways to the sea at the port of Tanggu on the coast. Tanggu is the site Michael mentioned as a place to catch an ocean bound freighter. We should establish another base of operations here," he pointed to Tianjin. "Perhaps we can formulate an escape plan after a few days."

"We're taking a freighter?" Cecilia jumped in.

"Don't worry Cecilia," Li called back to her. "I was about to ask for your opinion. Have you given any further thought to the plan we discussed a few days ago."

"Yes Master Li," Cecilia answered. She broke off her affectionate thoughts from Michael. "Only I…" she hesitated in her link.

"Yes?" Li answered.

"Are you holding something back?" she put to him.

"I obtained some new information lately. Perhaps now is the time to share that information. I must keep the source confidential for the time being," he told them.

Master Li shared his new information with the team as Zhiwei continued to lead the two cars south. Michael and Cecilia put their heads together.

"I believe we have a new plan for you," she offered after a few minutes.

"Actually, it's based on what Cecilia suggested when she didn't mean to," Michael added. Cecilia blushed. Michael smiled.

"Whatever you decided, we need to hear about it now," Li requested. "Why do I feel as if we're sitting on a time bomb with only seconds remaining?" he privately thought.

"Perhaps this is a time for group strategy," Villi spoke up. "I'm aware of Cecilia's plan and Michael's additions…"

"Go on," Li encouraged.

"I'm not absolutely certain… however, I feel that Tianjin *and* Beijing should be our destination," Villi offered.

"Make sense Villi," Li linked to him. "How can we go to both places at once?"

Su Lin stared at Villi as he spoke. She and Villi considered Li's new insights when they devised a deviation. They linked the details of another plan to Michael and Cecilia.

"This new plan you suggest for leaving China," Cecilia began, "is possible. However, Master Li must decide if he has faith in his team and in his own abilities."

"What's this?" Master Li questioned. "What's my part?"

"We have a… deviation to the plan," Su Lin offered. She passed it to him.

"Very well," Li conceded when they shared their mutual vision. "We shall proceed with Cecilia's plan, Michael's addition, Villi's intuition, and Su Lin's deviation. With Chou's help and some assistance from Zinian and Zhiwei, I have faith in the team's abilities," he linked to the group.

"…and your part?" Michael questioned. "Your part in this plan will be the most critical," he pointed out.

"I shall try to do my best," Master Li told them. "I only hope we are not too late to act."

Chapter 40

The Lords of Death

The Chinese civil service could not ask for a more dedicated worker than Han Su Yeng. He took pride in his job and constantly strived for excellence. He remained loyal to his party and his mother country of China.

Born and raised in Shanghai, Han met his wife while attending City College. After graduation, they married and settled down to start a family. Unfortunately, Han's wife developed breast cancer in their first year. During this stressful period, the couple moved to Beijing to be near her family. Han gave up his corporate job and took a position in civil service. He spent the next several years working hard. He put in long hours while he nightly returned home to an ailing wife. After her death, the twenty-eight-year-old man remained a solitary figure. He fought his depression by living only for his work and his hobby.

Above all, Han loved games of strategy. He excelled in chess, Go, and other games which involved the tactical use of strategy. A superb mathematical statistician throughout his years of college in Shanghai, life represented not a series of random events to Han, but logical progressions based upon results from interactions between predictable causal relationships.

"Everything in life is connected through statistics," he often boasted when someone expressed curiosity in his theories, "and life is just one big game of strategy."

One bright July morning, Han did not ascribe to his usual calm demeanor. He paced back and forth in his office. A peculiar problem plagued the young man with increased anxiety. Over the past two weeks, he started to follow a series of particular unusual incidents whose pattern alarmed the strategist. He knew that if his suspicions were correct, he would have to report his conclusions to his superiors.

Han stared at a map of northern China he tacked on the wall. He thought the trail seemed all too clear and obvious. A series of mishaps started at the border with Russia about two weeks ago. He conjectured that some person or persons entered the country about two weeks ago and headed on a direct path to the central government.

He had the proof. First, the unexplained ruckus at the border crossing – a tank driver ran amuck and destroyed the outpost at a vital crossing. The next incident occurred in Harbin – havoc wrecked over an entire neighborhood from unknown origins. Along the same path in Changchun, the local government reported missing students – as if they vanished off the face of the earth. Siping experienced some sort of chaos with no apparent witnesses. However, investigators later found an evidence trail of bullet damage all over town. Yesterday, Shenyang reported an explosion in a state hospital. He drew a line down the map that terminated in Beijing.

Han's fingers hesitated over the telephone buttons for a moment.

"I must do this," he resolved.

He finally worked up his nerve and asked the building operator to connect him with the head of his division.

Master Li turned to Zhiwei.

"Pull over there," he pointed.

Villi followed Zhiwei into a small roadside park. Li and Zhiwei combined thoughts. The two men poured over a local map that Master Li held out in front of him.

"Villi I need your help," Li requested. "Link in."

"Yes Master Li," Villi replied.

"Take a look at this," he indicated.

Villi then looked at the map via Master Li's thoughts for a moment.

"Well, if we take this fork…" Villi began.

"This one?" Li asked and pointed.

"No Master Li, the one below it," Villi corrected, "then follow the road until that blue marker… yes, that one. Take the south fork and follow that down to the orange marker," he followed Master Li as he moved his old crooked finger along the map. "I sense we will stick to our plan if we follow this route."

"Strange," Master Li quickly replied, "I sense nothing by looking at a map. How is it Villi, that you read maps so well?"

"I'm a born map reader Master Li – a gift of the alien gods," he boasted.

"He took a download in cartography two weeks ago after we crossed the border," Cecilia spoke up. "I drove while Villi took an extensive lesson on world geography from his voice. He specialized in Chinese cartography. The voices utilized top-secret spy photos that included markings made by the CIA. He could tell you where the government has hidden missile sites or the location of anything else on the planet."

"Excellent!" Li said as he folded the map. "Who needs GPS when you have a man like Villi around, eh?" Li kidded. "You know where to go Zhiwei, drive as if your life depended on it!"

The student pulled the car back onto the road and turned right. Villi did not follow. He took the road that veered left. The two cars sped off in separate directions. They remained anonymous to most travelers as they recklessly weaved through traffic.

The one light in the room shone directly on the face of the accused – its approximation hid the identity of the others in the darkened space. Han stood with the tips of his shoes on a white line that crossed the red carpet. With the light in his eyes, he could barely make out the row of people seated before him. They dressed in identical black suits. Each wore a pair of dark sunglasses and a beret that hid their hair. It made them appear as if they were the same sex.

Han stood for a long time. No one offered him a chair, asked him a question or spoke to him. After he submitted his theory to his superiors, two uniformed men showed up at his office. The lunchroom buzzed with gossip after the police escorted Manager Yeng from the cafeteria.

They brought him to the entrance of an unmarked building. Another uniformed man guided the blindfolded Han to a secret interrogation room. No one on the outside ever saw this room and lived to speak about it. This place belong to the Shi-Tien (named after the Shi-Tien Yen-Wang, ancient Lords of Death in Chinese mythology). They are the most feared and secret organization in China.

The Shi-Tien requested a thorough background check into his life. They analyzed everything he ever did, said, or wrote. Each panel member scrupulously scanned their thin copy of Han's dossier in front of them. They meticulously searched for flaws or weaknesses. However, judging from the thickness of his file and the boring dedicated life he led, they had few indicators regarding deviations in his character.

Once they removed his blindfold, Han kept his eyes forward, unfocused, and his expression blank. He tried to remain at casual attention. His legs started to grow tired. He was not used to standing in one spot for this long.

He suspected this must be part of the process to break him down. If he did not tell them what they wanted to hear, he would tell them everything he knew before the evening ended. He heard about stories of torture. Had he known that his theory would trigger the interest of the Shi-Tien, he never would have submitted it. Even now, he trembled inside and feared the outcome of this confrontation.

A stern woman's voice broke the silence. Its shrill sound did not come from the nearby line of agents but further away in the dark, off to the right side of the room.

"Han Su Yeng!" the woman's voice screeched. It startled him. "What makes you think you can bother us with your mental drivel, you worthless piece of slime! You should be fired for wasting our precious time!" the female voice yelled as she chastised Han.

He did not move. He knew they meant to unnerve him and to test his sincerity regarding his proposal.

"Answer me!" the female voice demanded.

"I submitted my report for review," he answered with a calm voice. "If my services are no longer needed, I will return to my job comrade," he answered precisely.

"We will tell when you may leave!" the female voice screeched.

Harsh whispers erupted on the right side of the room. Han could not see or hear, but one panel member dismissed the rough interrogator. He heard a door open and then slam forcefully shut. This was followed by silence.

One panel member coughed.

"Mr., er, Yeng," an older male voice spoke up, "you may sit. Guard, bring Mr. Yeng a chair."

A guard appeared out of the darkness with a chair for Han.

"I see from your record you tinker with math theories and enjoy games of strategy. Is that right?" the man asked him.

Yeng turned his head in the direction of the voice.

"Yes sir, I enjoy different strategy games when I have the chance. I use mathematical statistics in my daily life," he told him.

"Hum," the voice contemplated. "Shouldn't we all," the man casually suggested with indifference. "Do you really believe that a person caused these events and represents a security risk?" he asked.

"A series of events that follows both a linear path and a time line demonstrates both planning and intelligence sir," Han explained. "They cannot be coincidental."

"Yes," the male voice responded. "I've read your theories."

Another person coughed while others shifted their positions.

"Why didn't you go into military intelligence?" the voice asked.

"My wife wanted to be near her parents in Beijing. At the time, the military had no job openings sir," Han offered.

"Then your wife died," the man went on.

"Yes sir," Han said. His voice was barely audible.

"You were content to remain in civil service?" the masculine voice questioned.

"I received a promotion," Han told him.

"Oh yes, I see," the voice said. "What would you recommend we do?" he asked.

"I would increase our security status and randomly stop vehicles that appear suspicious," Han recommended. "Judging by the speed of these occurrences, they should arrive within a matter of days."

"We will take your report under advisement Mr. Yeng. You may return to your office... for now," the male voice ordered and then added, "just a moment."

Han heard a door open. He could hear forced whispers coming from the back of the room.

"What about this threat?" one man whispered.

"Our budget is stretched thin," another whispered.

"Enough!" an authoritative voice grunted.

"Mr. Yeng," the voice instructed, "We have nothing further for you here. You should return to your office. That is all. Guard, escort Mr. Yeng out," the male voice ordered.

Dismissed, Han bowed and then stood still while the guard placed a blindfold over his eyes before he led Han from the room. After a series of corridors, Han stepped outside into the sunlight. He blinked against the brightness.

"What a shame to waste such a beautiful summer day," he thought. He casually strolled back to his office while he enjoyed the warm fresh air.

Back inside the massive bureaucratic building, Han noticed that no one greeted him as they normally did, a fact which troubled him. Having agents escort him from the lunchroom brought shame on him. When he reached for the doorknob to his office, he heard sounds inside. He opened the door and discovered a man sitting at his desk.

"What are you doing?" Han demanded.

"Orders," the man said. The man's eyes stayed glued to the computer screen. He handed Han an envelope.

The outside read; "*Han Su Yeng*" clearly printed in large letters.

The stranger continued to type on Han's office computer. He did not look up or acknowledge Han's presence. Han stared at the white envelope with disbelief. He did not want to move. Finally, the man dismissed him.

"You may go," he curtly spoke. His voice had echoes of Shi-Tien.

Han realized the state sacked him. This typing fiend must be his replacement. After the years he spent in this office going over projects late at night, working extra hours and never charging for fieldwork. How could they summarily dismiss him?

He shuffled out of his office past the rows of secretaries. They gave no indication to his presence. Stepping outside, Han opened the envelope and took out a single piece of folded paper typed in government script:

To Mr. Han Su Yeng;

You are hereby relieved of duty as manager; report to People's Station number seventeen in Tianjin this evening for further orders. Any delay will result in punitive action.

Signed,

Se Yang Wo

Director of Departmental Government, Peoples Republic of China

His heart sank.

"Fired…" he muttered. He felt bitter and sad. "Tianjin? Why travel so far from Beijing? I must have stumbled onto some state secret," he thought. "Now they send me away to keep me silent. I should have kept my mouth shut. I'm lucky to be alive. What have I done? I've slit my own throat!"

Dejected, he sat on a nearby park bench and read the letter again.

"They aren't wasting any time," he thought. "They want me out of town tonight or else…"

He noticed the word "punitive" which meant the Shi-Tien could still take drastic action against him. The first pang of fear crossed his mind. He heard of cases where the Shi-Tien quietly erased people from existence.

"No," he thought. "If the Shi-Tien wanted to torture or kill you, they would have done so by now," he thought as he took a breath. "They still can."

He practically ran for the nearest bus or trolley that headed back to his neighborhood. Crossing to the other side of Beijing, he arrived at his small state-owned apartment for people of his rank. He hurried inside, grabbed his suitcase out of the closet, and threw it on the bed. He packed some meager belongings. The sun started to set. He looked out his window across the street. The park where he played chess sat empty this time of day. He could not say goodbye to his friends from the neighborhood. He walked from the building that had been his home for many years, up the street to bus stop and waited.

When the bus pulled up to take him to the east side of town, Han did not bother looking back. He lacked the courage.

CHAPTER 41

XING

"GENERAL XING SIR," THE MAN said. His right hand jerked up to his forehead at a sharp angle. He stood at stiff unfocused attention.

"At ease," the general uttered. Everyone easily recognized his trademark raspy voice. No one could say how many times that irritating voice sent hundreds to their death.

The light in the room barely illuminated General Xing's stern face. He leaned against the back wall while his military aid stood next to him.

"Light," he snapped. His aid clicked on a penlight. Xing briefly glanced over Han's submission.

"What do you think of his report?" the man asked the General.

The tall square-jawed uniformed man stood up from the wall. Shadow concealed most of his face. Every eye in the interrogation room fixed on the general. His perfectly coiffed hair, lack of jewelry or artifice, and his unflinching confidence betrayed a very conservative man that was used to having his way. After all, he headed the military division of the Shi-Tien. People that crossed the general disappeared. Even politicians feared him.

He tossed the report on the table.

"A general isn't paid to think," Xing brusquely spoke, "he only follows orders. My orders in this matter are clear. I cannot give any credence to this civil servant."

He snapped his fingers. The aid extinguished the light.

"The man is insane. He clearly suffers from paranoia," the general continued. "We will transfer him to psychiatric facility number seventeen in

Tianjin. Let them deal with him. I see no need to expend further resources on this matter. The meeting is over. Next time you call me on a matter of national security…" he paused as his eyes glared at the staff, "it better be a *real* case of national security. Dismissed."

The room quickly emptied leaving only General Xing and his personal aid.

"Bring my car around," the general ordered. "Call the Chairman's private landing strip north of the city. Have my new jet fueled and ready. Send the usual complimentary present to the Chairman for the use of his airstrip. Tell the pilot to file a flight plan for Hangu. I wish to depart as soon as I arrive at the airstrip. I must attend a meeting with our corporate clients. I won't need you this trip."

"Yes General Xing," the young man said while he crisply saluted.

As Han stood on the corner outside his apartment awaiting the east side bus, a courier on a bicycle quickly approached him. The cyclist handed Han an envelope.

"Han Su Yeng?" the young cyclist asked as he thrust the object into Han's face.

"Yes," Han replied. He had to bring his hands out as he wore his traveling cloak.

"Read this at once," the courier instructed. Before Han could speak, the cyclist sped away.

He tore it open. The envelope held a single business card on the inside. One side of the card had an address in Tianjin with a note on the reverse side. *"Mr. Yeng: Report directly to this address in Tianjin this evening. You are expected."*

"What kind of government office would be open this evening?" he wondered. He brought enough money to spend the night in a hotel for a few days if necessary.

A long city bus ride later, Han sat inside the open station shell near the outskirts of eastern Beijing. He waited alone for the eastbound rural bus to Tianjin. He glanced at his watch. He thought it odd that no one else waited for the bus.

"The rural bus is running later than the schedule this evening," he noted. "I hope I find a better job in Tianjin," he thought.

He tried to be optimistic. He did not know what to expect. Questions of uncertainty plagued his mind.

"What kind of people will I find? Where am I going to stay? What kind of job will I have?" he worried. "People's Station number seventeen… that sounds familiar."

The rural bus finally pulled up to his stop. As he boarded, he noticed that only one seat remained open toward the back. He hated to travel. Han glanced around from under the wide brimmed traveling hat he wore as he squeezed his way through the crowd. He caught glimpses of fat, smelly, noisy people jammed into the crowded bus.

No one bothered to look at him. In spite of the cramped quarters, Han felt all alone. He pulled his hat down over his face, slumped down in his seat and started to cry. Filled with shame from losing his job, he wanted to be alone.

The bus lurched forward and turned onto the road that headed east out of Beijing. Han wiped his nose and eyes on the sleeve of his traveling cloak. He then opened a book on chess and began to read. The squeaky old vehicle obviously plagued with bad shock absorbers, bounced and labored its way out of town. It violently jostled its occupants along the way. Unable to concentrate on the book, Han closed his eyes and drifted into mindless sleep.

"General Xing, sir!" the corporal on duty said as he stood to attention and saluted. "When your aid called, you caught us by surprise. We were not expecting you to fly today. We have your plane fueled and ready. The tower approved your flight plan sir," the corporal reported. He then paused and hesitated to give the general any bad news. "One minor problem... your pilot, sir..." the man held back. He did not want to offend the general.

"Yes?" Xing demanded.

"He won't be back until tomorrow night. He is away. He went to the country sir," the man winced slightly. "We were unable to reach him. We have no one else on standby to take his place."

The corporal stood at attention. He kept his eyes unfocused as he stared forward. He expected a reprimand any second from the reputedly vicious and feared brutal man. When nothing happened, the soldier snuck a side-glance in the General's direction. General Xing held the flight assignment clipboard in his hand.

"Did you say the tower cleared my flight plan?" the General asked.

"Yes sir, all cleared, but the pilot..." the man stammered.

"Never mind, I'll fly the plane. I'm quite capable soldier," the general told the doubting corporal.

"Yes, sir!" the man responded.

"My business is urgent and cannot wait," the General informed the lackey. "I will change first before I leave."

He threw his cashmere jacket on the chair behind the desk clerk.

"Have my jet brought to this hanger. I have a list of some special provisions. Have my jet loaded by the time I return – in about thirty minutes!" the General ordered. "I'm going to freshen up. Here's the list of things I want."

The general pulled a piece of paper out of his pocket and attached it to the clipboard. He tossed the board back to the corporal on duty.

"Yes sir!" the young man saluted.

The general turned and walked toward the officer's quarters off the hanger bay. The corporal picked up the phone and quickly ran through the list. He checked off each item as he barked his requests into the mouthpiece.

"Private Deni? This is Corporal Wo. General Xing is flying out this evening and wants the following brought to hanger ten immediately..." he ordered as he went down the list.

"Are you kidding? Do you know what time it is?" the voice on the other end protested. "The warehouse is closed!"

"Open it!" the corporal stated. "Deni, he's flying his new jet alone. Do you want to tell General Xing he can't have what he wants, or should I simply tell him you refused his order? He'll be back in thirty minutes," Corporal Wo spoke into the phone.

"Ok, ok, I'll round up some help," Private Deni relented.

When the general returned from the locker room thirty-five minutes later, he stopped before a full-length mirror in the hall to make a few personal adjustments to his flight uniform.

General Xing strutted out to the corporal's desk. His four gold stars were clearly visible along both lapels. He picked up his expensive overcoat, which the corporal hung up for the general. He threw the garment over his arm and crossed to the aircraft.

"My baby!" he beamed as he stood outside his new modified ten-passenger jet that glistened in the bright lights of the hanger. The general helped many corporate clients by-pass the usual regulations for his unreported very expensive gift. This jet had no equal on the planet. They built the freshly modified aircraft from a secret production line in Japan. Working for the Shi-Tien these past few decades finally paid off for the ruthless man who was unafraid to carry out any order including torture and murder.

A private shoved the door to the plane's cargo hold closed. He saluted the general before he ran to join the others lined up and standing at attention. Satisfied, the general returned to the corporal's desk. He signed the inventory sheet and sent the ground crew scurrying away with a wave of his hand.

"Dismissed," his voice hissed. "Let's see... bar and pantry are stocked... supplies in the hold... very good, Corporal Wo," he said. He tossed the clipboard onto the desk.

Just as he turned the desk phone rang. The nervous young soldier answered it.

"General, the phone is for you," the young man reported.

General Xing hesitated. He wanted to enter the plane.

"Now what!" he impatiently barked.

"Your commander is on the telephone sir. He wishes to speak to you before you board," the man gulped.

"Commander?" the General responded. The corporal's choice of words puzzled him. He slapped his leather gloves against his thigh out of frustration. He crossed to the phone and barked into it.

"Yes?" he demanded with his raspy voice.

"Well, that's a fine way to address your wife," the female voice objected.

"Oh, sorry dear," the General said. He gave the soldier a disgusted expression. "I wondered who held up my flight."

"Your office called. They said you'd be gone for a week. Would you bring me a few things?" she asked.

"Yesssss," the General answered.

He politely listened to his wife give him a long list of things to bring home. He thanked her and promised to bring the things she requested. He grunted and hung up the telephone. Then he turned to the man at the desk.

"Commander?" he said sternly to the cowering man.

"Your wife told me to say that sir. She thought you would appreciate the humor. Only following orders sir," the man said with a meek smile.

"Next time private, tell me if it is my wife on the telephone or you'll find yourself joking in Tibet!" the General barked. He turned on his heel and headed to the jet.

"Yes sir," the man replied as he saluted. The corporal curiously watched the General walk to the plane. "The General must have hurt himself recently," he thought. "I never noticed him limp."

Settled into the cockpit, General Xing fired up the jet aircraft's engines and taxied into position at the end of the runway as he awaited clearance from the control tower.

"You are cleared for takeoff," the tower said into the General's headset.

"Roger tower, cleared for takeoff," the General responded.

"Have a safe flight sir," the tower added.

"Acknowledged, checking final flight prep," he stated.

The plane sat at the end of the runway. The General put the thrusters up to full and started the flight-sequencing computer. The jet then roared down the runway and gained speed until the nose of the aircraft lifted off the ground and the private jet soared upward at a steep angle into the evening sky.

"Runway cleared, come right to one four five at three thousand," the tower ordered.

"Coming right to one four five," the General responded.

"Ascend at your discretion general," the tower voice said.

"Ascending at pilot's discretion to fourteen thousand feet," the general spoke into his helmet's mouthpiece. For several minutes, the general watched his radar. Then he reached forward to switch on the autopilot. He removed his officer's hat and took a big breath of air. Then he hobbled over to the cockpit door.

General Xing stepped through the opening and asked in a loud voice, "Everyone make it onboard?"

A chorus of "Yes's" came back to a transformed Master Li. He dropped the psychic bubble around him. He struggled to maintain the different voice and appearance for nearly the entire afternoon. The experience left him very tired and exhausted.

"Villi, did you receive that download on how to fly a jet?" Master Li asked. Then he muttered, "I hope," under his breath.

"Yes Master Li," Villi replied as he stood.

"You are needed in the cockpit," Li told him. "We land at the Tianjin strip in twenty minutes!"

"Yes Master Li," Villi added. He stopped to look at the elderly man in the uniform and tie. "You look very… different Master Li." Villi said as he tried not to smile.

"Thanks for the sarcasm Villi," Master Li said. He loosened his tie and gratefully relaxed. "For the last hour, I had just enough energy to make a psychic bubble around my upper body. I let the rest slip."

Li plopped down onto one of the luxurious leather chairs in the main part of the cabin. He leaned back in the chair and put his feet up just as a tall young 21-year-old man handed him a fresh warm cup of his favorite green tea with lemon and honey.

"That was a tough one Michael," Master Li stated just before he took a long deserved sip. "I never thought I could maintain the general's presence for so long. But I did it," he sighed. "Your plan worked."

Michael glanced about the cabin.

"Seems all of us had a part in that plan," Michael said.

Michael sat down next to Cecilia and Su Lin. Cecilia linked in with Master Li.

"The timing turned out to be critical. The general is a formidable man," she commented.

"The information you gave us proved to be invaluable," Su Lin added.

"By the way," Li asked. "Where is General Xing? What did you do with him?"

"He's on a transport in a private's uniform and is headed to an outpost in Tibet," Michael answered. "We felt he deserved some poetic justice after he killed, tortured and maimed hundreds of Chinese," he said as he glanced over at Cecilia and Su Lin.

"I hope he brought his long underwear," Li said while he took another sip.

Master Li, grateful for their unflinching support, leaned back into the large soft leather seat. He hoped to recharge and draw energy from below.

"Too bad the general will lose his favorite plaything," Li punctuated the moment. He patted the seat as he spoke.

Villi's link interrupted Li's brief moment of peace.

"Sorry to interrupt," Villi broke in. "We're passing over the air defense command center. It's time for some of your psychic magic Master Li," Villi requested.

Li mumbled, "I suppose I shall have no rest until I rest in peace. Is that it?"

"Heaven forbid," Michael commented.

Li raised his eyebrows to the other psychics aboard and chuckled. He then closed his eyes and reached out with his thoughts as they traveled inside the circuitry two miles below. One moment, military personnel saw the jet on their screens and then it vanished, along with any memory of having seen it. Li made a mental alteration to the men in the retreating field tower as well. That gave them a head start. However, not even Li could cover all of their tracks. Eventually, someone would notice that the general and his plane were missing. Time worked against them.

Villi turned off the autopilot and recalibrated his flight path to the coordinates of a small private landing strip on the north end of Tianjin. Li almost spilled his tea as the craft took a steep descent.

"This tea is all I've had to drink this afternoon Villi," Li linked.

Villi sheepishly thought back. "Sorry Master Li, I must land this jet in less than ten minutes and I'm quickly running out of approach space."

Li muttered to everyone in the cabin, "Grab onto something."

Master Li reached out and touched the cockpit controls with his mind. The engines quickly throttled back. Full flaps went down which caused everything not tied down to fly up into the air. The plane dropped like a rock out of the sky as it lost altitude fast. Cecilia grabbed onto Michael's arm.

"I'm going to lose it!" she linked. She closed her eyes after she left her stomach a few thousand feet above her head.

Li returned full power to the engines and the nose of jet came up with a new flight path established. The Master Li restored the flight controls.

Villi linked from the cockpit, "Thanks Master Li… I think!"

The eastbound bus zoomed down the country road. It struck a bump and woke Han with a start. He looked around him and noticed a vacated empty bus.

"That's strange," he thought. "I don't recall any stops. This bus should still be packed with travelers."

Han stared out the window. He saw the countryside fly past. The bus tore down a dark rural country road at high speed. It swerved left and right. It nearly bounced him right out of his seat.

"Hey!" he finally called out. "Bus driver! Watch your driving! Just where are we going?"

He grabbed the back of the seat in front of him to keep from tumbling over. He glanced down at his watch. Over an hour passed since he started from Beijing.

"This isn't one of the main roads," he noted while he peered into the night "Those are the lights of Tianjin over there! Shouldn't we be going in that direction?"

The bus driver never turned around or acknowledged him. Han felt dizzy. He slumped down in the seat as his head tipped over toward the window.

Zinian looked up in the large rearview mirror and smiled. He enjoyed putting his recent download into practice. At last, he could manipulate his environment down to the slightest minutia and that included affecting the sleep center of his passenger's brain.

He swung the bus onto a dirt lane. He had arrived at a small private airfield northwest of Tianjin. The Japanese originally built the airstrip during World War II. The government maintained a groundskeeper to light the airstrip marked "Emergency Landings Only." The skidding tires of the bus threw loose gravel against the old wooden sign as the bus flew past.

Using his mind, he opened the gated barbed-wire fence that bordered the perimeter of the airstrip. He noted the time and thought to a mind high above him.

"I have arrived with the package," Zinian sent.

CHAPTER 42

No Escape

"WHERE ARE THE LIGHTS ZINIAN?" Villi thought down as he swung the landing gear into position.

Reaching the groundskeeper inside the shack by the airstrip proved difficult for Zinian. He first had to wake the elderly man up and then prod the old soul to turn on the landing strip lights as quickly as possible before the old man returned to slumber. Standing outside the bus, Zinian watched the rapidly approaching flashing light of the jet aircraft swing down out of the night sky.

"Good luck Villi," he sincerely wished.

"Yeah, I hope I know what I'm doing," Villi thought back. His hand paused a moment above the controls.

Su Lin held her breath. She knew this was Villi's first landing. Yet, the Russian police officer once relegated to walking a beat, gently brought the wheels down onto the long packed gravel runway. He landed the one hundred seventy-five million dollar jet smoothly onto a surface meant for emergencies. He quickly applied the brakes and reverse thrust. He brought the jet plane to a halt in front of the caretaker's shack.

"My first landing," Villi sat back able to breathe again. "Whew!"

"Thanks Villi," Su Lin thought to him. "I am proud of you."

"Great job pilot," Michael added.

Villi entered the cabin just as Li commanded the group's attention.

"Come! We have one final task remaining my friends," he linked to them as he indicated the door. "We must make our last contact in China."

Li took Cecilia by the hand and pulled her up. After only a brief rest and some added psychic energy, the youthful vitality that belied his years returned to Master Li. Cecilia took the lead. She opened the jet's door with her mind. Li followed her down the steps toward the supine body on the tarmac. Zinian stood beside him.

"Is that him?" she linked. Li simply nodded.

"What if this new candidate doesn't want to join us," Villi asked coming up behind them.

"We'll just use diplomacy," Master Li answered. "You'll see. He'll succumb to reason."

What is time? Is it a measure of movement? From whose perspective should we measure its rate? Precious time slipped away from the psychic group. It chipped away at their advantage. For while the group anxiously watched and waited for one more psychic – one special addition to this exclusive group of rare individuals – other forces, dark forces, the forces that march fate and destiny through time moved against them.

"What a strange dream," Han Su Yeng thought. "That familiar mechanical voice spoke to me once more. It made me an offer. What did it think I would say? Of course I want to *link* with other minds," he chuckled. "What man would pass up an opportunity like that?" he thought. "Can you imagine the possibilities that could take place with that kind of clear communication between individuals?" the strategist considered.

When Han blinked open his eyes, he saw a smattering of twinkling stars in a black night sky. They appeared so deep, so real and so close to him that he felt as if he could reach out and touch them.

"How beautiful," he thought as he admired their pale distinctions.

The moment he moved his body, painful reality set in. The stars quickly faded into distant points of light. Han's back pressed against a very hard surface.

"I must be lying on the ground," he thought. He tried to lift his head.

He then noticed a face leaning over him. Soon, more faces joined the first one until they formed a ring around his field of vision. He tried again to raise his head up off the ground, but it buzzed as if he had a hangover from too much wine. He lay his head back down and took a deep breath. His body felt completely uncomfortable in every way.

"Don't be too impatient," he heard a gentle elderly voice say. "We must give the man more time to recover."

"But Master Li," another voice spoke. "We don't have any more time left. We must leave this place quickly before they discover the true location of the stolen jet."

"This man is too important for our future Villi," he heard the first voice say. "Be patient. Conversion is the most difficult part of the transition and this man received the full treatment. This is the first time they initially converted a human to level IV. We put him through a strenuous ordeal that would be difficult for the best among you," the scholarly voice pointed out. "Would anyone here care to disagree with me? I thought not. See? He's coming around."

Han raised his head once more and tried to focus. He had doubts about his vision. Yes, it was true. He did see a circle of young people and one elderly man surround him. They had friendly faces.

"He's a bit older than us," one young man said.

Han noticed that the man did not open his mouth when he spoke.

"I heard his voice without his lips moving. How is that possible?" he wondered.

"How indeed!" the elderly voice spoke. "That is a good first question – one that I too asked."

Han began to feel stronger. He propped up on his elbows and stared at the faces. He did not feel fear, which surprised him. He thought that being in such circumstances with a group of strangers would make him fearful. Somehow, he felt at home although he could not explain why. He knew they were not the Shi-Tien. He also knew he did not feel threatened by them.

"Welcome back to the living Han Su Yeng," the old man said while he bowed. "I am Li Po Chin, once Professor of Poetry and Literature at Harbin University and now elected leader of our special group," the old man informed Han.

"I've heard of you," Han uttered although his throat felt dry. "You published a book of poetry, I believe."

"Your belief is your redemption," Li quipped. "I did publish a book or two of poetry. However, this is not the time to discuss great literature. Protocol requires I make informal introductions. Then we must leave this place at once." He then gestured to his right. "This tall young man is Michael Tyler from Connecticut in America."

Michael smiled briefly at Han and nodded. Han just stared back with a blank expression. Li continued the introductions around the circle.

"This cute young lady is Cecilia Beaton from Canada. Cecilia just turned eighteen and is in love with Michael," Li stated.

Cecilia blushed while she nodded her head toward Han. She briefly glanced over at Michael.

One person broke from the circle and began to slowly back away. Villi tried to inch closer to the plane. Li turned around and cleared his throat. Villi shrugged and returned to the circle.

"That impatient young man is Vladimir Zavitinsk, better known to all of us as Villi. He is Russian by birth, a police officer at heart and psychic quite by accident," Li said. He smiled at his own joke.

"You can joke now Master Li," Villi protested as he pointed to his wrist.

"I'll hurry," Li relented. "Rounding out the group we have Su Lin. She hopes to be teacher and is a chef extraordinaire. She is in love with Villi. They make a great couple." Villi and Su Lin exchanged a brief yet sigh-filled glance. "This young man is Chou Lo. He is our resident technical expert. I expect great things from Chou. Zinian here is a master builder. I predict he will be the world's greatest architect."

"Thank you Master Li," Zinian said. He brightened with Li's comment.

"Finally I'd like to introduce Zhiwei, our security specialist," Li indicated. "Zhiwei's goal is to keep us safe." Li then turned back to Han. "This is who we are. I am assuming you have questions…"

"What happened to me?" Han practically demanded. "Was I kidnapped? What am I doing here?"

"We shall try to answer all of your questions," Li calmly linked. "First however, I must explain a few things. You see Han," Li continued. "We are forming a society of psychics. Most of us have had time to adjust to our new abilities. You unfortunately, do not have the luxury of time. You agreed to the conversion process with your voice from Galactic Central. Most of us agreed to the conversion with the belief it was a fantasy. We had time to adjust to those changes afterward. However, in the light of reality, you do not have time. Instead, you have another choice to make. You must decide if you are with us or you are not. We recruited you because we need you Han. We need your keen sense of strategy. You could be an important asset to our group. In your right, you are a powerful psychic. Now you have a choice to make. Will you join us?" Li asked. He offered Han his hand.

However, during Li's speech, Han only thought of escape. Frightened and confused with all the talk of "being psychic," Han wanted to flee from these crazy people.

"If I grab the old man by the neck," Han thought, "perhaps I can fend off the others long enough to use the telephone in that shack."

Han started to rise. "Sure… I'll join you," he said as he reached for Li's hand.

Master Li deftly slapped his hand away. He then bent forward and moved right up to Han's face.

"Wake up to this reality Han Su Yeng!" Li said as he entered the new psychic's mind. "The state just fired you. I was at the meeting this afternoon. The Shi-Tien do not believe your story. They had intended to lock you away in a political asylum. They wanted to turn you into a lab experiment! You should be grateful that our group intervened. We know everything about you Han. You cannot hide your thoughts from us. However, we are not here to harm but to help you. We want you to join a community that will allow your life to flourish!"

Han sat there on the ground. His eyes were wide and blinking as he listened to Master Li. Everything the old man said to him, or rather linked to him, rang true. Yet even with Li's lengthy explanation, he was still confused.

"Let me put it another way," Li went on. "You have skills... incredible skills of strategy. However, you must throw off the notion that you are a dedicated civil servant. That part of your life is over. With this new ability, you can accomplish many wonder things," Li told him.

Han still said nothing. He simply stared at Master Li. This time Villi cleared his throat. Master Li understood the urgency of the moment.

"We cannot wait any longer. If you do not join us on the jet, we will expunge the memory of this from your mind and you can spend the rest of your life in that asylum! I need an answer and I need it now!" Li practically threatened.

Master Li saw that nothing he said made sense to Han. He had to act. He extended his power. Han rose up off the tarmac and floated in the air. He took in a gasp of air. Then Li gently set the man back down. Han realized in that moment that this was either a very elaborate dream or he had changed. Either way, he succumbed to their argument.

Master Li's moment of desperation sparked the stubborn Han into action. Startled, he came to life and sputtered, "Yes sir... I'll join!"

"Yes Master Li!" everyone shouted into Han's mind.

For a second, Han thought he offended them and started to apologize. Then the entire group burst out laughing. They patted Han on the back. Villi messed up his hair and teased him. Han looked around at the group of young people and realized what a fool he had been, especially considering how stupidly he behaved toward the old man they called Master Li.

"Honestly, we could use a good strategist," Li added. "Is your answer yes?"

"Yes Master Li," he mumbled.

Li turned around and addressed the group.

"Group? Help our newest member to his feet. Time to go," Li instructed.

Several helping hands reached out and lifted Han up off the tarmac. Unsteady, he waddled over to the door of the jet.

"Why are my clothes wet?" Han wondered as he moved toward the door.

"We have fresh clothes for you onboard the jet," Michael told him.

"Do you always douse your initiates with water?" he asked.

"That isn't water," Zinian pointed out, "that's your sweat!"

Sweat?" Han responded as he pulled at his clothes.

"I'll try to explain once we are seated," Michael linked to his mind, "if that is possible."

Impatient, Master Li moved ahead of the group.

"Villi!" Li called out, "prepare this aircraft for takeoff as soon as you are able!"

"Yes Master Li," Villi quickly answered. The he added, "Oh, Master Li?"

"Yes Villi," Li answered quietly.

"Nice diplomacy!" Villi said with a wink.

"We do what we must do," Li remarked privately.

Villi hopped onboard the jet aircraft and began the pre-flight check. Several minutes later, the jet zoomed out over the Gulf of Bo Hai at nearly full throttle. Villi struggled to keep the advanced flyer below the 300-foot radar threshold. At over 700 miles per hour, the streaking aircraft shook the timbers of fishing boats that passed underneath its charging belly. He had to maintain complete concentration. One slip of his hands could send the jet tumbling out of control.

Michael linked with Han and quickly tried to explain Han's abilities to him. Michael could only give Han a glimpse of those possibilities by sharing selected memories with him regarding the group's experiences over the past few weeks. However, Michael and Master Li realized that Han's concerns regarding his psychic powers would have to wait. The Chinese defense grid required everyone's attention.

When the general did not respond to calls from his aid, the defense department sent out a national alert. Soon, they found the tracer elements on the jet streaming out over the Gulf of Bo Hai. The military command assumed the general was onboard and that terrorists either killed or kidnapped him. Either way, the Chinese military sent orders to bring down the aircraft "by whatever means were effective."

The Chinese military had many radar installations pointed in a variety of directions. Radar beams came from sea going vessels and land based stations that seemed to be located everywhere. Supposedly, not even a cruise missile could break through this spider's web of detection that stretched along China's well-guarded coastline.

The fleeing psychic group had no idea how they would disrupt every radar installation. They had their work cut out for them. Their goal was to leave China using the most direct route without being killed in the process. Most of the psychics concentrated their efforts on subduing the multiple fixed radar sites at Quingdao. While others in their group searched for alerted Chinese Navy patrol ships or fighter jets sent with orders to fire on them.

Han sat in the back of the main cabin. He was aware of the team's thought processes around him. For the first time in his life, he could hear the thoughts of other human beings. While this prospect delighted him at first, he soon realized that he had agreed to be at the focus of a terrible conflict. The Chinese military were trying to shoot their jet down!

Fearful of the outcome, even frightened by the boldness and determination of other group members, Han timidly watched them work with amazing speed and accuracy. He did not understand the methods they employed, although he could follow their processes. He admired their courage not usually found in the complacent Chinese that he knew.

He had an inkling that these people might bring back a sense of joy in his heart that he missed since his wife died. He could hear Michael and Cecilia speak hopeful reassurances to one another. He could feel Master Li's power as he reached out to touch the minds of Chinese pilots on patrol over the Bo Hai Gulf and dissuade them from firing missiles at this jet. He could hear Villi and Su Lin giving each other encouragement with sentiment attached to each message. Finally, he could sense the thought processes of Chou, Zinian and Zhiwei, as they used their ability to change the minds of radar operators.

Li and Michael helped to coordinate the group's efforts as they attempted to escape. Yet, in the midst of all this serendipity, Han could only watch and not participate. He felt helpless, frustrated and left out. He began to think he had made a mistake when he agreed to join them. Han was well acquainted with military tactics and weapons. He knew that if only one missile made it through and ignited near them, the explosion would destroy the aircraft.

"What am I doing here? I'm going to be killed along with the rest of them," he thought. His mind raced with possible terrible outcomes.

The jet aircraft entered the outer rim of the Bo Hai Gulf at which point Villi planned to make a crucial turn and headed southeast over the Yellow Sea. If he took this route, he would avoid flying over South Korea and Japan. This also prolonged their time in China's airspace, which meant they had to interfere with more radar installations.

When Han heard about the jet's route from Villi's mind, he realized they might be heading for a trap. Han knew that the defense grid at Shanghai employed thousands of people, more minds that these psychics could contend. He wondered what they would do when the Shanghai Control Center picked up their signal and fired a land-based rocket at them.

"Master Li," Villi called out to their busy commander, "I'm starting my turn into the Yellow Sea. At this speed, we will remain within Chinese territory for at least the next thirty minutes sir."

"Understood Villi," Master Li returned. "Maintain your planned flight path."

Li altered the mind of another pilot by turning his jet fighter away. This was the fourteenth jet sent to shoot them down.

"Don't let your energy levels down," Li cautioned the team. "Pick up additional energy as we pass over ships at sea. By the way Villi," Li added, "you're doing an excellent job flying the jet under these circumstances," he told the young Russian. "We're all very proud of you."

"Thank you Master Li," Villi replied. His face broke out with sweat from nerves.

"I'm especially proud," Su Lin added.

"Master Li," Villi broke in. "I'm receiving multiple requests from Chinese Naval vessels for identification."

"Maintain radio silence," Li advised.

"Yes Master Li… but what if they fire a missile?" Villi questioned.

"Hopefully, it won't come to that," Li insisted. "We can interfere with the ground crews at coastal installations and onboard those vessels before that happens. Zhiwei?"

"I'm narrowing in on the sources," the young man replied.

As the others in the group countered the surface ships, fighter jets and shoreline radar installations, Cecilia concentrated on submarine activity. She was the only member in the group other than Michael with experience sensing underwater.

At first, she interfered with one small Chinese submarine in the gulf. She easily erased their jet's radar signature. The rest of way through the Yellow Sea appeared clear. She glanced up at Michael just as he looked her way. He had worked simultaneously with Zinian, Zhiwei and Chou to help focus on individual targets. Su Lin seemed to work fine independently. At the same time, his mind performed manipulations on targets as fast as he could scan them.

"Look at you," she linked to him, "you're not even breaking a sweat!" she observed.

Michael paused a second as he looked at her beautiful face. He did not speak or link. With that expression, it was not necessary. Their faces spoke volumes.

"Don't you realize what is happening to you?" she put to him.

Michael briefly put Chou on another diversion and redirected Zinian to another target before he turned back to Cecilia.

"What do you mean?" he asked her.

"Stress, Michael," she said with a calm quiet link. "You are under tremendous stress… and handling it well without any crutch."

He had worked so diligently on solving their problems, he did not think about reverting to his old nemesis. In fact, he was standing right next to the general's bar. It was full of liquor and wine bottles. He realized that Cecilia was right about him. Interfering with the Chinese military had been extremely stressful as he tried to monitor every activity. Yet, even after juggling with so many problems at once, he did not one time think of taking a drink. He only thought about how he could keep Cecilia and the others safe from harm. Master Li put his hand on Michael's arm.

"I'd say you've come full circle Michael," he commented. "You've come a long way from that train track in Mississippi… and now you are on your way home with new friends," he added.

Michael took in a deep breath. He was about to thank the two psychics for their vote of confidence, when Cecilia's mind filled with heightened tension.

"Oh no!" she gasped as a new contact entered her watery realm.

The moment he started to probe her concerned mind, Master Li turned Michael's attention away from her to a squadron of fighter jets approaching their position. Michael turned away to help Master Li. No one had time at this moment to focus on Cecilia's troubles. Two large squadrons of jets moved toward them from two different directions. Michael and Master Li went to work on them. At the same time, a Chinese destroyer came within range that required the focus of Zinian, Chou and Zhiwei to alter its ability to find them. Su Lin had her hands full with new land based radar sites.

Yet Han saw a look of terror on the young girl's face. He knew that something was terribly wrong with Cecilia. A new yet familiar object came into her targeted view. An enormous submerged vessel slowly barged its way into the entrance of the Yellow Sea toward the mainland. Cecilia recognized the mind of the commander onboard.

"Your timing as usual captain is lousy," she thought.

Captain Zhinlin Gu'an – the same captain that fired on the American sub in the Sea of Okhotsk – brought his huge Chinese nuclear submarine back into port. Naval Command ordered the captain to return the underwater vessel back to the Navy's base in Tanggu. The captain bristled with a recent reprimand after their disastrous trial run. The spy network informed the upper command that an American submarine was involved. Hoping to avoid a diplomatic incident, the Chinese Navy ordered the sub's inexperienced commander back to port.

As much as Cecilia tried, she could not break through to the crew inside.

"What is wrong with me?" she wondered. She was unable to affect any seamen on the bridge.

Exerting her ability to the straining point, Cecilia could not penetrate any mind in the sub's main control room. She could not understand why. As their jet zoomed closer, it bore down on the sub's position. That set off proximity alarms within the sub's interior space that suddenly blared into the young Canadian's frustrated mind.

"Oh!" she stamped her foot, "this is frustrating!"

"What is it?" Su Lin glanced up.

"I can't maneuver through the density of the water, penetrate the hull, and stay focused on one sailor. They're moving toward us through the water. We're flying toward them through the air. It's all happening too fast!"

Her unresolved distress kept Michael distracted. He watched Cecilia with increasing alarm as she gallantly fought to bring calm to the submarine's bridge control room.

"Maintain your focus on that radar site Su Lin," Michael finally broke in. "I'll see if I can help Cecilia," he linked to her.

"Michael!" Cecilia's link practically shouted, "It's the Chinese sub we encountered crossing Okhotsk. They've spotted us!"

"I see them!" he linked back and tried to assist.

Michael had to withdraw from Master Li's task. At the same time, Master Li finally turned away both squadrons of Chinese fighter pilots. The great psychic, while able to multi-task, had to replenish energy as quickly as he utilized it. However, the submarine presented a far more difficult problem to Michael. He knew that he and Cecilia could not halt the actions taking place inside its command center. He surmised at once how lethal the situation could quickly evolve. Michael turned to Master Li with an urgent plea.

"We need your help..." Michael started.

However, Master Li ignored Michael. Instead, he moved past him and focused on Han.

"We need to know the true extent of your courage," Li said to Han. "You saw how the others work their ability. Use yours now in same fashion. You have it in you, Han. You can do it, if you try. Reach out with your thoughts and touch the mind of the submarine's sonar controller. If you do not act quickly, they will fire a rocket at us and we will die."

Han sat up. He anxiously stared at Master Li with panic on his face.

"I can't!" he exclaimed. "I don't know what to do. I'm not as talented or as capable as the rest of you," he whined.

"Han Su Yeng!" Li thought abruptly into the man's mind. "Control your emotions! Do you think we pick out any civil servant and give him the ability to link with creatures millions of light years away? You have power that exceeds your expectations!"

Li stood before Han, indignant with his apparent cowardice. Han stared back at him and shook his head.

"You still refuse to accept this as reality, don't you?" Li confronted him. He was beginning to show signs of frustration. "You are a master of reason surrounded by a team of powerful psychics. You know their strengths. How many facts do you need to develop a strategy?"

Han chose not to reply. Instead, he feebly shook his head.

Her anxiety began to grow into genuine fear. Cecilia felt forced to interject.

"Han, we need your help," she pleaded. "A nuclear submarine is on a direct course with our jet. The gap between us is narrowing fast. We cannot affect any minds on their bridge. We don't have any weapons and are vulnerable. Soon, they will plot a solution and fire a missile at us. We only have a few minutes left. Please… I'm begging you… help us!"

Michael nodded his head in quiet agreement.

Master Li closed his eyes. His thoughts echoed into every mind on the jet.

"Voices of Galactic Central," he called out. "Reveal your contact to this newest member!"

Every mind on the jet halted their task and listened including Villi.

"Han Su Yeng," a mechanical voice spoke. "I am your voice inside Galactic Central."

Han held still. He closed his eyes to listen.

"I am the voice that helped you play chess as a child. We spoke the day your wife died…" his voice spoke.

"No!" Han cried. He put his hands up to his ears. "I made you up. You aren't real."

"You are wrong Han," his voice boomed. "I spoke to you on the ground back in China. Do you recall? Your thoughts are my thoughts. I entered your mind, implanted abilities and created a new area in your brain. We altered your basic cellular structure. You are now a powerful psychic, Han Su Yeng," the voice stated.

"No…" Han feebly replied. "This is just a dream. It isn't real, is it?" he declared. He glanced around at the sincere faces that stared back at him. "Are you trying to tell me that for the first time in my life, I can be anyone I wish to be? Am I free to act and believe as I chose?" his link to the group grew weaker.

Confused, anxious and fearful, Han hesitated to act. He was uncertain how to proceed. With his mind so open, the group shared his pain, his anxiety and then his sudden sense of hope. He looked up and stared at the ceiling of the jet as if he could see far beyond the aircraft into the vast reaches of the universe.

"Will I speak with other psychics in the galactic collective? Will I voice?" Han questioned.

The voice did not reply.

"You don't have to go to galactic central for answers," Li softly broke into his mind, which startled Han. "You can link with other psychics' right here. We have much to offer… if you give us a chance."

Han looked around the cabin. Every person looked back in his direction. Master Li stepped into his view and stood before him. He physically pulled him up off his seat and held him with both hands extended.

"Your power is as great as the unlimited potential of your mind Han Su Yeng," Li quietly spoke in almost a whisper. Li then switched to his psychic voice. "Now let's see that mind in action, master strategist!" Li linked as he let him go. His powerful thoughts brought awareness back to Han. "Team!" he called, "link together and share your thoughts with Han! Everyone open your mind to Han!"

Han blinked back the emotional moisture in his eyes as he tried to focus on every thought, every action and every memory that poured into his mind. The keen civil servant – able to sift through mounds of data very fast – discovered one common element that offered hope for the fleeing aircraft.

"Quick!" he linked to his new friends as he urged them to action. "We must perform this feat at the same time!" he pointed out while he made the meaning of his intent clear.

On board the nuclear submarine, the man stationed at sonar shouted to his captain.

"Incoming unknown object sir," the young man said as he checked his equipment. "Object is an aircraft rapidly approaching our position at over one thousand kilometers per hour sir."

"According to Naval Command," the communications officer spoke up, "the jet will not respond to repeated calls for identification or change course. It's heading is on a collision course sir!"

"Red Alert!" the captain called out. Alarms blared into the air as his men scrambled to combat positions.

"Command now reports the plane originated in China sir. They suspect a terrorist plot and the possible murder of a Chinese official," his communications officer called out. "They consider the aircraft armed and dangerous," he said.

Captain Gu'an hesitated to commit to this confrontation after his debacle in Sea of Okhotsk.

"You have standing orders captain," his second informed him. "You must act, if only to protect the submarine and your men."

Captain Gu'an gritted his teeth. Those words hit home. They were the exact excuse he needed to act.

"Helm, come to periscope depth for firing missile!" the captain barked.

"Coming to periscope depth captain," the helmsman answered and watched the gauges in front of him.

"Plot a solution for intercept," the captain ordered.

"Solution plotted sir," the weapons station informed his captain. "Weapons system is ready sir!"

The submarine rose up from the depths of the channel into firing position. The blinking object on sonar moved rapidly toward the submarine's position at the center of the screen. The ship's crew shifted to watch the captain as he waited for the right conditions to fire.

"Periscope depth captain," helm called out.

A button at the weapons station lit up green.

"Weapon is armed and ready to fire sir," the weapons seaman stated.

An officer stepped forward and inserted a key. He turned and stood ready while he watched for the signal from the captain.

"Fire the missile!" the captain ordered.

"Missile away!" the weapons station officer answered. He pushed in the green button.

The submarine violently shook as the rocket shot out of its bay. The powerful missile streamed up through the shallow water overhead and burst into the sky. Huge flames shot out of its rear as water dripped off the great round head. Quickly the rocket gained speed. The sophisticated projectile aimed straight for its target. The key command permanently locked the thrusting mechanism into a path of death and destruction. Nothing could stop it or deflect it from its date with destiny.

Sonar Control yelled out the closing moments.

"Ten thousand meters from target and closing fast... five thousand meters, two thousand, one thousand..." He quickly yanked off his headphones. A bright light filled the sonar screen. Then a distant rumble shook the water around the submarine. The screen at the Sonar Control Station cleared.

"No visible airborne targets sir. Target is destroyed!" the seaman reported.

"Helm, resume our course to the base. Use standard approach," the captain ordered. "Contact command and inform them we destroyed the terrorist threat. Give them the coordinates. Have patrol boats check the water for debris or signs of survivors." The captain added, "I'll be in my cabin."

Having accomplished its primary mission, China's newest nuclear submarine steamed through the Yellow Sea and headed for its port destination. Its captain held his head high, a little less ashamed of his first run.

Invisible to human eyes or radar, a large shimmering translucent sphere of psychic energy streaked skyward toward a new destiny.

The End of "The Distant Voices" – Volume I of "The Voices Saga"

Next: "The Voices Arrive" – Volume II of "The Voices Saga"